He loves me not
. . . he loves me

www.**booksattransworld**.co.uk

He loves me not ... he loves me

Claudia Carroll

BANTAM PRESS

LONDON • TORONTO • SYDNEY • AUCKLAND • JOHANNESBURG

TRANSWORLD PUBLISHERS
61–63 Uxbridge Road, London W5 5SA
a division of The Random House Group Ltd

RANDOM HOUSE AUSTRALIA (PTY) LTD
20 Alfred Street, Milsons Point, Sydney,
New South Wales 2061, Australia

RANDOM HOUSE NEW ZEALAND LTD
18 Poland Road, Glenfield, Auckland 10, New Zealand

RANDOM HOUSE SOUTH AFRICA (PTY) LTD
Endulini, 5a Jubilee Road, Parktown 2193, South Africa

Published 2004 by Bantam Press
a division of Transworld Publishers

A catalogue record for this book is available from the British Library.
ISBN 0593 053079

Typeset in 12.5/15pt Bembo by
Falcon Oast Graphic Art Ltd.

Printed in Great Britain by
Mackays of Chatham plc, Chatham, Kent

1 3 5 7 9 10 8 6 4 2

Papers used by Transworld Publishers are natural, recyclable products
made from wood grown in sustainable forests. The manufacturing
processes conform to the environmental regulations of the country of origin.

For Anne and Claude, who are absolutely nothing like the parents in this book.

ACKNOWLEDGEMENTS

At the risk of sounding like a starlet on Oscar night, I really do have so many people to thank that I don't know where to begin, but here goes:

Huge thanks to Marianne Gunn O'Connor; there wouldn't be a book without her. I often think she should have a plaque on her office door that says 'Dreams Come True Here'.

Thanks to Pat Lynch at the agency, surely the calmest and most patient person in the northern hemisphere.

Thanks to Francesca Liversidge, Sadie Mayne and everyone at Transworld.

Thanks to Anita Notaro, Kate Thompson and Patricia Scanlan for their constant encouragement and gentle guidance, guardian angels one and all.

Thanks to Clelia Murphy for putting up with me during the long hours cooped up together in dressing rooms, with me about to fling my computer off a wall.

Thanks to Vicki Satlow in Italy for telling me that she sang Paddy's drunken love song down the phone to Marianne.

Thanks to Susan McHugh and Sean Murphy, the best couple on the planet, for the twenty-four-hour technical support.

Thanks to everyone in *Fair City*, especially Niall Matthews,

Brien Gallagher, Ann Myler, Johnny Cullen, Tony Tormey, Tom Hopkins and Zoe Belton for all their kindness and help during the last year.

Thanks to Maureen McGlynn and Eleanor Minihan.

Thanks to my family in Scotland, the Hearnes, for all their help when I was researching this.

Finally, I've been lucky enough to have been blessed with the nicest bunch of friends anyone could ask for. Special thanks to Karen Nolan, Larry Finnegan, Marion O'Dwyer, Pat Kinevane, Alison McKenna, Lise-Ann McLaughlin, Hilary Reynolds, Sharon Hogan, Madge MacLaverty, Fiona Lalor, Siobhan Miley and Elizabeth Moynihan.

Chapter One

OK, so it wasn't a Friday, but it was still the thirteenth. If Portia had never been superstitious before, she was now. As she stood in the freezing Drawing Room of her family's ancestral home, Davenport Hall, with her mother wailing in the background, she found herself idly wondering, the way you do in times of crisis, could this really be happening?

'It can't be true, my darling. It simply can't be true,' howled Lucasta for the umpteenth time that morning. 'How could he just bolt off into the blue without a by-your-leave? We were married for thirty-six years and to think that your father has abandoned me . . . ME! I was debutante of the year in nineteen sixty-six and everyone said your father was the luckiest man alive to have landed me . . .' And at the thought of her bygone youth and beauty, she spiralled off into a fresh bout of hysterics. 'I know I told him to bugger off, but how was I to know the bastard would actually leave? The one time in his worthless buggery life he actually did what I asked!'

Portia sighed deeply as she went to console her mother, yet again.

The unseasonable March sunshine streamed through the enormous bay window which dominated the room, bathing mother and daughter with warmth, which neither of them felt inside. To an outsider, they looked like an odd pair. Lucasta, Lady Davenport, although only in her mid-fifties, looked a great deal older, a legacy of her fondness for one gin and tonic too many. Her waist-length hair, which had been so admired during that debutante year, was now grey and matted and certainly hadn't seen the inside of a hairdresser's since the moon landings. Dressed in her trademark wellies, moth-eaten navy jacket and layer upon layer of heavy wool jumpers, she looked like she'd just mugged a homeless person and then ripped the clothes off their back. Yet, even though her red face was all puffy and swollen from crying, you could still tell that, in her youth, she would have been considered 'a handsome woman'.

Portia, her eldest daughter, was another story. Tall, thin and pale, with her light brown hair tied neatly behind her neck, she was as white as a ghost today. Not from shock, but from worry, sheer worry. As she handed her mother another fistful of tissues, she looked wearily around the room. At the filthy windows with their cracked panes; the high Georgian rose ceilings, which hadn't seen a lick of paint in decades and were now covered in cobwebs; the threadbare Persian rug on the floor, which stank to high heaven from all the generations of cats that her mother freely allowed to sleep there; and at the huge, bare, light patches on the walls, which marked where the Davenports' paintings had once hung.

In Portia's grandfather's time, the family's art collection had been quite renowned, one of the most impressive in the country. A Gainsborough and a Reynolds, no less, had hung in that room; Portia could remember seeing them as a child. She never even knew they were famous until, when she was at school, she recognized one of them from the cover of an art history book and thought: That's hanging in my house.

All gone now. All sold off, at way below their market value, to pay off her father's gambling debts. Portia sighed deeply. No point in dwelling on that now, what's done is done, she reminded herself. As she looked out of the bay window, she could see the distant figure of her younger sister, Daisy, furiously galloping on her favourite mare over the parkland surrounding the house.

It's even worse for her, the poor darling, thought Portia as she gently soothed her mother. She actually liked him.

Jack, Lord Davenport, known as 'Blackjack' because of his addiction to the game, was by now, Portia calculated, halfway to Las Vegas. Always one to do things in style, it wasn't enough for him simply to walk out on his wife and daughters, cleaning them out of the little cash they had, but, for added entertainment value, he had taken Sarah Kelly with him. Sarah Kelly was a stable hand on the estate. Sarah Kelly was nineteen.

It's all my bloody fault, as usual, thought Daisy as she galloped past the rose garden, the wild March wind full in her face, I hired the stupid little slapper. In her defence, though, it had looked like a good idea at the time. She had taken Sarah on last summer to help out during the tourist season. But I was explicitly clear about her job description. She was to help me muck out the stables and clean up horse shit, I never said anything about running off with Papa, Daisy wailed to herself, large tears now starting to roll freely down her face. How could he do this to us? How could he just run off with that thick-ankled shit-shoveller? She galloped on, past the old tennis courts with their nets rotting away, past the orchard and on towards the surrounding hills, which were still part of the Davenports' land. Whenever Daisy was this upset, there was only one place for her to go.

Davenport Hall had an equestrian centre close to the house, which at one time provided some badly needed income for the family. The idea was that visiting tourists could spend a day at Davenport Hall ('This stunning example of Georgian architecture in the heart of County Kildare' as the Bord Fáilte brochure boastfully and rather misleadingly declared). Those who were up for it could go out pony-trekking over the acres of beautiful woodland around the Hall, past the River Kilcullen with its own salmon trap, and up as far as the Mausoleum, a magnificent neo-classical monument where nine generations of the Davenport family were buried.

A stranger arriving here for the day could easily be forgiven for thinking how wealthy the family were, with all that land . . . and as for the Hall itself! From the outside, Davenport Hall looked so grand, you'd think royalty lived there. It dated back to the mid-eighteenth century and at one time was considered the finest house in the province of Leinster. Designed by James Gandon for his old drinking buddy, the first Lord Davenport, the Hall boasted eight enormous reception rooms, a Ballroom, a Library, a Portrait Gallery (where, legend had it, Edward VII and his Irish mistress had once lost a fortune at cards), and no less than sixteen bedrooms. To the naked eye you would think that only a Lottery winner or else Michael Flatley could afford to live there. Until you opened the front door and saw the sorry state into which Davenport Hall had fallen.

If any tourists were unfortunate or misguided enough to find themselves there, on crossing the threshold of the once grand entrance hall, the first thing that struck them was the freezing cold. Such cold, in fact, that even in deep winter it was often warmer outside the house than inside. Daisy would often throw a blanket around her and say, 'I'm just popping outside for a thaw.' But the cost of renovating the

Hall's ancient heating system was out of the question for the cash-strapped Davenports. However, once the unfortunate visitor had acclimatized him or herself, it was the smell that hit you next. A truly revolting aromatic blend of cat pee and damp, it was not for the faint-hearted. If visitors were particularly unlucky and it happened to be raining, then dodging the puddles on the floor caused by the gaping holes in the ceiling was the next ordeal. Portia had remortgaged the Hall a few years previously to have the roof repaired, but Blackjack, true to form, had run off with the bank's money . . . to the Curragh races. The cash lasted him for about an hour.

The Yellow Drawing Room, where Lady Davenport and Portia now sat, was probably the only hospitable room in the house: at least there was always a fire burning there and if you sat right on top of the hulking stone fireplace, it was possible to feel the merest flicker of warmth. Which was exactly what Portia was trying to do when the door burst open.

'For God's sake, Mrs Flanagan, do you ever think of knocking?' cried Lucasta from the chaise longue where she sat surrounded by snotty tissues.

'Ah, would ya ever relax, luv,' replied Mrs Flanagan in a thick North Dublin accent. 'I thought youse would like a cuppa tea,' she added, cigarette ash dangling precariously from the fag at the corner of her mouth.

'Thank you, Mrs Flanagan, you're very kind,' said Portia. 'Come on, Mummy, sugary tea is good for shock.'

'Oh, bugger that, Mrs Flanagan, get me a very stiff gin and tonic please, easy on the tonic,' replied her ladyship.

'Woulda thought it was a bit early, even for you, luv,' said Mrs Flanagan as she waddled towards the drinks cabinet in the corner of the room. Bless her, thought Portia. She's the only one of us who's taking this completely in her stride.

'And you know yer're miles better off without the aul' bastard anyway,' continued Mrs Flanagan as she splashed liberal dashes of tonic on her ladyship's gin.

'Blackjack was a wonderful husband,' said Lucasta primly, 'and I said go easy on the tonic.' Teary-eyed, miserable and bereft as she was, she still managed to watch Mrs Flanagan pour her drink like a hawk. Being an abandoned wife was one thing, but watery gin was quite another.

'Yeah, well, you keep thinking that if ya want, luv,' replied Mrs Flanagan, 'but I couldn't stand the aul' gobshite. Miserable git. And he couldn't pick a horse to save his life. Did youse not explain to Sarah Kelly that she was supposed to shovel the shite into a bucket, not run off to Las Vegas with it— AH JAYSUS!' she screamed out as she tripped over one of Lucasta's particularly mangy cats. 'I swear I'll drown them all one of these days. They have me heart broken,' she growled, handing over the drink.

'Oh Mrs Flanagan, you really must be careful with little Gnasher,' said her ladyship, holding the cat close to her and stroking it. 'In a past life, he was the Shah of Persia, you know.'

Mrs Flanagan, not a great believer in past life regression, merely muttered under her breath. She was never one to be easily intimidated by her blue-blooded employers and frequently put Lucasta in her place, but not today. Changing her tone, she handed Portia her tea and gently said, 'So how are you doing, luv?'

'It's Daisy I'm most worried about, to be honest, Mrs Flanagan. She was always Daddy's girl,' said Portia, checking for dead spiders before gingerly stirring her tea in the cracked china cup. For once, Mrs Flanagan had produced the good china, clearly considering this break-up of the family to be an occasion worthy of the Royal Doulton.

'And you know how emotional she is at the best of times.'

'Ah, don't talk to me. Do you remember the time one of her horses had to be put down? I thought she'd need psychiatric help, she was so devastated, God help her. And when she split up from that fella . . . what was his name again?'

'Sean Murphy,' Portia answered. Sean was the local vet and the only single, eligible man for miles around, whom Daisy had briefly dated a couple of months ago.

'Yeah, lovely-looking fella, but when it was all off, I've never seen anyone so upset as Daisy was. My God, you'd think they'd been married for years, and she'd only been going out with him for a couple of weeks.'

'Well, this is certainly worse,' Portia calmly replied.

'I'd paste that little trollop Sarah Kelly to the wall if I had her now . . .' continued Mrs Flanagan, her tone growing nasty. 'Never liked her. Anyone with a pierced ear and a pierced nose and a chain going between the two of them is not to be trusted. What did she think, that someone was going to rob the nose on her or something—?'

'You know, Mrs Flanagan, I really think I'd better go and find Daisy,' Portia interrupted. She didn't mean to be rude, but there was going to be enough gossip in the town about what had happened without her adding to it.

'Ah yeah, go on so, luv,' replied Mrs Flanagan, a bit embarrassed. The last person she'd ever want to offend was Portia, who was so good to her and so lovely to work for.

'I'll see you at dinner then,' said Portia, kissing her mother on her cheek. 'I think we can all guess where Daisy's gone.'

And off she went. Mrs Flanagan watched her walk out through the rotting French doors and on to the terrace, over the south lawn and on towards the hills, calm and composed with her head held high.

And she thought her heart would break.

Portia had thought that the walk would do her good, but

she was mistaken. Her head kept pounding with the worry of it all. It wasn't the fact that she would most likely never see her father again while he lived, but what were they going to do now? How would they live? Blackjack had thoughtfully cleaned them out of every last penny that she'd scrimped and saved for over the years. And now here she was, thirty-five years of age, trying to manage this great white elephant of a house and its vast estate with virtually no help whatsoever. And still the tears wouldn't come. On she walked, out of breath now, but almost there. She was at the top of one of the hills, which overlooked the south face of the hall, and she could see the neo-classical Greek columns of the Davenports' mausoleum coming into view. Sure enough, there was her sister's beautiful white mare, Kat Slater (Daisy was something of a soap-opera addict) grazing beside the limestone steps.

'Daisy?' Portia called out, breathless. 'Are you there, darling?' A few stifled sobs from inside the domed temple gave her an answer.

'I thought I'd find you here,' Portia went on, tripping up the four steps to the central flagstone area, with its ornate, moss-covered, Grecian stone benches evenly set all around the edge of the dome. It was here that their Davenport ancestors had been buried and it was a favourite spot for both Daisy and Portia. In more carefree days, they would often ride up there together, sit down and admire the magnificent view. You could see three counties so clearly from that spot, rolling away into the distance. When they were younger, the sisters would often sit side by side, munching on their sandwiches and wondering what would become of their lives. The girls had always been close, in spite of a fourteen-year age gap between them. In fact, Daisy often looked on Portia as more of a mother figure than Lucasta had ever been.

'Oh Portia!' Daisy cried out, almost knocking her over as

she hurled herself into her sister's arms. 'I'll never trust any man ever again, as long as I live! Mrs Flanagan is right, they're all just a shower of worthless fuckheads.'

'There, there, darling, you get your cry over with,' Portia said soothingly, handing her a great wad of Kleenex.

'You know, there's heaps we could do,' said Daisy, blowing her nose. 'We could tell him we're building a greyhound racing track on one of the fields. That might lure him back. Or we could pretend we won the Lotto, or we could ask Mummy to do one of her love spells . . .' She trailed off, seeing the stony look of disapproval on Portia's face.

'Daisy, I know how much you loved him, but honestly, darling, do you really think that's going to bring him back? He went of his own free will, you know, no one kidnapped him.'

Portia could see Blackjack's note, all tear-splodged, in her sister's tightly clutched hand. She could still make out the opening line: *My dearest girls, this is the hardest letter I've ever had to write . . . etc., etc.*

Typical of him, she mused bitterly, he addressed the letter to us to save himself the bother of writing to Mummy, so we'd have to do his dirty work for him, and certainly not for the first time either. But she kept her thoughts to herself.

'I just can't believe I'll never see Daddy again!' cried Daisy, almost on the verge of hysteria now.

Portia looked calmly at her, as if she were seeing her for the first time. Even though Daisy had had no sleep, hadn't eaten in God knows how long and had been weeping buckets, she still looked stunningly beautiful. She'd just turned twenty-one, and with her model-thin figure, light blond ringlety hair and deep blue eyes, she was a Davenport to her very fingertips. Portia could remember from old the magnificent family portraits that used to hang in the Long Gallery, with generation after generation of blond, blue-eyed lords and the various local heiresses they'd married. Back in old God's time the Davenports had been famous for their good looks, and Daisy was certainly carrying on the tradition.

Thank goodness one of us is. The family features have certainly passed me by, she thought, though without a trace of self-pity. She'd always loathed the way she looked, with her shapeless figure, mousy brown hair and pale, freckled skin.

Not that it mattered. Davenport Hall wasn't exactly a lap-dancing club, awash with single, eligible men. In fact, if a good-looking man landed at their door, they'd immediately presume he'd come to burgle them. Except that he'd need to be one of the world's dumbest criminals; anything of any value at the Hall had been flogged off years ago.

'Darling, don't cry any more, you'll give yourself the most awful headache,' Portia said as her sister continued to wail. But, highly strung and emotional as Daisy was, Portia knew there was no point in reasoning with her in this state. The protective big sister in her took over as she put her arm around her and held her close. 'We'll be fine, darling. I just know we'll be fine. I'll ask Steve to call over tomorrow. He'll know just what to do.'

The Steve that Portia was referring to was a solicitor in the local town of Ballyroan. He was a family friend of many years' standing, ever since he'd first come to live in the sleepy hamlet, while still a young law graduate. He was newly qualified as a solicitor and anxious to start work when a friend of his father's, Tom MacLaverty, suggested he apply to his firm, NolanMacLaverty, of Ballyroan, Co. Kildare.

As a city boy, Steve initially baulked at the idea of relocating to such a remote backwater when an honours graduate like him could easily get work in some flashy Dublin firm; but, to this day, he still remembered driving to Ballyroan for the first time. He could vividly recall that clear summer's day, seeing the town at its very best: with its wide streets, the fountain in the middle of Main Street, the cinema which was still screening *The Rocky Horror Picture Show* (always packed on Friday nights) and more pubs side by side than he'd ever seen before.

'How do they all stay in business?' he'd naively wondered. He needn't have worried. In fact, at one point Ballyroan had made it into the *Guinness Book of Records* for having the highest number of pubs per capita than anywhere else in Europe. He remembered the lush, green acres of land that enveloped the town, the most beautiful, peaceful, restful sight he'd ever seen. Right there and then, he'd decided he wanted to spend the rest of his life in this spot.

Twenty years on and Steve had never looked back. He loved it here. He loved the friendliness of the people, who'd always stop for a major chat with you on the street. (There were times when he thought he should just plonk his desk right in the middle of Main Street; he certainly spent more time talking there than in his office.)

And the law practice was booming. Steve had a natural way with people: a friendliness and an instinctive knack of making people trust him. He would never dream of putting a clock on his clients and then charging them according to timesheets as plenty of lawyers would. That just wouldn't be his way of doing business. Instead he'd chat away to people, advising them on conveyancing and making their wills, all the normal work of a country solicitor. But he took the time to explain things really clearly to his clients and never forced them into signing anything or agreeing to anything they didn't want to. And NolanMacLaverty's clients loved him for it. Pretty soon, people took to phoning the office and asking to speak directly to young Steve Sullivan, instead of Sean Nolan, who could be a bit intimidating, or Tom MacLaverty, whom they'd known for years, but was rarely sober enough in the afternoons to dispense good, solid advice.

So when Tom MacLaverty's boozy lunches finally caught up with him and he died a few years ago, Steve naturally became a partner and renamed the firm NolanSullivan. Sure, his old college pals who were making a fortune working on the various Tribunals in Dublin Castle told him he must be mad, that he could make ten times as much money if he came back to Dublin, but to no avail. In a nutshell, Steve loved his job and the peaceful calm of rural life.

And he loved the Davenports. They'd first met over twenty years ago, when Steve, as a rookie solicitor, was sent over to the Hall to sort out 'a delicate matter' for the family. He vividly remembered arriving there for the first time, driving through the entrance gates, past the gate lodge and on up the two-mile drive to the Hall itself. He remembered being nervous as he knocked at the huge oak entrance door, and then been shown in by the fifteen-year-old Portia, grave and pale and old enough to be deeply embarrassed by the situation.

Her father, Lord Davenport, had gone on a gambling spree at nearby Naas races and had bet more than he had on him. The bookie at the racetrack had indulged him, probably impressed by his noble punter. But it was a different story when his lordship had lost over ten thousand pounds on a single race and hadn't a penny to pay up. The police were called and Blackjack was unceremoniously dumped in a Kildare Town prison cell for the night, until bail could be arranged. Except that his lordship's family didn't have a single penny to bail him out.

The solicitors were called, and so the twenty-one-year-old Steve found himself standing in the Yellow Drawing Room, deeply mortified and wondering how on earth he could explain the situation to Blackjack's teenage daughter.

He needn't have worried. Portia had handled the whole thing beautifully. She calmly shook hands with Steve and explained that her mother was looking after her new baby sister and couldn't come downstairs. She then asked how much her father had lost this time? She never even flinched when Steve told her, she only said that the matter would be taken care of and that a few nights in a police lock-up mightn't do her father any harm.

Steve only found out days later that she'd had to sell off an exquisite Fabergé egg, which had been in her family for over a century, to raise the cash. He had never forgotten meeting Portia that day, how his heart had gone out to this teenager, surrounded by all the trappings of wealth and privilege, without two brass pennies to rub together.

And they'd remained the best of friends ever since. God, when he thought of the scrapes he'd got the Davenports out of over the years . . . The time that Lucasta, in a misguided effort to raise cash, decided to organize school tours to visit the estate and the health and safety authority had closed them down within a week. It had simply never occurred to her ladyship to bother with such boring, mundane details as making sure that there were adequate toilet facilities for the coachloads of schoolchildren that arrived. One small boy found a fingernail in the Davenport jelly Lucasta forced them all to buy, and then, to cap it all, a three-foot stone gargoyle fell from the Ballroom ceiling on top of another particularly unfortunate child, who remained in a critical condition for weeks after. Rumour in the town had it that when doctors in the accident and emergency department of Kildare hospital heard that the kids had just come from a tour of Davenport Hall, they immediately gave them all tetanus jabs, just to be on the safe side.

13

Then there was the time that Daisy, aged sixteen, thought she could raise cash by giving guided ghost tours of the Hall: she invented the headless ghost of some distant ancestor and gave visitors a ghoulish rendition of his demise. The problem was that she did such a good job of terrifying her guests that none of them slept a wink that night. The next morning, after a sleepless night listening to the normal creaking of the Hall and imagining the very worst, her guests checked out, bleary-eyed, demanding their money back and vowing to report the Davenports to the tourist board. One even tried to sue for mental distress and anguish. Steve certainly had a job sorting that particular one out! Needless to say, insuring themselves against any of these mishaps was something that would never occur to any of the family, even if they could afford it.

So over the years, Steve had got to know the Davenports intimately. They were friends. (They were clients too, of course, but ones who rarely paid, and he was far too soft-hearted to be a tough creditor. After all, you couldn't get blood from a turnip.) And there was nothing he wouldn't do for them. So when Portia phoned later that day and asked him to come over, he cleared his diary and said he'd be there first thing next morning.

'Actually,' he added, rather theatrically Portia thought, 'I was going to call over to see you anyway. The fact is, I have some news which may be of great interest to all of you.'

Chapter Two

Portia had just drained the last drops of a lukewarm cup of coffee the following morning when she heard the sound of Steve's car scrunching up the gravelled driveway outside. Looking out of the estate office window (a posh title for what was really only the old playroom, never used now), she saw him slowly clamber out of his great black Jeep, bringing a briefcase and a thick wad of files with him. He wasn't handsome, with his ruffled dark brown greasy hair and that slightly unkempt, almost scruffy look he always had about him. In fact, he reminded her of a great big cuddly bear, tall and broad, a gentle giant of a man and a bachelor through and through.

Portia often thought how different he'd look if he ever married. A wife would smarten him up: make him wash his bloody hair for starters and then get him out of those corduroy trousers and 1980s stripy shirts and into trendier gear. He certainly was a man who would be either made or marred by his wife or girlfriend. She'd be a lucky girl who got him though; he might not be Colin Farrell, but he had a heart of solid gold. Anyway, these were thoughts for more leisurely times, she decided as she ran down the great oak staircase and tripped across the black and white marble floor of the huge, domed entrance hall to meet him.

'Thank God you're here, Steve,' she said, standing on tiptoe to hug him. He hugged her back, noticing that she was even thinner and paler than usual. Hadn't slept for days, by the look of her. Portia, for her part, was finding it hard to let go of him. She'd been through so much in the last few days; it just felt good to have a man's strong arms around her, for once. Steve would sort things out for her. Didn't he always?

'There's no problem that can't be solved, Portia. Where's your mum?' he asked, gently releasing her grip.

'Doing energy clearings on anything Daddy ever laid his hands on,' Portia replied.

Lucasta was known to be a great believer in clearing negative energy by chanting, burning incense and ringing bells a lot. 'May the goddess of purity and beauty cleanse what has been soiled by the negative spirit of my bastard ex-husband!' she could clearly be heard chanting from the Library.

'She's been at it all morning,' Portia explained – not that she needed to. Steve was too well used to Lucasta's various eccentricities to bat an eyelid.

'And Daisy?' Steve asked. 'I need to speak to the three of you together.'

'Out riding, I think. She's taking this badly, Steve, you know how close she was to him.'

'Will you find her for me? I'll grab some of Mrs Flanagan's finest instant coffee and I'll meet you in the Library. That's if your mother doesn't sense any negativity around my aura today and ask me to leave,' he said, a wry smile playing round the corner of his mouth.

He wasn't kidding. Lucasta was famous for throwing people out for the flimsiest reasons: their star signs weren't compatible with hers; their channels were blocked; she didn't like the colour of their aura; or they'd somehow pissed her off in a past life unbeknownst to themselves. She'd once accosted a terrified bailiff, who'd come to take back the TV, on the grounds that his spirit guide had brutally assaulted her in the eighteenth century. It worked; she got to keep the TV, free of all repayments.

'Give me five minutes, Steve,' Portia replied.

As she went outside to find Daisy, she already felt a bit better. God, it felt good to have a normal adult to talk to!

Poor Portia had a job dragging Daisy back into the house, after she'd eventually tracked her down, bawling her eyes out in the gazebo.

'Bloody hell, Portia, do I have to talk to him?' she had wailed. 'He's so boring and dreary and I hate the way he just stares at me all the time.' It was a sort of joke in the family that Steve seemed to have an eye in Daisy's direction. He certainly reddened a lot on the rare occasions she spoke to him.

'I mean, for God's sake, Portia, he's an old man. He must be at least forty years of age. Does he even have his own teeth?' Daisy ranted as she strode towards the house, her blond curls gleaming in the sunlight. 'Why the hell can't he find someone his own age to leer after?' she thundered on with all the venom of youth towards middle age. 'Does he think I'm completely desperate? Who died and made me Anna Nicole Smith?'

'Darling, he's here to try to help us, so just try and be civil, that's all I'm asking you,' Portia cajoled as they went into the Library.

Steve was waiting patiently, sitting in the huge green leather armchair by one of the bookcases. Lucasta was twittering around the shelves, chanting and squirting Toilet Duck as she went, not particularly caring where it landed.

'May the goddess of all that is pure cleanse this room of all negativity and . . . Oh hello, dears.' She broke off her chant as the girls came in. 'I'm just getting rid of any last vestiges of your father's spirit,' she said, as if this were the most normal thing in the world. 'You chant, you spray some bleach and then you burn some bergamot incense to expel negativity. Works a treat,' she added cheerfully, splashing the Toilet Duck along the shelves as she worked her way around the room.

'Mummy, is it a good idea to burn anything near where you're squirting bleach?' Portia asked tentatively.

'Don't be ridiculous, sweetie, you're such a worrier. Typical Capricorn,' her mother tossed back.

'Ahem, I've got another meeting in town later this morning, so if you don't mind . . .' Steve said, taking a huge folder stuffed with papers from his black leather briefcase and accidentally dropping a bunch of them on the floor. Daisy silently rolled her eyes to heaven, irritated by his haplessness and making no attempt to conceal it.

'Go on then, let's get this over with,' she said, rudely for her. Portia darted a warning look at her but said nothing.

'OK, let me get to the point,' he continued, more than a little nervous under her gaze. 'Blackjack is probably living it up in Las Vegas as we speak, with his nineteen-year-old girlfriend. And, of course, the ten thousand euros he cleaned out of the safe.'

'Oh Steve, must you?' Daisy wailed, her enormous blue eyes welling up with salt tears.

'Sorry, Daisy, I'm terribly sorry,' Steve apologized, reddening. 'I didn't mean to upset you even more, it's just that . . .' He trailed off. Ballyroan was a small town, and Blackjack had provided the gossips with ample fodder for years. His philandering ways were well known locally. Sarah Kelly certainly wasn't the first affair he'd had and probably wouldn't be the last either. It was hard to blame Steve for being matter-of-fact about the whole thing.

But still Portia sighed. Ten thousand euros he'd taken. Ten thousand. When she had it spelt out to her like that, it hit her all over again. When she thought of how she'd sweated blood for that money! The tiny frozen tour groups she'd patiently guided through the Hall, trying her best to ignore their looks of disgust at the state of the place. (She often thought that no living person could have heard the phrase: 'What a total waste of money that was,' spoken in Japanese quite as often as she had.) The pony-trekking she and Daisy managed to scrimp a few hundred euros out of in the summer months; and the miserable amount of money she eked out from selling rhubarb, mushrooms and home-grown herbs to the organic greengrocer's in Kildare. Unfortunately, they were about the only thing she could manage to grow by herself, since she was unable to afford help on the home farm.

Anyhow. No point in dwelling on the past. It was time to move on.

'Sorry, Daisy,' Steve repeated, looking sympathetically at her. 'It's just that, well, I think I may have a way out of this for you all.'

He'd finally got their attention. All three women turned to look at him, intrigued. Even Lucasta momentarily put down her bleach and incense.

'I had a phone call a while ago from a film production company called Romance Pictures,' he went on, consulting his notes as he spoke. 'They're coming to Ireland to shoot a film, and it seems they've been considering Kildare as a possible location. Apparently, there's a lot of outdoor filming involved, actors chasing each other on horseback, that sort of thing, and they were looking for a few local pointers. So I suggested they send their location scouts to look at the Hall because the landscape around here is just so beautiful, it's perfect. Then I received a follow-up call from them yesterday and, in a nutshell . . .'

'Go on,' said Daisy, intrigued, her blue gaze trained on him.

'Well,' he continued, 'the production company seem to think that Davenport Hall would be the perfect place to shoot the entire film. They've even offered Daisy a job as horse wrangler—'

'Horse wrangler?' Daisy interrupted. 'What the hell is a horse wrangler when it's at home?'

'Basically, they'd want to use all of your horses in the film, and not only that, they'd need you to coach the actors in how to ride properly. You'd be in charge of every horse that they use for filming.'

'You mean I'd get paid for doing what I'm doing now for nothing?' Daisy asked, brightening.

'You've got it,' Steve replied.

'But what about the house itself?' said Portia, a little worriedly. 'Surely they don't want to film inside here?'

'That's exactly what they want,' replied Steve. 'The location manager checked out the Hall from the Bord Fáilte brochure and thinks it's the perfect place to film. It's a period movie so the age of the house is just right; it saves them a fortune in building expensive sets in a studio somewhere. Much easier just to shoot the whole thing here.'

'Steve, you know perfectly well I wasn't referring to the age of the house,' Portia interjected.

'Well, what then?' he asked, sensing the worried note in her voice.

'Oh, just look around you,' she went on, 'we've got to be realistic here. Look at the state of the place! It hasn't been painted since the Emergency, the curtains are only being held together by dust and cobwebs, and chunks of plasterwork are constantly falling on top of us from the ceiling. And that's on a good day. When it's raining, I sometimes have to put up an umbrella inside the house, the roof leaks so badly. And don't even get me started on the cold! On the hottest day in July, when people are sunbathing in the town, we still have to wear at least three layers of woollies, so we don't get frostbite. In winter, I have to scrape frost from the inside of the windows, just to see out. So please don't expect me to believe for one moment that someone wants to make a film in this house, because unless it's a movie version of *Fawlty Towers*, I can't understand why.'

Steve took a deep breath. He knew he'd have to tread carefully here.

'Well, you see, Portia,' he began, pulling all of his lawyerly tact into play, 'the fact is that they love the house exactly the way it is.'

'On the verge of being condemned, do you mean?' she asked, incredulously.

'Maybe it's a Hammer House of Horror production,' giggled Daisy.

'No, it's not a horror film,' said Steve.

'What, then?' chimed both girls in unison.

'The title is *A Southern Belle's Saga: Brent's Return*. It's a sequel, they tell me. The storyline seems to be that the heroine . . . I forget her name . . . emm—' He broke off, searching through his notes.

'Magnolia O'Mara,' said Daisy, suddenly breathless with excitement. *A Southern Belle's Saga* was one of her desert island favourite films of all time.

'Yes, that's it,' Steve went on. 'Anyway, the heroine comes to live in Ireland among her Irish ancestors, but she's fallen on hard times and so she rents out, emm . . . let me just quote from the blurb the film production company sent me . . . Ah yes, here it is. Yes. "Magnolia O'Mara, newly settled in Ireland, rents out a decaying, decrepit manor house, miles from anywhere. She then tries to start a new life away from the Deep South, still torn asunder by the ravages of Civil War and away from Brent Charleston, the only man she ever truly loved." '

'Now you're making sense,' Portia said, sitting back in her chair, the mystery solved.

'Just think, Mummy,' said Daisy, clearly enamoured of the whole idea, 'there'd be film stars all over the house and we'd get to meet them and maybe they'd invite us to the premiere in Hollywood!'

'Oh, how thrilling, darling,' replied Lucasta, her cleansing ritual forgotten as she got swept up in the idea of hobnobbing with Hollywood's A list. 'Maybe I'd get to meet Shirley MacLaine, we were great friends in a past life, you know, and I've always fancied that yummy Marlon Brando, if he'd only lose about ten stone . . .' she went on, never doubting for a second that Hollywood royalty, no matter how overweight, would be magnetically attracted to her.

'Steve, who's starring in the film, do you know?' asked Daisy, beside herself with excitement, her tears long forgotten.

'Oh yes,' he replied vaguely, 'I wrote the name down somewhere.' He leafed through yet another mound of papers.

'Yes, here we are,' he said, putting on his glasses to read the tiny typewriting on the page he produced. 'I'm afraid the star isn't anyone I've ever heard of, some actor called Guy van der Post.'

'Guy van der Post!! But he's the sexiest man alive,' gasped Daisy, almost falling off her chair with shock. 'Did you see him in *Unbelievable Cruelty Two*? He was amazing, he's just so talented,' she said dreamily, his talent clearly having nothing to do with her interest in Guy van der Post.

'I'm afraid I missed that film, Daisy,' said Steve. Only Portia seemed to notice that his soft brown eyes never left her face.

'And just think, my dearest,' said Lucasta, 'he's going to be making a film here, with us! Oh, how exciting! I don't suppose you found out what his star sign is, Steve?' she asked.

'Emm, no, I'm afraid that didn't arise,' he replied tactfully. 'What do you think, Portia? You're very quiet,' he added as he watched her walk slowly to the window and idly wipe some of the filthy dust from the shutters.

Portia looked at him, calm as ever. She had been inwardly marvelling at both her mother and sister and this great talent they shared for completely overlooking anything remotely disagreeable. Ten minutes ago, Daisy had been sobbing her heart out for the loss of her father and now all she could think about was some actor with a very silly name.

'How much?' was all she said aloud.

'I think you'd better sit down for this,' he replied.

'All right,' said Portia, doing as she was told.

'Have a look at this,' he went on, 'and that's only their first offer. I'm sure we could do much better than this.' And he handed her a sheet of paper with a figure written on it. Lucasta and Daisy watched her face intently, knowing the final decision would rest with her. Now that Blackjack had deserted them, there were no two ways about it: Portia was the boss.

She glanced at the sum of money offered and went even whiter than usual. It wasn't a fortune by any means, but it more than made up for what Blackjack had cleaned them out of. A thousand thoughts raced through her head, all fighting for airtime.

Throughout her life, Portia had dreamt of restoring the Hall to its former glory and running it as a fabulous, five-star country house hotel. She'd even gone to college in Dublin to study Hotel Management after she'd left school, probably the happiest and most independent time of her life. It was a four-year course and by her third year she was top of her class, an A student brimming with ideas for the renovation of her ancestral home and then . . . disaster struck. Blackjack casually informed her that in an attempt to double her college fund at the racetrack, he'd lost it all, leaving her with no choice but to return home. True, the money Romance Pictures were offering wasn't nearly enough to carry out the full scale of work she would have wished, but at least she could get part of the roof repaired, maybe even expand the home farm, hire some help and generate a decent income there. It wasn't exactly a win on the National Lottery, but it was certainly a very welcome and timely windfall.

'Where do I sign?' was all she could stammer, her voice sounding as if it came from the next room. 'Quickly, before they change their minds.'

She never even heard Steve's reply, Lucasta and Daisy were too busy cheering and screaming like a pair of teenyboppers at a boy band concert.

'Ladies, ladies, just a moment please, I'm not quite finished,' Steve said, raising his voice to make himself heard. 'That's not all there is to it, I'm afraid.'

'What can you mean?' asked Daisy impatiently. 'Don't we just sign on the dotted line and have done with it?'

'If only life were that simple,' he replied, smiling shyly at her. 'No, Daisy, I'm afraid that the film company have stipulated a non-negotiable condition to the deal going through. One rather important condition.'

Chapter Three

The next few months went by in a daze for Portia. She couldn't believe how quickly everything moved along, once Steve had agreed a deal with Romance Pictures. Soon, huge film production trucks were rolling up outside Davenport Hall and unloading miles of cable, electrical equipment, cameras and lights. So much lighting that Daisy had asked if the entire film were going to be floodlit. Johnny Maguire, the first assistant director on the film had laughed at her.

'Not a chance, love,' he'd said, in a flat Dublin accent. 'You need around sixty lights in these dark rooms just to make them look normal,' he added, pulling on a cigarette. 'When was the last time this house was rewired, by the way?'

Portia was relieved that her mother arrived along just then to change the subject. The house certainly hadn't been rewired since the rural electrification programme of 1936.

'So when can we expect Guy van der Post to arrive?' Lucasta asked, breathless with excitement. 'I think we'll put him in the Mauve Suite when he gets here, Portia darling, it's the only bedroom that's not haunted.'

It had transpired that the only non-negotiable condition Romance Pictures had to shooting at Davenport Hall was that the leading actors all be housed there. It seemed that the producer, one Harvey Brocklehurst Goldberg, was a keen advocate of method acting and was insisting the cast stay at the location, to make their living there seem utterly believable on film (little realizing how ill prepared Hollywood's pampered elite would be for the Spartan rigours of Davenport Hall; the US Marines would have had a hard time getting used to the stench of cat wee alone and at least the army are issued with gas masks).

'Well,' Lucasta went on, pausing only to light a cigarette, 'the Mauve Suite *is* haunted, but only by the spirit of Tiddums the Fourth, a very benign ghost.' Tiddums IV was a favourite ginger cat of Lady Davenport who'd died tragically in a freak accident the previous year, when he'd fallen asleep in the kitchen's huge Aga.

Johnny must be well used to dealing with eccentrics, Portia thought to herself. He never batted an eyelid.

'Ah, Guy van der Post won't be here for a few weeks yet, love,' replied Johnny. 'He's in Thailand shooting the end of the new James Bond movie. I think he's playing the baddie, you know, the one who gets to wear a tuxedo and say, "Not so fast, Mr Bond." '

'Oh, we're just so thrilled to have a Hollywood star staying here!' her ladyship twittered on, totally oblivious to the fact that Johnny and his crew were trying to work. 'It'll be such fun! I'm going to host the most enormous party for you all; you can meet all our lovely neighbours. Some of them are working class too, so you'll have lots in common . . .'

She would happily have gone on, only Portia gently but firmly steered her towards the house.

And then there were the trucks. Dozens of them rolled up the driveway of Davenport Hall and parked in the forecourt in front of the main entrance. Portia and Daisy had no idea what they could all be for, there were so many of them. Johnny had kindly shown them around and patiently explained what each one was used for. There was an entire double-decker bus for catering alone, a truck for make-up and another for wardrobe. In fact, the whole front lawn looked like the circus had arrived. Then there were the three Winnebagos parked right beside the rose garden.

'Is that some sort of kosher food?' Lucasta had asked innocently when they were pointed out to her.

'Far from it, love,' Johnny had replied. 'This is where the stars hang out when they're waiting to do their scenes.'

'Do you mean like dressing rooms, Johnny?' asked Daisy, her eyes like saucers.

'Not like any dressing rooms you've ever seen before. Take a look at this one!' said Johnny, opening the door of the first one they came to with a flourish. The neat writing on the door bore the legend 'Ms Montana Jones'.

'I know that name,' said Portia, racking her brains to think where she'd heard it before.

'Oh! Montana Jones!' said Daisy in amazement. 'I love her! She was in that film *Servant in Seattle* with Hugh Grant.'

Daisy was constantly reading magazines with titles like *Dish the Dirt*, *National Intruder* and *Secrets the Stars Never Wanted You to Know*. Consequently, she was very well up on all her Hollywood gossip.

'In fact, wasn't there a big scandal about her recently?' she asked, crinkling her forehead as she tried to remember.

'Oh, yeah,' said Johnny sagely. 'She borrowed around five million dollars' worth of jewellery from Tiffany's for the Oscars last year and, emm, forgot to return it the next day. At least, that's what she said in court.'

'No, Johnny, I remember now,' Daisy contradicted him. 'At her trial, she said that she got so completely rat-arsed drunk at the Oscars that she forgot all about giving back the jewellery. And apparently, she only had two glasses of white wine, you know.'

'Two poxy little glasses of vino? I'd have that for my breakfast,' said Lucasta. She wasn't joking.

'Two glasses of white wine in Hollywood means you're a dangerous, raving alcoholic,' said Johnny, shaking his head sadly. 'The poor girl spent six months in the Betty Ford Center after that and her career never recovered. No one would touch her. That's why she's doing this film, you know. She's trying to claw her way back to the top. Anyway, take a look at this.'

With a flourish, he threw open the door of Montana Jones's Winnebago and the Davenport ladies trooped in after him. It was an amazing sight.

'It's more like a hotel room than a dressing room,' gasped Daisy. And indeed it was. Over thirty feet long, it had a huge double bed at one end and a full dining room at the other. To the left, there was a fully equipped gym, complete with treadmill and rowing machine, with a door leading off to a steam room and sauna. In the central living area, there was an exquisite leather sofa facing a wide-screen TV with a DVD player.

'Wow!' said Daisy. Her mother and sister were too speechless to do anything but ooh and aah.

'Yup, Montana certainly likes her home comforts,' said Johnny. 'And wait till she gets going on the catering staff! She's vegetarian, vegan, wheat-intolerant, lactose-intolerant . . . In fact, I think the girl lives on blades of grass and nothing else.'

'So that's how she keeps her amazing figure,' Daisy said thoughtfully. It was extraordinary, seeing how the stars lived. Like gods and goddesses from another world, she thought. God help them when they saw the inside of the Hall.

He loves me not . . . he loves me

★

A few days later, in the middle of all this chaos, the phone rang. Portia nearly broke her neck tripping over the electric cables, which the film crew had carelessly strewn all over the estate office in her rush to answer it. (No such luxury as an answering machine at Davenport Hall.)

'Hello? To whom am I speaking?' asked a particularly cultured woman in a South Dublin accent. The sort of accent that pronounced 'Dart' as 'Dort'.

'Oh, hi, it's Portia speaking. Emm, can I help you?'

'Yes, put me through to one of the family, please.'

'Do you mean one of the Davenport family?' Portia asked, wondering if this was a hoax call.

'Obviously I mean one of the Davenports,' came the curt reply. 'Now really, I've got caterers arriving in a few minutes and a florist who's about to have a nervous breakdown and I don't have all day, so if you could get one of them to the phone I'd be most grateful.'

'Well, this is Portia Davenport speaking, so I suppose I count as one of the family,' said Portia politely, not quite knowing what to make of the stranger's odd manner.

'Well, you should have said! There was I thinking I was wasting my time with some lackey. This is Mrs de Courcey speaking. Susan de Courcey.'

'Oh, hi!' said Portia, at a loss as to who this unpleasant woman could be. It momentarily flashed through her mind, was it someone else they owed money to? A new bank manager, perhaps?

'My party planner is just putting the final touches to the guest list for tonight, and we were astonished to see that you hadn't bothered to RSVP your invitation. We sent it to you weeks ago.'

Portia racked her brains. An invitation? To what? No,

29

definitely nothing had arrived; at least, nothing that she'd seen although Lucasta frequently hijacked the post and used it to line her cat-litter trays, causing untold problems for Portia when their phone, gas and electricity bills mysteriously went missing and they were suddenly cut off without warning.

'And I said to my party planner,' Mrs de Courcey went on brusquely, 'that's the landed gentry for you, probably too busy hunting, shooting and fishing to answer a simple invitation.'

'Well, I can assure you that no invitation has arrived here,' answered Portia, taking an instant dislike to this incredibly rude woman. 'May I ask what the invitation's for?'

'Our housewarming party, of course,' said Mrs de Courcey. 'I've invited our two hundred closest friends, mainly legal people, so I don't think you'd know any of them. But my party planner assures me that the correct etiquette on such occasions is to invite the neighbours too, and I'd hate to think we'd get off on the wrong foot . . .'

Portia said nothing. This awful woman and her party planner had already got off on the wrong foot with her.

'So shall we say eight o'clock tonight then?' Mrs de Courcey asked, not bothering to disguise the impatient tone in her voice.

'Emm, well, we're sort of caught up in the middle of some-thing here,' Portia said, unsure of how to explain the film crew who'd descended on them. 'But I will do my best to get there. I'm so sorry about not replying to your invitation . . .' Portia tailed off, thinking: Why am I being nice to this obnoxious woman?

'Well, if you do decide to grace us with your presence, the address is Greenoge Stud Farm, on the Dublin Road. You can't miss it,' came the curt reply as Mrs de Courcey hung up.

And indeed, you couldn't miss it. Portia and Daisy had often driven by that land on their way to and from the town and had noticed the mad frenzy of building work going on there in the past few months. They were used to city people relocating to the country in search of a quieter life, retired couples who sold their Dublin homes for huge amounts of money and moved to smaller and more manageable houses in the peace and tranquillity of Ballyroan. But Greenoge Stud was different. After Davenport Hall, it had more land attached to it than any other property in the area. Portia had only ever seen glimpses of the vast, custom-built house through the scaffolding that surrounded it, but her curiosity was certainly roused. They must have built their home completely from scratch. Who were these people and why had they come to live here? No shortage of money, obviously, she thought wryly to herself as she went in search of her mother and sister to pass on the invitation.

Her timing couldn't have been worse. As she ran down the staircase, dodging cable wires, she met Mrs Flanagan waddling across the marble hall, autograph book in hand.

'Get out of me way, would ya!' she said to Portia, all but elbowing her aside in her rush to get to the main entrance. At the same moment, Lucasta stuck her head around the Drawing Room door.

'Oh, thank God you're there, Mrs Flanagan,' she groaned, 'I really feel most dreadfully unwell, you know. My head is thumping, my mouth's all dry and my hands are shaking uncontrollably.'

'Are you all right, Mummy?' Portia asked, concerned. 'What's the matter?'

'Well, the only logical explanation is that someone's trying to contact me from the other side. I'm such a natural conduit for lost spirits—' began her ladyship, hoarsely.

'Ah, there's one spirit that's been near you all day, and that's a bottle of Paddy Power Gold Label,' Mrs Flanagan

31

interrupted rudely. 'There's nothing wrong with you, only a good, old-fashioned hangover, ya fecking eejit. Now grab the camera and get out here quick,' she ordered, expertly unlocking the heavy oak door.

'What's going on?' Lucasta asked, confused.

'Ah Jaysus, what do ya think, that the coal delivery man is here? There's a stretch limo after coming up the driveway this minute, and I'd be very surprised if it's your husband coming back to ya, wouldn't you?'

Chapter Four

As Mrs Flanagan and Lucasta, closely followed by a curious Portia, trooped out into the warm sunshine, they were just in time to see the longest stretch limo you could imagine scrunch up the gravelled driveway.

'Oh God, wait for me!' Daisy cried at the top of her voice as she raced around the side of the house in her jodhpurs and wellingtons and clambered up the dozen or so stone steps two at a time to join them. You'd think they were expecting royalty, Portia thought, but for the sake of politeness, she slipped in between her mother and sister. What a line-up we make, she thought dryly to herself, they'll think they're at a Royal Command Performance at Drury Lane. All that's missing is the red carpet.

'Please let it be Guy van der Post arriving,' Daisy whispered to herself.

'Ah Jaysus, no, I'm not ready for Guy just yet!' Mrs Flanagan replied, clearly every bit as star-struck as Daisy. 'I'm not even in me good housecoat! I hope it's Montana Jones, and if it is, I'll defrost some of me calf's kidney and liver stew for the dinner tonight in her honour.'

The limo rolled to a stately halt right by the foot of the

steps. (Where in God's name did they find a limo in Ballyroan? Portia asked herself. They must have driven directly from Dublin.) All four of them strained to peer through the windows but, alas, they were too deeply tinted to see anything at all. A chauffeur, clad in uniform, sprang out and elegantly held open the car door. Daisy was about to faint when a slightly overweight, middle-aged man stepped out, smoking a cigar and putting on sunglasses as he did so to protect his eyes from the glare. He was short and stocky and wearing denim jeans with a chunky cable-knit Aran sweater, which had obviously been a recent purchase as the label was still hanging off the back of it. He was accompanied by a woman, about the same age as himself. She was tiny, barely five feet tall, and certainly wasn't attractive, with mousy brown hair parted severely to the side and a tired, pinched look on her face. But she had an air of authority about her that somehow let you know that here was someone you didn't mess with. She also carried a neat clipboard and, oddly, a stopwatch.

'Well, that's what I call one helluva stately pile!' the man exclaimed to his companion in an American drawl as he surveyed the Hall. 'And the scenery on the drive here! I just know we're gonna have a lotta fun on this shoot,' he went on. 'Well, I guess I'd better introduce myself. I'm Jimmy Pearlman, at your service, ma'am,' he said, shaking hands with Portia. 'You know, this is my first visit to your country and I am deeply honoured to be here! I just cannot wait to really immerse myself in your culture. I wanna drink all of your Guinness, eat all of your bangers and mash and listen to as much of your great bagpipe music as I can. I even bought one of your Aran ganseys at the airport as a tribute to my Celtic hosts. It's itching like bejaysus and I may have to be cut out of it, but it's worth it to outstretch the *lamh* of friendship. So, as you say here in your beautiful Emerald Isle, the top of the morning to you all.' (He'll be congratulating us on how well we speak the Queen's English next, Portia thought wryly.)

'Are you the producer, Mr Pearlman?' asked Daisy, puzzled.

'No, honey, better than that. I'm the director. I get to spend the producer's money,' he chuckled, flicking cigar ash on the steps. 'Gee, you sure are pretty. Ever thought about getting into movies yourself?' he went on, a slight leer coming into his voice as he scanned Daisy's lovely face. 'You have a great profile,' he went on, 'kinda like a young Reese Witherspoon.'

A young Reese Witherspoon? Portia thought. Surely Reese Witherspoon was still in her twenties? She had a lot to learn about how prejudiced Hollywood could be against actresses who had the audacity to age.

'I know who you are!' Daisy blurted out, the mystery solved. 'You're James D. Pearlman! Oh my God, I can't believe I'm meeting you!'

'That's right, ma'am,' he replied, delighted at being recognized, 'but everyone calls me Jimmy D.'

'Yes, I know exactly who you are now,' Daisy went on. 'You were nominated for an Oscar for directing *Titanic Two: The Iceberg Strikes Back*, and that was the year that James D. Brooks won but you only heard the first part of his name being called out and you thought you'd won and were halfway to the stage when you realized your mistake and . . .' Daisy trailed off, realizing that this might not be the most tactful story she could be telling.

'Longest walk of my life, back to my seat that night,' said Jimmy D. 'And you must work here too, right?' he asked Lucasta, anxious to change the subject.

'Well—' Lucasta began, about to launch happily into her life story, before he interrupted her.

'Let me guess. I can see your back history now,' he said, moving his hands in front of his face as though painting a picture. 'You're a faithful old family retainer, kinda like that old bird in that black-and-white movie with Laurence Olivier – what was it called? Oh yeah, I got it, *Wuthering Heights* – and you've slaved away in the kitchens for decades, with a secret lust for the Lord of the Manor you've been hiding for years—'

'Ahem,' Portia gently interrupted, judging this conversation to have gone on for long enough. 'I think this might be a good opportunity to introduce my mother, Lucasta Davenport.'

'Well, it's a very great pleasure to meet a real live member of the aristocracy,' Jimmy D. said, taking her hand and kissing it, totally unfazed at his mistake. An easy one to make too, given that her ladyship looked like she permanently slept in a hedge.

Too eccentric to take any offence at this jibe at her appearance, Lucasta innocently asked, 'And is this the famous Montana Jones I've been hearing so much about?' gesturing to Jimmy D.'s companion, who was tapping her Biro impatiently against her clipboard. At this, her tired, pinched face broke into a smile, instantly softening her appearance.

'I'm afraid not, your ladyship,' she said in an accent that was hard to place. She sounded English, Portia thought. 'My name is Caroline Spencer. I'm Miss Jones's personal assistant,' she added in her clipped tones, shaking hands with everyone there.

'Yeah, luv, but where's Montana? I want to get her autograph and maybe a picture of her arriving at the Hall,' Mrs Flanagan said, camera in hand.

'No one speaks directly to Miss Jones except through me. And she doesn't do either autographs or photos, ever. So I'm awfully sorry about that, but if you don't mind, we have an awful lot of luggage to unpack, so if you could show me to Miss Jones's room right away, please?' she said briskly.

'Yes, certainly, I'll show you,' said Portia, sensing that this was not a woman you messed with.

'Thank you,' Caroline replied. 'And I may need some help with the suitcases.'

Twenty minutes later, Portia, Daisy and Mrs Flanagan, who didn't stop moaning once, were still carrying luggage out of the limo, into the house and up the six flights of stairs to the Edward VII Room.

'But where's Montana?' hissed Daisy at Portia as they passed each other on the stairs for about the twentieth time. Portia, who was struggling with a huge Louis Vuitton vanity case labelled 'Vitamins', said, 'I don't know. How could she have slipped in without our noticing?'

'Thank you very much for your help, that'll be all,' Caroline called to them from the top of the stairs. 'Oh, and I'll need to speak to your housekeeper later on about Miss Jones's food allergies,' she added briskly.

'Mrs Flanagan will love that,' Daisy said wryly. 'The only allergy she's ever heard of is to penicillin.'

As they walked back out to the limo, to check that they'd unloaded everything, they both noticed waves of cigarette smoke coming from inside the car door.

'Anyone in there?' Daisy called out.

A long silence followed.

'Hello?' Daisy called out.

'Oh shit,' came the reply at last, followed by a long sigh. 'OK. Get in the car.'

Without hesitating, Daisy and Portia both climbed in.

And there she was. Montana Jones. In the flesh. Although it was very hard to make out her face, so huge were the dark sunglasses that she was wearing. She also had a baseball cap on, pulled right down over her eyes. Daisy, who was used to seeing photos of her in the glossy magazines, dressed up to the nines, swanning down a red carpet at various award ceremonies with some gorgeous guy on her arm, couldn't believe that this was really her. She seemed so tiny and thin and frail. Casually dressed in denim jeans and a deep blue fleece jumper to keep out the Irish cold, she looked like any normal teenager would. In fact, she was so completely unrecognizable, that she could have been almost anyone.

She doesn't look anything like a proper movie star, Portia thought as they introduced themselves in the back of the car. She looked far too normal.

'Is the old she-witch gone?' asked Montana. 'If Caroline caught me having a cigarette she'd report it right back to the producer in LA, and I'd be on the next plane home.'

'Just for having a cigarette?' Daisy asked incredulously.

'Honey, I just got out of rehab. If I drink sparkling water instead of still I'm straight back in there again. That's why Caroline's watching me like the CIA, to make sure I don't fall off the wagon again. You wanna know something? They're making me do urine tests every day on this movie to make sure I'm clean. The insurance company will pull out if anything shows up. I mean, like, how humiliating is that?'

Portia found it hard to believe that here she was, sitting in the back of a limo chatting casually to a star like Montana Jones about her urine.

Daisy was busy gushing, 'Oh Montana, is it OK if I call you Montana? We're just so thrilled to have you here, I'm such a fan of yours from way back, ever since you made your screen debut with *Disastrous Liaisons* . . .'

And Montana let her gush on, smiling politely and thanking them for having her to stay. Yes, of course Daisy could call her Montana. Yes, she'd be delighted to pose for photos with her. Yes, she'd even tell her what Guy van der Post was really like. Three cigarettes later and Montana was inviting Daisy to come out to visit her in LA.

She's not at all what I expected a star to be like, Portia thought as she made her way back to the estate office. She had expected Montana to be vain, spoilt, self-centred and a pain in the arse, and was stunned to find that she was actually just shy, insecure and self-effacing. It's a real lesson, she thought, not to judge books by their covers, film stars included. I like her already, she concluded. She's one of us.

Daisy and Montana would quite happily have spent the rest of the afternoon in the back of the limo, only they were rather crudely interrupted by Caroline Spencer. She came clicking down the stone steps on her kitten heels, calling out, 'Miss Jones? Miss Jones, are you still in the car?' And then, sticking her head inside the window, she spotted her charge and added in her crisp, Mary Poppins-like tones, 'Really, Miss Jones, I can't be running all over this vast house looking for you all day, you know. Now, it's four-thirty p.m. and we know what that means, don't we?'

Daisy turned wide-eyed to Montana, who responded by rolling her eyes heavenward.

'Yes, Caroline, thank you, Caroline, I'll be right there,' she answered sullenly.

'And what's that smell?' asked Caroline, sniffing at the air like a bloodhound. 'Do I smell cigarette smoke?' The colour suddenly drained from Montana's face as she turned imploringly to Daisy.

'Yes, that is cigarette smoke you smell,' Daisy coolly replied, taking the hint as she looked her straight in the eye. 'I have a sixty-a-day habit, you know.'

'Hmmph,' was all Caroline grunted in reply as she stumped back into the Hall. The girls waited till she was out of sight before collapsing into fits of giggles.

'Oh, you absolute doll,' Montana cried, hugging Daisy tightly. 'You covered for me! I'd be out of a job if that bitch caught me smoking. You know what she wants me for?'

Daisy shrugged.

'An afternoon nap, how juvenile is that? Christ, they treat me like a five-year-old since I got clean. Boy, am I glad you're gonna be around, Daisy. At least we'll be able to have a little fun. Say, do you have mini-bars in the rooms here? How about we celebrate my arrival here with a couple of beers?'

'But what about Caroline and the urine tests they make you do every day?' asked Daisy, puzzled.

A dangerous, devious glint came into Montana's eyes. 'Honey,' she purred, ' I may have just thought of a way around that . . .'

Chapter Five

They were already running an hour late for the de Courceys' housewarming party by the time the three Davenport ladies were ready to leave. As they clambered into their ancient, mud-splattered Mini Metro, Portia glanced at her watch for about the hundredth time that evening. Nine p.m. Would they ever get there? Mind you, she'd had some job persuading Lucasta and Daisy to go to the party in the first place.

Montana Jones and Daisy had bonded in a seriously big way ('My new best friend!' as Montana had called her) and it had taken all Portia's powers of persuasion to drag Daisy out of the house. The pair of them had spent all afternoon gossiping (and drinking, judging by the smell of booze coming from them) on the huge four-poster bed in Montana's room.

That is to say, after Montana had recovered from the shock of realizing that this was where she was expected to stay for the next few months. In fairness to her though, once she'd taken in the full horror of her bedroom (the filth, the dust, the freezing cold, the peeling wallpaper and the prevailing smell of damp), she adopted an admirably positive attitude.

'OK, sure, so it's not the Beverly Hills Hotel, but what the heck? It'll help me with the part. My character lives here and so will I.'

She never even flinched when it was pointed out to her that the lump hammer beside her bed was to bang on the pipes in order to get some hot water running in her bathroom. The plumbing at Davenport Hall was ancient, bordering on dangerous, and this was the only way to enjoy the luxury of running water anywhere in the house.

Few other method actors would have endured so much for their craft.

'Why is it called the Edward the Seventh Room, anyway?' she asked Daisy.

'Oh, he stayed here once, I think,' Daisy had replied vaguely, never a great one for knowing the history of the house. 'I know,' she giggled, 'you'd think he'd lived here for years, calling the room after him like that.'

'Well, I thought Edward the Seventh was the title of a movie,' Montana had replied, and the two of them had collapsed drunkenly into hysterical laughter on the bed. 'Now, lock that door to keep ol' hatchet-face Caroline away and let's have ourselves another beer.'

Montana had also taken it on herself to give Daisy a Hollywood-style makeover, plastering her naturally beautiful, blemish-free, porcelain skin with inches of heavy make-up. As if this weren't enough, she decided that Daisy needed to show off her figure a bit more, and proceeded to dress her up in one of her more outlandish movie-star outfits.

'Honey, let's get you out of these jodhpurs and woolly jumpers, that look is just sooo two thousand and two,' Montana had said, in her Valley Girl accent. She'd then dressed her in the thinnest, flimsiest piece of metallic gauze, which basically served as a bra and nothing else. It was completely see-through and was worn with an equally revealing pair of

1960s-style hot pants, which clearly showed off Daisy's knickers. In short, Montana had transformed Daisy from a naturally beautiful, casually dressed country girl into a Versace-clad, over-made-up Beverly Hills slapper.

'What do you think?' she asked Portia, twirling around to show off her new sartorial splendour. 'Montana says I look like a movie star.'

'And so you do,' Portia had replied, shoving her into the car. 'Julia Roberts when she was a streetwalker in *Pretty Woman*.'

And then there was Lucasta. By the time they were due to leave for the party, she'd already moved on to her fifth gin and tonic. Portia had found her in the Drawing Room, knocking them back and flirting outrageously with Jimmy D.

'And you know, even though I'm dealing with the pain of a broken marriage on a daily basis, I simply wouldn't dream of letting that get in the way of my finding happiness with someone else,' she said, pointedly gazing at Jimmy D.

'Well, I think that you're a mighty strong lady, with everything you've been through,' Jimmy D. had replied, sipping a pint of Guinness and chomping on a cigar, completely oblivious to the fact that her ladyship was throwing herself at him.

Eventually, Portia had managed to prise the gin and tonic out of her hand and get her into the car. There was no time for Lucasta to change, she'd just have to go looking like a bag lady. Not that Portia was entirely happy with her own outfit. The only decent thing she had to wear to this sort of occasion was a pink woolly twin set and her jeans. Not very glamorous, she knew, but she had no choice. Ballyroan wasn't exactly the fashion capital of Ireland, and even if it was, she hadn't the money for luxuries like new, trendy clothes. Anyway, she reasoned, they were only putting in an appearance, just to be neighbourly.

And then, of course, the car had broken down on their way. It often happened; it just needed a little water and Portia was well able to fix it herself. But it did mean another delay as she ran into O'Dwyer's pub in the town with the empty plastic bottle she kept in the boot for emergencies like this.

'Here, Portia,' Mick O'Dwyer, the friendly landlord, had said to her as he handed over the replenished bottle of water. 'Is it not high time you bought yourself a new car? Things can't be that bad up at the Hall!' he joked.

'Got to dash, Mick, we're on our way to a party and we're so late,' was all she said in reply as she ran out of the pub door.

'In response to your question, Mick, yes things are indeed that bad up at the Hall.'

Mick turned around only to see Shamie Joe Nolan, Jr, Ballyroan's local TD (and easily one of the best-known members of Ireland's Parliament, the Dáil). He and his wife, Bridie, were standing at the crowded bar, patiently waiting to be served. Even though the pub was packed to the rafters, it was impossible to miss them. Shamie was wearing a red tartan peaked cap on his head, which brought out the broken veins on his huge, bulbous nose, and his wife was dressed in an out-landish mother-of-the-bride blue suit, with a bright yellow buttonhole and brassy blonde hair to match.

'Ah Shamie, how are you? And Bridie, you're looking as gorgeous as ever tonight. What can I get you?' Mick asked, tactfully ignoring the fact that Bridie looked like she was on the game.

'I'll have a pint and my lady wife will have a gin and tonic, thanking you, good sir!' Shamie replied, hauling himself up on to a bar stool that had just become free and shouting as loudly as if he were haranguing the Opposition leader during a heated debate.

'You are one ignorant fecking gobshite, so you are, Shamie,' his wife hissed at him under her breath. 'Pints is only what knackers drink, ya thick eejit.' Then, raising her voice and suddenly dropping her Kerry accent, she called out to Mick, 'He meant to order a chardonnay, thanks very much.' As Mick nodded and went to get their order, she went on, 'And shift yer fat arse off that stool, me shoes are killing me and I need to sit down.'

Shamie obeyed and made a great show of seating his wife; after all, in a small country pub you never knew who'd be watching.

'There you go,' said Mick, delivering their drinks at break-neck speed. 'How did your clinic go tonight by the way, Shamie?' he added, whipping the proffered fifty-euro note from his hand and ringing it into the till.

'Well, there's a lot of talk about what's going on above at Davenport Hall, to be honest with ya,' replied Shamie, and then, raising his voice so most of the pub could hear, 'and keep the change out of that fifty for yourself there, Mick, good man.' Twenty years in politics had taught him that it never did any harm for people to think you were generous to a fault.

'It's all very fecking well for film stars to come here to make a picture, but what good is that going to be to Ballyroan?' said Bridie, sipping her screw-top white wine and crossing her fat, pork-ham-and-sausage-roll bare legs with studied elegance. 'Of course, that's the Davenport family for ya. They're all too fecking cracked in the head to think about the disruption this'll bring to the town. Once Lucasta Davenport is making a quick buck, that's all she gives a shite about. And as for Blackjack fecking off with some teenager, it's a disgrace. Landed gentry, me arse!'

Shaking his head, her husband said, 'It's a terrible thing for this town to have a family of lunatics running the Hall. I

45

mean, what did we fight the War of Independence for only to get shut of the Anglo-Irish anyway? When ya think of the amount of prime land that lazy shower are sitting on and them letting the ground rot from under them—'

'Shut the feck up or people will think yer're in the Labour Party,' hissed his wife.

Reddening, Shamie changed tack. 'And when you think of how this town is only crying out for a motorway to put us on the map, and them inbreds at the Hall with two thousand acres sitting idle, it's a fecking disgrace!' he said, banging his fist on the bar.

'Well, maybe it's high time the Davenports got a kick up their behinds,' said Bridie. 'All it would take is the right word in the right ear.'

Her husband smiled down at her. 'Jaysus, I did well the day I married you, Bridie. You're the perfect wife for a politician, do ya know that? Eva Peron eat yer heart out! I'm telling you, love, the day will come when I'll have a ministry of me own above in Dublin, and won't you be the last word in style arriving to meet the girls for lunch in a chauffeur-driven ministerial Merc!'

His wife glowed, excited by the thoughts of what lay ahead. A ministry for her husband, and then who knew? The Taoiseach was getting on a bit and was always on the lookout for a successor . . . She could see herself now, Ireland's first lady – and by Jaysus wouldn't she give them a run for their money? A style icon, a Jackie Kennedy for the noughties, that's what she'd be. (She'd get her roots done twice a month, develop an eating disorder like royalty and open an account on Frawley's of Thomas Street, to hell with the expense!) All it would take was for her to steer her husband in the right direction. A bit like Macbeth in that boring aul' Scottish play they once had to sit through at her son's school, all he needed was a wife who'd give him a right good kick up the arse.

'I'm only saying, stranger things have happened, Shamie,' she replied. 'Look at the time they found some fecking medieval ruins in Foxrock, and you still got an eight-lane dual carriageway built over it, in spite of the gobshite conservationists protesting. And you were dead right! Do ya remember that great speech ya made in the Dáil, in front of half the Cabinet, when ya stood up and said, "I mean, for feck's sake, what's more useful? Getting into the city centre ten minutes quicker on the motorway or a few fecking piles of ancient aul' rocks that are of no use to anyone?" '

'Yeah, the papers really sat up and noticed me after that,' replied her husband, fondly reminiscing about the amount of column inches that speech had generated. ('SHAMIE NOLAN GETS HIS ROCKS OFF', the banner headline in the *Evening News* had read.)

'And what about the time ya took on that lazyarse shower of nuns in the convent in Balbriggan?' Bridie went on. 'I never heard the like of it before or since. There were only half a dozen eighty-year-old Little Sisters of the Poor sitting on nine hundred acres of land! And ya bought that up for half nothing and got the shopping mall up in no time.'

'They were the little Sisters of the Rich by the time I'd finished with them,' laughed Shamie.

'Well, this could do the same thing for yer career all over again,' insisted Bridie. 'Think of what ya could do for Ballyroan, Shamie! Think of the tens of thousands of young people in this country who can't get on the property ladder! For feck's sake, you'd get six housing estates on the Davenport land alone. Young people could buy starter homes here and commute to Dublin – young people with votes! Will ya use yer fecking head!'

'And all it would take would be an aul' bit of rezoning,' said Shamie, lost in thought, 'and, of course, a fabulous new motorway to Dublin . . .'

'I'd say the Davenports would be delighted to get shut of the place,' said Bridie. 'Sure, haven't that family been there long enough?'

Chapter Six

And so, nearly two hours late, the Davenports' bashed-up Mini Metro eventually pulled up beside the de Courceys' house. It had been relatively easy to find: there was a long line of Mercedes, BMWs and more soft-top convertible cars than Portia had ever seen parked in the driveway, all with Dublin registrations. Portia parked discreetly under a tree, as far away from the door as she could, in the hope that no one would see her car and laugh.

'Oh my God, it's like something from a magazine!' Daisy exclaimed as the three of them trooped up the pink-gravelled driveway towards the house. ('Pink gravel!' Lucasta had sniggered. 'What the fuck next?' and Portia, for once, had to agree with her.)

The house was an enormous flat-roof bungalow, entirely new and ultra-modern in design, with wall-to–wall glass windows looking out on to the immaculate front garden. Portia had heard the phrase 'manicured lawn' before, but had never seen anything like this. Davenport Hall was a wilderness in comparison.

'Wow, they must have had the garden landscaped,' she said, noticing the tasteful shrubberies and beautiful bay trees in

twin ceramic pots standing neatly on either side of the front
door.

As they approached the door, however, they were suddenly
illuminated by bright security floodlights, making them completely visible to the other guests inside the glass walls of the
house.

'Jesus, what's that?' said Lucasta as she stumbled over with
shock, temporarily blinded by the glare and knocking over
one of the bay trees as she did. There was a loud crash as it
toppled over, smashing the ceramic pot into a thousand tiny
pieces.

'Oh Mummy, are you all right?' Daisy cried out, bending
down to help her mother up. However, she'd momentarily
forgotten that she was only wearing a tiny pair of hot pants.
As she bent down, the hot pants came down too, so that the
entire houseful of guests was now treated to the sight of
Daisy's bare bum wriggling about as she dragged her mother
to a standing position. As far as they were concerned, it looked
like she was mooning at them.

Unaware that her family was providing a sideshow for other
guests, Portia rang the doorbell. It was one of those elegant
bells that chime resonantly throughout the house, unlike the
one at Davenport Hall, which sounded like a foghorn.

The most immaculately dressed woman Portia had ever
seen answered the door, with perfectly coiffed fair hair,
groomed to within an inch of its life. Her make-up was
impeccable and made her look far younger than her sixty-odd
years. The dress she was wearing was simple, black and almost
certainly cost a four-figure sum. The whole look was completed with a string of pearls and a pair of elegant, strappy
sandals which most definitely were not purchased in
Ballyroan. (Fitzsimon's, the only shoe shop in the town, still
considered the Dubarry Hush Puppy to be the height of

chic.) In short, she looked a million dollars. Unfortunately, however, the same could not be said of the three new, rather scruffy arrivals on her doorstep.

'Yes?' she said in that South Dublin accent Portia immediately recognized from the phone call earlier. 'Have you come about the hedges? Isn't it a bit late to start gardening? And besides, I have guests, so if you call back tomorrow that would be much more convenient,' she concluded, about to slam the door in their faces.

'Well, actually, I think we have been invited,' Portia said apologetically. 'You must be Susan de Courcey? I'm Portia Davenport, we spoke earlier, and this is my sister Daisy.' Their hostess said nothing, but coldly shook hands with each of them. Portia could feel her looking them up and down, taking in their appearance. 'And this is my mother, Lucasta,' she concluded, wondering again why she was being polite to this awful woman. But then, she thought, she'd forced the others to come out in the first place, why not stay for a few minutes, put in an appearance and then get the hell out of there?

'Oh, you're Lady Davenport?' asked Mrs de Courcey, momentarily impressed at meeting aristocracy. 'Well, do come in, then,' she said, finally holding open the door for them.

'Thank bloody God for that,' said her ladyship. 'I'm dying for a drinkie. Where's the bar?' She all but knocked Mrs de Courcey over as she barged inside, followed tentatively by her daughters.

Neither of them had ever been inside a house like it in their lives. Everything was open plan, so that when you walked in the door you were immediately in the living area. It had been designed with stark Japanese minimalism, in total contrast to Davenport Hall, and it seemed to be painted white everywhere. The first thing that struck you was the heat; it was boiling hot even though the night outside was freezing. Then there was the deep-pile white carpet that felt so incredibly luxurious underfoot, like walking on cotton wool. A pianist was tinkling away, playing Cole Porter tunes at the grand piano beside the door.

Dotted around the walls were some tasteful oil paintings and a few watercolours that seemed to have been chosen to go with the house, they blended in so perfectly with their surroundings. To the left, in a sunken area you stepped down to, was a long white sofa facing a rectangular coffee table. Facing it was an elegant white marble fireplace with a giant plasma TV screen above it. To the right was a dining area with a magnificent mahogany dining table which could easily seat twenty people, and ahead, a curved staircase made of glass brick and covered in the same white carpet which was such a feature of the house.

And then there were the guests! There must have been over two hundred people elegantly standing around quaffing champagne from fluted crystal glasses. Waiters dressed in black tie hovered discreetly in the background waiting to replenish people's glasses. These people just oozed wealth and privilege, Portia thought, noticing how beautifully dressed all these skinny women were. (God, they look like they've thrown up everything they've ever eaten in their lives! she thought, scanning the room.) It seemed that every single one of them was wearing black, and designer labels at that, perfectly complemented by the dazzling diamond jewellery they wore around their fingers and throats. She spotted Steve in the throng, chatting to one of these elegant creatures: a woman wearing a backless dress, which showed off her suntan to perfection. (The dress was black, what else?) Apart from him, though, she didn't recognize a single soul.

'We must look like the Beverly Hillbillies compared with these people,' whispered Portia to Daisy. She had never felt so scruffy in her whole life, and was suddenly aware of the picture she and her family cut. Lucasta, with her filthy waist-length grey hair, wearing a tweed skirt, muddy flat brogues, laddered tights and the navy wax jacket, which would have to be surgically removed from her. She literally lived, ate, drank and slept in that stinking jacket and normally kept the pockets permanently stuffed with cat biscuits, as treats for the dozen or so strays she kept at the Hall. Daisy, looking like an over-painted trollop trying hard to be Jennifer Lopez in that ridiculous outfit; and Portia herself, feeling like a middle-aged frump in her Marks & Spencer woolly twin set. She found herself wishing fervently that she'd at least washed her hair before she came out. These women looked like they'd spent all day in the beauty salon getting ready for the party.

'May I offer you a glass of champagne?' a waiter who'd magically appeared at Portia's shoulder asked.

'Yes, thanks,' Portia replied. She rarely drank, but thought she'd need something to get her through this ordeal.

'And a beer for me,' Daisy added, oblivious to the stares her outfit was attracting.

'About bloody time someone offered me a drink,' said her ladyship. 'Large gin and tonic, please, and do you have a light?' she asked, fumbling in the huge pockets of her jacket and producing a bashed-up packet of cigarettes.

'I'm afraid there's absolutely no smoking in this house,' snapped Mrs de Courcey. 'I loathe the smell.'

'And these must be our new neighbours,' said an elderly and rather overweight man, joining their group. He was dressed in black tie and wore a cummerbund, which only served to attract attention to his bulging waistline. 'Susan, do introduce me, darling.'

'This is my husband, Michael,' said Mrs de Courcey,

carrying out the introductions without a flicker of enthusiasm. 'That's Chief Justice Michael de Courcey,' she added, as if they should have heard of him.

'Do you know, we've only been here a few days and already I've heard so much about your family,' he went on, peering over the half-moon glasses perched on the edge of his nose. His voice was loud and booming and seemed calculated to intimidate, probably from years of pontificating from the bench.

God, he's a bit scary, Portia thought to herself. Wouldn't fancy coming up in court in front of him with an unpaid TV licence.

'I hear you have some notable celebrities staying with you at present, you'll have to introduce me. I'm something of a movie buff myself, you know,' he boomed on. 'Now, can any of you ladies name all of the Magnificent Seven?' he said, with all the swagger of someone about to launch into a well-rehearsed party piece. 'Well, can you?'

There was a short silence as Portia and Daisy looked at each other, both of them suddenly feeling very small, as though they were back in school and unable to answer a simple question about the Battle of Waterloo.

'Dopey, Sneezy, Grumpy,' Daisy muttered under her breath, but thankfully, the Chief Justice didn't hear her.

'Yes, that question does seem to separate the men from the boys, I find,' he said, shaking his head sadly as though speaking to two dimwit students. 'Well now, there was Yul Brynner, Steve McQueen—' he recited by rote, before his wife cut across him.

'Oh shut up, Michael, no one's interested. But, you know, our housekeeper has been marvellous about filling us in on all the local gossip, particularly about your recent domestic troubles. I understand your husband' – with a perfunctory nod to Lucasta – 'has abandoned you, traded you in for a younger model so to speak. Bad luck.'

Lucasta, thankfully, was too engrossed in downing her gin and tonic to feel the full force of this insult. But Portia and Daisy did. 'You know, it's enough to give happily married men ideas!' she went on, patting her husband's bulging waistline under the misguided impression that she was being funny. He at least had the good grace to look embarrassed by this, Portia noticed.

'How dare you?' Daisy blurted out, cutting her short. 'You have no idea what a wonderful man Daddy is. If he were here now, he'd smack you one for saying that—'

Thankfully, she was interrupted by Steve who, with impeccable timing, had just arrived at her side. 'Hey, girls,' he greeted them cheerfully, unaware that the third Gulf War had been about to break out. 'Nice outfit by the way, Daisy,' he added, unable to take his eyes off her see-through top.

Portia kissed him on the cheek, delighted to see at least one friendly face at this awful party.

'Oh, hi, Steve,' Daisy answered dully, taking in Steve's characteristically unkempt appearance (crumpled corduroy trousers and a patterned jumper, which looked as though one of Lucasta's cats had thrown up on it). She would gladly have continued berating her hostess, only, just then, she spotted her ex-boyfriend, Sean Murphy, in the throng.

Oh God, please don't let her cause a scene, Portia thought. Don't let's give these awful people any more ammunition against us than they already have. Daisy had a habit of tearing strips off anyone who crossed her, anytime, anyplace, any-where, particularly when fuelled by alcohol.

'I don't bloody believe this,' she said, striding towards Sean, gunning for a fight. 'That bastard dumped me and broke my fucking heart and I'll bloody well sort him out now. My blood's up.' Portia could see Sean Murphy going white in the face as Daisy marched towards him. But there was no stopping her. Once the volatile Daisy was up for a fight, God help anyone who got in her way, especially after an afternoon spent knocking back one beer after another.

'Oh Steve, it's going to be a long night,' Portia sighed as she half-heartedly sipped her champagne.

'Don't worry, I'll keep an eye on Daisy,' he said protectively. 'I'll make sure she doesn't douse him in paraffin and chuck him on the fire.'

'How the hell am I going to get the pair of them out of here?' asked Portia, knowing full well that it would be near impossible to drag Lucasta home until the free booze ran out. She could see poor Sean in the corner of the room being accosted by a semi-naked Daisy; there was no way her sister was going anywhere until she'd drawn blood. Lucasta was by now perched beside the pianist and was singing along to 'Night and Day', her favourite Cole Porter song. 'She'll be up on that piano next, doing her impression of Michelle Pfeiffer in *The Fabulous Baker Boys*,' she added wearily. When in her cups, Lucasta had no doubt that she sang like Charlotte Church, whereas she actually sounded more like Ozzy Osbourne after a vodka-fuelled night on the tear. And that was usually before she launched into her party piece, a self-composed little ditty entitled 'Soap up your Arse and Slide Backwards up a Rainbow'.

'Look, go outside and get some air,' Steve said gently. 'Give them an hour and then I'll help you get them home. There's just a few old friends from law school here I want to catch up with. One hour, Portia, that's all.'

Portia did as she was told. It felt so good to step outside into the crisp night air, away from the awful de Courceys and their pristine home. She found herself strolling to the bottom of the garden, champagne glass in hand, where she found a stone bench perched beside a Japanese-style water feature. As she plonked down, grateful for a little peace and quiet, all she could think was: Thank God I'll never have to socialize with these dreadful people again. True, Ballyroan was a small town, but they were so isolated up at the Hall that it was easy enough to avoid anyone you didn't want to see.

'Had enough already?' came a man's voice from the darkness behind her.

'Jesus!' screamed Portia, nearly leaping out of her skin and spilling the dregs of her champagne down the front of her jumper. 'Who's there?' she asked, peering into the sculpted hedgerows behind her.

'I'm so sorry, I didn't mean to startle you,' he replied, stepping from the shadows. Portia glanced up. A tall, fair-haired man, about her own age, stood in front of her. He was wearing a beautifully cut suit, black of course, and was lightly tanned as though he'd just returned from a holiday. His eyes were a deep blue and twinkled as they took in this strange lady, all by herself, doused in champagne.

'Were you trying to escape from all those legal eagles inside?' he asked, sitting down beside her. 'You certainly don't look like a barrister or a solicitor,' he added, smiling. 'Let me guess, you're a socialite who's dodging your ex-boyfriend inside. Or maybe you're the religious type and you've come out here to contemplate life, the universe and everything. Or maybe, like me, you just slipped out for a quiet smoke,' he concluded, offering her a cigarette as he lit one for himself.

'None of the above, I'm afraid.' Portia laughed, amused that anyone could describe her as a socialite. 'I just slipped out for a breather,' she went on, 'and I think as far as the hostess is concerned, my family are *personae non gratae* tonight.'

'Who are you with?' asked the stranger, exhaling smoke into the night air, his eyes studying her face keenly.

'My mother and younger sister,' she replied, wondering who this handsome man could be. Not a local, anyway; she wouldn't have forgotten meeting him before. Probably a friend of the family who'd come from Dublin.

'And why would you think you and your family are unwelcome here?' he asked, stretching his long legs out in front of him.

'Well, let's just say we don't exactly fit in with the gathering inside. I'm sure they're all lovely people and everything, but I don't think country folk like us are quite the type of guests Mrs de Courcey wants at her elegant soirée. If you'd seen her face when we arrived – I was half expecting her to delouse us. I could have sworn she was looking over her shoulder to see where we'd parked our caravan.'

The stranger said nothing, but chuckled to himself. Portia found herself gazing at him from the corner of her eye. God, he was gorgeous-looking. She was so out of practice when it came to chatting up men, she was afraid she'd come across as a stalker or a serial killer. She couldn't remember the last time she'd flirted: the 1980s probably. Anyway, she thought resignedly, why would any guy as divine-looking as this one give her the time of day? He was probably only being polite, and would soon drift inside to join his girlfriend. Or wife. And yet her companion seemed in no hurry to leave her.

'And what do you think of the house?' she asked, figuring she might as well be hanged for a sheep as a lamb. 'Did you ever see anything like it? I was afraid that de Courcey battleaxe would berate me for leaving imprints on her cashmere carpets, just by standing on them. It's almost as though she had her guests interior designed; they all seem to be colour-coded. Do you think these people ring each other up beforehand, just to make sure that they're all dressed to blend in?'

'Yes,' he said, looking at her with interest, 'gatherings like this aren't exactly my cup of tea either. A load of boring legal people talking about the Tribunals in Dublin, how much dosh they're all making out of them and how white-collar crime is really paying these days. No one in Ireland goes to prison any more, it seems, you just sit in front of a Tribunal for a few months and then nothing happens. No, give me a good old-fashioned knees-up any day. And as for the women! They're all afraid to smile in case they get wrinkles and they're all terrified to sit down in case their fabulously expensive dresses happen to crumple. The thirty-something ones are the worst,' he went on, warming to his theme. 'It's almost like they're interviewing you for the role of husband-to-be. Honestly, they must think I'm blind or something. Do they think I can't see them looking down to clock whether or not I'm wearing a wedding ring?'

Portia just smiled; this guy obviously had a lot of women chasing after him.

'I'm not, by the way,' he said, smirking at her.

'You're not what?' she asked, at a loss.

'Married.'

'Oh,' was all she could manage to say, trying very hard to sound casual and uninterested.

'I'm sorry,' he went on. 'You're very patient to put up with my rantings; most women would have told me where to go. I've been working on Wall Street for the past few years and Manhattanites tend to say it like it is. You must forgive me, I'm just bitter and twisted.' He twinkled at her, looking neither bitter nor twisted.

'What a change it must be for you, coming back to Ireland after so long,' she went on. 'I presume you're living in Dublin?'

59

'Well, as a matter of fact—' he began, when suddenly they were interrupted by a voice calling from the door to the garden.

'Andrew? Andrew, are you there? Senator Callaghan wants a word with you!'

Portia would recognize those strangulated vowels anywhere. It could only be Mrs de Courcey.

'Be right there, Mum,' he answered as he sprang to his feet.

'Oh Christ,' said Portia, squirming inside. 'I had no idea that this was your home. There's no way I'd have gone on like that if I'd known . . .' She trailed off. Bloody typical, she thought, the first interesting guy over sixteen and under seventy that I've met in decades and I have to insult his mother, and his house for good measure.

'Don't apologize,' he said, offering his hand to help her up. 'Between you and me, I actually agree with you.' He winked at her conspiratorially. 'I'm only here temporarily until my own apartment in Dublin is ready and then I'll throw a proper housewarming. One you can smoke at for starters,' he added, stubbing out his cigarette.

'Well, I see you've met the neighbours then, Andrew,' said Mrs de Courcey as she waited for them by the door. 'What was it again? Patricia, isn't it?' she asked.

'Portia,' she replied, unable to contain herself. 'I'm named after a character in Shakespeare's *Merchant of Venice*, actually, not after a stripper in a Chris de Burgh song.'

Mrs de Courcey said nothing, merely eyed Portia up and down, her eagle-eyed gaze noticeably resting on the stain where she'd spilt her drink on her jumper. It looked like she'd drooled all down her front.

'Well, it's lovely to meet the girl next door, so to speak,' Andrew said, politely shaking her hand. 'At least, to meet you properly.'

'And you,' was all Portia could manage in reply, fully aware of his mother glaring at her.

Andrew smiled down at her. 'I think you've finally met your match, Mum,' he said, steering Portia back towards the house.

'Andrew, please, the Senator is waiting,' snapped Mrs de Courcey, barging on ahead of them.

As they went back inside, Portia's heart sank. Her mother was singing her lungs out at the piano, belting out her favourite show tune, 'Memory' from *Cats*. Except that the woman hadn't a note in her head. She was drowning out any conversations that may have been going on and was blissfully unaware that she was making a complete show of herself. Other guests were tactfully moving away from the piano, one by one, as Lucasta screeched her head off tunelessly.

As if this wasn't bad enough though, Daisy was standing at the marble fireplace loudly and drunkenly berating Sean Murphy for having dumped her and not giving a damn who overheard.

'You ASSHOLE GOBSHITE!' she almost roared at him. 'Did you ever ONCE consider MY feelings? You never once introduced me to your family or your friends—'

'But, Daisy, we only ever went on three dates, it's not like it was serious or anything,' Sean was trying to say. But in vain; there was no stopping Daisy once she got going.

'SHUT UP and listen!' she snarled drunkenly at the poor terrified Sean. 'You were just using me for sex, you tosser. What sort of bastard are you that you think that's an acceptable way to treat your girlfriend?'

'But, Daisy, you were never my girlfriend, I only ever called you once . . .' Sean tried to interject, deeply embarrassed and probably feeling like he was re-enacting the bunny-boiler scene from *Fatal Attraction*. In vain, Portia looked around to see where Steve had got to, but he was deeply engrossed

61

in conversation with Andrew's father, the Chief Justice.

'I'm awfully sorry about the sideshow,' said Mrs de Courcey to the distinguished Senator, well within Portia's hearing. 'I'd no idea our new neighbours were, emm, so colourful, shall we say?' she added.

Portia could take no more. 'Would you excuse me?' she whispered to Andrew as she left his side and headed straight for the piano. 'Time to leave, Mummy,' she said softly into her mother's ear, closing down the lid of the piano as she did so. 'Party's over.'

'Don't be a bore, sweetie, I'm only warming up,' said Lucasta, gulping back another gin and tonic.

'I know, Mummy, and that's why the party's over,' replied her daughter, gently but firmly steering her towards the door.

'Need a hand?' came a voice from beside her. She looked up. It was Andrew.

'Would you mind telling my sister that it's time for us to leave,' she asked calmly. Bugger it, there was plenty of time to be mortified tomorrow. 'You can't miss her, she's the girl dressed in next to nothing screaming her head off beside your fireplace.'

Andrew said nothing, merely nodded and went off to find Daisy.

As Portia struggled to the door with her drunken mother, she was aware that the room had gone deadly quiet and that, probably, all eyes were on them. She finally made it outside, dragging her mother in her wake, and got as far as the car. Once again, the security lights came on full blast, just in case there was anyone inside who hadn't noticed them leave. The cold night air suddenly hit Lucasta, making her drowsy and easy enough for Portia to bundle into the back of the car. Daisy was another story, however. Portia looked up to see Andrew practically hauling her out of the house, as she continued to hurl drunken abuse at the hapless Sean Murphy.

'BASTARDS! YOU'RE ALL FUCKING BASTARDS!' she was roaring at the top of her voice as Andrew helped load her into the front seat.

'She's just tired and emotional,' he said, smiling at Portia, greatly amused by the whole situation. 'She'll be fine when she sleeps it off.'

Portia couldn't look him in the face. As she got into the driver's seat, she was aware that he was standing beside the car waving her off. Please let the bloody car start, was all she could think. Please, dear God, just let it start. On the fourth attempt, it finally did. Oh, thank Christ, she thought as she drove back down the driveway. In her rear-view mirror, she could still see him waving as her car spluttered great clouds of blue smoke from the exhaust into his face.

As Andrew strolled back to the party, deep in thought, his mother came to meet him at the front door.

'Really, Andrew, Senator Callaghan has to leave now and you've hardly said two words to him all night,' she said, angrily twirling the pearl necklace around her neck.

'I was just seeing our guests off, Mum,' he answered coolly.

'Well, just so long as that's the last you see of them. You were an awfully long time chatting with the tall skinny older one. What was her name again?'

'Portia,' he replied, thinking how poor an actress his mother made. Of course she remembered the name, this was just her subtle way of showing disapproval.

'Well, whatever her name is, she and her family behaved like an absolute sideshow tonight. If I'd wanted a cabaret, I'd have booked one. Poor Elizabeth Montgomery is still talking about Lady Davenport screaming her head off at the piano. And the young blonde daughter who was dressed like a trollop most definitely used the "see you next Tuesday" word.

Your father had to have a lie down when he heard her. And I'm quite certain I saw her ladyship slipping a bottle of Cristal under her jacket as she was being dragged out of the door.'

He was about to retort when his mother delivered one of her trademark killer lines.

'I mean, for goodness sake, Andrew, what will Edwina say?'

Chapter Seven

Portia barely slept a wink that night. It was well after three a.m. when she finally got to bed and sleep just wouldn't come. All night long she lay there, listening to the grandfather clock in the hall booming away the passing hours. And thinking. Wondering if she'd ever be able to look any member of the de Courcey family in the face again.

Ordinarily, she wouldn't really have cared; after all, her family had been the talk of the town many times before and no doubt would be again. But this was different. Her mind kept coming back to Andrew and the way his eyes had danced when she was slagging off his mother's party. She'd been so completely starved of male attention for so long that it was impossible to trust her own instincts. Portia was probably the least vain creature in the world and so had no faith in her ability to attract men.

He's just come back from New York, where he was probably dating scores of women whose lives are like something out of *Sex and the City*, she reasoned with herself, suddenly getting a mental picture of him living in Manhattan, surrounded by models and Broadway actresses. Anyway, she thought, he was probably only being charitable by giving me the time of day. Why would someone like him look twice at me?

She was suddenly filled with self-loathing at the way she looked, hating her lank, mousy-brown hair, her pale, freckled skin and her shapeless rake-thin figure. She was tall, over five feet ten, and at one time had been thought reasonably pretty, with her even features and bright blue eyes, but years of slaving away at Davenport Hall, stressing about how the next bill was going to be paid and what they could do to survive had taken its toll on her.

Right, she thought, lying on her back and staring at the ceiling, at least that's one problem I can solve. Like it or not, she was going to give herself a makeover.

Breakfast at the Hall was a desultory affair the next morning. Daisy slid into her accustomed place at the kitchen table as white as a ghost and, unusually for her, not saying a word. But when Mrs Flanagan plonked down a plate full of rashers and sausages in front of her, she could take no more. She wordlessly ran out of the room and into the downstairs bathroom, from where everyone could clearly hear her throwing up.

'Better out than in,' Mrs Flanagan said cheerfully.

'Really, Mrs Flanagan, must you make such a Godawful racket?' Lucasta had growled as yet another plate was unceremoniously clattered down in front of her.

'Ah, eat yer breakfast and don't be annoying me,' replied Mrs Flanagan, well used to dealing with her ladyship after she'd overdone it the night before.

Portia knocked back the last of her orange juice, grateful at least for not having the mother and father of all hangovers, as Lucasta and Daisy did. But even for someone as good-natured as she was, it was bloody hard to have sympathy for either of them, after their joint performance the previous night.

Lucasta slurped the last dregs of her tea and stood up to go.

'Do you know, I've had the most wonderful idea, darling,' she said to Portia as she shoved fistfuls of uneaten rashers into her pocket to feed her cats with.

'Yes, Mummy, what about?' asked Portia, groaning inwardly.

'About what to do with my share of the money we're getting for the film. I thought it might be rather jolly for me to go into business. My horoscope says this is an awfully good month for me to embrace new ventures.'

Lucasta consulted her horoscope on a daily basis and rarely took any decision without first checking to see if her planets were favourably aligned.

'Oh Mummy, what are you thinking of now?' asked Portia, remembering all too clearly the occasion when an unfortunate visitor to the Hall had found mouse-droppings in the home-made chocolate-chip cookies Lucasta had forced him to buy, her last foray into the business world. Then there was the time her mother had tried to sell her own original pottery to unsuspecting American tourists staying at the Hall, even though the earthenware cups and saucers she tried to make in her knackered kiln looked like big blobby, semi-pornographic lumps. Never one to miss a sale, however, she passed them off as handmade modern art sculptures, without batting an eyelid.

'I've had a road to Damascus revelation, darling, and I really think I could be on to something.'

Portia braced herself. 'What now, Mummy?' she asked.

'Davenport bottled water! Straight from the old well by the orchard and into Tesco's, sweetie. Aren't I simply a genius to think of it? It's a licence to print money, you know, nobody drinks anything but water from bottles now. What do you think?'

'Mummy, you can't! Bottled water is supposed to come from two-thousand-year-old underground springs, not from a filthy old well like that. It's totally unsanitary; Daisy used to pee in there when she was small. And I know for a fact there's at least one dead cat down there.'

'Oh really, must you always be so negative? I'm only trying to do my bit, you know. Right, I'm off to phone Steve, he'll advise me what to do. I've nothing more to say to you, Portia, your channels are completely blocked.' She flicked her long grey mane of hair over her shoulder as she swept out of the door.

Oh, just let her, Portia reasoned to herself. It's just another of her get-rich-quick schemes that'll fall flat on its face.

'Thanks for brekkie, Mrs Flanagan,' she said. 'I'm just popping outside to see if the film crew needs anything.'

'Let me know when Guy van der Post gets here, will ya, luv?' replied Mrs Flanagan. 'So I'll have time to wax me moustache, trim the hair on me mole and shave me legs for him.'

In film parlance, today was 'Day One; Principal Photography', as the shooting schedule declared. This meant the first day of actual filming, as opposed to all the setting up that had been going on for the last few days.

Well, they've certainly got perfect weather for it, Portia thought as she headed towards the gravelled forecourt of the equestrian centre, where they would be filming for the rest of the day. On her way, she bumped into Johnny Maguire, who was bellowing into a walkie-talkie. 'Yeah, Jimmy D., I copy, we'll get the talent out straight away.'

'Hi, Johnny, how's it all going?' she asked, catching up with him.

'Good morning!' he replied, as cheerful as ever, striding confidently over cable wires as he chatted to her. 'So far, so good, I think. We've been here since first light this morning setting up and now I think Stalin's ready for the first shot of the day.'

'Stalin?' asked Portia, puzzled. Was this a new actor she hadn't heard of yet?

'Yeah,' Johnny chuckled, 'it's what the cameraman has nick-named Jimmy D. Wait till you see him in action, you'll soon understand why! Do you want to stick around and watch us do this shot?' he asked. 'You're very welcome to.'

'Thanks, Johnny, that would be terrific,' she replied, already feeling perkier. This was such a great distraction from dwelling on the dismal events of last night. 'Are you sure I won't be in the way?' she added.

'No worries, Portia, you can see it all from here,' he said, gesturing to an empty canvas chair well behind the camera, beside a makeshift desk covered in what looked like sound equipment.

The whole scene was a hive of activity – and the buzz! Portia had never seen anything like it. Everywhere she looked there were people coming and going, men carrying lights and cables, women dashing around with clipboards. Ahead of her, just inside the stable forecourt, she could see Caroline Spencer animatedly chatting to Jimmy D., who looked as cool and unruffled as he always did. He was chomping away on his trademark cigar and sporting a pair of bright green tartan trousers and a jacket to match, which even Rupert Bear would have blushed to wear in public.

Suddenly, Portia's attention was caught by a giant crane, about twenty feet above her head. She gasped aloud when she realized that there was a cameraman up there, intently focused on the lens and oblivious to the height and speed he was moving at.

'Don't worry, he's perfectly safe, he's just lining up the first shot,' said Johnny, seeing the alarmed look on her face. 'That's

Ivan Lamar up there, one of the best cameramen in the business. He's Czech, and has worked on just about every movie that's come out of Eastern Europe in the last few years. He's even worked with Polanski. They were bloody lucky to get him for a pile of shite like this.'

'Sorry?' said Portia, thinking she was hearing things. 'Do you mean the film's not going to be any good?'

'Ha, ha, ha,' came a raucous machine-gun laugh from behind her. 'She mustn't have seen a script yet, Johnny!'

Portia turned around to see a skinny, pimply guy with a set of headphones around his neck. He was in his early twenties and had that skin tone peculiar to Irish people, which goes bright red and freckly when exposed to more than five minutes of sunshine. He'd obviously been standing around in the sun for some time, as the tip of his nose and his neck were raw red, while the rest of him was blue white. On his right arm was a tattoo, which said simply, 'Fuck Yis'. The look was completed by a pair of combat trousers, which clearly showed the tip of his bum, and a T-shirt emblazoned with the legend: 'If you think my face is bad, you should see my hairy hole.'

'This is Paddy O' Kane, our sound man,' said Johnny, introducing Portia. 'He's just come off the latest Courtney Cox Arquette movie, *Screech Three*, so he's a bit full of himself, but don't worry, Stalin will soon have manners put on him.'

'Piss off,' said Paddy sulkily. 'So this is your gaff, is it?' he said to Portia. 'I'm glad the crew aren't staying up there; it's like the house in *Psycho*. Would you not be terrified getting into the shower?'

'Where are you staying?' Portia asked out of politeness; why, she didn't know.

'Some Jaysus kip of a b. & b. in the town run by a mental case. There's fuck all to do here except talk shite to culchies.

And how am I going to see Arsenal play on Saturday? None of the pubs have Sky Sports.'

Portia was unsure how to answer this last remark, when suddenly Johnny's walkie-talkie crackled into action. She immediately recognized Jimmy D.'s voice saying, 'Talent on set, Johnny. We're almost there.'

'Copy that,' Johnny replied into the walkie-talkie. Caroline then rushed by them, heading in the direction of Montana Jones's Winnebago.

'Hope to Jaysus she's sober,' Paddy said, covering his ears with headphones and fiddling with the recording deck in front of him. 'You heard about her at the Oscars last year, didn't you?' he said, miming someone knocking back drink after drink as he did.

Johnny was about to snap his head off for being so cheeky, when suddenly a silence descended around them.

Montana Jones had left her trailer. It seemed that all the crew and all the technicians turned to watch her as she walked the short distance from her Winnebago to the set. And, boy, was she a sight to behold. She was kitted out in her full costume, which was a Victorian riding habit made of the most exquisite crushed velvet in a shade of sapphire blue which perfectly complemented her eyes. The attention to detail on the costume was astonishing; from the neck down it was covered with oceans of cream lace with delicate touches of mother of pearl hand-sewn into it, so that it shimmered as it caught the light.

Then there was Montana herself. Portia had only ever seen her once, the previous day, when she'd arrived wearing a baseball cap and slightly scruffy jeans, not looking anything like a movie star. But to see her now! She seemed to be wearing a dark brown wig, with thick glossy curls cascading down her back, held in place by a jaunty tricorn hat, with an ostrich plume which fell seductively over one eye. Her make-up was so flawless, you'd think she wasn't wearing any at all; she just seemed to glow naturally from within. The wardrobe and make-up people had done a terrific job; Montana's transformation was truly amazing. This vulnerable slip of a girl, who only yesterday was cowering in terror in case her personal assistant caught her having a sneaky cigarette, now looked every inch a fully-fledged Hollywood star. More than a star, a goddess, in fact.

'Oh my God,' Portia couldn't help saying aloud, 'she's breathtaking!'

'Ah, she's not a bad-looking aul' bird,' Paddy replied, tweaking at the sound deck like an expert DJ warming up for a rave in Ibiza, 'she scrubs up well, all right. But have you seen her without all that slap on her face? Jaysus, she looks like she should be out in Dublin airport sniffing luggage.'

Portia could recall seeing the original film, *A Southern Belle's Saga*, one Christmas, years ago now, on the flickering black-and-white TV set in her father's study. She remembered getting hopelessly swept up in the narrative, and shedding copious tears when the heroine, Magnolia O'Mara, finally lost Brent Charleston, the only man she'd ever really loved, at the end of the film.

And now, here was Montana Jones, Magnolia O'Mara to the very life, about to take up the story, here at Davenport Hall!

Portia fervently wished that Daisy were here beside her, instead of barfing down the loo. She must have seen *A Southern Belle's Saga* over a dozen times and could quote freely from any scene at will. Well, she reasoned, they'll be filming here for at least the next twelve weeks, plenty of time for Daisy to catch up.

'Quiet on set, please,' Johnny shouted through a

megaphone. 'Tense up, everybody, we're going for a take.'

Portia could see Montana shuffling through a few crumpled bits of paper, probably looking over her lines one last time, she thought. Jimmy D. was strolling back towards a canvas chair, which said 'Director' in block capitals on the back, the only person who was unflappably cool and calm in the middle of all this frenzy.

'OK, people,' Johnny continued to roar through the megaphone in his hand, 'scene one. Let's get this in one take if we can.' Paddy began to madly adjust sound levels on the equipment in front of him.

'Roll sound!' Johnny blared.

'Speed!' called Paddy from beside where Portia was sitting.

'Roll camera!' Johnny shouted next.

'Shot!' came the heavily accented reply from the crane above Portia's head.

'Mark it!' said Johnny, as a young crew member sprang out in front of Montana's face with a clapperboard in his hand. 'Scene one, take one,' he said, bringing the clapperboard down with a loud thud.

'And . . . action!' said Johnny, loudly enough for them to hear him in Ballyroan. Then silence.

You could have heard a pin drop as Montana slowly lifted her head and surveyed the scene around her.

'Oh my, oh my,' she began in a Southern drawl, 'it feels so good for me to be back here in the Emerald Isle, land of my forebears, ancestral home of the O'Mara clan, among my own people once more and away from the rigidities . . . the rigidities . . . the rigedd . . . SHIT!'

Portia was on the edge of her seat. Surely that couldn't be part of the script?

'Line, please,' called Montana, momentarily slipping out of her southern accent.

73

Jimmy D. sighed as he consulted the script in front of him.

'Cut!' Johnny called out.

'Brutal accent,' Paddy said, whipping off his headphones. 'Southern belle, my arse.'

Portia could see Jimmy D. walking slowly towards Montana, still smoking his cigar. They were too far away for her to hear what was being said, but she could see Montana gesturing wildly and waving the script under Jimmy D.'s nose in a very aggressive manner. After a few moments, however, Jimmy D. went back to his canvas chair and nodded at Johnny.

'Make-up checks!' Johnny called as a youngish man with his hair dyed green rushed over to Montana. He was carrying a shoulder bag stuffed with lipsticks and make-up and proceeded to dab a powder puff across Montana's beautiful face.

Montana didn't speak to him, merely nodded her thanks.

'OK, people, we're going for take two,' bellowed Johnny. And then came the same routine all over again.

'Roll sound!'

'Speed!' said Paddy.

'Roll camera!'

'Shot.'

'Mark it!'

'Scene one, take two.'

'And . . . action!'

Again, a hush descended as all eyes focused on Montana. Again, she slowly raised her beautiful face to the sky and said, 'Oh my, oh my. It feels so good for me to be back in the Emerald Isle, land of my forebears, ancestral home of the O'Mara clan and away from the ridig . . . rigid . . . rigidities . . . HOLY SHIT! You can write this crap but you sure as hell can't say it!'

'CUT!' called Jimmy D., stubbing out his cigar as he strode

towards her. This time Portia had no difficulty in hearing their conversation.

'You'd just better get your act together, Montana, or you're out of here,' Jimmy D. roared at her. God, he was terrifying when he got going, no wonder the crew nicknamed him Stalin. 'I hired you when no one in LA would touch you with a fifty-foot bargepole and you repay me by showing up on set without even doing me the courtesy of LEARNING YOUR GODDAMN LINES!'

'I'm a professional actress, I'm here to do the best job I can, Jimmy D., but you cannot ask me to say this absolute HORSE SHIT! I mean, for Chrissake, how in the hell do you expect me to deliver a line like "and away from the rigidities imposed on a woman of my class and breeding by the dictates of society back in Atlanta, Georgia, where I've been living apart from my husband Brent for the last three years"? I can't do it, Jimmy D., Meryl fucking Streep couldn't make a line like that work!' She was screaming right back at him now, tears running down her face.

'OK, people, take five!' Jimmy D. called out as he followed Montana back to her trailer.

'Jaysus, it's going to be a long day,' said Paddy, wearily taking off his headphones. 'Do ya fancy a cuppa tea?' he asked Portia.

'Yes, that'd be lovely, thanks, as long as I'm not in anyone's way,' replied Portia.

'Catering wagon's this way,' said Paddy as they headed towards a double-decker bus parked on the grass in front of the Hall. All of the crew seemed to be heading in that direction, probably glad to be out of the line of fire.

As she stepped on to the bus, she was amazed to see that there were tables laid out in front of the bus seats, groaning with Danish pastries, croissants, bagels and hot cross buns. A rich, aromatic smell of freshly ground coffee hit you next, as the caterers rushed up and down the bus, pouring out tea and coffee for everyone.

'Mmm, yummy smell,' said Portia.

'Yeah, that's the one saving grace about this gig; the grub's all right,' replied Paddy, plastering tomato ketchup on a Danish pastry and stuffing his face with it.

Portia slipped into one of the empty bus seats beside Paddy, whereupon one of the caterers plonked a cup and saucer in front of her.

'Tea or coffee?' she asked.

'Oh, coffee, please,' said Portia gratefully as her cup was filled to the brim. It tasted divine, nothing like the watery instant stuff Mrs Flanagan served up. Just then, the green-haired guy she'd seen powdering Montana's face sat down opposite her.

'Hi, we haven't met, I'm Serge from make-up,' he said, shaking hands with her. 'Oooh . . . somebody needs their eyebrows plucked!' he added, immediately scanning Portia's face. 'You look so natural, honey, but we could do a lot more with this face. You want me to do your eyebrows for you now?' he asked, magically producing a tweezers from his pocket.

'You're very kind, maybe another time?' Portia laughed. It was impossible not to like these people, they were all so warm and welcoming to her.

'Say the word, honey,' replied Serge. 'You Irish *cailíns* have such great skin to work on, not like back in LA where everyone's so Botoxed it's like working on corpses. And as for you,' he added, turning his attention to Paddy, 'I really wanna highlight your hair for you. I think a few blond streaks at the front would make you look so . . . virile.'

'Piss off,' replied Paddy as he doused tomato ketchup all over a freshly baked bagel. 'No way am I going around with a head full of dye.'

'Honey, I wasn't talking about the hair on your head,' replied Serge nonchalantly as he winked at Portia.

Just then, running round the side of the Hall, Daisy appeared. As she raced towards the catering bus, it seemed that every man there turned to look at her, momentarily forgetting about their tea and sticky buns.

'Woooah, who's yer one?' asked Paddy, leering out of the window at her. 'I wouldn't think twice about bending her over the pool table and letting her play with me cue. Ha! Ha!'

'That's my younger sister, actually,' said Portia primly as Daisy clambered on to the bus.

'There you are, Portia, I've been all over looking for you,' she panted, introducing herself to Serge and Paddy. 'Hello, you're very welcome, I'm Daisy.' She smiled at each of them, looking ravishing and not at all as though she'd been throwing up all morning.

'Well, aren't you a doll!' exclaimed Serge, immediately running his fingers professionally through her long blonde curls. 'What great hair! What do you use? Who's your colourist? Tell me everything!'

'Never been inside a hairdresser's in my life,' Daisy answered truthfully. 'Portia cuts it for me when it gets too bushy.'

'Howaya, Daisy?' said Paddy, red in the face. 'I work on sound and I tell you, you can play with my boom anytime! Ha, ha, ha!'

Daisy, who'd been provoking this sort of reaction in men since she was about three, let it pass. 'Portia, could you come back to the house straight away?' she asked.

'Well . . .' said Portia, indicating her half-drunk cup of coffee.

'Emergency,' said Daisy, not taking no for an answer as she steered her sister towards the bus door. 'See you guys later!' she called out, unaware that every man's eyes were still following her, until she was out of sight.

'What's up?' asked Portia, imagining the worst as they picked their steps over the electrical wires that lay strewn like plates of spaghetti at the main door.

'Be patient, sis,' was the only reply she got.

As they went into the freezing cold, damp entrance hall, Portia nearly fell over. There, sitting on the huge oak sideboard beside the door, was the most magnificent bouquet of flowers she'd ever seen in her life.

'Well, they must have arrived for Montana,' she began, 'probably from some deranged fan in Ballyroan who found out she was staying here and—'

'Portia,' interrupted Daisy, holding out a small white card, 'they're for you.'

She was serious. The card simply said, 'Miss Portia Davenport'. 'They arrived about half an hour ago,' said Daisy, breathing down Portia's neck as she ripped open the envelope.

Just to say thank you so much for livening up an otherwise impossibly dull evening. Call me: 0863319677. Andrew de Courcey. P.S. Am also enclosing something for your mother and sister.

'What? What did he enclose?' said Daisy, impatiently grabbing the envelope from Portia. Two Solpadeine tablets fell out on to the marble floor.

'Well, he's got a sense of humour, I'll give him that.' Daisy giggled in spite of herself.

Portia suddenly felt weak. She got as far as the staircase and slumped down, still holding the card in her hand.

'You OK, sis?' asked Daisy, sitting down beside her, suddenly worried.

'I'm just a bit stunned, darling,' Portia replied, her voice sounding as though it was coming from another room, 'but I'll be fine.'

So engrossed was Daisy in making sure her sister wasn't about to pass out that she never even noticed a black

Harley-Davidson motorbike thundering at a rate of knots up the gravelled driveway. Nor did she see the driver dismount, whip off his helmet and immediately clip on a pair of designer sunglasses, slinging a rucksack over his back as he strode towards the film set.

If she had, she'd have passed out cold.

Chapter Eight

It had taken some doing, but eventually Daisy had persuaded Portia to pick up the phone and call Andrew. Mind you, they had to do a couple of dry runs first, with Daisy acting out the role of Andrew answering the phone, before Portia felt confident enough to do it for real.

'Right, pretend I'm him, and I've just sent you these magnificent flowers and I'm sitting in my mother's all-white, Snow Queen palace, thinking: Why hasn't she called to say thanks? She seemed like such a lovely girl!' Daisy said, doing a lousy impression of a man and waving the phone in the Library menacingly under Portia's nose.

'Oh darling, I'm just so out of practice at this. What do I say to him then?' Portia wailed, clenching and unclenching her hands nervously.

'Come on, Portia! You're only making a polite phone call, it's hardly the Duke of Edinburgh Awards, you know,' replied Daisy in her best sergeant-major tone of voice. 'Now, get a grip. What are you, a man or a mouse?'

'OK,' said Portia, taking deep gulps of air, 'you're right. It's not as though he's going to ask me out or anything. I mean, why would he? He probably just feels sorry for me and—'

'*Dial!*' said Daisy, in her most threatening manner.

'You have to stay in the room with me!' Portia pleaded. Oh God, she thought, what's wrong with me? I'm thirty-five years of age, why can't I just pick up a bloody phone? Suddenly, she thought back to all the beautiful people at the de Courceys' party last night. Would any of those women have the slightest difficulty in calling a man like Andrew? Not on your life, they'd be confidently chatting away to him right now. Bugger it anyway, she thought. What's the worst that can happen? She found her fingers dialling his number. Daisy said nothing, just turned to look out of the filthy French windows, concealing her triumph.

It rang. And it rang. Portia's stomach was doing somersaults until she heard a voice answer, 'Hello?' It was unmistakably him.

'Emm, hi. It's, eh, Portia. Davenport. You know? From last night?'

Shut up now, Portia, her inner voice said. *From last night? I sound like a prostitute.*

'Well, hello, Portia Davenport, from last night,' said Andrew, sounding cool and relaxed and sexy all at once.

'I was just phoning to say thanks for the flowers. They're . . . emm . . . nice.' Put the phone down now and run away, very, very fast, the same inner voice said. It's never too late to emigrate to Bolivia.

Portia could see Daisy rolling her eyes to heaven as she looked out of the window.

'I'm very glad you think they're nice,' replied Andrew. 'I'll tell you what else I think would be nice – dinner tonight, say about eight? Would that be nice enough for you?'

'That would be lovely,' she replied, stunned.

'Good. I'll pick you up at seven-thirty.'

Portia started to panic. How would she explain the film

crew and the general chaos at the Hall? His parents' house was an oasis of calm and tranquillity compared to the asylum she was living in. God, he'd run a mile if he saw the squalor of Davenport Hall, and that was before you factored in Montana, Jimmy D. and half of Hollywood who'd descended on them in the last few days.

'I've a better idea,' she said, amazed that she could finally think clearly. 'How about meeting in the town instead? Do you know O'Dwyer's pub? I'll see you there at half-seven.'

'Looking forward to it,' he replied as she hung up.

'YES! You did it! I am so bloody proud of my big sister!' cried Daisy, throwing her arms around the shell-shocked Portia. 'Now that wasn't so bad, was it?' she went on. 'After all, you're only calling a bloke on the phone, it's hardly brain surgery.'

Portia couldn't answer. She sat very still, playing absent-mindedly with the phone cord in front of her. So this is what it feels like to be a normal woman who goes on dates. Oh Christ, she was so out of practice. She'd had boyfriends in the past, of course, but had been pretty much chronically single since she turned thirty.

Daisy often bemoaned the fact that they were so utterly isolated, living in the back arse of County Kildare among men who looked like they'd been hewn from the rocks, as she so poetically put it. 'We're just like all the women who were left unmarried after the First World War,' she used to say, 'when a whole generation of young men was completely wiped out and so you had all these single women and no men. There's nothing wrong with us, it's just, well, can you name me two eligible bachelors in the whole of Ballyroan?'

And, apart from the unfortunate Sean Murphy and Dickie McGhettigan, who played the fiddle in O'Dwyer's pub on a Saturday night (and hadn't a tooth in his head), she wasn't joking. The highlight of Portia's social calendar up till this point was the Ballyroan Annual Ploughing Championships, held on one of the Davenports' fields at the back of the Hall, which was hardly the Monaco Grand Prix. She had long since given up all hope of ever meeting anyone, and had accepted that she'd remain single for the rest of her days. Ordinarily, this wasn't something that caused her any great pain; if her history of boyfriends past had taught her anything, it was that she was far, far happier as a single girl than as part of a couple with a guy who treated her badly and made her miserable. And it could safely be said that her track record here was certainly nothing to envy.

Her first boyfriend, Tom Malone, had been one of her tutors during her happy years at college. They'd dated for a full six months before it even occurred to Portia that he only ever stayed over at her tiny student bedsit; she was never invited to stay at his enormous, four-bedroomed townhouse. He fobbed her off by saying that he lived with his deeply Catholic mother who would be horrified at the very idea of Tom entertaining overnight female guests. Then, on his birthday, she decided to be impulsive and romantic and arrived on his doorstep with a bottle of champagne. His wife answered the door with Tom standing behind her, pretending he didn't even know who Portia was.

Then there was Simon McGuinness, a farmer from Kildare whom she'd met at a hunt ball several years ago. On paper, he seemed perfect for her: they were both country-lovers and he always treated her like a princess. He seemed attentive, kind and sensitive (or so Portia thought), the type of guy who would hold open a door for you, hand you a wad of Kleenex as you sniffled over a chick flick and then go out and buy you tampons. She had fallen head over heels in love with him and invited him for a weekend's shooting at Davenport Hall.

However, Daisy picked that very weekend to be expelled from yet another boarding school and happened to be wandering around the Hall in her school uniform just as Simon arrived. He took one look in her direction and spent the entire weekend making overt passes at her, right under Portia's nose. Daisy at the time was fifteen. Following that episode, he was unceremoniously dumped and subsequently only ever referred to within the family as 'Sleazy Simon, the scumbag git'. Various dates followed for Portia after that, but the general rule of thumb was that anytime someone attractive came into her life, he would meet Lucasta and Blackjack, take one look at Davenport Hall and run screaming into the arms of someone whose family were . . . a little more normal.

Daisy, however, wasn't going down without a fight. Despairing of the lack of talent in Ballyroan but fully determined to find love, she had even tried Internet dating at one point. She patiently spent hour after hour reading profiles of men she found sexy on the ancient old computer in the freezing estate office. When eventually she did meet an interesting guy in an online chatroom and they agreed to swap photos, she immediately packed the whole thing in. He'd sent her his wedding photo, with his wife's bouquet in her severed hand clearly visible.

'We're going to have to speak very nicely to Montana and ask her if she has some kind of half-decent outfit she can lend you to wear,' Daisy was chirping on, 'and there's a sale on in Fitzsimon's shoe shop in Ballyroan, maybe we could pop into town and get you kitted out there.'

'If what Montana kitted you out in last night is anything to go by, forget it. I'd prefer not to, thanks,' said Portia. 'In fact, I think I'd actually rather go out in one of Mrs Flanagan's housecoats instead. The Beyoncé Knowles look just isn't me, somehow.'

Daisy playfully punched her, reddening at the thought of what she must have looked like the previous evening.

That afternoon passed by in a blur for Portia. Without knowing what she was doing, she found herself heading for the halting site of caravans and trucks that the field in front of the Hall had become, frantically searching for the one with 'HAIR AND MAKE-UP,' written in block capitals on the door. Eventually she found it and, bracing herself, gingerly knocked.

'Come in if you're good-looking and available!' Serge called from inside.

She obediently stepped in.

'Well, honey, what can I do for you?' asked Serge as he put down the clutch of make-up brushes he was soaking in disinfectant.

'Oh Serge, I know you're awfully busy and everything, but the thing is . . . I was sort of hoping you could help me out,' she stammered.

'*Mi casa es su casa*,' said Serge. 'What's up?'

Portia found herself blurting out the whole story, about the awful party the previous night, the incredibly snotty de Courceys, the sleek, groomed, beautiful women that filled their house and finally, Andrew. Her date with Andrew. Tonight.

'And just look at me, Serge,' she went on. 'Queen Victoria had a sexier, more up-to-date image than me. I know you're up to your eyes, but is there anything you can do to help me?'

'Well, stick a halo on my head and call me your fairy god-mother,' replied Serge. 'Do you see this?' he asked, waving a make-up brush in front of her face. 'This is not a make-up brush, it is a magic wand. Sit right down, honey, I'm gonna turn you from Queen Victoria into Mrs Victoria Beckham.'

★

Meanwhile, Daisy, in her capacity as horse wrangler on the film, was about to start her first afternoon's work. Montana Jones had finally been coaxed out of her Winnebago and back to work, but only after several hours of the ugliest threats being hurled at her by Jimmy D. Chiefly, this involved him letting her know in no uncertain terms that if she failed to behave on set or to deliver her lines as scripted, he would personally see to it that she spent the rest of her jaded career shovelling French fries into chip bags at her local McDonald's on Sunset Boulevard.

It worked. Just after lunch, she emerged from her trailer, meek as a lamb and ready for her close up, Mr De Mille. So, once they'd completed the scene she'd walked out on that morning at the equestrian centre (with Montana word perfect this time) Jimmy D. nodded his satisfaction and said, 'OK. Next scene, the stable interior. Let's go!'

Given that the crew only had to relocate from the forecourt of the stables, the setting up of the following scene didn't take too long. As the lighting men and electricians ('sparks', as Johnny called them) shifted mounds of cables and lamps around the particular stable they were going to film in, Daisy decided the most useful thing she could do would be to keep out of everyone's way until she was needed. Her job was a doddle, she had decided. For God's sake, all she had to do was coax the horses on to the set when they were required, and take care of them when they weren't. Money for old rope, she reasoned to herself. So, to while away the time, she ambled over to Montana's Winnebago and tapped lightly on the door. Caroline, hatchet-faced as ever, opened it.

'Oh, it's you,' she said. 'I'm awfully sorry but I'm afraid Miss Jones is resting before her next scene and can't possibly see anyone, so if you don't mind . . .'

She was about to close the door in Daisy's face, when

Montana called from behind her, 'Daisy, honey! Boy, am I glad it's you! Say, would you do me, like, the biggest favour in the whole world?'

'If I can,' Daisy replied, peering in the door.

'It would be sooo cool if you could help me learn my lines for the next scene,' pleaded Montana. 'I got in such trouble with that asshole Jimmy D. for not being word perfect this morning that I really have to get my act together for this afternoon. Would you be, like, a total doll?' she went on, indicating to Daisy to come in.

'I'd be delighted!' replied Daisy, stepping inside.

Montana was still wearing the same Victorian riding habit she had on that morning, but she had thrown a bright orange fleece jacket around her shoulders, which looked not a little anachronistic.

'Oh, you are lifesaver!' Montana went on, thrusting three pages of typewritten script at Daisy. 'OK, here's what. I need you to pull me up on every little mistake I make, OK? Every freaking comma and full stop that I forget. Christ, it is sooo hard to learn these lines! Learning shit is so much harder than learning stuff that's well written.'

And so, for the next hour, they ran the scene over and over again, until Daisy was blue in the face and Montana was, indeed, word perfect. Neither of them even noticed the time passing until Caroline came rushing to the door of the Winnebago to usher Montana back on to the set. They were finally ready for her.

'Good luck!' Daisy whispered. 'You'll be brilliant, I'm sure.'

'Thanks, honey, I'll need it,' replied Montana, as both girls made their way towards the stables, picking their steps carefully, so as not to fall headlong over a pile of cables. 'Say, maybe you could smuggle a couple of beers into my room tonight, to help me relax after the shitty day I've had?' she whispered to Daisy, checking first that Caroline was well out of earshot.

Daisy hesitated for a moment, a worrying doubt niggling at the back of her head, but then nodded her consent. 'I'll see what I can do,' she replied. What the hell? After all, what harm could a few beers do Montana? This was Ireland, she reasoned; people put Guinness on their cornflakes, for God's sake.

Johnny greeted them at the entrance to the stable fore-court, ushering Montana on to a canvas chair with her name printed on it. She sat down obediently, looking straight ahead, as Jimmy D. was sitting right beside her. Neither one of them said a word or even acknowledged the presence of the other. Jimmy D. just stared furiously into space.

'Trouble at the top,' Johnny whispered to Daisy. 'And it's only day one!'

'OK, people, we're almost there!' he bellowed into the megaphone in his hand.

'What do you need me to do, Johnny?' asked Daisy excitedly.

'Easy,' replied Johnny. 'In this scene, Magnolia is saying goodbye to her favourite stallion whom she's forced to sell to raise money, so all we need you to do is to make sure the horse goes into the stable for us. OK?'

'Of course,' Daisy replied, 'but which horse are you planning to use?'

'Jimmy D. wants to use that black one in the field outside. Looks perfect,' said Johnny.

'Godfather Part Three?' said Daisy, alarmed. 'But he can't, he just can't! Godfather Part Three hates being stabled, he's un-believably highly strung, he'll bolt!'

'Sorry, Daisy, the decision's been made,' said Johnny, cutting her short. 'Can you get him in here right away, please, we're going for a take.'

Panicking inside, Daisy plucked up her courage and

approached Jimmy D. 'Look,' she began, 'couldn't you use any other horse instead? There's no way that Godfather Part Three will possibly—'

'Bring me solutions, not problems,' Jimmy D. barked at her. 'Get that horse in here and get out of my sight!'

Stunned at being spoken to like that, Daisy staggered outside. Paddy was twiddling away at his sound deck, having overheard the whole exchange on his headphones. 'Don't mind him, luv,' he said, seeing how shaken she was. 'If you saw his wife, you'd understand him being such a complete wanker.'

Unknown to any of the crew, however, just at that moment, Mrs Flanagan was waddling across the marble hall to open the front door.

'Holy suffering Jesus,' she said, almost fainting when she saw who her visitor was. 'It's you! You look just like yourself, so ya do!'

'Well, thank you, ma'am,' replied the stranger, in a not-quite-perfect Southern drawl as he whipped off his sunglasses, 'that is always mighty reassuring to hear.'

'I've never met a real celebrity before,' stammered Mrs Flanagan. 'Only aul' soap stars, and sure they're ten a penny.'

'Why, you mustn't think of me as a celebrity,' he replied, modestly. 'I'm just the same as you, only better-looking and richer.'

'Why are you talking in that funny voice? You didn't sound like that in *Space Bastards*,' Mrs Flanagan went on. 'Have you the flu or something?'

'Well, ma'am, I'm something of a method actor, you know. I like to immerse myself so completely in a role that I become whoever I'm playing for the duration of the shoot. I'm a perfectionist, can't help myself. I just give myself entirely over to the character.' Then, giving Mrs Flanagan the full mega-watt voltage of his cosmetically enhanced smile, he asked, 'So what did you think of my performance in *Space Bastards*? *Empire* magazine gave me three stars out of a possible five, you know.'

Mrs Flanagan paused, considering. 'I thought your bum was lovely in the shower scene,' she replied as she escorted her new guest to his room.

'And action!' cried Johnny into his megaphone.

'Oh, my precious love, my beautiful stallion, how on earth will I ever part with you?' Montana intoned, word perfect this time. 'It's just breaking my poor Southern girl's heart to think that my straitened financial circumstances are forcing me to sell you at the county fair!'

'Cut and print!' Jimmy D. called out, adding, 'Better, Montana, better.'

Montana said nothing, still smarting from the dressing-down he'd given her in front of the crew that morning.

'OK, people,' blared Johnny, 'we're moving out for the wide shot. Bring on the horse, quickly, let's get this in the can and we can call it a wrap for today.'

Daisy was outside, petrified. There was just no way on God's earth that Godfather Part Three was going to go inside the stable for her.

'Why are we doing this scene all over again, Johnny?' she whispered hoarsely. 'Haven't we just done it perfectly?'

'That was on a single close-up shot, Daisy,' Johnny helpfully explained. 'That means we only see Magnolia's face, very tight. Now we need the same dialogue all over again except this time we film from further back, so the shot is much wider. In other words, we see who Magnolia's talking to.'

'So how does Jimmy D. decide which shot to use then?' she asked. 'Whichever one turns out best?'

'That's up to the editor to decide, when we get the film

back to LA. If we ever get the film back to LA,' he added. 'Come on, Daisy, get the horse in here and let's get this over with.'

'But, Johnny—' she began, but it was too late. Before she knew what was happening, they were calling the shot, both cameras and sound were rolling and waiting. There was nothing for it but to do her best, try and coax Godfather Part Three inside the stable and just hope he didn't bolt for the hills. Gently, she tried to lead him by the bridle inside. But Godfather Part Three, already perturbed at all the unusual activity going on all around him, was having none of it. He started to whinny and jerk his head violently away from Daisy's grasp.

'We don't have all day, get him inside!' Johnny shouted impatiently, waiting at the stable's half-door. Daisy hastily adjusted his blinkers in the hope that would do the trick. No joy. Godfather Part Three was sensing trouble and was having none of it. He was agitated now and was thrashing about, neighing and whinnying as he violently pawed the sawdust on the ground around the stable.

There was nothing else for it, Daisy reasoned, she'd have to mount him and try to ride him inside herself. An experienced horsewoman, she'd normally have no difficulty in coaxing a reluctant thoroughbred into a stable, but Godfather Part Three was panicking now, frightened and out of control. Bravely, Daisy jumped on to his back but suddenly, at that moment, a loud bang like a shotgun exploded in the distance. It was only the Mini Metro backfiring as Lucasta drove up the driveway, fresh from her meeting with Steve, but it was enough to send Godfather Part Three over the edge. He reared up on his hind legs, violently pawing at the air, and then took off, galloping as far away from the stables as he could, with the terrified Daisy clinging on for dear life. In vain, she tried to grab on to the reins to slow him down, but the poor beast was beyond control now. On and on they went until Daisy saw the orchard wall, five feet high, looming closer and closer.

'No, Godfather, NO!' she screamed, to no avail. Over the wall they went, Godfather Part Three clearing it as easily as a national hunt show jumper, only clipping his hooves as he soared to safety. Daisy wasn't quite so fortunate, however. In mid-flight, she was thrown, banging her head off the wall and landing face-first in a dung heap thoughtfully placed just over the other side.

I'm OK, she thought. At least I think I'm OK. She was shaking like a leaf from the shock of it all, but was still able to feel her legs, which was a good sign. Gingerly, she tried to stand up. She was a bit wobbly on her feet, but no bones broken, at least. And then she looked down. I don't bloody believe this, she thought. From head to toe she was completely saturated in horse manure. It was in her hair, her teeth, all over her jeans and jumper and felt like it had seeped into just about every orifice.

'Jaysus, you scared the life out of me,' came a voice from behind. She turned round to see Paddy, breathless from having chased after her to see if she was OK. 'You looked like Lester Piggott winning the Grand National there for a minute. Wish to Jaysus I'd had money on ya.'

She couldn't reply, her mouth felt like it was full of dung. Paddy looked her up and down, taking in her appearance. 'So, you're in showbiz for the glamour then, are you, luv?' he asked, without batting an eye.

At just about the same time, the newly arrived stranger back at the Hall finally found himself alone in the Mauve Suite, which was to be his for the duration of the shoot. It had been something of a trial getting the ever-inquisitive Mrs Flanagan to leave him in peace, but after signing around a dozen autographs for her to give each of her nieces and nephews, posing for a few photos she insisted on taking and answering irritating questions like: 'How do you learn all them lines?' finally, he got to be alone.

The room was truly grim, he thought, but then he'd been used to being quartered in five-star, Philippe Starck-designed luxury for the past few years. However, he found himself casting his mind back to his first major movie role, when he'd played a prisoner on death row, wrongly accused of murder. (*Cell Block Redemption* it had been called; *Empire* magazine had awarded him four stars out of a possible five for his performance, he fondly recalled. It had launched his career.) In preparation for that part, he'd asked to live in a prison cell whilst filming and Warner Brothers had kindly obliged, building a custom-made cell for him on an empty back lot beside the car-park (and probably delighted not to have to shell out half the movie's budget on housing a budding star in the Beverly Hills Hotel).

Maybe it was just a hunch, but he really felt that this role could do something pretty amazing for his career. And it needed to. His most recent release, a musical based on the movie *Waterworld*, had bombed at the box office, oddly enough. Brent Charleston was a terrific part, one of the greats; this could be his own personal Hamlet, he thought. So why not stick it out in this rat hole of a house, as the character would, finish the shoot and then head back to his villa in the Hollywood Hills and wait till the Oscar nominations rolled in?

Great idea, he thought, undressing and slipping a towel around his waist as he headed for his bathroom.

Paddy had been terrific. He'd helped Daisy, still a bit shaken, all the way back to the Hall and had even managed to crack a smile out of her, regaling her with stories about Courtney Cox Arquette on the set of *Screech III* and the time the crew had substituted full fat milk for low fat when she was doing a breakfast scene and her reaction when she discovered what she'd been drinking. In spite of herself, Daisy giggled, leaning on him for support. When he'd safely deposited her at the front door, Paddy headed back to the set, to see if filming was entirely abandoned for the day.

'Might see ya for a few scoops later, then?' was his parting shot as he disappeared in the direction of the stables.

Finally alone, Daisy hauled her battered, bruised, dung-stained body up all four flights of the great oak staircase and into the family bathroom beside Portia's office.

'AGHHHH!' she screamed at the top of her voice, seeing a naked man's body sitting in the bath.

'HOLY SHIT!' he roared, on seeing the Yeti standing in front of him, dripping dung. In one swift movement, he was out of the bath with a towel wrapped around him. 'Who the hell are you?' he demanded. 'And what the hell are you doing in here? Get out before I throw your stinking butt out of the window!'

'I might very well ask you the same question—' Daisy began, but then broke off as the penny slowly began to drop. 'Oh my God,' she began, 'I do not believe it . . . I just don't believe it . . . You're . . . you're . . . You must have arrived when we were . . . I don't believe it! It's you!'

'Guy van der Post, at your service. And who might you be?'

'I'm . . . well, you see . . . I sort of . . . Oh Jesus, I don't believe I'm actually talking to you, in the flesh! But what are you doing in here? Your room has an ensuite bathroom.'

'It is correct to say that there is a bathroom off my bedroom, but one without a modern amenity such as running water,' snapped Guy, at the end of his tether, but still managing to keep his Southern accent up.

'But didn't Mrs Flanagan explain to you how the plumbing works?' stammered Daisy, as she squelched from one foot to the other. 'There's a lump hammer beside your bed and you have to bash the water pipes in the bathroom with it a couple of times to get it going, but then it works just fine . . .' She trailed off, realizing that here she was, talking to one of the biggest movie stars in the world about lump hammers and water pipes whilst stinking of horse shit.

Ever since she first heard that Guy van der Post was coming to stay at the Hall, she'd dreamt about their first meeting, imagining their eyes gazing longingly at each other from across a crowded room, or, in one of her wilder flights of fancy, that he swept her to safety after she was thrown from her horse, scooping her up effortlessly into his manly grip.

'I don't mean to be rude, ma'am,' drawled Guy, by now completely overpowered by the smell, 'but if you don't wash yourself soon, that's gonna harden.'

Chapter Nine

Portia couldn't believe it. She just couldn't believe the transformation. Never one to pamper herself, she'd been in heaven
all afternoon as Serge fussed round her, primping and preen-
ing at her hair and make-up, all the while filling her in on the
latest gossip from the world of movies. ('Now I don't wanna
say anything that'll get me into trouble or anything, but you
just make a sentence out of these words for me, honey. Certain
A list movie star ... dead gerbil ... rumours all true.')
However, in between telling tales out of school, he'd worked
nothing short of a miracle. In the space of a few short hours,
he'd ruthlessly chopped her lank, mousy brown hair and then
run easy-meche blonde highlights through it; given her a
facial, plucked her eyebrows, waxed her legs (she thought she
was having her legs amputated, the pain was so acute),
polished her fingernails and, the pièce de résistance, applied
make-up to her face, the first time since her debutante ball
that she'd worn any.

'Well, look at you, honey!' he said, whipping off the plastic
gown he'd covered her with. 'Andrew will just want to hurl
you over the back of his mother's feng shuied cream sofa and
have you right there and then, baby!'

Portia took a long look at herself in the mirror. She couldn't believe it. Serge had taken about ten years off her. Her hair was shining, cut into a perfectly executed, shoulder-length shaggy bob, and the light blonde highlights completely flattered her skin tone as they caught the light. Her make-up was so natural, you wouldn't think she was wearing any, except that her skin looked healthy and glowing. In short, she looked and felt a million dollars.

'Honey, it's the biggest transformation since Ashtanga yoga came into Madonna's life,' said Serge, delighted with his handiwork.

'Oh Serge, I really don't know how to thank you . . .' she began.

'Honey, save it,' he replied, dismissing her heartfelt gratitude with a wave of his hand. 'You can pay me back by fixing me up with one of Andrew's chums, lucky bastard whoever he may be. I want someone tall, dark, sophisticated and independently wealthy, that's not too much to ask, is it? I know this is Ireland and everything, but there must be some guys out there who've derooted the potatoes from their ears and are up for action,' he went on, keenly examining Portia's reflection in the mirror as though checking for last-minute blemishes on a work of art.

'I'll do my very best, Serge,' she laughed, feeling better about herself than she'd done in ages.

'And make sure you score!' he called after her as she skipped down the steps of the make-up truck. 'I'll need a blow-by-blow account of every teensy little detail tomorrow! Only the unedited version for me, thanks!'

Portia grinned and waved back at him as she headed back to the Hall, silently blessing him for making her feel so special, if only for a few hours.

The feeling didn't last for very long. No sooner had Portia

97

crossed the threshold of the Hall door, which seemed to be permanently open these days, than Daisy accosted her, hurriedly blurting out her tale of woe.

'Darling, you mustn't take it to heart,' Portia counselled wisely as they walked upstairs together and down the long corridor that led to her bedroom. 'It wasn't your fault, you know. Whether you're a movie star or not, accidents will happen.'

'But you should have seen me, Portia,' wailed Daisy, plonking herself on her sister's huge wooden four-poster bed. 'I was like the abominable snowman except I was covered in horse dung. All he could see of me were the whites of my eyes. It's taken me the guts of three hours just to clean myself up.'

'You still whiff a bit though,' replied Portia as she searched through her wardrobe, frantically looking for something to wear that didn't look like she'd bought it in a charity shop.

It was typical of Daisy to be so absorbed in her own drama that she never even noticed Portia's changed appearance. Not that Portia minded really, but some small acknowledgement of her radically altered new look would have gone a long way.

'And the worst is yet to come,' Daisy went on. 'They're all downstairs in the Long Gallery having sherry before dinner. You've got to come with me and give me some moral support. I need you,' she implored, her blue eyes like saucers.

It was an unspoken tradition at the Hall that the family and any unfortunate guests that happened to be staying would all assemble for aperitifs in the freezing Long Gallery before dinner. It was a house rule rigidly upheld by Lucasta, even if dinner consisted of pizza from the local takeaway in Ballyroan, followed by tinned peaches for pudding, as it frequently did. 'Happy hour, I think,' Lucasta would say from as early as three in the afternoon. 'Bar's open!' she'd call out loudly as she headed for the Long Gallery surrounded by whatever mangy stray cats she happened to be feeding that day.

'No can do, I'm afraid,' replied Portia as she whipped out a crisp white shirt from the back of the wardrobe. 'I'm meeting Andrew, remember?'

'Oh Jesus, Portia, I'm so sorry, I totally forgot. What in hell will you wear?'

'This,' replied Portia, turning from the mirror to face Daisy.

'Wow! You look sensational!' said Daisy, momentarily forgetting about Guy van der Post as she took in Portia's new image. She looked incredible, with her newly highlighted hair and fabulous make-up, dressed simply in denim jeans which showed off her long legs to perfection, black boots and the white shirt she'd successfully rooted from the back of the wardrobe.

'You're like a teenager!' Daisy gasped. 'He'll take one look at you and propose on the spot!'

Portia laughed as they went downstairs and headed towards the Long Gallery together. The huge oak double doors were open and Portia could hear her mother accompanying herself on the piano as she belted her lungs out. 'My Heart Will Go On' from the film *Titanic* was tonight's opening number. Through the door, Portia could see Montana and Caroline on the couch deep in conversation while Jimmy D. puffed on a cigar and made small talk with Steve. Over by the fireplace, smoking a cigar and gazing at his own reflection in the mirror, was an outrageously good-looking young man, wearing a tweed jacket and a cravat with his jeans, as though trying to look the part of the country squire, but not quite pulling it off. He can only be Guy van der Post, Portia thought to herself, delighted to have an excuse not to join them all.

'Have a ball tonight,' whispered Daisy. 'Are you sure you

won't come in for five minutes? Please? Just to help me break the ice with him?'

Portia hugged her. 'You just walk right up to him and be yourself, darling. Look at you. How could he resist you, even though you do still smell a bit dungy?' She laughed as she headed for the entrance hall, leaving Daisy to enter the lion's den alone.

Although Portia didn't realize it, she wasn't the only one nervously heading out to meet someone that night. At just about the same time, a middle-aged, balding man dressed in a beautifully cut bespoke suit was strolling into the famous Octagon bar in Kildare's fashionable K Club Hotel. The bar was jam-packed but he soon picked out the person he was due to meet. It was easy enough to spot him, he was always wearing that ridiculous tartan peaked cap.

'There ya are now, Paul, yer're looking great so ya are, great aul' tan, the weather must have been good down in Marbella?'

'Yes, thanks,' Paul O'Driscoll replied curtly. The sooner they got this over with the better. He checked discreetly over his shoulder to make sure no one was watching, before sitting down beside his companion. 'Look, Shamie, I have no objection to meeting you, but for God's sake does it have to be here? Half the County Council drinks in the K Club! Couldn't you just call into my office on Monday morning and we could talk privately then?'

'Ah, will ya relax, Paul, don't be aggravating yer ulcers on my account. No, I just wanted a bit of a chat with ya about a favour I might need in the not-too-distant future.'

Paul began to sweat into the expensive silk shirt he wore under his Savile Row suit. He could still remember the Huguenot graveyard episode all too clearly, which Shamie had successfully bribed his way into having rezoned a few years back. (He then built a Leisureplex over it with an adjoining nightclub, which he named R.I.P.s.) 'Sure them aul' Huguenot bones are well disintegrated by now,' had been his reasoning at the time, 'and anyway, the dead can't vote.' The sleepless nights that Paul had suffered and the blood he'd sweated over that! Christ, if the papers had found out about his involvement, he'd have been ruined. He shifted un-comfortably in his seat. There was nothing for it but to nip this in the bud now.

'Look, Shamie, I really don't feel that I can be of any more use to you . . .'

Shamie put down his pint and regarded him the way a dog looks at a rabbit before it devours it whole.

'Wouldn't it be a desperate thing altogether,' he began, his voice suddenly low and threatening, 'if your lovely young wife was to find out where the money that paid for your villa in Marbella came from? Or the money that pays for your kid's private school fees, or your expensive clothes . . .'

'All right, all right, you've made your point,' Paul answered, thinking the sooner they got this over with, the sooner he could get out of there. 'Where this time?'

'Ah, nowhere for you to be getting uptight about. Only an aul' rundown manor house in Ballyroan that no one gives a feck about, by the name of Davenport Hall.'

Chapter Ten

Almost as soon as she walked through the door of O'Dwyer's pub, Portia regretted suggesting it as a possible meeting place. She was so unused to socializing (unless you counted the rare occasions when they entertained at the Hall), she'd entirely forgotten that it being Saturday night, the place would be packed. She could barely squeeze herself through the door as she glanced around the room for any sign of Andrew, trying her very best to look cool and unconcerned, but terrified she might come across like an escapee from an asylum.

'Ah Portia, how are you?' said Mick the landlord from behind the bar as he frantically rushed around trying to serve six customers at once. 'We don't often see you out and about at the weekend. What can I get you?'

She was about to order a glass of white wine when a voice from behind said, 'I'm so sorry I'm late, have you been waiting for long?' She turned around to see Andrew, dressed smartly in a black suit, with an exquisite turquoise silk shirt underneath, which looked like it had cost a bomb. He looked just as tanned and gorgeous and sexy as he'd done the previous night, with his blue eyes twinkling as he eyed her up and down.

'Wow, you look good,' he said approvingly as he took in her glamorous, sexy new look.

'Well thanks, and thanks again for the flowers, they're magnificent by the way,' she replied, blushing deeply as she felt his eyes running all over her body.

Just try really hard not to blow it, her inner voice kept quietly nagging at her. Meet his gaze and don't gush too much, you're starting to sound deranged.

'It's my pleasure,' he replied, smiling. 'I thought you might be able to use a little cheering up after the party. Actually, I envied you leaving when you did; the whole night was such a bloody bore, I'd gratefully have slipped into a coma. My mother tried to keep me in conversation with the esteemed Senator, in the vain hope that this would be a useful legal contact for me, but, I kid you not, he spent twenty minutes describing in minute detail how he'd sponsor me for member-ship to his elite golf club. The man was practically measuring me up for a Pringle jumper. I nearly ran screaming out of there.'

Portia found herself laughing, liking him even more for being so unsnobby and not wanting to join posh golf clubs.

'Your mum and your sister were the biggest laugh I had all night,' he went on, still twinkling at her. 'I love meeting people who know how to let their hair down and have a good time.'

'If having a good time were an Olympic event, my family would be gold medallists,' replied Portia, suddenly wanting to change the subject. Too little couldn't be said about Lucasta and Daisy's behaviour the previous night. 'I don't think your mother was overly amused by them,' she trailed off weakly.

'Look, it's so crowded and noisy in here, do you fancy going straight to the restaurant instead? We could have a drink in the bar there, if you like,' he said, as though reading her thoughts and sensing she'd like to talk about something else. About anything else.

Portia readily agreed as he led her by her elbow out into the cold drizzly night.

Before she knew where she was, she found herself sitting on the soft, cream leather passenger seat of Andrew's brand new Mercedes sports car, being whisked through the Kildare countryside to God knows where. He playfully refused to tell her where they were going, but just kept glancing sideways at her as he sped along the dark country roads.

'Trust me,' he grinned, 'I'm a gentleman. Do you think I'd haul you down to the back of some deserted field and have my wicked way with you?'

Wish you would, she thought, smiling back at him in what she hoped was a seductive Mona Lisa way, but was afraid made her look more like a leering crone.

A few minutes later, they hit the motorway and it wasn't long before she started to pick out signs saying, 'Dublin 60km'.

'So we're going to town then?' she asked.

'Wait and see. You aristocrats are all so impatient!' was the jokey reply she got as he rolled his eyes up to heaven in mock irritation.

About half an hour later, they approached the outskirts of the city, a road Portia knew well, although it had been months since her last trip to town. In fact, she remembered it clearly; she'd been driving Lucasta to one of her past life regression therapy sessions in the city centre. The day had firmly lodged itself in her mind, because Lucasta had been fully expecting to be told that she had been Marie Antoinette or, at the very least, Cleopatra in a past life. She was utterly devastated to be told that her most recent incarnation was as a root vegetable. This did have one advantage however; it shut her up on past lives for some time, much to Portia's relief.

Very soon, they veered off the motorway to splash through the rain-soaked, winding streets of the capital city. Portia noticed that they seemed to be heading for the centre of town, and was proved right when she saw that they were approaching St Stephen's Green. Andrew luckily found a parking space right on the Green itself, and immediately pulled over, springing out of the car to hold the passenger door open for her.

Manners as well as looks, was all Portia could think as she slipped out, trying to look as graceful as she could. The rain was down to a light drizzle but it was bitterly cold, and she was relieved when he said the restaurant was only across the road. As they dodged the oncoming traffic, she looked up to see where they were heading for, and dimly made out a sign, which read: 'L'Hôtel de Paris'.

'I've read about this place,' she said. 'It's only recently open to the public. You know, apparently you practically have to give a blood sample to get a table in the restaurant. I'm impressed you got a reservation.'

'Well now, you hardly expected me to take the lady of the manor to the local chipper, did you?' he asked jokingly as they tripped up the stone steps to the entrance door.

L'Hôtel de Paris was an imposing Georgian house, which had been semi-derelict for decades, until it was sold at auction about two years previously. A wealthy Dublin investor had eventually seen the potential of the house and bought it lock, stock and barrel at a bargain basement price. He subsequently poured several million euros of his own personal fortune into gutting the original building and completely renovating it from top to bottom. No expense had been spared in transforming the house into one of the most luxurious, opulent, state-of-the-art hotels in the country. The moment Portia and Andrew walked through the main door, they were warmly greeted by the concierge, who treated them like old friends he hadn't seen in years. Portia's jacket was whisked off her and before she knew where she was, they were being ushered into the hotel bar, with menus placed discreetly in front of them.

'Wow, take a look at this place!' Portia exclaimed, unable to help herself as she took in the magnificent varnished wooden floors, the crystal chandeliers and then the bar itself, which was entirely made of mahogany and shaped like a horseshoe. Andrew ordered them both a champagne cocktail as Portia sat back, luxuriating in a dark green leather sofa. She found herself chatting freely to him, without any of the uncomfortable gaps in conversation that sometimes befell her when she was feeling nervous or a little shy, as she often did.

As she sipped her cocktail, she found herself telling him all about Davenport Hall, about her father running off, and about the film, which had entirely taken over the house in the last few weeks. He seemed genuinely interested, asking her all sorts of pertinent questions, but without being intrusive. Portia honestly couldn't remember the last time someone had paid her any attention; it always seemed to be her role to wait in the wings whilst her mother and sister took centre stage. It just felt so warm and wonderful to open up to someone who asked about how *she* felt, for a change. Far too soon for her liking, they were being escorted by the maître d' into the restaurant.

'SOAP UP YOUR ARSE . . . AND SLIDE BACKWARDS UP A RAINBOW . . .' screeched Lucasta from the grand piano in the corner of the Long Gallery, blissfully unaware that she was drowning out any conversation within a ten-foot radius. Daisy slipped past her and went to join Montana and Caroline on the moth-eaten sofa, dislodging one of her mother's cats from a cushion as she sat down. Steve was standing beside the stained-glass windows that dominated the room, deep in conversation with Jimmy D., who was talking at the top of his voice, saying, 'You know, I think we may shoot a scene in here. I'm seeing a ballroom, I'm seeing dancers, I'm seeing hoop skirts, but, hell, this lighting is all wrong. These windows just have to go,' he said, waving at the six-foot-high windows.

'The stained glass?' replied Steve, shocked. 'I think you may run into a few problems there. They were brought over from a monastery in France by the second Lord Davenport. They date back to the eleventh century, if I'm not mistaken.'

'Hey, I once took over the entire island of Manhattan for a shoot, you think a couple of windows are gonna slow me down?' replied Jimmy D., not brooking no for an answer.

'Well, Daisy!' said Montana delightedly. 'I sure hope you're feeling better, honey, that was some tumble you took today,' she added, rising to kiss her warmly on each cheek, Hollywood-style.

'Well, I suppose I was rather lucky really,' Daisy replied. 'The horse shit actually broke my fall. Without it, I'd probably have broken my neck. Sorry if I still smell a bit.'

'I'm very pleased you're not hurt,' replied Caroline in her clipped tones, 'but we lost over an hour of production today because of your fall and, you know, in this business, time is money.'

Daisy was about to snap her head off when Montana, sensing trouble, hastily interrupted.

'Say, Daisy, have you met Guy? He just got here today, I'm sure he'd love to meet you,' she said, gesturing over to where Guy was standing, still transfixed by his reflection in the gilt mirror above the fireplace. He appeared to be measuring how much his moustache had grown in the last few minutes.

'Well, we sort of bumped into each other earlier,' Daisy

began, unsure whether or not to go into the graphic details of how they'd met. 'Mind you, I don't think that he'd have recognized me, actually. Would you introduce us properly, Montana, please?' she implored, her tummy filling with butterflies.

'Guy, there's someone I want you to meet!' Montana called over to him, but to no avail. He completely and utterly ignored her, even though he was only a few feet away from where she was sitting. 'Oh shit, I totally blanked, he's so immersed in his character, he's not answering to any name other than Brent,' said Montana wearily. 'Not even asshole,' she added under her breath. As though making a point, she said, 'Brent, could you come over, please?'

'Why, that would be my pleasure,' Guy replied in his Southern drawl as he joined the three ladies on the couch. 'And who might this delectable creature be?' he asked, lightly taking Daisy's hand in his and pressing his lips against it.

'Oh, that tickles!' Daisy giggled, feeling the handful of hairs that passed for Guy's moustache brushing against the back of her hand.

'This is Miss Daisy Davenport who's working as horse wrangler for the duration of the shoot,' said Caroline crisply.

'I think we may have met earlier actually,' said Daisy, blushing to her roots. Guy continued to hold her hand in his, in no rush to let go.

'Well, I think that I'd have remembered meeting someone as pretty as you,' he replied, holding her gaze.

'Oh, will you shut up, Guy, you make me wanna hurl,' said Montana impatiently. 'I'm sorry, I meant Brent.' Then, turning to Daisy, she added dryly, 'Guy's a method actor, honey. He's very influenced by Daniel Day-Lewis, ever since they made *Thugs of New York* together.'

'Hey, *Empire* magazine gave me three stars out of a possible five for my role as Bill the Baker in that movie, you know,' Guy interrupted her, momentarily forgetting his Southern accent in exasperation. 'I can't help noticing that you haven't been awarded anything in quite some time now, Montana – oh, unless you count that Golden Raspberry you picked up last year for *The Hours Part Two: How the Time Drags*.'

Montana refused to rise to the bait, but jokingly said to Daisy, 'And surely you heard about the time when Guy was shooting *Space Bastards* and to help him get into character, he spent the entire shooting period wearing an astronaut's suit? This was in LA, during July, in forty-degree heat, by the way. He lost over twenty pounds in weight and had to be rushed to hospital twice during filming to be treated for dehydration, for fuck's sake!' She laughed, but with a slight edge in her voice.

'Why, that's nothing compared to the time you played the title role in *The Diary of Anne Frank*,' drawled Guy, by now back speaking in his Southern accent.

'What about it?' asked Montana, wondering what was coming next.

'Oh nothing, it was just unusual that Anne Frank was naked in almost every scene.'

'The nudity was entirely justified by the script, Guy – sorry, I mean Brent,' Montana almost spat at him. 'And it's the mark of a fine actor to do theatre work.'

'Honey, that show was so far off Broadway, it was in Harlem!' Guy sneered at her.

Daisy was unsure what to make of the rivalry between Guy and Montana, or even if they were joking with each other for her benefit. However, she was saved from wondering by the timely interruption of Mrs Flanagan, who waddled into the room saying, 'Right! Youse can all come in for yer grub now, or, as they say in Dublin: "Yer dinner's poured out!"' She almost had to shout, to make herself heard over Lucasta's squalling at the piano.

'Really, Mrs Flanagan,' Lucasta hissed at her as their guests filed out of the door to the Dining Room. 'Can't you use the dinner gong when we have guests?' she added, bashing down the lid of the piano.

'I turned the gong upside down and I'm using it as a salad bowl,' replied Mrs Flanagan. 'And in case ya recognize the soup tureen I'm using tonight, yes, it is the chamber pot from yer bedroom. And if ya don't want it, don't eat it.'

'We're awfully sorry, but I'm afraid we have a strict policy of no jeans allowed in the restaurant area,' the hostess informed Portia and Andrew as she came briskly from around her desk to meet them.

'I mightn't look like I've just stepped off the catwalks of Milan,' Andrew replied, smiling, 'but this suit cost me a packet and it most definitely doesn't look much like denim to me.'

'I was referring to the young lady,' said the hostess, peering over her glasses at Portia.

'Oh Jesus,' said Portia, glancing down at her blue denim jeans. 'Andrew, I'm so embarrassed, I had no idea that there'd be a dress code.'

'Couldn't you make an exception, just this once?' said Andrew, turning his charm up to its highest voltage. No go.

'I'm afraid it's policy,' replied the hostess.

'Have you met my dinner guest?' he then asked, changing tactics. 'This is Miss Portia Davenport, daughter of the ninth Lord Davenport, perhaps you may have heard of him?'

'I don't particularly care if her father is Archbishop of Canterbury, no jeans allowed,' she replied, brushing past them to greet an incredibly glamorous-looking couple who'd just arrived, neither of whom was wearing jeans. Portia turned to

Andrew, her face scarlet from sheer mortification, when a voice from behind said, 'I don't believe it. Andrew!'

'Edwina?' replied Andrew, stunned. Portia turned around to see an exquisitely dressed woman standing behind them holding the arm of a very familiar older man, who looked like he'd had one sunbed session too many. She was about thirty years of age, blonde and beautiful, with a perfect size-ten figure, emphasized by the skin-tight black silk dress that fell in elegant folds down to her ankles. She was impeccably made up, with just a hint of lip-gloss, and wore one simple diamond cross around her neck.

The whole effect was dazzling, which was more than could be said for that produced by her companion. He looked ancient, wizened and grey, with long, lank shoulder-length white hair scraped back into a greasy ponytail. He was about half the height of his dinner companion, and was wearing leather trousers with a shirt opened to the navel revealing a very orange-looking suntan, topped off with a pair of wraparound sunglasses. In short, he looked like a right eejit.

'It's great to see you,' purred Edwina to Andrew, kissing him on each cheek. 'It's been, what, six weeks now? How have you been?'

'Very well thanks, glad to be home,' Andrew replied flatly. If Portia hadn't been so overwhelmingly embarrassed about being refused admission, alarm bells would have been ringing in her head right now.

'And your parents?' asked Edwina, her eyes not leaving his face. 'Your mother took me to lunch in the Unicorn last week and was telling me all about the new house. It sounds wonderful. I'll have to come and see for myself soon.'

'You're welcome anytime,' was all Andrew said in reply.

'Won't you pass on my very best love to them? And tell

your mother lunch is on me next time she's up in Dublin shopping.'

What? Portia thought. She's friendly with his mother? And seems actually to like her? The plot thickened.

'Excuse me, Mr Morrissey? Your table's ready,' the hostess interrupted. 'It's your usual seat, in the VIP section.'

'Would you like to join us?' Edwina asked, glancing at Portia for the first time. 'Trevor and I are just having a quick bite before the MTV music awards later in the Point Depot. You're very welcome to join us.'

So that's why her companion with the orange skin tone looked so familiar. He was Trevor Morrissey, the rock musician, nicknamed the grandfather of Irish rock, who still toured occasionally, in between hip-replacement operations.

He looks like a dried carrot, Portia thought, never having seen skin that colour before in her life.

'We'd love to but . . . we can't,' said Andrew, unable to think of a lie to explain their hasty departure from the restaurant. 'Another time, Edwina,' he added as he ushered Portia out of the door. They'd got as far as the car before it struck Portia that he'd never even introduced her.

'Davenport bottled water. It's going to make me a million, you know. Easy as eggs,' Lucasta announced to the guests seated around the dining table as she helped herself to yet another gin and tonic.

Steve sighed deeply. 'Lucasta, we've been through this a thousand times already today. You can't just stick labels on a couple of bottles and smack them in a supermarket. For starters, you'd have to get the mud removed, then you set up a limited liability company, register it, then apply to the Department of the Environment for them to come out and inspect the spring you're talking about. If, indeed, such a spring exists.'

'Oh, sweetie, I need positivity around me right now, you really must try not to be such a Taurus, darling. This is going to make us all so rich, rich, rich!'

Steve was about to answer, but wisely decided against it.

Suddenly there was silence in the room. Mrs Flanagan trundled into the room, wheeling a squeaking trolley in front of her. 'Right! Grub's up!' she hollered, leaning over to stub out her fag in an ashtray on the sideboard.

'I sure am looking forward to some home-style Irish cooking,' said Guy as he sat himself down beside Daisy.

'Bacon and cabbage, Irish stew, oysters and Guinness, the more traditional the better for me,' said Jimmy D., knife and fork in hand, with his mouth practically watering.

'Ya can't get much more traditional than this!' said Mrs Flanagan as she passed around a stacked-up pile of plastic trays as expertly as an air hostess. 'Take one each and pass it on,' she announced to the table at large. There was a general air of puzzlement as everyone helped themselves to a tray from the top of the pile.

'Is this some kind of Irish custom?' Montana asked innocently.

'Now mind your fingers, they're straight out of the microwave and they're very hot,' cautioned Mrs Flanagan, positioning herself behind Guy's chair and leaning forward to grab the tray in front of him. With a flourish, she whipped off the plastic wrapping which covered the tray, and said, 'Chicken à la king with pilau rice on the side. Enjoy yer dinner, everyone!'

There was a stunned silence around the table, broken only by the clinking of the ice in Lucasta's gin and tonic.

Eventually Montana spoke. 'I sure am sorry, but I can't eat

anything that ever had a face,' she said, pushing the plastic tray away from her.

'There's more than one food group on that tray, luv,' said Mrs Flanagan. 'Eat the rice, so and you'll be grand.'

'I'm afraid Miss Jones doesn't eat carbohydrate after six o'clock in the evening,' Caroline explained, looking down her nose at the TV dinner in front of her.

'Ah Jaysus, luv, no wonder you are the size you are,' replied Mrs Flanagan, looking sympathetically at Montana. 'Sure there's more meat on a butcher's pencil.'

'I sure am sorry not to eat this, emm, lovely meal,' said Montana sweetly, 'but I have to be so careful not to carbo load.' Mrs Flanagan wasn't in the least offended but did look a bit puzzled. 'You see, the camera puts about seven pounds on you,' continued Montana by way of explanation.

'Right, well, I suppose that's the end of any chance I had of being a Bond girl then,' replied Mrs Flanagan, cheerfully waddling her fourteen-stone frame out the door.

'Is this normally the sort of food y'all eat here at the Hall?' Guy asked Daisy in his Southern accent.

'Well, it's not exactly Michelin-starred here,' she replied, mortified. 'We're not really used to entertaining, you see.'

'It's just that I have a fine bottle of Jack Daniel's up in my bedroom that's crying out to be drunk, preferably in the company of a beautiful woman,' he murmured to her.

Daisy may have been mistaken, but she could have sworn she felt his hand graze against her thigh under the table. 'That's if you have no objection to a liquid dinner,' he whispered in her ear. 'I find myself in need of a little alcoholic fortification tonight.'

This time she wasn't mistaken. His hand was on her leg, slowly working its way upwards. Daisy found her breathing getting heavier. Jesus Christ. Guy van der Post was feeling her up! One of the most famous movie stars in the world was groping her under the dining table! Never one to let an opportunity slip through her fingers, she leant in to him, so that her lips were brushing against his earlobe. 'Excuse yourself from the table now,' she whispered urgently, 'and I'll meet you upstairs in five minutes.'

It had been so easy, almost too easy. Tony Pitt almost had to pinch himself in disbelief as he waited for something to go wrong. And yet what could possibly go wrong now? he asked himself. Wasn't he home and dry?

He'd always prided himself on how quick he was off the mark; there was no one on the staff at *National Intruder* to touch him. Of course, he'd heard rumours about Montana Jones, fresh out of rehab, filming in Ireland, of all places, in some stately pile. And with Guy van der Post (known in the showbiz circles Tony aspired to be part of as 'Ed Wood', a reference to his tree-stump-like performances) who had once been one of the hottest things in Hollywood and now couldn't get arrested if he tried. Tony well remembered the days when a shot of Guy leaving a nightclub (usually with Leo or Ben or Tom in tow: the 'crap pack' as they were known in journalistic circles) would have fetched him a fortune. But lately, that had all changed. Guy van der Post was still a big name, but he hadn't made a hit movie in some time and his old crap pack buddies seemed to be deserting him one by one, or so Tony's sources said. Not that his sources in LA were impeccable (one was a driver who worked at Paramount and another had just been promoted to a senior street sweeper on the Warner's backlot) but a story's accuracy was never something that bothered his bosses back in the States. 'Just as long as you can get a picture,' Tracey Reeves, his editor, always said, 'we'll fill in the rest.'

So Tony found himself on an Aer Lingus flight to Dublin and then, without delaying for a moment, en route to County Kildare in his hired car. But Christ Almighty, nothing prepared him for the Irish road system, or lack of signposts anywhere. Eventually, after asking for directions about a dozen times, he stumbled on the sleepy town of Ballyroan almost by accident.

He checked into a b. & b. (where, conveniently, some of the film crew were sequestered too; that could be useful later on, he thought) and waited for nightfall. Then, at about ten p.m., he told his landlady he was heading out for a stroll, and started off towards Davenport Hall. It was relatively easy to find: the huge entrance gates were a giveaway (someone had written in graffiti across the brick gateposts, 'All hope abandon ye who enter here.' Very encouraging). Tony had expected to encounter huge, burly security men on the long walk up the driveway, but no one attempted to stop him. And then, after a marathon walk in pitch darkness, here it was, the Hall itself. Sure, it looked a bit run down, Tony thought, but was probably fabulous and opulent on the inside, a bit like that place in County Monaghan where Paul McCartney got married.

As he skirted around the perimeter of the Hall, he was careful to stay well back on the grass (the gravel on the forecourt would be too noisy underfoot and there could be guard dogs about, he was taking no chances). He searched frantically for an open door or window or, better yet, a room full of people he could photograph from a safe distance. He could hardly believe his luck when, walking around the edge of the east wing, he heard voices, laughter, the clink of glasses. Looking up, he saw a dining room full of people, through an open window, and YES! There was his prey, Montana Jones, playing with the food on her plate, looking moody and sulky. Better still, through his telescopic lens, he could just about make out Guy van der Post, sitting with his back to him and feeling up a very pretty blonde girl. Bingo!

The trip's been well worth it for this alone, he thought as he huddled down in the overgrown grass and shot off his first roll of film.

Chapter Eleven

'Two batter burgers with chips and two Diet Cokes please,' said Andrew. 'That it?'

'Oh, and an onion ring please,' said Portia. 'For some reason, I have a huge craving for an onion ring.'

'And an onion ring!' Andrew called out to the chipper, almost having to shout to make himself heard over the din of late-night revellers in the queue behind them. 'God, you're an expensive date, Portia, you'll be looking for paper serviettes next,' he said, twinkling down at her. She said nothing, but blushed prettily at him.

Her sane mind told her that she'd effectively blown any faint whiff of a chance she may have had with this man, not only by getting him thrown out of the snootiest restaurant in town but then by having the gall to suggest they grab a bag of chips each and eat them on the beach. In the lashing rain. But the weird thing was that she didn't care. She was having far too much fun with Andrew to mind that this was probably the last time she'd ever see him. What the hell, she thought, may as well go out on a high note.

'Well, this is certainly one date I won't forget in a hurry,' said Andrew as they dashed back to his car, clutching greasy chip bags dripping with vinegar and giggling like a pair of teenagers. 'It's been years since I've seen the inside of a chippers.'

'You mean you can't get a battered sausage in Manhattan? How on earth did you cope?' Portia replied, tongue firmly in cheek as she clunked the car door behind her.

'Where to now, my lady?' he asked, running his fingers through his fair hair, which was damp from the rain.

'If you're going to have fish and chips, there's only one place for it and that's Killiney Beach,' she replied, being careful not to let vinegar drip on to the cream leather upholstery.

'Do you know Dublin well?' he asked as they splashed through the streets, heading southwards towards the affluent suburbs of Ballsbridge, then Dalkey and on towards the seaside town of Killiney, past queues of soaking-wet party-goers waiting for taxis.

'Actually, Daisy and I used to come to town a lot when we were small—' she began before breaking off. 'Why are you laughing at me?'

'Because you're so funny.'

'Explain!'

'You're the only person I've ever met who refers to the capital city, which houses over a million people, as "town", that's all.'

'If I could just be permitted to finish my story, thanks,' said Portia, pretending to be annoyed with him, though she wasn't really. 'We used to be sent up here when Daisy was still in nappies to stay with our grandmother who lived here, in Killiney, actually.'

'I thought you were a tenth-generation blue-blooded Davenport. Don't tell me you have middle-class blood flowing in your elegant veins, my lady.'

'I meant my grandmother on my mother's side, smarty, and, by the way, I'm not a lady.'

'What a thing to admit to!'

'My father is a lord so Mummy is automatically a lady, but Daisy and I just get lumped with "the Honourable" before our names. Not that either of us could be bothered using it.'

'The Honourable Portia . . . it certainly has a ring to it. So who was your granny in Killiney then?' he asked, pulling the car over to the side of the road so that they were looking out across the moonlit beach.

'Mummy's family were called Elgee. She was an only child and grew up here, in a house that was quite close to the beach. Daisy and I often used to visit Granny here. I suppose we were the opposite of most normal people, in that we were country bumpkins who'd spend our holidays in the city.'

Again, he roared laughing.

'What is so bloody funny?'

'With blades of straw in your hair, no doubt. Poor little rich girl.'

'Only someone who'd never seen the inside of the Hall could ever accuse me of that! Rich? The only member of my family who ever had two pennies to rub together was this granny, who left a fortune after she died.'

'So what happened to the money?'

'She left it to the cats' and dogs' home. I think she realized that if she gave it to Mummy, my father would get his paws on it and lose the lot on a horse.'

'Ozzy and Sharon Osbourne eat your heart out! To think that I imagined Americans to have the monopoly on dysfunctional families. Is your father really all that bad?'

'Andrew, he once put Daisy up as collateral in a card game. She was about six months old at the time. Thank God he happened to win, that's all I can say. If a social worker knew half of what she and I endured as children, we'd have been packed off to reform school immediately. And probably been a lot better off.' Andrew glanced over at her, and wisely judged it best to change the subject.

'Look, the rain's eased off a bit, do you fancy a stroll along the beach, my honourable friend?' Portia readily agreed, although she wasn't entirely sure what to make of the 'friend' reference.

Still munching on their chips, they clambered down the half-dozen stone steps that led to the strand, with Andrew thoughtfully holding Portia's hand, so that she wouldn't slip. Descending on to the sandy beach, they sauntered out towards the sea, looking for all the world like a honeymoon couple out for a moonlit stroll. Unused as she was to male attention, Portia still had the wherewithal to realize that it simply wasn't good manners to hog the entire conversation as she had been. Tentatively she raised the subject that had been hovering at the back of her mind ever since they'd left the restaurant.

'Andrew, may I ask you something?'

'Fire away.'

'That girl we met at the restaurant, who is she?'

He sighed deeply and kept on walking in silence. Portia glanced sideways at him and saw that he was staring straight ahead with a blank expression on his face. Oh God, she thought, had she said the wrong thing?

'I'd no intention of prying, Andrew, if it's something you don't want to talk about . . .'

'It's OK. I suppose I was just wondering when this would come up.' His tone had changed too. He sounded preoccupied and distant. 'Do you really want to know?'

'I was just curious, that's all. She seemed to be on very good terms with your mother,' she answered, regretting she'd ever brought the subject up in the first place.

'Edwina and I were together for eight years and were engaged to be married this summer. Next month, in fact.'

121

Portia felt as though she'd been punched in the stomach. She could physically feel the blood draining from her face and was grateful that it was dark and that she could turn her face out towards the sea, pretending to be engrossed in the view.

'You've gone very quiet, my lady,' he said, his tone softening a bit. 'Look, Portia, I'm thirty-five years old. You just don't get to my age without accumulating some sort of baggage. Most people my age are married, divorced, separated or struggling with single parenthood. I consider myself lucky to have got this far in life relatively unscathed.'

Well, that settles that, she thought. The only reason he asked her out was that he was on the rebound from the beautiful, elegant Edwina. They walked on in silence, and eventually came to a small wooden bench facing out to sea. They both sat down, Portia grateful for the chance to look straight ahead and not directly at him. Christ, she thought, I must look like a car crash compared with bloody Edwina in her bloody designer evening dress who's probably never even *met* anyone who was turned away from a posh restaurant in her life.

After a long silence, Andrew eventually pulled a pack of cigarettes from the inside pocket of his jacket and lit one up. He must have sensed her insecurity because, turning his whole body to face her, he gently brought the subject up again.

'You know, Edwina would never in a million years have sat on a beach eating chips in the rain with me.' He was rewarded with a slight smile from Portia as she continued to look out to sea, pretending to be absorbed in the view. Another silence. This night is turning into a play by Samuel Beckett, she thought.

'Portia, will you let me explain?' he asked. 'I know there's nothing worse than people who go on and on about their exes, but I really feel I owe you an explanation. Edwina and I spent eight years together in New York living the high life, eating out all the time, going to the theatre, throwing dinner parties, weekends at the Hamptons. Christ, we would have gone to the opening of a fridge. I was expected to network constantly with my job and, looking back, she was almost a trophy girlfriend. She thrived on that lifestyle. Everyone said she was the perfect woman for me.'

'Uh huh,' was all she could manage in response, shifting nervously on the soaking-wet bench. She flicked at a vinegar stain she noticed on her jeans, suddenly feeling extremely self-conscious and wishing this conversation could end. She started to feel a rumble of anger bubbling up inside her. Was this the only reason he asked her out? To talk about his ex-fiancée? What was she, his therapist?

Sensing her discomfort, he went on, 'I know I'm not explaining this very well. On paper she may have been my perfect partner, but the reality was very different. I began to notice that we never spent any time on our own together, we were constantly surrounded by people, buzzing around us. On the outside, it may have looked like we had the perfect relationship but inside, I don't think I've ever been lonelier. It's as though we surrounded ourselves with people to avoid ever being alone together.'

'And you were to be married next month?'

He sighed deeply. 'Oh, Adare Manor was booked and we were to go to South Africa on safari for our honeymoon, but you know, the wedding seemed to be more about seating plans and gilt-edged invitations than whether or not we wanted to spend the rest of our lives together.'

'So you called the whole thing off?'

'Let me tell you something,' he said, stubbing his cigarette out on the ground. 'A couple of months ago, just after

Christmas, I had one of the worst days in work I can ever remember. I lost a huge corporate case for the firm I worked for and I rang Ed to talk about it. I really needed to confide in someone and just blow off some steam. The minute she picked up the phone she launched into a tirade about the life expectancy of ice sculptures for the wedding centrepiece. I can remember trying to explain to her that, for once, I needed to talk and she just fobbed me off like I was being monumentally selfish in the middle of her horrific day. I remember leaving the office on Wall Street and walking uptown just to clear my head. I got as far as Union Square and sat down on a bench to have a cigarette and a think. I looked around and noticed this young professional couple sitting right opposite me. He had taken off his tie, she had kicked off her shoes and they had tossed their briefcases on the grass. They were chomping on sandwiches and roaring with laughter at some gag one of them had cracked. It sounds so mundane, but I can remember sitting opposite them and thinking: That's what a relationship is. It's snatching time together because you can't bear a whole day apart, laughing at some private joke with that amazing intimacy that couples have. And I can remember thinking: That's it. That's what I want. That's what I want and I don't have it. Oh, I knew exactly what lay ahead for me that evening. I knew I'd go back to our Park Avenue apartment and that she'd be all dressed up to go out for the night, she'd tell me I'd ten minutes to get ready and to wear such and such a suit. There wouldn't be any time for conversation, just on with the whirl. Maybe in the taxi she'd elaborate on her day and tell me the minutest detail about the bridesmaids' bloody knicker elastic. That's when I decided enough was enough.'

'Oh my God. How did she take it?'

'Ed's made of very stern stuff, you know. She decided to

come back to Ireland with me, as we'd planned to do anyway when the wedding was still going ahead. She said she needed the break.'

Portia thought quickly. What the hell? She might as well know one way or another. 'And do you think you may get back together again?' she asked, trying to keep the wobble out of her voice.

Andrew sighed and stared out to sea. 'If my mother has anything to do with it, we will. She absolutely adores Edwina, they're like mother and daughter. I think she took the break-up far worse than either Ed or myself.'

Well, that's that then, Portia thought. I was just a handy little diversion to pass a Saturday night with while he's visiting his parents in Ballyroan. Serves me bloody right for ever thinking that I could land a bloke like this. And anyway, how could I compare with Edwina? God, she even has his dragon lady of a mother eating out of her hand. She glanced down at her watch. Two-thirty a.m.

'It's getting late. Don't you think it's time we got going?' she said, rising to her feet.

'Whatever you say, my lady,' he replied, a little startled at the suddenness of her decision to leave. She walked briskly ahead of him, frantically racking her brains to think of a topic of conversation that wouldn't involve Edwina, and eventually gave up. All conversational roads seemed to lead back to the unalterable fact that he should have been getting married the following month.

Bugger it, she thought, they could just go home in silence.

'Well, that is certainly one experience I won't forget in a hurry,' drawled Guy as he stretched out to replenish the whiskey glass that lay empty beside him on the bedside table.

'Mmmmmm,' was all Daisy, her long, lean body naked

beside his, could murmur in reply. She snuggled up into the crook of his arm, still a bit woozy from the shots of neat Jack Daniel's they'd knocked back together and dreamily thought that she must be the luckiest girl alive. She could scarcely believe it, here she was, in bed with Guy van der Post, the sexiest man on earth! From the corner of her eye, she could dimly make out the outline of her hastily discarded clothes strewn all over the floor at the far corner of the darkened room. In fact, was that her see-through pink bra hanging off the edge of the four-poster bed? She giggled knowingly to herself, wanting to savour every second so she could think back over the whole evening in minute detail later. Beside her, Guy had slowly sat up and was knocking back the dregs of whiskey from the bottom of his glass. Turning to face Daisy, he lay back down beside her and stroked a loose blonde curl away from her semi-comatose face.

'You sure are one mighty pretty lady,' he murmured, putting his arms around her and noticing as he did, that his tan was beginning to fade a little. Damn this freezing Irish weather anyway! For crying out loud, it's June, does the sun never shine in this hellhole? He made a mental note to himself that he'd put in a request for a sunbed to be installed in his trailer asap.

He cast a quick look down his naked body and decided that in all other respects, it was in pretty good nick. Sure, his abs were a tiny bit flabby, but that was good for the part, after all Brent Charleston famously consumes nothing but neat whiskey in the script. A couple of extra pounds around his waistline would be entirely in keeping with the character.

He thought back to life in LA and how he'd regale the rat pack of young, twenty-something movie actors he hung around with there with tales about this shoot, the minute he got back. Christ, that dinner tonight was something else . . .

Were this family completely crazy or what? The mother should have been locked up years ago by the look of her. If it hadn't been for Daisy, he'd never have got through the miserable evening. And when he thought of what a bitch Montana was being towards him, when she should be thanking her lucky stars to be working with an actor of the calibre of Guy van der Post with her stock as low as it was in Hollywood! Well, he'd show her and that's for sure. Just wait till their first scene tomorrow, he'd wipe the fucking floor with that smug bitch. He'd show her what movie acting was all about; she wouldn't know what hit her.

He chuckled to himself, thinking what a great story this whole experience would make to tell Leo and Ben and Tom back home. Not that Leo and Ben and Tom were exactly hanging around with him any more. No, he had to admit, since his last movie had turned out to be such a turkey, there had been something of a downturn in his life. He wasn't even getting seen for parts which should have been straight offers for him. This was such a lousy business, he thought, furiously kicking at the bedclothes. You make ten hit movies back to back, then one minor flop, just one bad call, and you're right back on the shitheap. And it had looked like such a winner on paper too! '*Waterworld*, the musical . . . *Moulin Rouge* in bikinis!' the tag line had run. How could it have turned out to be such a loser?

Well, he'd change all that. Just wait till this movie came out, he'd be back on top of the A list before you knew it. Hell, all he had to do was put up with Montana for a couple more months and then he'd be home and dry. Guy glanced down at the half-asleep Daisy, looking like an angel beside him. Yip, this shoot sure had some interesting diversions to offer, he thought, then, taking one final gulp of whiskey, he chuckled softly to himself.

'What are you giggling about?' whispered Daisy, sleepily fondling the nape of his neck and snuggling in even tighter to him.

'Why, I was just thinking what a lucky man I am to have a beautiful woman like you in bed beside me,' he replied, without even pausing to think.

It had begun to drizzle again as Portia and Andrew hit the motorway that would take them through Kildare and then, via the back roads, on to Ballyroan. Apart from a few polite comments about the appalling weather, they hadn't exchanged a word since they left the beach.

Eventually, however, Portia could take no more. So what if he was on the rebound from Edwina? she thought to herself. After all, he's a lovely guy and, let's face it, they were pretty thin on the ground where she came from. Maybe they'd turn out to be just friends, was that so awful? Apart from Steve, she hadn't a single male pal in the world. She turned sideways to face him, just as a car swished past on the far side of the road, momentarily lighting up Andrew's face. God, he looked divine, she thought, even in this light. His ice-blue eyes were focused on the road ahead and the gold signet ring which had his initials engraved on it glinted at her from the corner of her eye. Even the way he handled a car was sexy. Small bloody wonder Edwina had followed him all the way back to Ireland. She must have been secretly hoping to wear him down, aided and abetted by his mother, no doubt. For a split second, a rush of pity came over kind-hearted Portia for the other woman. To have your wedding called off at the last minute must be horrific, but to have lost someone like Andrew in the process must be soul-destroying.

'Andrew?' she began tentatively, as they arrived at the outskirts of Ballyroan. He glanced sideways at her.

'Yes, my lady? I was just wondering if you were intending to speak to me again.'

'Of course I'm still speaking to you.' She smiled. 'Why wouldn't I be?'

'Because that was something of a bombshell I landed on you back there.'

'Well, I was a bit taken aback, but the thing is—'

'Sorry to interrupt but it's left here for Davenport Hall, isn't it?' he asked, turning the car and deftly avoiding the potholes all around.

'Yes, and straight ahead on through the gates,' she replied as they pulled up to the huge stone pillars at the entrance to the Hall.

The gates loomed ahead of them, twelve feet high, held together by rust and badly in need of a lick of paint. Needless to say, there was absolutely no lighting whatsoever on the two-mile driveway to the Hall itself, making it something of an assault course for the unfortunate night-time visitor. As Andrew skilfully negotiated the pitch-black dirt track that led to the Hall, Portia seized her moment.

'You know, I'm not very good at this, but I just wanted to say that . . . well, I had a really good time tonight and, of course, it goes without saying that if you ever need to talk about—'

'You had a good time tonight?' he interrupted, glancing at her from the wheel.

'You sound surprised.'

'Of course I'm surprised. I thought I'd blown it by droning on about Edwina.'

'Well, you haven't,' she replied, grateful that it was pitch dark and that he couldn't see her face, which was probably tomato red by now. 'Of course you're entitled to talk about her, I mean, you were meant to be getting married this summer after all. And that's what I'm trying to say. I know you're only in Ballyroan for a short time, Andrew, but we are neighbours and, well, I'm here if you ever do need to talk.'

He said nothing, but smiled to himself.

As the car twisted past the tennis courts, he eventually said, 'I was just thinking how utterly different to Edwina you are. In fact, how utterly different you are to anyone I think I've ever met.'

Not used to being complimented, Portia wasn't quite sure how to take this.

'Because I get asked to leave posh restaurants?'

'Because you're beautiful and funny and sexy and warm-hearted and have absolutely no idea that you're any of those things. I think you're probably the least pretentious person I've ever met in my whole life, which is saying something, con-sidering you're a titled member of the aristocracy.'

Before she could reply, they'd arrived at the gravelled drive-way in front of the main entrance to the Hall. Oh God, thought Portia, what do normal women do in these situations? Invite him in for coffee? Peck him chastely on the cheek and jump out of the car? They should have night classes to guide out-of-practice single women through these social minefields, she thought. Bloody, bloody hell, who invented the concept of dating anyway?

She was saved from wondering any further by a loud, thundering crash from inside the Hall. In a flash, both she and Andrew had leapt out of the car and rushed to the main entrance door. Shoving the door open, Portia switched on the lights only to discover that a huge plasterwork stone harp of Leinster from the dome in the great hallway had fallen on to the floor beneath, smashing several of the Kilkenny marble tiles on the ground to smithereens.

'Oh, thank God no one was hurt,' Portia began, when

suddenly they both heard an ear-piercing scream from the top of the staircase.

'Leave this house, evil spirit, I condemn you to the flames of hell!' screamed Lucasta, running down the stairs in her long white flowing nightie, with her mane of grey hair loose about her shoulders. 'Oh hello, darling, did you have a nice time? And this must be Andrew, whom I've heard so much about—' She broke off, as though suddenly finding herself in the middle of a garden party. With her talent for blocking out anything disagreeable, she clearly had absolutely no recollection of Andrew having seen Portia physically hauling her into the car the previous night.

'Mummy, what's going on?' asked Portia, almost afraid of the answer.

'It's Great-aunt Cassandra again. The silly cow has been wandering around the Hall all night, and now look at what she's done,' replied Lucasta, indicating the smashed plasterwork harp on the marble floor.

'Your great-aunt is still alive?' Andrew said to Portia, totally unfazed by the sight of her ladyship in her nightie, looking like the mad wife from the attic in a very poor amateur dramatic production of *Jane Eyre*.

'No, she died in nineteen sixty-nine,' replied Lucasta, 'but, you know, she was a bitch in her past life and is now a bitch in death.'

'Cigarette?' said Andrew, nonchalantly producing a pack from his pocket.

'Oh, you are an angel,' said Lucasta, greedily grabbing one and taking a light from the elegant cigarette lighter Andrew proffered her.

'And her ghost walks the corridors at night?' he asked as calmly as if they were discussing the local weather report.

'Dreadful bore, isn't it?' replied Lucasta. 'And, you know, no one minds her wandering around a bit during the day, dozens of spirits live here and I do my best to make them feel welcome. I don't do any exorcisms or anything to piss them off, but Great-aunt Cassandra is really the giddy limit. She's so bloody violent.'

'Mummy, don't you think you should go back to bed?' Portia interjected.

'Has she done this sort of thing before?' asked Andrew, sounding genuinely interested.

'All the bloody time, darling. Constantly smashing things all around the Hall and wreaking havoc. I mean, look at that.' She indicated the smashed harp on the ground. 'Someone's going to have to clean that up, you know.' (This was said without the smallest attempt to help Portia, now crawling about on her hands and knees trying to pick up some of the massive pile of stone debris.)

'It's the cats, you see,' Lucasta went on. 'She always hated my cats and vowed on her deathbed that she'd come back to get them, dead or alive.'

'And what did she die of?' Andrew asked, politely bending down to help Portia.

'Toxoplasmosis. Served her right, really,' Lucasta replied, swishing her long grey mane behind her as she went back to bed.

No sooner was she out of sight than Andrew and Portia collapsed into a helpless fit of giggles, sitting side by side together at the bottom of the stairs.

'I love your family,' was all Andrew could blurt out, shaking with laughter. 'That film crew should be making a documentary about this house and the Davenports, not some rehash of *A Southern Belle's Saga*. Miles more interesting anyday. Your mother is a walking sitcom, I'm mad about her.'

Portia beamed at him. 'I can't believe she hasn't scared you away. Mummy can be a lot to take, you know. And that's before you even get started on Daisy.'

'It would take more than that to scare me away,' he answered softly, slipping his arm around her waist. All Portia could remember after that was him bending down to kiss her, slowly and tenderly at first but gradually becoming more and more intense. She responded, surprising even herself with the depth of feeling she had for this man she barely knew.

'I've been wanting to do that for hours,' he said, taking her face in his hands and kissing her again. Portia couldn't bring herself to speak, she just locked her arms around his neck and kissed him back, running her fingers through his hair and pressing herself as close to him as she could.

If she'd thought for one second that her every move was being photographed right then, she'd probably have fainted.

Chapter Twelve

There was no rest for the wicked; at least, not at Davenport Hall. It was barely after seven a.m. when Daisy came bounding into Portia's bedroom, exuberantly jumping up and down on her four-poster bed just as she used to do as a small child.

'Darling, do wake up, I've got such heaps to tell you!' she pleaded, inadvertently kicking Portia as she spoke.

'Oh God, what time is it?' replied Portia, sleepily opening her eyes and sitting up.

'Just after seven, lazy lump,' said Daisy, roughly pulling the bedclothes off and plonking herself down beside her.

'Are you completely insane? It's the middle of the night,' said Portia, still half-asleep.

'Is not, Guy's make-up call was for six a.m. Ask me how I know that!'

'All right, darling, how do you know that?' asked Portia, realizing she wouldn't get a minute's peace unless she played along.

'Because I spent the night with him! So are you stunned?'

Portia sat bolt upright, now wide-awake.

'You did not!' was all she could stammer at Daisy. 'But you

134

said the first time he saw you you were covered in horse dung and that you'd never look him in the face again.'

'Well, that just shows what a wonderful guy he is, that he could see beyond his first impression of me.' Daisy sighed dreamily. 'We had the most amazing night together and now I'm completely in love with him. I just want to go back to LA with him and have his babies.'

'Daisy, do take it one step at a time,' begged Portia, knowing full well how apt her sister was to jump headlong into a situation. She'd be sending out wedding invitations next. 'You've just spent the night together, let's not talk about your moving to Hollywood and having babies just yet. You know next to nothing about him; he's from another world entirely.'

'Oh, listen to you, Nancy Drew, why must you always be so fucking negative about everything?' cried Daisy, her mood changing dramatically. 'Why can't you just be happy for me?'

'Darling, of course I'm happy for you. I'm just saying let's take it slowly, that's all,' Portia replied calmly, well used to Daisy snapping her head off.

'Oh, I know, I know,' replied Daisy, relenting a little. Try as she might, it was impossible to stay angry with Portia for any length of time. Much better simply to change the subject and get the hell out of there. 'Anyway, breakfast's ready in the catering truck, so you'd better get up, lazy arse,' she added chirpily, hopping off the bed and slamming the door behind her.

Portia lay back on the huge goose-down pillows and smiled wryly to herself. Ironic that here she was lecturing Daisy on the perils of falling head over heels for a guy she barely knew, when that was pretty much what she'd done herself.

Her mind wandered back to Andrew and how hard it had been to let go of him when she kissed him goodnight at his car door last night. He'd behaved like a perfect gentleman at the end of the night, had thanked her for a wonderful evening and told her that he'd call her and, deep down inside her, she knew he would. There was no awkwardness on her part or pushiness on his about him not being invited to stay over. For all that he'd awoken something romantic inside Portia that had been slumbering for years, her practical, resolute side kept telling her not to get swept away in the excitement of the moment, as Daisy had done. If he were a nice guy, he'd call: simple as that. Yet a huge rush of adrenalin came over her even when she just thought about him. It had been hard enough to try and get any sleep, she'd been so busy dreaming about him, but she snuggled back under the covers in the hope of dozing off for a few minutes at least. She stretched her long thin white arms in front of her and yawned. The last thought that went through her head before nodding off was about Daisy . . . she really must be knickers about Guy van der Post. She was so caught up with him that she'd never even asked Portia how she'd got on last night.

'What right have you, Brent Charleston, to come chasing after me all the way to the Emerald Isle and making such demands on me? What makes you think that I'd ever want to leave the O'Maras and return to Atlanta ever again, as long as I live?'

God, I'm on form today, Montana thought to herself as she skilfully allowed a tiny tear to trickle down her cheek whilst turning to gaze out of the carriage window, making sure the key light hit her beautiful face as she did.

'I swear you are the most stubborn woman that ever lived, Magnolia. Now you'll do as I say and come home with me or, by heaven, I won't be responsible!'

God, Montana was particularly brutal today, Guy thought, almost spitting his dialogue back at her. Had she done any work at all on her Southern accent? he wondered to himself.

She sounded like a Californian Valley Girl auditioning for a part in a daytime soap opera. When he thought of the meticulous attention to detail he was bringing to his character, how he was living and breathing the part of Brent Charleston during this shoot – why, he was even prepared to cultivate saddle sores on his ass for the sake of his art. Whereas Montana's approach to her role appeared to be just turn up on time and try to remember the lines. I wonder how many studio bosses she had to sleep with to land this part, he thought bitterly to himself.

'And cut!' yelled Jimmy D. from his director's chair where he'd been intently watching the scene on a tiny, flickering monitor in front of him.

'Take five, everybody,' he growled at the crew as he strode purposefully towards the carriage they were shooting in, ignoring the huge golf umbrella his assistant held out for him (as the rain was pelting down by now).

'And we're taking five,' Johnny repeated into his walkie-talkie for the benefit of the make-up and wardrobe people who were out of earshot. They were shooting the carriage scene down by Loch Moluag on the edge of the Davenport estate, but because the dirt track the carriage was on was so narrow and entirely enclosed with great oak trees, there was only room for the cameraman and his focus puller, while the rest of the crew were dotted around the lake, clad in huge green raincoats, patiently watching the action on live monitors.

Montana and Guy sat uncomfortably close together in the carriage, each studiously ignoring the other as Jimmy D. strode through the mud and down the dirt track, addressing them both through the open window. His voice was low and threatening.

'Just in case it hasn't occurred to either of you to actually read the goddamned script, Brent and Magnolia are supposed to be *in love* with each other.' A huge purple vein was now starting to throb at his left temple. 'I wanna see chemistry, I wanna see sparks fly, I wanna see two people who can't keep their hands off each other, not a squabbling pair of assholes who look like they should be doing dinner theatre in Santa Barbara.'

'You know, Jimmy D., this is really difficult for me,' Guy replied, totally unfazed by the dinner theatre reference. 'It's like working opposite a plank of wood. I'm giving, giving, giving all the time here and getting zero in return. How in hell am I supposed to play the scene when she won't even make eye contact with me?'

'Giving, giving, giving?' Montana snapped. 'The only thing you ever give away for free is syphilis.' Then, whipping off the radio mike Paddy had neatly pinned to the collar of her riding habit, she added, 'You try swapping places with me and see how you like it, Jimmy D. It's bad enough that Guy's been eating enough garlic to wipe out an entire village of vampires, but the smell of whiskey from him is making me wanna hurl. Oh, but then I guess he was too busy with Daisy last night to even have time to brush his teeth this morning.'

'Jaysus, is that true?' an incredulous Paddy turned to ask Daisy, having overheard everything on his headphones. Daisy, who was perched uncomfortably on a canvas stool beside him, immediately pretended to be too absorbed in a fistful of script pages in her hand to have heard him. News travelled quickly around film sets, or so it seemed.

'Did you shag that fucking eejit?'

Although she was wearing a huge anorak, which covered most of her face, she still felt herself burning bright red from the back of her neck up.

'Say no more,' Paddy continued, miffed. 'But I'd love to

know what that wanker has that I don't. I mean apart from his house in the Hollywood Hills and his money and his vintage car collection and his vineyard in the Napa Valley and his bleedin' loft conversion in New York, and, if the *National Intruder* is right, his penis extension. But apart from all that, what in the name of Jaysus do ya see in him?'

'Oh Paddy,' Daisy began, seeing that he was genuinely hurt. 'I can't explain how I feel about him, it's just . . .'

'You can spare me all that womany shit,' he replied, sadly putting his headphones back on. 'All I'm saying to ya is . . . you could have done an awful lot better for yerself.'

'You can put him through,' Steve said to his secretary, wondering why on earth Paul O'Driscoll would be calling him.

'Steve, how are you?' came the nervous voice from the other end of the phone.

'Just heading out for a meeting actually,' Steve replied, 'and I'm running late.' He was on his way over to Davenport Hall as it happened, to give Lucasta a full report on her bottled-water idea. (A ten-page report his junior had worked on for hours, which Steve knew full well Lucasta would end up using to line a cat-litter tray.)

'I won't keep you, just to ask you if you'd come along to an extraordinary meeting of the Kildare County Council on Monday next if you're free. The local development planning committee have received a submission that we need to discuss.'

Steve, who had been gathering up bundles of files and folders as he was talking, suddenly stopped dead in his tracks. The County Council *never* held extraordinary meetings, for any reason.

'The development planning committee? Paul, what's going on?'

'Eight o'clock next Monday then, in the Dunville Arms Hotel in Kildare town. I'll explain when I see you.'

Tony took one final glance at the photos he was just about to email to the *National Intruder*. Fantastic stuff. Guy van der Post undressing a gorgeous blonde on the staircase of this dilapidated stately home while Montana Jones sat alone at dinner with a face like a bulldog sucking piss from a nettle. The mileage they'd get out of this one! A story suddenly flashed through his quick-thinking journalist's brain. Guy having an affair with a beautiful Irish girl right under his lover's nose . . . true, Montana and Guy had never been an item, but whoever let the truth get in the way of a good story?

Then there was that other couple, the tall fair-haired guy and that sexy-looking woman he was kissing on the stairs in the early hours of this morning. Pity neither of them was famous in any way, but Tony had such fantastic shots of them kissing each other so passionately, it seemed criminal to waste them.

Another story was starting to ferment in his head . . . the Lord of the Manor and his housekeeper, locked in a torrid embrace. He could be a character a little like Princess Diana's brother, proud and arrogant, while she could be a poor, working-class girl slaving away at this stately home to earn enough money for her mother's hernia operation. What a back-up story to Guy and Montana's that could be!

HE WAS THE ALL-POWERFUL EARL OF IRELAND AND SHE WAS A HUMBLE SCULLERY MAID. SOCIETY KEPT THEM POLES APART UNTIL ONE FATEFUL DAY THEIR EYES MET ACROSS THE COAL SCUTTLE. CAN THEIR LOVE CONQUER THE SOCIAL DIVIDE?

He loves me not . . . he loves me

The *Intruder*'s readers would lap it up, and, let's face it, it had been a slow season for celebrity gossip. Not a divorce, a bust-up or a brawl in months, which never made for healthy circulation figures. He even had a headline: 'SEX AND INTRIGUE AT DAVENPORT HALL! THERE MUST BE SOMETHING IN THE IRISH AIR . . . EVERYONE'S AT IT!'

And who the hell was to know it wasn't true? Hadn't he the pictures to prove it?

'How marvellous you're looking, Susan, it's wonderful to see you,' chirped Edwina as she rose to peck her mother-in-law-elect delicately on each cheek, being ultra-careful not to leave a lipstick stain. 'And congratulations on your new home . . . I hear it's utterly divine!'

'How sweet of you, my dear, you must come down to see us as soon as you can,' replied Mrs de Courcey, as she grace-fully accepted the proffered housewarming gift, though making no attempt to open it. Very poor etiquette to open a present in front of the donor, an appallingly middle-class trait, she always thought.

'Now, Edwina darling, just because Michael and I have become country bumpkins doesn't mean we don't expect to see you as often as possible. We do hope the new house won't be too unsophisticated for a girl-about-town like you.'

Edwina protested at this, as she knew she must, and purred that, at her next window of opportunity, she'd be straight down to visit.

'And you know, Susan, I'm devastated not to have been at your housewarming the other night, but I had given my word that I'd model at the Peter O'Brien couture show, and I'd have hated to let him down.'

Mrs de Courcey smiled benignly at her as she sank into a luxurious tapestry chair in the chic Dublin restaurant the

Hibernian. It was just after one and the 'ladies who lunch' set had started to arrive in Lainey-clad force. She recognized some of them and blew a few air-kisses across the room, fully aware of the envious glances she was attracting. After all, she was having lunch with Edwina Moynihan, one of a new breed of Irish supermodels. What a wonderful daughter-in-law she would make! And what stunning grandchildren she and Andrew would give her!

'Of course, Andrew was distraught that you weren't there.'

Edwina hesitated slightly before answering, as though making a decision about whether or not to confide any further.

'Do you know, I bumped into him last night, Susan, can you believe it?' she said, hoping she sounded suitably casual. 'In the Hôtel de Paris of all places! He was with the most oddly dressed girl . . .' She trailed off, very deliberately. That was all she needed to let slip.

What was left of her smile stayed frozen on Mrs de Courcey's impeccably made-up, Botoxed face.

'Yes, I know who you mean, Portia Davenport. A neighbour. From a family who seem to be so inbred that they must have been marrying their cousins for the last two hundred years at least. I really prefer not to talk about the way they behaved at the housewarming. It was utterly shocking. And, I have to admit, she did pretty much hurl herself at poor Andrew the other night, you know how needy and persistent these unmarried thirty-something women can be. I'm quite sure she pestered him into taking her out and, of course, you know how soft-hearted Andrew is.'

Edwina relaxed into a smile. 'Well, Susan, you know I'd be the last person ever to pass comments about another woman, but she should have had a huge D for Desperation tattooed right across her forehead last night. And if you'd seen her outfit! She may as well have been wearing wellies. Those Town and Country types really are a law unto themselves. I presumed Andrew was taking out a traveller for a bet.'

'Yes, the "too posh to wash" brigade, I call them.' Mrs de Courcey laughed cruelly as she turned to attract the attention of a passing waiter.

'But really, you must try to put that unfortunate Davenport woman out of your head, Edwina dear. It's most unlikely he'll ever see her again.'

Portia couldn't believe her eyes when she woke to hear the grandfather clock in the hall chime midday. She never slept in, ever! As she hurriedly pulled on a tracksuit and tripped downstairs to grab some coffee, she overheard voices coming from the old servants' kitchen.

'How in the name of Jaysus am I supposed to get lunch organized when you have two hundred bleedin' bottles of water all over the kitchen table?'

Oh God, Portia groaned, Mrs Flanagan in one of her moods. All she needed.

'I am *trying* to run a business here and a little support and encouragement wouldn't go amiss!' Lucasta screeched back at her. 'I watch costume dramas on TV, you know, I know how the aristocracy is meant to be treated by staff. Housekeepers are supposed to use phrases like: "You rang, my lady?" not: "What the fuck do you want now?"'

Portia sighed deeply to herself and opened the door, wondering what fresh hell this could possibly be. There sat Lucasta, amid stuffed ashtrays, surrounded by dozens and dozens of empty wine and spirit bottles, patiently soaking them in hot water and removing the labels one by one.

'Oh, good morning, darling,' said her mother, glancing up, 'you're just in time to help me.'

'Mummy, what on earth are you doing?' Portia asked, almost dreading the answer.

'Richard bleedin' Branson here has decided to save herself the bother of getting perfectly good water from the well out-side for her new business venture,' sniffed Mrs Flanagan disapprovingly. 'Oh no, because that would be what a normal person would do.'

'Well, I would go down to the well but . . . it's raining,' said Lucasta like a sullen six-year-old. 'And don't use that dreadful sarcastic tone with me, Mrs Flanagan. I've a good mind to sit you down and make you watch every Merchant Ivory film ever made as a lesson in how employers should be spoken to. You can treat them as training videos.'

'If you think I'm going to lick yer arse on the money you pay me, yer've another think coming. Jaysus, I'd earn more working in McDonald's.'

'Yes, but you'd need to be able to cook before you'd get a job in McDonald's!'

'Mummy, stop it!' Portia pleaded, well used to intervening in the scraps she and Mrs Flanagan regularly indulged in. 'Now please tell me what's going on?'

'This,' said Lucasta, theatrically waving an empty wine bottle right under Portia's nose, 'is your future. Eau de Davenport. Organic spring water. Practically pure. Yes, I could be unimaginative and spend a fortune mining for water underground, but why bother? Much easier just to use good old-fashioned tap water. It's all the bloody same anyway. And you know, I'm not leading customers astray in any way, the labels on the bottles will clearly say "Eau de Davenport" and that's precisely what they'll get. Do you know, I feel just like that Michael O'Leary. I've got entrepreneurial vision just like him. Eau de Davenport could very well become the Ryanair of the bottled-water business.'

'And where on earth did all these empty bottles come from?' asked Portia, attempting to shift some of them off the huge pine kitchen table so Mrs Flanagan could at least have some space.

'Well, darling, you'd be amazed how much booze we get through in this house,' replied Lucasta, looking a little sheepish. 'I was just saying to Andrew that I simply can't believe the amount of bottles lying by the bins outside—'

'Andrew?' Portia interrupted. 'Do you mean he's here?'

'Yes, darling, he's been here all morning helping me. He's just outside bringing in some more bottles.'

'Lovely fella,' said Mrs Flanagan approvingly as she mopped up some water Lucasta had sloshed all over the flagstone floor. 'Now, Guy van der Post is definitely more of a ride than him, but I think he could be a bit high maintenance. No, there's a lot to be said for a bloke that's more normal, like. Jaysus knows, it's a rarity in this house.'

Before Portia even had time to gather her thoughts, the back door opened and there he was – laden down with as many empty bottles as he could carry, drenched to the bone and still managing to look super-sexy.

'Good morning!' he said, grinning at her as he unloaded some of the bottles on to the kitchen table. 'And please allow me to introduce myself,' he went on, twinkling at her just as he'd done the previous night, 'I'm your mother's new business partner.'

Chapter Thirteen

'OK, people, that's a wrap for today,' Johnny wearily called into his walkie-talkie as the crew slowly began to pack up their equipment and head for the hills, every one of them soaked to the skin.

'Jesus H. Christ, I've been on some miserable shoots in my time but this is one for the records,' moaned Jimmy D. as they both trudged up the dirt track (which, by now, was virtually a mudslide) at the edge of Loch Moluag and on the mile or so towards the Hall.

'Ah, cheer up,' Johnny replied, lighting up a cigarette, 'think of the fabulous cordon bleu meal that the mad housekeeper will have waiting for you when you get back.'

'We've been working on the exteriors for two weeks now and I barely have ten minutes of usable film in the can,' continued Jimmy D., ignoring the jibe about Mrs Flanagan's culinary efforts. 'What the fuck is Harvey Brocklehurst Goldberg gonna say? He could close down the whole shoot if this continues. Hell, it's happened before.'

Johnny didn't reply, but hauled his weary bones on through the driving rain in silence. It had indeed happened before. Only a few years ago, he'd been Assistant Director on a huge,

big-budget American blockbuster about the Normandy landings (shot on Dollymount Strand in Dublin) called *D is for
Deliverance*. Within three weeks of production, the backers had
pulled out and the entire film collapsed, with the result that
no one, cast or crew, ever saw a penny of their wages. The crew
promptly nicknamed the film *D is for Dole*.

It had indeed happened before.

'Oh Guy, you were so wonderful today,' gushed Daisy breathlessly as she threw her arms around his neck. 'I was watching
your scene from the monitor and you were just *magnetic*!'

'You really think so?' he replied, pouring himself a large,
neat glass of Jack Daniel's. 'Well, you know, the script is good
and the director is good, but obviously, not as good as me.'
Somehow, Guy always managed to sound like he was giving
an interview on *The Johnny Carson Show*.

'That bit where you took Magnolia's hand in yours and told
her that you loved her so much that you wanted to smack
her across the face . . . I had tears in my eyes, it was all so
real!'

This, needless to say, was music to his ears. 'Honey, just for
that, I'm gonna let you watch me shower,' he drawled as he sat
on the sofa of his Winnebago struggling to wrench off his
Victorian riding boots whilst simultaneously knocking back
the whiskey. He also had a towel draped around his neck,
which made him look, and behave, like a boxer after a prize
fight.

'Mmmm, what a perfect end to a dreary day, my darling,'
she replied, slipping out of her wet gear and sashaying to the
bathroom, divesting herself of jeans and all the layers of woolly
jumpers it was necessary to wear in June in Ireland if you
didn't fancy a bout of pneumonia. Then, ruffling her blonde
curls and looking like a young Brigitte Bardot, she turned to

him seductively from the bathroom door and said, 'And if you're very, very good, I just might join you.'

'Caroline, I need you to take an urgent message to Daisy for me,' Montana commanded as Serge patiently unclipped the enormous hairpiece which was practically stapled to her head.

'Do you mean now, Miss Jones?' replied Caroline as she picked up various discarded bits of rain-drenched period costume Montana had dumped carelessly on the floor.

'Yes, now. Whatever,' hissed Montana, who'd had quite enough attitude for one day.

'Well, good luck, honey,' Serge chipped in, his mouth full of the hairclips he was deftly removing. 'I saw her disappear into Guy's trailer just now, and honey, that pair are sooo hot to trot! I've never seen a Winnebago jiggle up and down like that before; I was afraid they'd cause a mudslide.'

'Not that Mr van der Post's extra-curricular social activities are of any concern to us,' snapped Caroline.

'Oh, keep your pantyhose on, Mother Teresa,' sighed Serge, who was by now removing Montana's expertly applied make-up with what looked like a large trowel. 'Don't you know that gossip is the teat at which the crew of any film set suckles?'

'What was the message, Miss Jones?' asked Caroline, choosing to ignore Serge and his mixed metaphors.

'Just give her this,' replied Montana, curtly handing over a scrap of paper she'd been scribbling on, 'and tell her I'll see her later.'

As Caroline picked her way through the lashing rain and across the muddy forecourt towards Guy's trailer, she was unable to resist. Curiosity had got the better of her and besides, Romance Pictures were paying her far too much to renege on her duties now. Montana Jones was her charge whether she liked it or not, and Caroline was being paid to keep her on the straight and narrow for the duration of the shoot. She tore open the note, making sure to shield it carefully from the pouring rain with her umbrella: *Daisy. The well has run dry. Urgent. And if you're reading this, Caroline, you're even more of a sad bitch than I thought.*

Unmoved by this dig at her, she was about to shove the note hurriedly back in its envelope, when she was suddenly startled by a voice from behind her.

'Why do all the best women go for wankers?' It was Paddy, drenched to the bone, hauling an armful of sound cable back to base and looking sadly in the direction of Guy's trailer. 'I was even going to ask Daisy to go for a Super Macs tonight.'

Caroline gave him one of her 'how dare this pile of chopped liver address me?' killer glares before knocking rapidly on the trailer door. 'Is that so, Paddy. Super Macs. How on earth could any woman refuse?'

'If you're going in there, just let her know, discreetly like, that she coulda had me.'

'So, without further ado, I declare the motion to apply for rezoning passed by twenty-two votes against one!' And with a flourish, Paul O'Driscoll banged his gavel down, thus bringing the extraordinary meeting of the Kildare County Council to a close.

'Jaysus, that couldn't have gone better,' Shamie Nolan proudly declared to anyone who'd listen. Then he turned to his wife, Bridie, who had outdone herself in the style stakes tonight: she was wearing a bright pink, badly copied Chanel suit, complete with a corsage, which might have been passable if worn by Sarah Jessica Parker, but made a middle-aged politician's wife look like she was soliciting. 'Listen, luv, I'll just get in a few rounds for the lads, to thank them for coming at

such short notice, like. Would you ever have a word with Steve
Sullivan for me?'

'With the greatest of fecking pleasure,' she replied with an
edge in her voice. 'You just leave that gobshite to me, Shamie.'

Then, pausing only to check that the false tan hadn't
dribbled down her legs in the lashing rain outside, she
marched up to poor Steve, who sat alone at the end of the
hotel room, staring out the window and fiddling with a Biro.

'Well, I hope yer're fecking delighted with yerself,' she
began. 'Ya do realize that all yer've succeeded in doing here
tonight is pissing off your local TD who, I might add, has
thrown an awful lot of legal business in your direction over
the last few years.'

Steve sighed sadly, with the air of someone who already
knew that the battle was over and lost. 'Bridie, you don't
understand. The Davenports are old friends of mine. The Hall
and the land are all they have. There have been Davenports
living there for over two hundred years, it's their heritage, it's
all of our heritage.'

'Heritage me hole. If they'd taken better care of the Hall in
the first place, this never would have happened. Sure my
eleven-year-old, Shamie Junior, went on a school tour there
and fell clean through a rotting floorboard. The poor child had
to be rushed to the accident and emergency in Kildare and
given penicillin shots for two weeks.'

'I'm sorry to hear that. I hope he was OK.'

'Shamie Junior is a girl. Anyway, the point is, the Hall
should have been condemned years ago—'

'No, Bridie,' Steve interrupted, unable to take much more
of this conversation. 'The point is that no member of the
Davenport family is going to allow the County Council to
condemn the building, serve them with a compulsory
purchase order, knock it down and rezone all of their land for

150

residential purposes. Over their dead bodies will that ever happen.'

'Except that Lucasta and the girls aren't the legal owners, are they, Steve? The legal owner of Davenport Hall is Lord Blackjack himself, now out in Las Vegas having a grand aul' time of it, from what I hear. And the family's heritage never kept him awake at night, now did it? Sure it's well known in the town that Blackjack would sell his own liver for cash. I'd say he'd be delighted with the few extra bob. More money for him to spend on his teenage girlfriend.'

There were no two ways about it. Andrew was in love. Davenport Hall had completely and utterly captivated him. At his insistence, Portia had spent an entire evening patiently giving him a guided tour of the Hall, the Dining Rooms, various Drawing Rooms, the stinking Music Room, the Billiard Room, the freezing Ballroom, the Long Gallery and the Master Bedrooms, with Andrew tirelessly asking questions about the history of the Hall and the few artefacts lying about that miraculously hadn't been flogged off.

'Why is the Ballroom separate to the rest of the Hall?' he'd asked, his keen, educated eye not missing a thing.

'Wow, hardly anyone ever notices that,' replied Portia, genuinely impressed. 'It was built at a slightly later date, eighteen hundred and one, in fact. You see, the fourth Lord Davenport was big mates with the Prince Regent, who was having an affair with Lady Coyningham from Slane Castle at the time. He used to come over quite regularly to see her and would stop off here en route for a few stiff brandies and to water his horses. So Lord Davenport almost bankrupted the family adding on the Ballroom, thinking it would impress his royal guest, but no sooner was it completed than the Prince dumped his Irish mistress and never set foot in the country again. So that Lord Davenport died in penury, you know, and they say his dying words were, "Set fire to the fucking Ballroom and give thanks that at least I managed to live longer than that fat Hanoverian bastard." '

Andrew threw his head back and howled with laughter. 'Go on,' he said, encouraging her, 'more anecdotes from the family archives, please and, by the way, why is the Powder Room locked? I'd love to see inside.'

'Because the bins aren't collected till Thursday,' Portia replied sheepishly, 'and if we keep them outside, we get rats.'

She couldn't believe it though; she'd never shown the place to anyone who seemed so genuinely interested in period houses before. In fact, usually she was mortified leading people from one manky room to another and seeing the disgusted look on their faces when they saw the dilapidated state it had fallen into. Not Andrew. He couldn't see or hear enough and seemed genuinely fascinated by the tales Portia could tell about the antics of her colourful ancestors.

There was the family legend about the brutish Lord Davenport who'd had an affair with Emily Brontë and was rumoured to be the inspiration behind the character Heathcliff, which he particularly enjoyed.

Then there was the story of George Davenport, the second lord, who was a founder and active member of the United Irishmen. His good friend Robert Emmet had recruited him in the 1790s, probably because of his vast wealth rather than anything else; poor George Davenport was known locally as the thickest revolutionary Ireland ever produced – which was no mean feat. In fact, it was reckoned by historians that his misguided republicanism actually resulted in British rule being extended in the greater Kildare area by at least twenty years.

During the 1798 rebellion, he was entrusted with one

simple task, which his lordship still managed to make a complete pig's ear of. Emmet charged him with storing several tons of gunpowder and hundreds of rifles sent over from France until the glorious day when Leinster would arise in rebellion. But poor dim old George foolishly hid the ammunition in the coach house and then forgot all about it. One fateful night, legend had it, he was groping a dairymaid at the back of the coach house and afterwards lit up a pipe, throwing a taper from his lantern carelessly aside where it landed on a keg of gunpowder. Eyewitnesses claimed that the explosion could be seen from as far away as County Carlow. His lordship was killed instantly, thus passing on the land and title to his nine-year-old son, Frederick Davenport, who unfortunately only retained the title for a year. He died in suspicious circumstances, thus passing the Hall on to his uncle, whom locals immediately nicknamed 'Richard III, the nephew killer'.

All that's known of poor young Frederick's stewardship at the Hall was that he hated his governess and, upon ascending to the title, sacked her immediately and closed down every school for miles. He may not have been the most impressive ancestor the family had produced, but he was certainly by far the most popular among the children of Ballyroan.

Andrew roared with laughter, egging Portia on to let more family skeletons out of the closet. He didn't even complain when they discovered that one of Lucasta's cats had given birth on a Georgian ottoman and was now using it as a litter tray. Eventually, they both collapsed, exhausted, on the huge Louis XV armchairs in the Yellow Drawing Room, which at least had the remains of a fire flickering in front of it.

'Did you ever see the film *Pacific Heights*?' Andrew asked as he lit a cigarette and sat back, surveying the room around him. Portia shook her head. 'Well, it's about a tenant who refuses to leave the house he's living in. I think that could well be me.'

'Do you fancy a drink?' Portia asked, rising to go to the drinks cabinet at the other end of the room (and, indeed, the only corner of it which wasn't covered in dead flies and cobwebs, it was so well used).

'Gin and tonic would be lovely, thanks.'

As she fixed the drinks, she called over her shoulder to him, 'You've no idea what a new experience it is for me to show the Hall to someone who doesn't bolt for the hills. Usually when I ask anyone, "Would you like a tour?" it's followed by hysterical laughter, then a deathly silence as they realize I'm serious, followed by an even more awkward pause while they think of an excuse to get the hell out of here.'

Andrew laughed again as she passed him a drink and sat down on the rotting Persian rug beside him. He slipped his arm around her shoulder and casually started to coil her hair around his finger.

'Portia, have you any idea how amazing this house could be if you did something with it?' he asked, moving a little closer to her. 'I know it would take money, but with a new roof and the place refurbished from scratch, this could be one of the most beautiful houses in the country.'

'It would take money? Andrew, you're talking millions here!' She laughed. 'I think the last architect who visited the Hall was the man who built it, James Gandon. In 1770.'

'Look, do you remember L'Hôtel de Paris in Dublin?'

She nodded, looking straight ahead into the last dying embers of the fire. She would hardly have forgotten the night she'd met Edwina and her geriatric date.

'That hotel was derelict until a few years ago, when Dermot O'Brien took it over, gutted it and restored it to what it is today. Now it's one of the most successful hotels in the country. If you salvaged this house, you could open it to the public and make a fortune. Or what about turning it into a golf club and hotel or even a health spa?'

Portia sighed, taking a sip of her gin and tonic. 'It would be a dream come true for me to restore this house to what it once was and then run it as a country house hotel. And I know it would be successful. But in a million years, I could never afford it. Even the money Romance Pictures are paying me is barely enough to cover the cost of getting a small part of the roof renovated. And at that, I have to wait till the film wraps before I can even get started. According to Jimmy D., scaffolding on the side of a listed building isn't very Victorian.'

'So why don't you get an interior designer in to help you renovate the bedrooms and get your hotel up and running?' he asked, puzzled.

'Easy to tell you've never lived in a Georgian house before, Mr Park Avenue.' She smiled back at him. 'Because if Laurence Llewelyn-Bowen himself were to decorate for me, I'm afraid even the most luxurious bedroom wouldn't compensate guests for pelting rain gushing down on top of them. No, I'm afraid it has to be the roof first and, at that, it'll only be a portion of it. A lot of my money was guzzled up by the cost of settling Mummy's account at Oddbins.'

'But look at Lord Harry Fitzherbert, he makes a fortune from renting out Navan Castle as a rock venue.'

Portia giggled at the thought of U2 or Bruce Springsteen staying at the Hall, sampling one of Mrs Flanagan's TV dinners, while twenty thousand fans used Portaloos outside. 'I think only hardened Glastonbury fans who actually enjoy swimming in mud and shite would feel at home here. It's so sweet of you to want to help, but honestly, Andrew, I just don't have that kind of money.'

He smiled down at her, with that twinkle in his eyes which made her stomach churn over. 'You mightn't be able to afford it, my lady, but I can.' His lips were nuzzling against her cheek now, then moving down and lightly kissing her neck, in the manner of someone who had all the time in the world. Portia snuggled in beside him, running her fingers through his hair and longing to kiss him properly.

'Great tour, my lady,' he whispered, slipping his hand inside her shirt and gently playing with her bra strap, 'but do you think you could show me the bedrooms again?'

Later that night, as Lucasta patiently waited for the photo-copier in Ballyroan's local Spar to do its work, she fell into chit chat with Lottie O'Loughlin, the owner (known locally as 'the oracle', such was her in-depth knowledge of half the town's comings and goings).

'Five thousand labels is a shocking amount of photocopying to be getting on with,' said Lottie, leaning over the counter, her curiosity piqued. 'Would this be anything to do with all the filming that's going on above at the Hall?'

'Oh no, darling,' replied Lucasta, picking up one of her cats which had hidden under the frozen-vegetable counter, 'this is all for my new business. Gnasher, do come out of there, you naughty bugger!' Then, producing one of the freshly photo-copied pages from the machine she waved it proudly under Lottie's nose. 'What do you think? *I* think it'll be the biggest thing since some genius said, "Why don't we try putting gin into the tonic?"'

Lottie grabbed one and read it aloud. '*Eau de Davenport. One hundred per cent water. Practically pure.*'

Each label was handwritten in Lucasta's schoolgirlish writing and bore the logo of a black cat drinking from a well with a sign stuck to it, which read, '*Fat free. Can be used as part of a calorie-controlled diet. Can also be used as a mixer. Signed: the Government.*'

'Isn't it wonderful?' chirped Lucasta. 'And the beauty of it is, the coppers can't come after me, there's not a word of a lie on that label.'

Lottie was about to reply when she was interrupted by another customer tapping impatiently on the counter and waiting to be served.

'Ah, Mrs de Courcey, how are you? What can I do you for?'

'I'm here to complain actually,' came the curt reply. 'My husband's copy of the *Irish Times* wasn't delivered this morning, for some reason.'

'Oh, we used to have the paper delivered to us at the Hall,' said Lucasta, who by now was on her hands and knees trying to extricate Gnasher from where he was stuck under the frozen-carrot display. 'But for some reason it just stopped, can't imagine why.'

Lottie coughed discreetly. 'Because you still owe me for three years' worth of deliveries is the reason why. By the way, have you met Lady Davenport yet?' she asked Mrs de Courcey, suddenly aware of an awkward pause.

'Yes, I believe I have,' replied Mrs de Courcey, whipping her leg up so that Lucasta's cat couldn't ladder her expensive, sheer Wolford stockings. 'At our housewarming party.' Then she dryly added, 'You were kind enough to perform a number of party pieces for our guests.'

Lucasta, who had been staring at this glamorous stranger, clearly racking her brains to remember where she knew her from, suddenly lit up. 'Oh, now I remember! Thank Christ for that, I was afraid you were someone we owed money to. So you must be Andrew's mother! Yes, I'd entirely forgotten about that night, I do hope I wasn't too completely sozzled. My daughter says I'm a tuppenny whore when I'm drinking gin. And I can't even argue with her because I never remember the next day. I could have shagged your husband for all I know.' She laughed innocently.

157

'I'm so sorry about your paper this morning, Mrs de Courcey,' said Lottie, not paying the slightest bit of attention to her ladyship's twitterings. 'I will of course refund you and deliver tomorrow's free of charge.'

Mrs de Courcey merely nodded and was about to turn on her Jimmy Choos to walk disgustedly out the door when Lucasta came over to her, blissfully unaware that she'd caused offence. 'You know, Mrs de Courcey, you simply must let me repay your hospitality. I'm having my annual Midsummer Ball next Saturday, to mark the summer solstice, you know, and pay homage to the Goddess of Samhradh and we'd be so thrilled if you could come. For fuck's sake, Andrew's practically part of the furniture now. And you could meet all the lovely film people who are staying, they're absolute darlings . . .'

Before she could reply, Lottie came running up to her.

'Hold on, Mrs de Courcey, you forgot your copy of this week's *National Intruder*.

Andrew managed to kick the door of Portia's bedroom shut, without either of them breaking the kiss they were locked in. They tumbled on to her four-poster bed, landing in a heap and knocking over a huge pile of dirty laundry on to the floor. Portia was rubbing her long legs against his as he pulled her shirt over her head, then bent down to kiss her breasts. Oh God, she thought, my bra . . . The last thing that had occurred to her when she was getting dressed that morning was that she'd end up in bed with him and so, with a jolt of embarrassment, she remembered that she was wearing a once-white Marks & Spencer bra and knickers set, now gone grey from a combination of age and being shoved down the back of the Aga to dry. Thinking fast, she rolled on top of him, pulling a sheet over her as she undid the heavy clasp of his Gucci belt and undressed him. He was too quick for her though; in one expert snap, he'd undone her bra and was now dangling it over her head, teasing her, hysterical with laughter.

'I think I've just had a boarding-school flashback,' he said. 'All my misspent teenage years chasing convent girls from the school next door have suddenly come flooding back to me. Very sexy, actually . . .' He bent down to kiss her again, his tongue rolling around hers like satin. She kissed him back hungrily and then remembered.

'Andrew, condoms.'

'Mmmm, what's that, darling?' he murmured, kissing her breasts.

'In the medicine chest in the family bathroom. Go on, Andrew, it's only down the corridor.' Then, smiling shyly at him, she said, 'Getting condoms is the boy's job, you know.'

'Hold that thought,' he said, kissing her forehead as he lightly sprang out of the bed, by now down to his underpants. And what a body, Portia thought as he left the room, delighted for a few moments' respite to whip off the knackered-looking knickers and shove them under the bed.

Andrew strode down the corridor, fully confident that no one would see him, and opened the door of the family bathroom. The light was on and there, sitting on the toilet with her interlock pants around her ankles, smoking a fag and reading *Model Makeover* magazine, was Mrs Flanagan.

'I've been waiting four days for me bowels to move, luv, can you just wait four bleeding minutes?'

'I'm terribly sorry,' said Andrew, totally unfazed as though he were at a dinner party. 'I'll just wait outside then.'

Minutes later, safely back in Portia's bed, he was recounting the story with tears of laughter rolling down his face yet again.

'So I waited in the corridor,' he said, barely able to get the sentence out. 'And, being a gentleman, I thought I'd better cover myself up a bit. So I grabbed the shield from the coat of arms on the landing and stood there, waiting for the lady to finish.'

'Then what?' asked Portia.

'Eventually, she came out, spraying Haze air freshener behind her, took one look at me and said, "Ah Jaysus, luv, if ya weren't carrying that bleeding shield, you would have made an aul' woman very happy!"'

They held on to each other, each of them giggling uncontrollably.

'I'm sorry, darling,' said Andrew, wiping the tears away, 'I promise we'll do it better next time.'

Chapter Fourteen

Jimmy D. sat back into the huge green leather armchair in the Library and fumbled about in his pocket for a cigar. And not just any cigar, a Havana. Three hundred dollars' worth. One he'd been saving for a really special occasion. He had just put down the phone on a particularly gruelling conversation with Harvey Brocklehurst Goldberg ('Golden Balls' was his nickname in LA, such was his talent for spinning money out of dross) and now, finally, for the first time in weeks, Jimmy D. could afford to breathe a sigh of relief.

Ella Hepburn had just signed. Ella fucking Hepburn! He took a great puff of the cigar and surveyed the dismal view out of the French windows. For the past few weeks, both he and Golden Balls had been under colossal pressure to cast the cameo role of Blanche Charleston, Brent's mother. No A list star worth their Botox jabs in Hollywood would deign to work with either Montana or Guy, let alone agree to stay in a shithole location like Davenport Hall. And besides, as any Hollywood agent would tell you, pitching the word 'cameo' at a star was just a well-known euphemism for 'really small shitty part we couldn't get anyone else to play'.

This left both producer and director with a huge dilemma.

161

The shoot had been going so badly, dogged equally by bad weather, bad morale and bad acting, that the whole movie needed a huge boost just to keep it afloat. Ella Hepburn was like manna from fucking heaven right now, Jimmy D. thought, chuckling softly to himself. Her name attached to this project could spell the difference between triumph and disaster for the picture.

Ella Hepburn . . . Jimmy D. could well remember seeing her in the old black-and-white movies his father used to take him to see when he was just a kid back in Colorado. At five years of age she had lisped her way into America's affections in a series of movies she'd made with Bob Hope called *And Baby Makes Three*. She'd been a star ever since, graduating from those awful, self-indulgent, angst-ridden teen movies of the 1950s and then, via about ten marriages and divorces (not even the *National Intruder* could keep track) several stints in the Betty Ford Center and a number of overdoses, had finally achieved official iconic status. She was one of those stars that you couldn't believe was still alive and going strong. And she had just signed to play Blanche Charleston.

Jimmy D. took another luxuriant puff on his cigar and surveyed the view (although the septic tank was all that could be seen clearly from the Library window). After two God-awful weeks, finally things were starting to look up.

Being the bearer of bad news was never a part of his job which Steve relished, particularly where the Davenports were concerned, but this time he had no choice. He could postpone the inevitable no longer. For God's sake, he fretted, all Shamie Nolan had to do now was apply to the planning authorities in Dublin (half of whom were his old golfing buddies) and the deal would be done. The Council would condemn the Hall and immediately slap a compulsory purchase order on everything the Davenports held dear: their home, their land and their two-hundred-year history.

The only ray of hope Steve could see was Blackjack. If he could just get to him before Shamie Nolan did, there might be a chance, albeit a slim one, to persuade him not to sell out. Steve sighed as he drove his Jeep up the driveway to the Hall. This was the same Blackjack whose compulsive gambling had driven his family to the brink of ruin time and time again and who wasn't exactly known for holding the Davenport title and lands in the highest esteem. (He reputedly once drank a bottle of Glenmorangie Scotch whisky and staked the Hall itself on a hand of poker. Miraculously, he'd won.) Steve knew in his heart and soul that the chances of Blackjack turning down hard cash for his property were slim to none. And then what would become of Lucasta and Portia — and of course Daisy . . .?

He was roused from these depressing thoughts by a car passing him on the driveway. He just caught a glimpse of Portia waving at him from the passenger seat of a flashy sports car but couldn't see who was driving. Shit. He badly needed to talk to her and as it was already well after lunchtime, the chances of Lucasta being sober enough to take in the enormity of the situation were slim. And he really didn't want to be the one to break the news to Daisy, but now it looked like he'd just have to. Lousy timing, he knew, what with the Midsummer Ball planned for that evening, but this time his back was really to the wall. Shamie and Bridie Nolan were bound to be invited and the chances of them deliberately letting slip what was happening to one of the Davenports was a virtual certainty. Better, he thought, far better for them to hear the news from him, first-hand. He dreaded telling them, but knew it would have to be done. He brought the Jeep to a crunching halt on the forecourt and, gathering up a bulging

163

stack of files, headed for the kitchen door, via the walled garden to the rear of the house.

'If I've told ya once, I've told ya a thousand times, I am not marinating yer bleedin' chicken wings until after *Emmerdale* so piss off and leave me in peace,' said Mrs Flanagan as she plonked herself down in front of the tiny portable TV in the kitchen.

'Have it your way then, let all the guests starve. You're such a typical Virgo about these things,' Lucasta snarled back at her. 'In a past life, you were definitely in the SS.' She was about to snatch the TV guide from Mrs Flanagan's hand when Steve walked in.

'AH JAYSUS! Me nerves!' screeched Mrs Flanagan on hearing the back door opening. Then she visibly relaxed on seeing who it was. 'Ah howaya, Steve? Sorry if I gave ya a bit of a fright there, luv,' she said. 'It's just that every time that door opens, I keep thinking it's going to be Ella Hepburn.'

'And why would you think she'd be coming to see you?' sneered Lucasta. 'To borrow one of your housecoats perhaps?' Then, turning to Steve, her cranky mood completely evaporated. 'Darling, it's so sweet of you to call, now I do hope you haven't forgotten about my Midsummer Ball tonight? You simply must be here, half the town are coming, it'll be an absolute triumph.'

'Emm, no, Lucasta, of course I'll be here, it's just that there was something important I needed to discuss with you, if you have a minute.'

'Oh, not now, darling,' said Lucasta, sweeping by him on her way out to the garden, 'I've got to commune with the Goddess of Samhradh to intone her blessing for the party and I've got to do it now. The Ascendant Masters don't like to be kept waiting, you know.'

Steve braced himself. That only left Daisy and God only knew how she'd take the news.

He loves me not . . . he loves me

'Mrs Flanagan, I don't suppose you have the least idea where Daisy is, do you?' He had to raise his voice to be heard as she was hurling a string of abuse at the TV, her standard reaction to any commercial that met with her disapproval.

'Those bastard kitchen towels are the greatest load of shite yet invented and yes, I have tried them wet yet,' she was shouting.

'Mrs Flanagan, I hate to interrupt, but I really need to speak to her.'

'Who?'

'Daisy. Have you seen her at all?'

'Ah, she's out riding,' Mrs Flanagan replied, her eyes not leaving the TV screen.

'Do you know which direction she took? I could follow her in the car.'

'Ha, ha, that's not the kind of riding I meant,' Mrs Flanagan cackled, still glued to the box. 'Ya obviously haven't seen this yet,' she went on, holding out a battered copy of the *National Intruder* for him.

Steve glanced at the cover and nearly fell over. Plastered all over the front page was a colour photo of a semi-naked Daisy pressed up against the banisters with her head thrown back as Guy van der Post passionately kissed her neck. He had one hand clearly on her naked breast and the other on her bottom, whilst her legs appeared to be wrapped around his. The banner headline screamed: STAIRWAY TO HEAVEN. GUY AND MONTANA IN IRISH SEX TRIANGLE.

Then, flicking the magazine open, his jaw dropped as he saw a picture of Portia sitting at the bottom of the great staircase kissing the face off Chief Justice de Courcey's son, Andrew. Had poor Steve not been so shocked about Daisy's antics, this headline would have made him laugh: A TRUE LOVE EXCLUSIVE. THE ALL POWERFUL EARL OF IRELAND AND HIS HUMBLE SCULLERY MAID GET JIGGY WITH IT.

165

As the final credits rolled on *Emmerdale*, Mrs Flanagan rose out of her armchair and was about to get back to work, when she saw that Steve was still there, transfixed by the *National Intruder*.

'Yeah, according to that magazine, they're all at it here,' she said, rolling up her sleeves. 'Jaysus, Steve, it'll be you and me next! Mind you, you'd have to smarten yerself up a bit first, luv. There's a lot of rides wandering around the house these days and you'd have to be able to compete, if ya know what I mean.'

Poor Steve just looked at her, utterly at a loss.

'Now don't get me wrong or anything,' Mrs Flanagan went on, waddling towards the freezer. 'I mean, yer're a lovely fella an' all, it's just, sometimes, ya can be a bit . . . I dunno, beige.'

'Beige?'

'Ah, ya need to start watching a bit of daytime telly, luv,' she went on, hauling out bag loads of chicken wings from the freezer. 'Now, I never miss *Oprah* and, I'm telling ya, no one does a makeover like she can. Read the fashion magazines, Steve, black polo-neck sweaters is what all the Hollywood stars are wearing now, not bleedin' patterned jumpers that look they're holding a grudge against ya. And what about yer hair, luv, are ya waiting on it to come back into fashion or what? Jaysus, Prince Charles has a trendier hairstyle than you.'

Steve said nothing, just took another glance down at the *National Intruder*.

'A nice, sharp haircut would take ten years off ya,' she said, noticing where his gaze had fallen. 'And then maybe Miss starstruck Daisy might start paying ya a bit of attention. And if she doesn't, there's always me.' Then, winking slyly at him, she added, 'So how's about it then, babe?'

★

Andrew had been an absolute pet. Not only had he driven Portia into Kildare and taken her shopping for all the booze for Lucasta's Midsummer party, he had even insisted on footing the bill and wouldn't take no for an answer. Portia tried to fight her corner but to no avail.

'Look, since I met you, I've practically moved into the Hall,' he reasoned with her as they loaded case after case of wine into the back of his car. 'The least you can let me do is pay my way. And I can well afford it. I am the Earl of Ireland, you know, or don't you read the *National Intruder*?'

Portia laughed. In fact she and Andrew hadn't stopped laughing since that ludicrous article had appeared, Andrew in particular getting great mileage out of the fact that she'd been cast in the guise of 'humble scullery maid'.

'Besides,' he went on, holding the car door open for her, 'can't you tell I'm trying to be the golden boy in your mother's eyes?'

She was highly amused at the idea that anyone would feel the need to inveigle themselves into her mother's favour. 'Well, that's certainly a first. The last time anyone tried to impress poor Mummy was when Blackjack was courting her. In nineteen sixty-six.'

'What did he do?'

'He bought a racehorse and named it after her. Lucky Lucasta, it was called, but talk about not living up to your name! The poor animal was as slow as a donkey, you'd think it had a milk float harnessed to it. In the end, Blackjack shot him.'

'Your father certainly sounds colourful,' Andrew replied. 'Have you heard from him since, emm, since . . .?'

'It's OK, you can say it; since he bolted.' Normally her father was a perpetual source of embarrassment to her, but for some reason Portia could be completely open with Andrew.

He never judged or, worse, feigned false sympathy, he just listened.

'No, I haven't but he did send Daisy a postcard. From Caesar's Palace in Las Vegas.'

'Caesar's Palace? Bit of a change from his ancestral pile, isn't it?'

'Oh, you needn't worry about him, he'll be in heaven there until the cash runs out. And it always runs out.' She smiled to herself.

'What's so funny, my lady?'

'Nothing, I was just remembering the Midsummer Ball last year, that's all,' she replied, slipping into the passenger seat of the car.

If someone had told her then that only a short year later she'd be hosting a film crew at the Hall, she'd have scoffed. If they'd told her that she'd meet someone like Andrew, who seemed so completely perfect he was like a dream come true, she'd have gone into a coma. In fact, that was it, she'd in-advertently hit the nail on the head. He *was* too good to be true. Unlike any previous boyfriend she'd had, he treated her well, made her laugh, didn't ogle Daisy every time he saw her, loved Davenport Hall and, most surprising of all, actually got on with her mother.

Way, way too good to be true . . .

As ever, he seemed to be reading her thoughts. Getting into the driver's seat, he paused for a moment, as though trying to make up his mind about something, then turned to face her full on. Taking her hand gently in his, he massaged it softly, his blue eyes not leaving her face. Portia sensed that there was something coming, but wasn't quite sure what. Oh God, she thought, please don't let it be anything to do with Edwina.

'Portia, I've lived in New York for so long that it's second nature for me to be upfront and direct about things. Don't you think we should at least talk about what's going on here? I mean, what's going on between us? Dare I say it, how we're feeling about each other?'

Portia couldn't bring herself to speak. Not that she had much to compare it to, but everything seemed to be going so well between them, what could he want to talk about? And then a sickening feeling came over her. Edwina. It had to be something to do with Edwina: what else could it be? He must have sensed that she was falling for him more and more each day and was probably about to tell her that he was just getting out of an eight-year relationship and wasn't looking for commitment and blah bloody blah. What else could he mean by a comment like 'how we're feeling about each other'? Her eyes welled as she dropped her gaze and looked out of the side window. Any other single woman of her age would know exactly how to react in this situation, she thought to herself, but not her. Someone more sexually experienced would probably have batted his comment skilfully away, while still flirting outrageously with him, playing it cool and keeping everything nice and light. Non-threatening for a man. If women's magazines had taught her anything, they'd taught her that men ran a mile if they felt a woman was in deeper than they were. God, she thought, what to do? The last thing she'd ever been in her life was a game player and she was far too long in the tooth to start now. There was so much she wanted to say to him, but she just couldn't do it, her heart was too full for her even to begin to tell him what was going through her head. Not now.

'Can we go home?' was all she could stammer lamely. 'I have to defrost the lamb kebabs for tonight.'

Andrew looked at her for a moment, with an odd expression in his eyes, and then wordlessly started the car, looking straight ahead of him.

They drove back to the Hall in silence, with Portia wishing she could kick herself black and blue every mile and pothole of the way.

Daisy was really in no bloody mood for this. Serge had promised her that he'd do her make-up and hair for the Midsummer Ball and she was already late for her appointment when she had the bad luck to run into Mrs Flanagan, up to high doh about the party.

'Shove that up on the flagpole for tonight, will ya, luv?' she had asked, throwing the Davenports' tattered family standard at her.

'Oh Mrs Flanagan, why do I always get the shitty jobs? You know I hate going up to the bell tower. Mummy says it's still haunted by Satan . . .'

'Well, if you'd prefer to disinfect the outside toilets instead, that's your choice.'

Daisy thought for a second, decided which was the lesser of two evils, then snatched the flag from Mrs Flanagan's hand.

'Ah, yer're a great young one,' said Mrs Flanagan, waddling back towards the kitchen. 'I knew ya wouldn't want Guy van der Post to see ya in a pair of Marigolds with a bottle of Domestos in yer hand.'

As Daisy climbed out on to the roof of the Hall, still breath-less from climbing up the two hundred spiral stone steps which led up there, she cursed the family tradition of always having a standard flying on Midsummer night. And the flag itself was a disgrace; it was raggedy, moth-eaten and so faded with age that you could hardly see the family crest. (It was a picture of two cats fighting, which bore the Latin inscription *'Quid Rides? De Te Fabula Narratur'* ('What are you laughing at? The joke's on you'). Daisy mischievously used to tell tourists it translated as 'All men are bastards'.)

170

'Do you ever keep your promises?'

Daisy almost fell off the roof when she saw that Montana had followed her to the top of the steps, with rollers in her hair and clad only in a very flimsy, see-through dressing gown. 'Montana!' she said, shocked. 'What on earth are you doing here?'

'What do you think?' she replied. 'That I've come to admire the tar paper? You know, I thought we had a deal, but you're obviously too busy fucking Guy's asshole brains out to remember. When are you gonna wise up to him, Daisy? Can't you see that he's just using you?'

Daisy said nothing, just glared at her in silent fury.

'You know, I thought we were friends so I figure the least you can do is keep your promise to me. I need another sample for my drugs test and I needed it yesterday, now are you gonna help me out, or what?'

A wave of anger slowly began to come over Daisy. How *dare* Montana speak to her like this and how dare she be so bitchy about Guy into the bargain? Stupid, selfish bitch, she thought to herself as the colour rose in her cheeks.

'Well?' demanded Montana.

Daisy thought for a moment, the mischievous side of her brain working overtime.

'Christ, Daisy, I have better things to do than stand on a freezing rooftop waiting on your Barbie brain to make a decision. Do we have a fucking deal or not?'

It was the Barbie comment that swung it. Daisy breathed deeply to suppress her fury and flashed her beautiful smile at Montana. 'You have nothing to worry about. I'll have it for you tonight.'

Montana didn't even bother to thank her, just turned on her kitten heels and clambered back down the stairs. As soon as she was out of sight, Daisy started sniggering. There was no doubt about it, Montana was asking for her come-uppance and by Jesus she'd get it tonight. As she slowly began to hoist the standard up the flagpole, waves of laughter got the better of her. Just wait till she told Guy! He would be so thrilled with her for helping him to bring Montana down a peg or two. He always said that Montana Jones was the George Bush of the film world, thick, talentless and utterly beyond all hope. Wait till he heard about this little prank!

'You'd think a prerequisite for being an actor would be that you could actually act, but a wooden sideboard would make a better Magnolia O'Mara than that talentless bitch,' he'd said to her in one of his more poetic moments, as they both snuggled up in his huge four-poster bed the previous night. 'Some actors should just stick to doing porn,' was his final word on the professional prospects of Miss Montana Jones.

As Daisy checked to make sure that the standard was flying straight, she paused for a moment to survey the view from the parapet. A childhood spent chasing over those very rooftops had left her fearless about heights; any normal person would have demanded a bungee rope before balancing precariously on the balustrade as she was doing now. It was a beautiful clear day and the roof was so high that she could easily see as far as Ballyroan. Glancing down towards the River Kilcullen on her left, she dimly made out Lucasta, standing in the river buck naked waving a stick around, doing her incantations. Daisy giggled aloud. This was an annual Midsummer ritual of her mother's to invoke the blessing of some pagan goddess on the night's festivities. Well, she thought, I certainly won't need some ancient goddess with a name that sounds like a panty liner with wings to help me have a good time tonight! Further afield, over towards the Mausoleum, she could see the film crew like tiny dots in the distance, beavering away, setting up a shot by the looks of it. She could also make out Guy in his

Victorian white linen lounge suit, looking like a Greek god, she thought lovingly. It was his favourite costume, he'd told her ('So how badly do you wanna fuck me in this?' were his actual words), and he made the girls in wardrobe launder it freshly for him each day.

Then, coming from a long way off, she heard a sound like blades whirring, growing gradually louder and louder. She hadn't noticed before, but there seemed to be a small gaggle of photographers and a TV crew beginning to congregate at the main entrance gates. Daisy tittered. They'd probably seen the *National Intruder* and wanted a follow-up story and more embarrassing pictures, if that were possible.

All of a sudden, everyone's attention was drawn upwards as a helicopter hove into view coming from the Dublin direction. Daisy momentarily forgot all about her hair appointment as she too almost gave herself whiplash from staring up. The helicopter came closer and closer as Daisy stood on the parapet, straining forward to see who was in it. It was at her eye level now, the gale from the blades whipping Daisy's hair and making it stand on end. The pilot seemed to be vainly searching for a spot on the forecourt to land on that wasn't entirely covered in either trailers or cables, but while he looked, poor Daisy was subjected to Hurricane Harry, causing her to sway on her feet.

The pilot appeared to give up on the idea of landing in front of the house, and in one great sweeping motion tilted the helicopter dramatically to the right and whooshed on towards a muddy-looking empty field just beyond the tennis courts. This was the end for poor Daisy though, who'd already lost her balance from the force of the wind. Just as the helicopter whipped out of sight, she fell. And fell. And fell.

Now I know just how Alice in Wonderland felt, was the insane thought that flicked through her mind. Everything's

173

happening in slow motion, I'll see a fucking white rabbit next. They say that just before you drown your whole life flashes before your eyes, but in Daisy's case, all she could think about were Lewis Carroll books. She was screaming for dear life without even knowing it, then suddenly . . . THUD!

There was a split second when Daisy wondered if she'd died and was now in some kind of Purgatory. She lay on her back looking up at the sky thinking: Funny that Purgatory looks just like the view from the roof of our Ballroom. A heartbeat later, she became aware of a searing, raw pain in her left ankle and looking down she saw that it was fast swelling to twice its normal size. For fuck's sake, she thought. The biggest knees-up of our calendar year and I've gone and sprained my ankle. Then, tentatively, she put her hand out to feel . . . plastic. Gently, very gently, she eased herself up into a sitting position. She was still alive anyway . . . she thought. Lucasta always said that Daisy was like a reincarnated cat with nine lives and now here was proof. Gripping on to the ledge with trembling hands she realized that she'd fallen down two floors on to the slate roof of the Ballroom, but miraculously, the black bin liners they had covering the leaky holes in the roof had broken her fall. Holy Christ, she thought, I owe my life to Tesco's extra-strength wheelie-bin liners.

Still trembling, she looked over to the field where the helicopter had just landed. The ground was ankle deep in mud from all the rain they'd been having and she could see the machine slowly starting to sink into it. Just then, the pilot opened the passenger door and out stepped . . . Ella Hepburn. At least, Daisy assumed it had to be her, even though she was at a distance. She was entirely clad in fur, even though it was June, wore sunglasses and was carrying what appeared to be a white fluffy handbag (but turned out to be a tiny Pekinese dog). She made absolutely no attempt to move, just stood there as though expecting a Chinese litter to arrive and carry her over the mud so her high heels wouldn't be ruined. A Queen Elizabeth waiting for Sir Walter Ralegh. If Daisy hadn't been in such acute pain, she'd have giggled. Bloody diva, she thought, wait till Guy sees the state of her. He'll crack up.

Just at that moment, Guy himself, followed by most of the crew, raced over to the helicopter and seemed to be bending down to kiss Ella Hepburn's hand. Brilliant, she thought, if I scream loud enough he'll hear me and carry me back inside. Swelling her lungs out to their fullest, like Kiri te Kanawa launching into an aria, she yelled his name so loudly they could have heard her in Wales. But Guy didn't respond. He seemed to be so engrossed in meeting his screen mother that Daisy's plaintive wailing fell on deaf ears.

A moment later, Guy whisked Ella Hepburn up into his arms, fluffy dog and all, and waded through the knee-deep mud towards the Hall.

Daisy could hardly believe her eyes. And he was even wearing the cream linen suit.

Chapter Fifteen

'Have the cap twisters arrived yet?' Lucasta asked, as she was about to make her grand entrance down the oak staircase.

'Half the bleeding town's here, freeloading bastards,' Mrs Flanagan snarled back at her, on her way to put last-minute squirts of Parazone into the upstairs bathrooms.

'Righty-oh then, let the games commence!' replied Lucasta, adjusting her turban. 'How do I look?' This was the one night of the year when she actually got out of her smelly wax jacket and made an effort to dress up. However, her idea of an appropriate outfit for the occasion was to wear her Midsummer High Priestess robes, which she'd purchased at a car-boot sale in Thurles about ten years previously. Lucasta was utterly convinced they made her look like a pagan goddess whereas a mad middle-aged witch wearing a white sheet with a hole cut out for the head was somewhat nearer the mark.

'How much would ya charge to haunt a house?' was Mrs Flanagan's parting shot.

Blithely ignoring her, Lucasta swept down the staircase to meet and greet. Half the town was indeed gathered there but the first person she bumped into was Steve. In spite of being horribly overworked, somehow he'd found time that afternoon to heed Mrs Flanagan's advice, at least partially. He was still stuck in one of his trademark 1980s candy-striped shirts, but had actually forced himself into having a drastic haircut. Mrs Flanagan had been right; it did make him look a full ten years younger.

'Jesus, Steve, is that you? I hardly recognized you, what have you done to yourself?' said Lucasta, peering at him. Then, effortlessly switching into hostess mode, she chirped, 'Well, it's too divine of you to come! You heard about poor Daisy?'

'Yes, I did, but actually there was some rather important business I needed to discuss with you, if you have a moment to spare—'

'Darling, I can't believe you'd want to talk boring business in the middle of a piss-up! Later, sweetheart, later, I must go and make sure all the bottles of Eau de Davenport are prominently placed at the drinks table . . .' And she was gone towards the Ballroom, where a trestle table with a bed sheet covering it doubled as a makeshift bar. She barged her way through the throng, being unable to get into the party spirit without a few stiff gins, and bumped into Paddy doing exactly the same thing.

'Ah howaya, emm, yer majesty?' he greeted her, unsure of how to address landed gentry.

'Who are you now?' Lucasta replied, pouring herself a triple gin with only a wisp of tonic going into it. 'Cap twister or a film type?'

'Emm, I'm working on the film, yer majesty,' Paddy replied. 'Jaysus, I never woulda worn this T-shirt if I'd known I was going to be meeting royalty.' (His T-shirt bore a picture of a pair of double D breasts and read, 'Suck 'em and see'.) Then, nervously trying to make an impression on the mother of the girl he fancied, he added, 'So, like, would the Queen be your sister then or what?'

'Well, I know my husband was related to her distantly,' Lucasta replied, infinitely more chatty now she had a drink in her hand, 'because I seem to remember him writing to her to borrow money, which he did to all of his bastard relatives, you know. I can't remember what happened, I suppose she told him to fuck off like the rest of them, silly bitch.'

Paddy grinned broadly at her, never for one moment expecting the Lady of the Manor to have such a foul mouth. 'You're not a bad aul' bird, you know,' he said admiringly. 'I've loads of mates who are, eh, let's just say associated with a certain republican movement and I'm going to tell them I met a posh Brit who was all right.'

'But I'm not British at all, darling. I may be drunk but I'm not British—' Lucasta began, puzzled as to what he meant, but Paddy interrupted her.

'So like, I know about Daisy and Guy and all, but do you think it'd be cool for me to chat her up, like?'

'Go ahead, she's sitting right beside the grand piano in the Long Gallery. She's immobile for the night, you know, fell off the roof earlier. Christ, I hope the big lump didn't tear the bin liners up there, or if it rains, we're all fucked.'

Shamie and Bridie Nolan were running a good hour late for the party, all down to their feckless and unreliable babysitter. The gormless teenager had had the gall to arrive forty-five minutes late, claiming that she was at Saturday evening Mass. 'Now, what kind of religious service would give you a hickey like that on your neck, is what I'd like to know!' Bridie had remarked acidly on their way out of the door. The final straw was when she discovered a huge ladder down the side of her tights as they were driving through Ballyroan. Several rows later, she finally got Shamie to pull his brand-new Jaguar over right outside Spar so she could dash in quickly to buy a spare pair. Bridie was especially proud of her outfit tonight and was damned if she was going to let a knackered-looking pair of tights ruin it on her. It was a purple and red confection, a copy of Posh Spice's wedding dress. The kindest thing you could say about it was that it was probably more suited to a Flamenco dancer or someone who pole danced in nightclubs for cash.

'Jaysus, Bridie, would ya get a move on or we'll miss all the food!' Shamie had said to her as she got back into the car clutching a new pair of tights (extra extra large size).

'Ah, feck off,' his wife replied, thrusting her hands up her dress to take off the laddered pair. 'If the food's anything like last year's then I'm doing ya a favour, ya eejit. Egg sandwiches and a few aul' vol-au-vents still frozen in the middle! Is that anything to serve guests? Jaysus, I couldn't go to the loo for a full week.'

Shamie laughed and scratched his head where it was itching beneath his tartan cap. 'Well, just think, me love, this could very well be the last time we'll be at any kind of social hosted by the Davenports!'

Bridie began to relax a bit. 'Thank Jaysus it's dark, at least no one will see me changing me tights,' she said, struggling to haul her chunky white thunder thighs on to the dashboard of the car as she inelegantly pulled the old tights off and the new ones up. She was by now almost straddling the gear stick with her enormous hips in the air; not a sight for the faint-hearted.

As Shamie swerved to the left at the gates of the Hall, suddenly a battery of flashbulbs exploded in their faces. 'Holy God! What in the name of Jaysus was that?' said Bridie at the top of her voice.

'Press,' replied Shamie, never unhappy to see any member of the fourth estate. Column inches were like mother's milk to a country politician with his sights set on higher things.

'They probably think we're more fillum stars after arriving!' he added, greatly tickled by his own gag.

'But they'll have seen me gusset!' shrieked his wife. 'I can just see the fecking headlines now. "Tight Squeeze", or even worse, "Tight Arse". Jaysus, Shamie, all I can say is, the night's off to a great fecking start.'

As his Jaguar sped over the potholes and on towards the Hall, the bickering continued. Bridie never even noticed that a few intrepid reporters, led by the *National Intruder*'s Tony Pitt, had begun to follow them on foot, scarcely able to believe their luck at the total lack of security at the Hall. ('Why in hell don't we try to get inside?' Tony had asked a colleague from the *Irish Press*. 'If someone can gatecrash Prince William's twenty-first birthday party, surely we can get in here?')

If Bridie had heard that, then she really would have had something to moan about.

With poor Daisy injured, Portia had barely had time to change for the Ball, never mind luxuries such as applying make-up. Andrew had dropped her back at the Hall earlier that afternoon and had silently helped to unload the cases of wine and beer they'd bought. He wasn't frosty or in any way rude, just silent, totally unlike his usual chatty, effervescent self. As they carried boxes into the Ballroom, Portia racked her brains to think of a way of bringing up the big subject. She so badly wanted to ask what it was he'd wanted to say to her, but hadn't a clue how to broach it. You stupid, stupid girl, she lectured herself as they both walked wordlessly back out to his car. Well, you've learnt a valuable lesson today. There's a time to discuss defrosting lamb kebabs and a time to keep your mouth shut.

She was spared any further agonies of indecision by the

sound of Daisy screaming like a banshee from the roof where the poor thing had been stranded for hours. Ever the gentleman, Andrew had gallantly helped carry Daisy down the stone steps and all the way to the Library, while Portia rushed downstairs for some ice to keep the swelling down. But he didn't stick around, he just muttered something about going home to change and that he'd see her later.

Portia said goodbye, surprised that he hadn't kissed her, and watched his car speed down the driveway. Something was gnawing away at her stomach, a disquieting feeling that all wasn't well with him. She knew she'd have to try to speak to him privately at the Ball tonight, which, given the number of guests her mother had invited, was easier said than done. She wished she had the guts to tell him how she felt, how the last couple of weeks with him had been the most amazing she'd ever known, about the butterflies that had permanently taken up residence in her stomach since they'd met, the sleepless nights spent thinking about him, the way her knees went weak when his eyes twinkled at her and this burning ache she felt inside, just watching his car drive off and knowing that she'd annoyed him.

And, worst of all, there was the voice in her head, ever present since they first met, which just kept repeating the same thing, over and over again.

Why on earth would someone like Andrew want to be with me?

It took a lot longer than expected but eventually the sisters had inched their way to Daisy's second-floor room, with Portia supporting her and Daisy squealing, 'Ow, ow, ow,' every step of the way. As luck would have it, Portia remembered that there was an old pair of crutches upstairs in the nursery, which had once belonged to their great-grandfather, Ernest

181

Davenport. He'd broken his leg in a Flanders trench during the First World War, which at the time was considered to be a very lucky injury; at least you got to go home in one piece to recuperate and your war was well and truly over. (To this day, the phrase 'break a leg' so beloved of luvvie types is thought to bring good fortune.)

So Portia trooped upstairs and rooted them out for Daisy, stopping to phone their local GP on her way. He wasn't there and his locum made such a pathetic excuse about not being available to call over to see Daisy that Portia put the phone down in disgust. Tales about the Davenports' complete inability to pay up even for urgent medical care had travelled far and wide, it seemed.

'Never mind, darling,' she'd said soothingly as Daisy practised using her crutches, 'Sean Murphy'll be here tonight, we'll get him to have a look at your ankle. I'm sure he wouldn't mind.'

'The fucking vet?' replied Daisy, outraged. 'Is that what things have come to?'

Portia said nothing, and left Daisy hobbling about the room as she went to get ready. Oh God, she thought, I'm so late! It was already eight o'clock and she was beginning to hear cars pulling up the gravelled driveway outside.

She'd planned her outfit so carefully for the Ball (a stunning white silk full-length evening dress which accentuated her height and slender figure to perfection. Even the snotty shop assistant in Kildare, where she'd splashed out on it a few days ago, had told her she looked like a Greek goddess and it wasn't often Portia was complimented). But now, there was barely time to change and tie her hair up before the front doorbell started clanging. She didn't mind a bit how she looked. Tonight, she had other things on her mind.

★

A few days earlier, at Guy's suggestion, Daisy had had the foresight to hire a DJ to really get things going at the party.

'I couldn't bear another Ball like last year's,' she'd told him. 'Mummy hired a ceilidh band who played the same bloody song over and over all night. At least, it sounded like the same song.'

The DJ was now really warming up, expertly bleeding one floor-filling number into another and totally unaware that large raindrops were now pelting through the torn bin liners on the roof and plopping right on to his sound equipment.

Portia had just at that moment come into the Ballroom and glanced around to see if Andrew was there when suddenly there was a great crackle and a puff of blue smoke right where the DJ had been standing. Portia and Steve were neck and neck in the race to see if he was badly injured.

'Are you all right?' Portia asked worriedly as he lay flat out on the floor.

'Don't touch me whatever you do,' replied the DJ, who was as white as a sheet, 'I think I could be live.'

'Can I get you anything? Some water?' she asked, terrified.

'Yeah, you can get me the fuck out of here,' he answered. 'I feel like I'm working on the *Titanic.*'

'He's OK,' Steve said reassuringly, 'although I think maybe he could do with some air.'

Before Portia knew what was happening, Serge was at her side, leaping up and down with excitement. 'Honey, I have waited all my life for a chance like this – my shot at being Boy George, or a sort of cuter version of Fatboy Slim! By the way, baby, you're looking hot, hot, hot tonight, in an understated Nicole Kidman sort of way . . . Andrew's a lucky son of a bitch. You just give me two minutes, I'll be right back!' In a flash, he'd run out of the rotting French door which led into the garden and disappeared into the darkness. Moments later he was back, drenched to the bone and carrying a portable CD player and a huge pile of CDs. 'No make-up bus I've ever worked in can do without mood music,' he said to Portia by way of explanation. Then, in one elegant movement, he leapt over the DJ's turntable, whipped on his headphones and started rooting through the stacks and stacks of CDs for any number performed by Barbra Streisand or the Village People.

'You do look wonderful,' Steve added, looking her up and down admiringly. 'The dress is a show stopper.'

'Thank you,' she answered, smiling at him. 'Great haircut, by the way, Steve, you look like your own younger brother.'

She was just about to offer him a drink when he took her aside, so Serge couldn't overhear. 'Look,' he said gently, with that tired, well-worn look coming into his eyes, 'I've been trying to get hold of you all day and I know this isn't exactly the time or the place, but the fact is . . . there's never going to be a right time to say this so I may as well tell you now.'

'Steve, what's the matter?' Portia asked, thinking it must be something to do with Daisy and those awful photos in the *National Intruder*.

'Let's find somewhere quiet where we can talk.'

I've had some shitty nights in my time, but this beats fucking Christmas, Daisy thought furiously as she sat alone in the Long Gallery, where Sean Murphy had just finished examining her ankle. It was just a sprain, he told her, nothing to worry about, but in the meantime, she was on the substitutes bench for the foreseeable future.

'Rest, ice, compression and elevation,' he'd ordered her, 'and absolutely no alcohol whatsoever.'

Daisy flashed her blue eyes at him, bitterly remembering the last time they'd met in the de Courceys' house, when she'd called him just about every name under the sun. This isn't the way you were supposed to meet an ex-boyfriend, she thought. She should have been in the Ballroom looking stunning with Guy by her side flirting with her and no one else and not caring who knew that they were a couple. 'This is who I'm with now, and compared with him, you're fucking destitute,' was the message she wanted to convey loud and clear to Sean bloody Murphy.

But she hadn't set eyes on Guy all afternoon. She'd given Mrs Flanagan strict instructions to let him know about her accident, that she was still in one piece, but was laid up in her bedroom, badly wanting to see him. But he never came near her. Something must have happened, she reasoned, he'd been delayed on the set or something, but still . . . he could have found five minutes to pop upstairs to see if she was OK.

'So where did you put it?'

Daisy was roused from her thoughts and looked up to see Montana, dressed in what looked like a pair of silk pyjamas.

'Listen, Daisy, I've got Caroline screaming at me for a sample and I need it right now. For the last fucking time, where is it?'

Daisy eyeballed her without flinching. 'In the fridge in the old servants' kitchen, Montana. And just so you know, the sample isn't actually mine either.'

'What did you say?' Montana's tone cut like ice.

'I drank a bit with Guy last night, so I wasn't exactly clean. But don't worry, the sample I got for you is as pure as a baby's, I can promise you that.'

'So where did you get it?'

Even though her ankle was throbbing, Daisy couldn't suppress a giggle. 'From someone called Kat Slater, actually.'

'Daisy, I don't know what the fuck is going on with you,

but, you know, I've been messed around here for the last time. If you think for one second—'

'OH SHUT UP!' Daisy shouted at her, unable to take any more abuse. 'Can you get it into your thick skull the favour I'm doing you here? If I were to let it slip to Jimmy D. or Caroline that your drugs samples aren't your own because you're back on the bottle, let's face it, you're off the picture and back to La La Land to pick up your porn career where it left off. Now bugger off and leave me in peace! Can't you see I'm injured?'

Montana was silenced. She gave Daisy the filthiest look imaginable before striding to the door. Then, as a parting shot, she said, 'By the way, if you're looking for Guy, he was last seen escorting Ella Hepburn to her room. And you wanna know something really weird? No one's set eyes on him since.'

'GET LOST!' Daisy yelled after her. Montana must take her for a right eejit if she thought Daisy would ever believe that there was something going on between Guy and a woman old enough to be his grandmother. He was just making her feel welcome, and running lines with her or something, that's all, she thought. Then the giggles got the better of her.

In a few days' time, in a laboratory somewhere in California, a sample would be sent for analysis in a test tube with Montana's name written on it. Daisy hadn't been lying when she said that the sample she'd procured (with great difficulty) belonged to a Kat Slater.

What she hadn't said was that Kat Slater was a two-year-old brood mare.

'You know, Susan, if you didn't want to come, why didn't you just say so in the first place?' Michael de Courcey was well used to dealing with his wife's legendary foul temper, but even he was at a loss to understand why she was so insistent on them going to the Davenports' Midsummer Ball. 'You've done nothing but badmouth the family ever since you met them. To be perfectly honest with you, I can't make out why you didn't just phone them and cry off. I'm quite happy to go in there alone, you know. Only really came to get a glimpse of the Hollywood elite at play, if the truth be known.'

Susan glared at him as she patted her gravity-defying hairdo. 'You know perfectly well why I'm here, Michael. One quick word in Miss Davenport's ear and then we're leaving. With or without Ella Hepburn's autograph.'

As they gingerly made their way up the steps to the main entrance door of the Hall, Susan caught a disapproving look in her husband's eye. Changing tack, she said, 'Darling, I'm doing that woman a favour. You saw those photos in that dreadful magazine. She's obviously decided to hurl herself at poor Andrew and you know how easily people take advantage of him. When she realizes that she's messing around with a man who's as good as married, she'll see sense. Portia Davenport will thank me in the long run, mark my words.'

Forty long years of marriage had taught Michael when to argue the toss with his wife and, more importantly, when not to. Anything for a quiet life, he thought as they walked through the great oak door and into the entrance hall.

'Oh, Andrew's mother's here! How lovely of you to come,' said Lucasta, spotting them through the crowd from across the hallway. Having completely forgotten Mrs de Courcey's Christian name she turned her full attention on to Michael. 'And this dishy man must be your husband,' she said, winking suggestively at the Chief Justice. 'All I can say is I see where Andrew gets his yummy looks from.'

'Actually, we've met before—' replied Michael before Lucasta interrupted him.

'Really? I must have been slaughtered drunk or I'd have

remembered meeting someone as hunky as you. By the way, where's Andrew?'

'He was unexpectedly called to an urgent meeting in Dublin. He'll be here later,' Mrs de Courcey crisply replied, distinctly unamused by the sight of her ladyship flirting with her husband.

'Isn't it too wonderful about Andrew and Portia?' Lucasta went on, slopping some gin and tonic on to the marble floor in her excitement. 'He really is the loveliest man! Do you know, I don't think Portia'd had a shag in about five years until Andrew came along and he seems to be dotty about her—'

Mrs Flanagan interrupted, in the nick of time. 'Howayis? Do youse want a drink or what?'

'I'll have a single malt whisky, if you have it,' the Chief Justice boomed at her.

'And I'll have some apple juice,' replied his wife.

'Is that it? Apple juice?' said Mrs Flanagan, not used to dealing with teetotallers.

'Yes. I don't drink.'

'Oh, you poor thing,' Lucasta cooed sympathetically. 'Are you an alcoholic?'

Mrs de Courcey, although possessed of a spinal cord of reinforced steel, could take no more.

'Forget it, I'll just go and find something to drink myself,' she said, stalking off, leaving her husband in Lucasta's firing line.

Just as Daisy thought the evening couldn't get any worse, it did. Bad enough that Guy hadn't come near her all day, but when she was finally reduced to seeking him out, she wasn't at all prepared for what she saw. Just as she hobbled out of the Long Gallery, she became aware of a hushed silence descending on all the guests in the hall below. She looked down from the first-floor landing only to see every head there turned up looking at her. Oh Jesus, she thought, do I have knickers on my head or something? A sweeping sound from behind made her turn just in time to see Ella Hepburn making her grand entrance down the staircase, head held high, looking just like Gloria Swanson at the end of *Sunset Boulevard*. She wore an impeccably cut white trouser suit with a long flowing red silk scarf trailing from her neck to the ground and was hugging her Pekinese dog close to her. Guy was at her side, looking like a devoted lapdog, making sure that the crowd parted like the Red Sea before her. A polite ripple of applause and a battery of camera flashes broke out, which Ella acknowledged with the merest hint of a wave as Guy ushered her into the Library and firmly shut the door behind them. Bloody hell, Daisy thought, that one would give the Queen Mother a run for her money. Then, gingerly manoeuvring herself on her First World War crutches down the staircase she followed them into the empty Library, where Ella was sitting bolt upright on a leather armchair with Guy at her feet. Never one to stand on ceremony, Daisy came straight to the point.

'Guy, what's going on? Didn't you get my message? I've been waiting for you all afternoon!' He said nothing, but excused himself from Ella's side and strode towards Daisy, who was by now close to tears.

'Can't you think about anyone other than yourself for a minute?' he hissed. 'Ella's had an exhausting journey and is still in deep shock about the room she's expected to stay in here. And she's allergic to your mother's cats; she says one tried to attack her earlier. She picked it up by accident thinking it was her mink muff. Not a pretty sight. You might have just a little consideration right now . . .'

Ella never uttered a word, just sat there like a silent movie star, smoking a Sobranie cigarette and letting Guy do all her dirty work for her.

'But, darling, I had this horrific fall and I just wanted to—'

Guy looked coldly at her. 'Me, me, me. Could you try thinking of other people, just for once?' he whispered, as though even a raised voice would upset the fragile Ella even more.

This was too much for Daisy. Her eyes welled up as she clumsily executed a three-point turn on the crutches and limped her way out of the door, where she immediately bumped into Paddy.

'Is that wanker giving you grief?' he asked, concerned. Daisy said nothing, just gulped back the angry tears that were choking her. 'And I wouldn't mind, only Jaysus, Ella Hepburn's about eighty-five,' he went on, under the impression he was making things better, 'and most of her films are shite. I wouldn't mind if she was someone who'd actually made a contribution to world culture, like, say, Cilla Black or someone, but she's brutal! And you'd think she'd been in *Dallas* the way she's going on.' Then, seeing that Daisy was genuinely upset he changed tack. 'Come on, luv, and I'll buy ya a drink at the free bar.'

Daisy forced a smile as she gratefully allowed Paddy to help her through the crowd. Had she been a little less tired and emotional she might have paid some attention to the bitter war of words that was going on in the hall between Shamie Nolan and, of all people, Chief Justice de Courcey.

Hold it together, Portia kept telling herself, just hold it together. Steve had steered her away from the throng and had taken her outside to break the news as gently as he could. However, as it was still bucketing down with rain, the gazebo beside the kitchen garden was just about the only spot where they could have an ounce of privacy. Portia was pacing up and down in the vain hope that the cool evening air would calm her down, but no such luck. She was still reeling from all that Steve had just told her and a dull pounding headache was starting to thud at her temples.

'Was I right to tell you?' he asked, genuinely concerned. She was so consumed with sheer panic that she barely heard the question. She couldn't speak, could barely breathe, she just turned to face him, her face as white as a sheet. 'Portia, I'm so sorry, but we will fight this, you know, I'll do everything I can . . .'

She couldn't answer, she just collapsed on to his chest, limp as a rag doll as the tears started to roll. Very gently, he steered her towards a wooden bench, sat her down and held her tightly to him.

'Shhh, calm down, we'll think of a way out,' he said soothingly. 'Come on, let's get you upstairs to your room, you're fit for nothing. I'll see if I can find some sort of sedative to help you sleep. You've had quite enough for one night, Portia.'

To an outside observer, they looked like two lovers having a secret tryst away from prying eyes. At least that's what Susan de Courcey thought, standing silently at the kitchen door, having traipsed over the entire Hall, determined to have it out with Portia. Well, well, well, she thought, staring at their silhouettes in the gazebo, just the ammunition she'd been waiting for. She barely even jumped when Daisy stumped into the kitchen on her crutches in search of a painkiller for her throbbing ankle. Taking the scene in, it only took Daisy a split second to cop what was happening. Andrew's battleaxe of a mother was spying on Portia; there was no other explanation for her being in the servants' kitchen. How fucking dare she? Daisy thought, full of indignation on her sister's behalf. The first time in years that Portia's actually got a boyfriend and his mother has to start behaving like Hercule fucking Poirot.

'May I get you something?' she spat at Mrs de Courcey, causing the older woman to turn her transfixed glare away from the gazebo. But Daisy had met her match. If she thought this was a woman to be easily intimidated by a slip of a girl wobbling about on museum-piece crutches, she was greatly mistaken.

'Yes, thank you,' came the reply. 'I came downstairs to get some apple juice.' The lie came easily to her; she never even flinched, just eyeballed Daisy, cool as a breeze.

'Certainly,' Daisy replied, smiling sweetly as she opened the fridge. Then, taking out the jug containing Kat Slater's urine sample, she poured out a full pint of it into a glass.

'Would you like some ice in that, Mrs de Courcey?'

Five in the morning and only a few stragglers remained. Daylight was already streaming through the huge, filthy shutters as Lucasta bashed away at the grand piano in the Long Gallery. She was blessed with the stamina of an SAS marine and traditionally partied all of her guests under the table. She was currently belting out a jaw-droppingly bad rendition of 'There's No Business Like Show Business' as a tribute to all her houseguests from the entertainment industry, oblivious to the fact that they'd all long since retired. Only Jimmy D. was present, dressed all in green, like a giant leprechaun, as if he'd somehow confused Midsummer with St Patrick's Day. He lay semi-comatose in a leather armchair with a lighted cigar about to fall from his hand. Daisy too was almost asleep, stretched out on a sofa with her crutches on the floor beside her.

This will go down as the most disastrous night of my life and that's really saying something, she thought. She had fully expected Guy to seek her out, apologize for his behaviour earlier and explain that he just felt sorry for Ella Hepburn on her first day or something, but he never did. She hadn't set eyes on him again all night. It almost killed her, but she'd even struggled on her crutches up to his bedroom door and had bashed on it like a woman possessed, but it was locked. Tomorrow, she thought, tomorrow. I'll deal with him tomorrow.

Just then, Paddy staggered in, pissed out of his head and barely able to walk. He immediately spotted Daisy in the corner, paused for a moment, then went over to Lucasta at the piano. He whispered a few words in her ear, swaying on his feet, then sat down on the stool beside her and proceeded to address the room.

'Ehh, excuse me, everyone, I know youse are all locked an' all, but if ya could just bear with me for a minute. This is just a love song I've been working on for a while now and it's dedicated to a certain young lady who shall remain anonymous, but she knows who she is, sitting over there with her crutches beside her.'

Then, expertly tinkering with the keys, he launched into his party piece.

'The minute I saw you
I nearly fucking died;
You are so beautiful,
An unbelievable ride.
Oh Daisy, I love you,
I hope you don't spew;
Please hear my love song,
I wrote it for you.
I know you are posh,
I know I'm a knacker,
But give me a chance, love,
I'll go like the clappers.

We've more in common
Than you might think.
Both our mas
Are poisoned with drink;
Your house is a shithole;
But that's all right.
If you were my girlfriend
I'd shag you all night.'

Daisy sat upright, fully awake now and watching him intently from the other end of the room. Well, she thought, looking at Paddy in a whole new light. If this didn't make Guy jealous, what would? Inching herself up from the sofa, she stretched her arms out to grab her crutches and gingerly hobbled over to the grand piano. Paddy saw her wobbling towards him and was about to leap up to help her when Lucasta roughly grabbed his arm and shoved him back down on to the piano stool.

'Thank Christ for someone musical!' she said, helping herself to one of Paddy's cigarettes. 'Serge's been playing that puffy gay shite all night long and now, at last, we can have some decent music. You must play something else, darling, or maybe we can sing a few duets together? Do you know "Save your Love" by Rene and Renata?'

'Was he a sweaty fat fella who threw some blondie one a rose in the video? Ehh, yeah, right, yer majesty, I do remember. Shitty song, but it's your gaff, if that's what ya want to hear,' replied Paddy, launching into it.

Daisy was standing beside them at the piano stool, by now swaying from exhaustion and unable to bear another minute of her mother's squalling.

'Maybe I'll see you later then, Paddy,' she whispered into his ear, 'if you'd like.'

Paddy looked up at her in stunned surprise, unable to believe his luck. 'My bedroom is on the second floor,' she went on. 'Take the left-hand corridor all the way down to the end, then go right at the bust of Napoleon, across the landing, up a small flight of stairs, past the armoire, left at the portrait of Granny Davenport, right down to the end of the passage and I'm the fourth room on the left. Will you remember?'

'Jaysus, yeah, no bother,' Paddy slurred, feeling as though all his birthdays had come at once.

Lucasta was screeching by now, but still managed to break off the caterwauling to say, 'Bugger off to bed and leave us alone, Daisy. Sex is sex and it's all very well, you know, but you can't beat a good sing-song.'

'Maybe see you later then?' Daisy repeated *sotto voce* as she hobbled out of the door.

Paddy winked back at her, red as a beetroot.

It was eight o'clock in the morning by the time Andrew arrived. He burst through the Hall door out of breath and the first person he bumped into was Mrs Flanagan. 'I'm so sorry I didn't make the Ball last night,' he began, 'but talk about having a good excuse! Do you know where Portia is? I know it's early, but I don't think she'll mind being woken up for this news.'

'Ah, still in bed, luv,' she yawned, wearily gathering up empty bottles from the hall table. 'Steve took her off last night. I saw them disappear upstairs together, early on in the night too.'

'Steve? Are you sure?'

'Yeah, luv,' she replied innocently as she waddled down the back staircase which led to the servants' kitchen. 'And he told me on no account were they to be disturbed.'

Andrew paused for a moment, then shook his head in

disbelief. Running up the stairs two at a time, he raced along the upper corridor to Portia's room. Pausing only to tap gently on her door, he waited for an answer. Silence. He knocked again. Still nothing. Then, whispering in a low voice so as not to disturb Daisy, whose room was opposite, he said, 'Darling, it's me,' before gently opening the door and stepping inside.

Two minutes later, he was gone, furiously slamming the Hall door behind him and this time not caring whom it disturbed.

Chapter Sixteen

'Now, don't forget to bring me back Celine Dion's autograph and a nice bit a costume jewellery that I can wear to the next gala dinner in Government Buildings. Something subtle now, Shamie, like a tiara with earrings to match. The golden rule is, what's good enough for Cher is good enough for me.'

'Not a bother,' replied her husband, dutifully writing out Bridie's shopping list. 'Anything else, me love?'

Bridie racked her brains as she sped along the MI motorway in North Dublin en route to the airport. She had just collected her husband from the Minister for Foreign Affairs' private residence in Howth and was now dropping him off in time to catch a flight to London and then a connection on to Las Vegas.

'Well,' she mused, 'a few spare sets of acrylic nails is always a handy thing to have and if ya happen to come across that fabulous antique shop where Michael Jackson went shopping with Martin Bashir in that documentary, anything from there will be perfect. They had beautiful life-sized stuffed tigers and all . . . in fact, Shamie, ya might as well open up an account there.'

'An account?' he replied, a bit perturbed by the amounts of cash his wife was intending to spend. 'Is that not a bit extravagant?' He was rewarded with one of Bridie's trademark turn-you-to-stone looks.

'Ah now, Jaysus, it's not that I'm being tight-fisted or anything, luv,' he said, backpedalling for all he was worth, 'but what if them fellas on the Opposition benches got wind of the fact that I'm spending this much on a new house? If that got into the papers . . .'

'Ah, feck off,' replied Bridie, unimpressed. 'If this is going to be our dream home then there'll be no cutting corners. It'll all be worth it when half the Government can come down to the Hall to visit ya at weekends. For God's sake, Shamie, you'll be like Tony Blair hosting weekends at Chequers.'

Shamie paused for a moment, contemplating the greatness which lay ahead. 'Jaysus, didn't we come a long way from selling slurry to cattle farmers, all the same, luv!'

'We did not sell slurry, we were in the waste management business, ya fecking eejit,' she replied, pulling her four-by-four Land-rover over at the drop-off point beside the entrance to the business-class departure lounge. 'Now, have ya got everything, tickets, passport, money?'

'All here, me luv,' he replied, patting the bulging pockets of his tweed tartan jacket.

'And the Minister didn't seem to think there'd be bother in tracking him down?' she asked for the umpteenth time.

'Not a problem in the world,' he replied, hauling from the seat behind him a huge suitcase covered in the same bright yellow tartan as his matching hat and jacket.

'Sure, how many seventy-year-old men with eighteen-year-old girlfriends are there going be in the big casinos?'

'Most of them, I'd fecking think, if that programme on Sky, *Las Vegas Uncovered*, is anything to go by,' Bridie replied, checking in the driver's mirror to make sure her mascara hadn't run.

'Don't you be worrying, luv, the Minister knows a fella in

the consulate in Nevada, who knows a fella, who knows a fella who'll sort me out. And if all else fails, sure, all we have to do is make a tour of every blackjack table in every casino in the city! How hard can that be?'

'You gave his mother horse pee to drink?'

Portia could hardly believe her ears. A rush of fury came over her but disappeared just as quickly when she remember the grim task that lay ahead of her that morning. She and Steve had agreed at the party that they should waste no time in communicating the bad news to the rest of the family, Mrs Flanagan included. Kind-hearted Steve had even volunteered to call over that morning to go over everything in detail with them and see what could be done. If, indeed, anything could be done.

'But I thought you'd be really pleased with me!' Daisy wailed. 'Mrs de Courcey's an old witch and she behaved monstrously last night. For God's sake, Portia, I caught her spying on you, probably checking to see if you're good enough for her precious Andrew. I felt like singing that song "Watching the Detectives".'

Portia rose wearily out of the bed with her head pounding just as relentlessly as it had done the previous night. Steve had managed to unearth a sleeping tablet from the medicine chest in the family bathroom which he'd insisted on her taking before she went to bed. It had certainly done the trick, she was completely knocked out all night, but was now feeling the ill-effects of it; she felt groggy and sluggish.

'I'm not even going to ask what horse pee was doing in the fridge in the first place,' she said, bending down to pick up her new white dress from the floor where it had fallen. For all the good an expensive outfit did me last night, she thought ruefully.

'It was . . . emm, fermenting,' replied Daisy. As Portia picked up a towel and headed for the bathroom, Daisy jerked upright from where she'd been sprawled all over her sister's bed, surprised at Portia's reaction to what was only ever meant as a joke. 'Don't go yet,' she pleaded, 'that's not even half of what I've got to tell you. Something really awful happened last night with Guy, and then I went and did something, well, a bit stupid . . .'

'Darling, I'll see you downstairs in five minutes,' Portia answered dully on her way out the door.

Whatever the awful thing was that happened between Daisy and Guy, she thought, it'll be a walk in the park compared with what I've got to tell her.

It was a rare, warm, sunny morning and as Portia stood under the tiny trickle of lukewarm water from the ancient shower in the family bathroom ('About as much water pressure as an old man spitting from the showerhead,' Daisy used regularly to complain) her mind raced. Yet she wasn't thinking about the huge threat that was now hanging over Davenport Hall like a giant sword of Damocles. No, just for a moment, she allowed herself to think about Andrew. He'd never even shown up last night, which was odd, to say the least. Nor had he phoned to let her know that he wasn't coming, which, considering how they'd been practically joined at the hip for the past couple of weeks, was nothing short of rude.

Mind you, once Steve had dropped the bombshell on her, the whole night had gone into a blur, but a few awful things did stand out. She remembered him sitting her down in the gazebo and crying and then feeling his arms around her and the smell of his aftershave. Then, in another hazy, woozy blur, she remembered him bringing her up to her room, laying her gently down on the bed, and then leaving her in peace to try to get some rest. The sleeping pill had acted quickly; minutes later she was comatose, in a deep, troubled sleep punctuated with wild dreams about Andrew.

She dreamt she was wearing a wedding dress, sitting in Ballyroan church, watching Andrew get married to Edwina. Weird. And what was even weirder was that, at the same time, she kept imagining that he was in bed beside her. At one point she stretched her arms out, fully sure that he was there; he'd arrived late, her subconscious mind told her, and come straight upstairs to her. His side of the bed even felt warm, but he wasn't there. Maybe he'd phone her later, she thought, stepping out of the shower and slipping a towel around her before padding back to her room in her bare feet. Or better still, just call over to the Hall as he'd done every single day since they'd met. She sighed deeply as she looked out of the window, where the film crew were madly setting up for yet another day's work.

If ever I needed him, she thought, I need him today.

Meanwhile, the door of Daisy's bedroom door opened and a head peeked round. The coast was clear. Good. Then, pulling a T-shirt inside out over his head, he tentatively crept along the second-floor corridor, being careful not to tramp on any floorboards which were too squeaky.

'Oh Paddy, lovely to see you, aren't you quite the early riser!'

'AHHHH JAYSUS!' Poor Paddy almost leapt out of his skin to see Lucasta standing behind him with her arms full of empty wine bottles.

'Ah, yer majesty, howaya?' he said nervously. 'I bet yer're wondering what I'm doing up here, well the truth is . . . emm—' He broke off, frantically trying to think of a good lie.

'I couldn't give a tuppenny fuck what you're doing here,'

201

replied her ladyship, 'but now that I've found you, darling, could you do me the most enormous favour?'

Twenty minutes later, Paddy found himself outside the gate lodge beside the main entrance gates to the Hall, where about a dozen journalists, radio reporters and a TV crew from a national news station had all gathered. The month of June, it seemed, was a silly season in terms of news and so the story about a semi-derelict manor house being taken over by a Hollywood film crew was now being classified as hot news. Especially when you threw a legend like Ella Hepburn into the mix; just a picture of her alone could earn a photographer upwards of ten thousand euros, easily.

Lucasta, in her permanent quest to generate a quick buck, had spotted the marketing potential of the situation immediately. She had driven down to the gates earlier that morning, a monster hangover notwithstanding, and had set up a picnic table covered in bottles of her Davenport water. Now, just as the press were arriving, she was waiting for them like a praying mantis. Nodding like a waggy dog at Paddy, she gave him his cue to 'casually saunter' over to the table.

'Good morning, yer ladyship,' he said in the stilted delivery of a particularly bad amateur actor but loudly enough for the press boys to hear. 'I am here because Ella Hepburn, that famous star of stage and screen, has sent me to buy some of your world-renowned Eau de Davenport. She says she will drink fuck all else— Oh *shit*! Sorry, yer majesty,' Paddy whispered the last bit, embarrassed at cursing when a TV camera was pointing at him.

'Lads, youse won't show that bit, will yis?' he called out to the assembled media. 'My ma would kill me if she found out I used bad language on the telly.'

'Keep going, sweetie, it's working a treat,' Lucasta hissed back at him.

'And as for them other legends of the silver screen, Montana Jones and Guy van der Post,' Paddy went on, as a battery of flashbulbs popped in his face, 'why, they claim that Eau de Davenport is good enough to wash yourself in.'

Then, smiling beatifically for the cameras, Lucasta whipped the cork from one of the bottles and gracefully handed it over to Paddy.

'How wonderfully kind of you,' she said. 'You must try some of my Eau de Davenport for yourself.'

Then, as rehearsed, Paddy took a few gulps from the bottle before turning back to the cameras, making sure that it was impossible for them to miss the label. 'Why, it's so amazing, I can't believe it's not alcohol,' he said in fake surprise.

'Now, don't forget the tag line,' Lucasta urged him under her breath.

'Oh yeah,' he replied, 'I forgot.' Raising his voice a few decibels he said, 'Eau de Davenport. Truly the drink of kings.'

'Well done!' she applauded him, delighted at the success of her free marketing scam. Then, addressing the assembled media, she said, 'Now then, darlings, how many bottles would each of you like to order?'

Serge was in a complete tizz. Caroline had just come thumping on the door of the make-up trailer demanding to know why he hadn't begun making up Ella Hepburn yet. 'We're scheduled to begin shooting the mother-and-son reunion scene in an hour's time; I cannot believe that you don't have her ready to go on camera.'

Serge nervously patted his chest and waved his hands in front of him, indicating to Caroline that he was having great difficulty breathing. 'In for two and out for four,' he kept repeating, inhaling and exhaling with the controlled precision of a yoga master.

'Are you all right?' Caroline asked, worried now. 'May I get you something?'

Serge nodded, indicating one of his make-up bags, which lay open on the table in front of her. Caroline began to root through it, eventually producing a tiny bottle of Rescue Remedy, which he immediately snatched from her. He didn't bother with the little dropper, he just unscrewed the lid and knocked the whole thing back in one gulp.

'Oh, that is so much better,' he said, feeling the warm hit from the brandy it contained rush through him. 'Honey, you have absolutely no idea how *très difficile* this is for me. Ella Hepburn! I've been watching her movies ever since I was in diapers, I had my first kiss at a drive-in where she was starring in *Cleopatra Two, Rise of the Mummies*, and in the club scene I'm part of in LA, she's like a living icon! You know when elderly people say they remember exactly what they were doing when they heard that Kennedy was shot? Well, I remember exactly what I was doing when I heard she was divorcing Kent Douglas for the second time. And now, here I am, about to do her make-up! Oh God, I am so unworthy!'

'You have exactly one hour,' Caroline replied, unmoved by his prima donna carry-on.

Serge breathed deeply, picked up his make-up bag and headed for Miss Hepburn's trailer. He paused for a moment to compose himself and to repeat his mantra. 'Living legends have feet of clay, living legends have feet of clay,' he whispered to himself before knocking.

'Yes!' came the reply from inside.

Taking another deep breath, he opened the door and stepped inside. 'Oh Miss Hepburn, I know I'm not worthy to apply your foundation, but just say the word and—'

'Yes! Yes! Yes!'

Serge almost passed out. Ella Hepburn was lying naked in

bed with Guy on top of her shagging her for all he was worth.

'Yes! Yes!' he groaned, on the brink of orgasm, completely ignoring Serge standing at the door with his jaw somewhere on the floor.

'Well, I guess this will add a whole new dynamic to the mother-and-son scene, won't it?' Serge said, unable to resist the quip before turning on his heel and banging the door behind him.

Later that morning, a scene of a very different type was unfolding in the Library of Davenport Hall.

'Now you listen here for a minute,' Mrs Flanagan said threateningly to Steve, as if somehow all this was his doing. 'I may be stupid, but I'm not completely thick. You can go on all ya like about County Councils and planning permission and land rezoning, but gobshite and all as he is I can't see Shamie Nolan going ahead with this.'

Steve wearily rubbed his eyes with the palms of his hands, wondering if, apart from Portia, any of them had taken in a single word he was saying. Lucasta was gaping at him in deep shock and Daisy had already started to bawl. The foresighted Portia had anticipated this reaction and was now handing out great wads of Kleenex to her.

'What Steve is trying to explain is that the matter is entirely out of our hands,' she said, deliberately keeping her voice calm. 'Shamie Nolan has already applied to the planning authorities in Dublin to have our land rezoned. Now, if he's successful and the planning application goes ahead, then all they have to do is issue a compulsory purchase order on us and we have no choice, we have to sell.'

'But, sweetie, I don't quite understand,' said Lucasta, still in shock. 'How can anyone force us to sell our home and our land if we don't want to? Can't we just tell them all to bugger off?'

Steve glanced over at Portia, knowing that one of them would have to explain, yet again.

'A compulsory purchase order is issued by the County Council only on a building which has first been condemned,' he said as gently as he could.

'But nobody would condemn Davenport Hall,' said Lucasta, aghast at the thought. 'It's our home! It's part of the nation's heritage! They simply couldn't do it—'

'Mummy, may I remind you that Daisy almost fell through the roof and nearly broke her neck only yesterday. We've got to be realistic, the Hall could be condemned in a heartbeat.'

'Oh Portia, you have such a cruel streak!' sobbed Lucasta, reaching out for the Kleenex.

'But isn't there anything we can do?' wailed Daisy, rocking back and forth in her chair, inconsolable.

'There is one ray of light,' Steve went on. 'But only one. Your father is the legal owner of the Hall, so if we can get to him and persuade him not to sell under any circumstances, there's a chance we could stall any condemnation order until the Hall could be renovated to pass the Council's safety standards, although where we get the money to do that is another matter entirely.'

Daisy sat forward, brightening a little. 'Steve, you're a genius,' she declared. 'Of course! That's the answer! Daddy would never consent to sell Davenport Hall in a million years, no matter how much money he was offered. Not in a million years!'

'In a million years, I never thought Blackjack would sell up this easily,' Shamie said into the mouthpiece of the phone, having to raise his voice because the connection from Vegas to Ballyroan was so crackly.

'Yer're a darlin' man,' replied Bridie from the comfort of her customized kitchen: 'I'm delighted with ya, Shamie, Donald Trump couldn't have done better. And how much did he sell for?'

'This is the best part, luv, I hope yer're sitting down for this,' Shamie shouted, barely able to contain himself. 'Two million. Only two million! Sure, once we get the planning permission, the land alone will be worth ten times that!'

'And did ya get everything signed, sealed and delivered, all above board?'

'Signed, sealed and delivered,' her husband replied, delighted with himself. 'Sure, Blackjack had the cheque ripped out of me hand before the ink was barely dry. So tell us, luv, how does it feel to be the new Lady of the Manor?'

Chapter Seventeen

Edwina had no difficulty whatsoever in finding Mrs de Courcey's room. As she clip-clopped on her Jimmy Choos down the corridor of Kildare General Hospital clutching a hand-tied bouquet of stargazer lilies, she was fully aware of the admiring glances she was attracting from a passing group of student doctors. Sensing that this stunning-looking woman was a bit lost, one of them even volunteered to escort her all the way up to the second-floor intensive care unit, where a sign on the door read, 'Immediate Family Only Beyond This Point'. Without even pausing to consider, she buzzed loudly on the intercom. A few seconds later, a surly-looking matron answered the door.

'May I help you?'

'Yes thank you, I'm here to see Mrs Susan de Courcey.'

'Are you her daughter?'

Edwina smirked. 'In a manner of speaking, yes; now can you please just let me in?'

'I'm very sorry, immediate family only,' replied the matron and was about to slam the door in Edwina's plucked, powdered face when one of the male consultants came down the corridor. In one expert movement, Edwina whipped the clip from the back of her straight, blonde hair, allowing it to tumble sexily about her bare shoulders.

'Can you help me at all, I wonder?' she asked him, flashing him with the full force of her perfect smile. 'It's just that I've driven all the way from Dublin to see a friend, and you know, it's not that I'd stay for long or anything, I just want to give her these.' She simpered, indicating the flowers.

He looked at her, utterly unable to resist. Few men could, when Edwina really chose to turn it on. 'Oh, I think we can make an exception just this once, can't we, matron?' he said, holding the door open for her. Edwina breezed through, not even bothering to thank him now she'd achieved her objective.

'Edwina, darling, you're so sweet to have come to see me,' Mrs de Courcey said in a feeble voice, lamely attempting to sit up in her bed.

'Let me help you,' her dutiful daughter-in-law-elect said, rushing to help prop up the pillows at her back. 'How are you feeling, you poor thing?'

'A little better, thanks, but still as weak as a cat,' Mrs de Courcey replied, with a look of suffering on her pale face that Mother Teresa would have envied.

'And have they any idea what the matter is?'

'Poisoning of some kind, but my blood tests all came back perfectly clear, so they don't really know what caused it. All I know is that I was feeling as fit as a fiddle one minute and then no sooner had I crossed the threshold of Davenport Hall than the most violent nausea I have ever experienced in my whole life came over me. It took Michael twenty minutes just to carry me to the car. What can I say, my dear? One evening in that madhouse and I wanted to die. I would actually have welcomed death just to get out of there.'

'Your picture is in the paper, you know,' replied Edwina,

producing a bundle of magazines and newspapers from the depths of her Hermes Kelly bag and spreading them all over the bed. 'Yes, look, there you are in a crowd of people. And isn't that Ella Hepburn in the middle?'

'Do you know, I feel so sorry for that poor woman,' replied Susan, sounding as weak as one of Lucasta's kittens. 'Unless she has the constitution of an ox, they'd better get a bed ready for her in here.'

'The papers certainly had a field day,' Edwina went on. 'Davenport Hall is getting more coverage then a royal marriage break-up these days. Oh, look at this,' she said, brightening as her eagle eye fell on a grainy black-and-white photo in the *National Intruder*. 'It's difficult to make out because of the rain, but isn't that Portia Davenport with some man?'

Susan sat bolt upright in the bed, all but snatching the paper from Edwina's grasp. It was indeed a blurry, long-lens photo of Portia and Steve, taken when they were in the gazebo, the night of the Midsummer Ball. It had obviously been shot from quite a distance, but it was still possible to make out that she was slumped against him and that his arms were locked tightly around her.

BEGORRAH, IT'S GOMORRAH! the banner headline ran. THERE'S MORE HOT SEX IN THIS TINY CORNER OF KILDARE THAN IN THE ENTIRE RED-LIGHT DISTRICT OF AMSTERDAM!

'For such a plain-looking woman, she certainly has no problem pulling, does she?' said Edwina, thinking aloud. 'I suppose ugly women just have to try harder.'

'Yes, that's right, I saw her with someone,' said Susan, instantly perking up, 'just before I was taken ill. Edwina darling, do you mind if I keep a copy of this? It's just that I'm sure Andrew will be in to see me later on. Now, ordinarily he wouldn't wrap his chips in the *National Intruder* but in this case . . .' She sat back on the bed and smiled wanly, looking almost as white as the starched pillows at her back.

Edwina took her hand and patted it soothingly, delighted. 'You poor, poor thing, Susan, it's been simply awful for you! But, you know, I didn't come all this way to see you just to talk about what's in the papers. I think I just might have some news that'll cheer you up.'

Daisy could take no more. For the third day running, she had spent the afternoon holed up in the estate office with Portia and Steve as they frantically tried to trace Blackjack's last known whereabouts. Daisy had remembered he'd sent her a postcard from Caesar's Palace in Vegas, but when they contacted there, they were told he had moved on. The receptionist's actual words were, 'Oh yeah, we did have this springtime/fall couple staying and he did strut around claiming to be an Irish duke or lord or some crap, but we get a lot of that here. Is he escaped from an institution or something?'

Meanwhile, Steve was trying to get hold of every member of the Kildare County Council that he could, to ascertain just how far the planning application had advanced. Portia sat opposite him at her huge walnut desk, calmly scribbling notes and chipping in with helpful suggestions. Daisy's sole contribution to the whole operation had been to pace up and down and burst into fresh bouts of tears whenever Blackjack's name arose, which was about once every five minutes. After a couple of hours of this, she thought she'd scream.

Steve had been on hold to speak to the chairman of the County Council for what felt like an eternity and was just about to be put through when Daisy erupted. 'How can you both be so bloody calm and sit there making phone calls when bulldozers could be waiting at the gates to turn our land into the next Ballymun Towers?' she howled.

A rare flash of irritation passed over Portia's face, but she quickly calmed herself. 'Darling, Steve and I are doing everything that's humanly possible to try to get us out of this mess. If you want to help us, fine; if not, why not go outside and get some air?'

Daisy thought about it for a moment, then excused herself. After the neutron bomb which had landed on her, she found herself desperately wanting to see Guy, to tell him what was happening and to see if he had any solutions to offer. She hadn't set eyes on him since she'd stormed out of the Library on the night of the Ball. It was almost as though he'd been avoiding her – he seemed to spend every spare second in Ella Hepburn's trailer and . . . who knew? Maybe he was just being attentive to her because he felt sorry for her or . . . well, who knew? But there sure as hell was only one way to find out.

'Don't mention anything, darling, will you?' Portia called after her. 'It's just that there are so many press and journalists around, we want to keep this in the family.'

'Yeah, the only way I can keep up with you these days is by reading the tabloids, it seems,' Steve quipped, smiling softly at her in an attempt to lighten the situation. But it backfired. Daisy's huge blue eyes welled with tears, remembering all the coverage about her and Guy and how the *National Intruder* in particular raved about what a beautiful couple they made. (LOOK AT THE ARSE ON THAT had been the actual headline, but she recalled it as fondly as if it had been a soft-soaped *Hello!* magazine lovey-dovey spread.)

'Daisy, I didn't mean to upset you—' he said as she picked up her crutches and stumped out of the room in high dudgeon.

'It's OK,' Portia mouthed silently at him. 'Long story.'

As Daisy inched her way down the staircase, she heard the phone in the Library ringing. And ringing. Fucking ridiculous that there's no mobile phone signal in this house, she thought furiously. She paused for a moment, then, sighing deeply, decided she'd better answer it in case it was someone important from the Kildare County Council, returning one of Steve's calls and unable to get through to the line in the estate office, which had been tied up for most of the day.

'Hello, Davenport Hall.'

'Daisy? It's Andrew.'

'Oh, hi,' she answered dully, unaware of what was going on, that there was anything wrong between him and her sister. 'Are you looking for Portia?'

'Yes. Is she there?'

Before she answered, Daisy happened to look distractedly out of the window and noticed that the crew were setting up in the old orchard. From a distance, she could make out Guy and Ella, he in his famous fucking cream linen suit and she in a Victorian hooped skirt confection. In a flash, her mind was working overtime. Never one to sit silently wondering what was going on inside any man's head, she was of the 'shoot first, questions later' school. It had got her into a lot of trouble in the past, but she didn't care. There was bugger all to lose by being direct, she figured, so she may as well just march or, rather, hobble up to Guy and demand to know what in God's name was going on. She was momentarily distracted from her plan of action by Andrew's disembodied voice on the other end of the phone, saying, 'Daisy? Are you there?'

'Emm, look, it's not a great time,' she muttered distractedly, anxious to be gone. 'She's busy upstairs with Steve, but I'll get her to ring you, OK?'

'It's urgent – absolutely vital that I speak to her, Daisy. Do you promise you'll pass on the message?'

'Yeah, yeah, whatever.' Then, banging the phone down and thinking no more of it, she went outside.

As she stumped past the catering bus, Serge spotted her and immediately discarded his non-dairy, gluten-free, low-carb snack and ran out after her.

'Well, hey, honey, how's your war wound?' he asked, indicating her ankle.

'Fine, thanks,' she replied. She was in no mood for trifles. 'Serge, are they filming at the moment?'

'Yeah, the end of the mother-and-son reunion scene.' But there was something in the look of steely determination in her eyes which made him add, 'Honey, you know you can't go near the orchard when they're shooting . . .'

Off Daisy went, not even waiting for him to finish his sentence. Serge followed at a discreet distance, never one to miss out on a good old-fashioned showdown.

'Mother, why have you followed me all the way from Atlanta to the O'Maras' family farm here in the land of saints and scholars?'

'Because, my darling boy, I cannot permit you to align yourself with that woman yet again, after the shame and disgrace she has already visited on the Charleston clan! Oh Brent, my darling baby, when will you realize . . . Magnolia's nothing but a harlot!'

'CUT!' Jimmy D. roared at the top of his voice. 'Somebody's walking through the goddamn shot!'

'I will personally disembowel whoever it is . . .' said Johnny, then broke off, recognizing that it was Daisy, who'd taken a short cut through a side gate into the orchard and was now hobbling towards where Guy and Ella Hepburn were standing side by side, blissfully unaware that filming was in progress.

'Guy, thank goodness—' she panted breathlessly.

'I hope you're satisfied with yourself,' Guy interrupted furiously. 'Ella and I have been rehearsing this scene for hours and we've just played it perfectly and now we've gotta do it all over. And frankly, I feel like I've already peaked.'

'But, Guy, you don't understand,' Daisy replied. 'We've just had the most dreadful news about the Hall, they've applied to rezone all of our land and want to put a compulsory purchase order on the house and—'

He laughed cruelly. 'You know, the sooner you face up to the fact that your house is a fucking dump the better. You should be thankful that anyone in his or her right mind wants to buy it at all. It's a shithole!'

'Davenport Hole,' said Ella Hepburn in her heavy, guttural, smoker's voice, the first words Daisy had heard her utter since her arrival.

'You know, I'd really prefer not to be having this conversation in front of Lucrezia Borgia here,' said Daisy, close to tears now.

'Ignore her,' Guy said to Ella dismissively. 'I only fooled around with her because that's what Brent Charleston would have done.'

'Honey, come with me,' said Serge, who'd come up behind Daisy and slipped his arm protectively around her shoulders. 'Let's just get you out of here.'

Too stunned to protest, she allowed herself to be led away, aware that everyone on the set was watching her. She took a final glance over her shoulder and wished she hadn't. Guy and Ella were running the scene over again, but this time his hand lay suggestively across her bottom, not a bit like a mother and son at all.

'Don't you worry one teeny bit, honey,' said Serge, fussing around the make-up bus, 'my magic coffee is just what you need, and then we're gonna talk this through. Like I always say, why would anyone need a psychiatrist when they have a hairdresser?' Then, grabbing a freshly brewed pot from where it had been percolating quietly in the corner, he filled a mug half full and topped up the rest with brandy.

'Now, you get that into you, honey, and your Uncle Serge will tell you a few horror stories about the male race,' he said, handing the mug over to Daisy, who, with her ashen face and a blanket thrown around her shoulders, looked like she'd been in a terrorist bomb blast. 'You know, an ex of mine broke up with me by text message once, can you believe that?' he went on, massaging her hands in his. 'And we'd been dating for three months! A lousy text message that said "Welcome to Dumpsville. Population: you!"'

They were interrupted by a gentle knocking on the door.

'Come in,' said Serge, as quietly and respectfully as if he were in a funeral parlour. In walked Montana, carrying a bunch of roses and looking sheepish.

'Daisy, I know this is a really shit time, but it's all over the set about Guy and Ella Hepburn and I just wanted to give you these and let you know how, like, really sorry I am.'

Daisy stared at her, speechless.

'And I know I've been, like, a total bitch to you lately,' Montana went on, sitting down beside her, 'when you've been such a doll to me from day one. There's no excuse for the way I spoke to you at the Ball, I just hated seeing you with that asshole Guy. You really deserve so much better than him. So now do you believe me about, like, what an unbelievable shit he really is?'

Daisy nodded weakly. 'It's just that it hurts, you know?' she sobbed. 'It really fucking hurts.' The brandy in Serge's coffee was beginning to kick in and the tears had started to roll. 'But you know, maybe, just maybe he'll get tired of her, realize he's made a mistake and want me back. What do you think?'

'Oh dear, oh dear,' Serge said, gently massaging her

shoulders. 'You're clutching at straws now, honey. You know, I hold Meg Ryan entirely responsible for this.'

'Meg Ryan?' said Montana, surprised. 'What has Meg got to do with it?'

'You mean you haven't seen this?' Serge replied, indicating a tatty piece of paper stuck to the back of the bus door. He went over to remove it, and read it aloud to the girls. 'It's just a little list I'm compiling. I call it: "The Movies of Meg Ryan and their Crimes against Humanity.

' "One: her movies perpetuate the belief that feeling, sensitive, single women everywhere will eventually find true love.

' "Two – and this is the one that pertains to you, honey: her movies peddle the notion that even if you start on the wrong foot with the man of your dreams, even if he cheats on you with your best friend, it doesn't matter, it'll inevitably end in marriage anyway.

' "Three: how dare her movies encourage single women to believe that all of their male pals, of whatever orientation, are up for grabs." '

Montana glanced across at Daisy, who had momentarily forgotten her tears. Serge was one of those people who are at their funniest when they're not trying to be.

'And just don't get me started on Miss Ella Hepburn!' Serge went on, by now in full rant mode. 'I got a good look at her when I was doing her make-up this morning and, honey, the amount of work she's had done! Let's just say there's a bucket in some cosmetic surgery clinic somewhere with most of her real face in it.'

A slight smile flickered across Daisy's beautiful, tired face. Montana noticed, and decided that now might be an appropriate moment to change the subject.

'Oh, by the way, you wanna know something? I owe you,

like, a really big thank you, Daisy,' she said. 'I totally forgot to tell you! My lab results came back from LA and your friend Kat Slater really did the trick. I'm as clean as a whistle, healthier than I've ever been!'

In spite of herself, Daisy began to chuckle. Large tears began to splash down her cheeks as laughter completely over-came her. For a moment, she forgot all of her cares in a helpless fit of giggles and, without quite knowing why, Serge and Montana both joined in until the make-up bus sounded like the canned laughter track on a US sitcom.

'Laughter through tears,' said Serge, 'my favourite emotion!'

At around the same time, Shamie Nolan's Jaguar was zooming over the potholes on the driveway up to the Hall.

'Jaysus, Mickey, if I have to go past that feckin' shower of bastard journalists once more, I'll go off me head,' said Bridie to her brother-in-law. 'They've been camped out at that gate all bloody week photographing anything that moves. I'm telling ya, I know exactly how Princess Diana must have felt.'

'Just think of the scoop you'll be able to give them when this story breaks, Bridie, or should I say, me lady!'

She laughed heartily at this as she pulled over just outside the main entrance. 'Come on, Mickey,' she said, hauling her huge frame out of the car door. 'Let's get this over with. Have ya got everything ya need?'

'I think so, yeah,' he replied, taking his architect's sketchpad, measuring tape and a small stepladder from the back of the car. 'Righty-oh, lead the way.'

Without further ado, they marched up the steps and Bridie bashed at the doorbell for all she was worth.

'Keep yer knickers on, will ya?' Mrs Flanagan could clearly be heard saying from behind the door (her standard greeting). Then, opening up and seeing who the visitors were, she said,

'Howaya, Bridie? What brings you all the way out here?' Then, a bit suspiciously, she added, 'Is Shamie not with ya then?'

'No, he's in the States on business,' replied Bridie, cool as a cucumber. 'This is his brother Mickey who's here to do me a favour.'

'Well, if yer're looking for Lady Davenport I'm afraid she's pissed,' said Mrs Flanagan, beginning to smell a very large rat. 'But Portia's up in her office. Did ya want to speak to her?'

'I did indeed,' replied Bridie. Then, unable to help herself, she added, 'You can just tell her the new owners have arrived.'

Chapter Eighteen

'I've come across some worthless shitheads in my time, but Blackjack Davenport beats fucking Christmas,' said Mrs Flanagan for about the tenth time in as many minutes, as she gazed morosely into space.

No one contradicted her.

This is like a scene from the final act of a Chekhov play, was the bizarre thought that filtered through Portia's mind. The decaying manor house that's been sold from under the noses of the family who'd lived there for centuries, the faithful family retainer, the beautiful willowy youngest daughter who'd spent the day crying for Ireland and the lady of the house anaesthetized with alcohol, all sitting in stunned silence around an empty grate wondering what would become of them. All we're short of is a bloody seagull circling us, she added ruefully to herself.

It had been a day of one devastating blow after another. She and Steve had worked side by side like lunatics firstly to track her father down in the vain hope that he could be persuaded not to sell; then, when they'd failed to contact him, the next Herculean task had been to try and persuade each member of the County Council not to condemn the Hall . . . and all for nothing. Once Bridie Nolan landed on the doorstep with an architect in tow, it was all over bar the shouting.

Bridie and her brother-in-law had spent the afternoon gleefully going over the Hall, deciding on what should be done and announcing its fate room by room. A few particular gems stood out like sore thumbs in Portia's memory.

'Well, for Jaysus' sake, Mickey, that monstrosity has to go for starters,' she'd said on seeing the antique Victorian full-size dining table in the Red Dining Room. 'Rip the whole thing out – including them ugly stone gargoyles in the ceiling; they remind me of Shamie's mother. Then the indoor heated swimming pool can go here, we can take up that manky aul' floor and make sure the pool has covers that slide over it when ya press a button, like in the James Bond films.'

'But, Bridie, sure none of your family can swim,' Mickey interjected.

'That's not the feckin' point, ya thick?, we can keep tropical fish in it, it'll be fabulous. And as for that,' she said, pointing threateningly at the minstrels' gallery in the Ballroom, 'I'd demolish it this minute if I could. What the feck use is it to anyone anyhow? Sure you'd never even get a karaoke machine up there.'

Not even the Library, probably the only respectable room in the Hall, containing as it did a considerable number of leather-bound first editions, escaped a lash from her acidic tongue.

'First thing tomorrow, Mickey, I want all them dusty aul' books belonging to the Davenports put in cardboard boxes for that happy day when they move out. Then we can rip out all the shelves and put in a full-length Mexican theme bar. And as for them ugly looking yokes,' she added, pointing to the original Georgian fifteen-pane sash windows, 'the sooner we get rid of them, the sooner we can get the double glazing in.'

Then, after another few hours of this, came the killer blow. Drawing himself up to his full height of five feet two, Mickey delivered his final pronouncement.

'I've had a decent look at the place for ya now, Bridie, and I have to tell ya, I've seen some right shitholes in my time, but Davenport Hall takes the gold medal. Sure, yerself and Shamie would only be wasting yer money trying to renovate the place, it's beyond hope. Ya may as well put a match to ten million euros as even try to salvage it. Sure the damp-proofing alone would run into millions.'

'So what do you suggest, Mickey?'

'Flatten the place quick as ya can when the fast-track housing gets under way, build yerselves yer dream home here on the original site from scratch and instead of Davenport Hall, call it Shamie Joe Nolan Junior Hall.'

Bridie thought for a moment, entranced by the idea, then reluctantly shook her head. 'Think of all the bastard conservationists, Mickey, they'd have a field day. You know what them tree-huggers are like, Shamie says they should all be bulldozed over.'

'For a smart woman, yer're not thinking straight, Bridie. You and Shamie are the rightful owners of the Hall now, and no doubt you'll get it insured for a fair few quid. Suppose someone left a cigarette smouldering in that dusty aul' library some night, and the whole place was to go up in flames . . . all I'm saying is, stranger things have happened.'

'Do you know, I had a premonition on my wedding day,' said Lucasta, smoking a cigarette and continuing to gaze into space. Portia, Daisy and even Mrs Flanagan all turned to look at her in surprise, momentarily shaken from the depression that hung like a fog over the four of them. It was unheard of for Lucasta ever to speak about her husband. Indeed, with that innate knack she had for airbrushing anything disagreeable out of her life, you could be forgiven for thinking that she'd been a widow for at least twenty years.

'What happened, Mummy?' asked a very red-eyed Daisy, looking and sounding as vulnerable as a four-year-old.

'Well, on the morning of the wedding, your grandfather was taking me to the church on the back of his new Vespa moped which he wanted to try out. And just as we were leaving my parents' house, he ran over my favourite cat, Fidelity, and killed him stone dead. Then as we arrived at the church, a single magpie did its business all over my veil. And, of course, your father hadn't even arrived at the church because his car broke down so he had to hitch a lift from a hearse, which happened to be going in the same direction. So just as I was wiping bird shit from my veil, I saw what I thought was a funeral procession arriving, but it turned out to be the groom. Then I remember a black raven getting caught in your grandfather's hair, causing him to fall and crack his head on the stone steps outside the church. As I rushed to help him up, some blood oozing from the side of his head went all over my wedding dress. I slipped in a puddle of the blood and landed on the flat of my coccyx and had to be carried up the aisle. Then the photographer got sick at the sight of all the gore and started to vomit on the altar. That's why there aren't any photos of the wedding, you know. It was like Sweeney Todd's bloody cellar.'

'But, Mummy, how could you have possibly gone ahead with the wedding? It seems to me that if you'd driven past a billboard on the side of the road with a sign saying, "Lucasta, do not marry Blackjack", the signs couldn't have been clearer,' said Portia.

'Signs? What signs are you talking about, darling?' replied Lucasta, puzzled. 'Do you think that if there'd been any kind of signs for me not to go ahead with my own wedding that I, of all people, wouldn't have seen them?'

Portia just caught Daisy's eye and a flicker of a smirk passed between them.

'No, darlings,' Lucasta went on, 'the premonition I had was crystal clear. We'd left the church and were driving up to the Hall for our wedding reception, when I glanced over to the field behind the Hall and there it was. A tractor.'

'You saw a tractor,' said Mrs Flanagan, struggling to see where this was going, 'in the middle of a field. In summer. On a country estate with two thousand acres. And that gave ya a premonition . . . Why?'

'Because at that moment, I knew. And I remember turning to my husband of ten minutes and saying, "Mark my words, Blackjack. The day will come when culchies will live at Davenport Hall." '

'Ah would you ever get up to bed,' replied Mrs Flanagan. 'Do you think I don't have enough to worry about without listening to you? Jaysus, if you'd brains you'd be dangerous.'

Portia knew she wouldn't get a wink of sleep that night. Unusually for her, she'd had a couple of her mother's gin and tonics and was now feeling the worst ill effects imaginable. As she lay on her bed, the whole room seemed to swirl around her in a sickening kaleidoscopic blur. Worry was gnawing at her insides, gripping at her till she couldn't breathe. What in God's name were they to do now? The Davenports had been in plenty of tight scrapes before, especially where money was concerned, but nothing, nothing, nothing compared with this.

Blackjack had never exactly been father of the year as far as Portia was concerned, but as she lay wide awake for yet another hour, she could see his face clearly in her mind's eye and a rage like she'd never experienced before came over her.

Two million he'd sold them out for, lock, stock and barrel. Typically, he'd not even bothered to phone his wife and daughters to tell them himself, but then he always was one for allowing others to do his dirty work for him. Then, furiously kicking the bedclothes off her, she found herself wondering how long that amount of money would last even him at the blackjack table. Had he walked through the door of Davenport Hall that night, she honestly believed that she'd have killed him. And that no jury in the land would have convicted her.

Five a.m. and daylight was beginning to creep through the cracks in the wooden shutters of her bedroom windows. From outside, she could already hear sounds of the film crew cranking up for the day, particularly Serge, whose voice would carry over the Grand Canyon.

'You know I cannot function in the morning without something hot and wet inside me, and I'm referring to caffeine, so no knocking on the make-up bus for at least ten minutes!'

Portia turned over. Years of being independent, self-reliant and alone had turned her into the least needy woman imaginable, but Christ, she thought, just once, just this one time, I so wish Andrew was in bed beside me. Just so she could feel his strong arms around her and know that there was at least something that couldn't be taken from her. She hadn't heard a single word from him since the party, nothing. Since they'd met, they'd rarely been separated. Not since the first night they'd kissed and then the night when they'd kissed again, but this time she had shyly led him by the hand to her bedroom and he'd gently but firmly shut the door behind them.

Something was up. She wasn't quite sure what, but something was definitely up.

225

Chapter Nineteen

Steve had been nothing short of saintly in the miserable days that followed. He had worked like a Trojan on behalf of the Davenports to see if there were any possible loophole in the sale of the Hall, anything at all that would prevent the family from having to move out.

'This is a listed building, Steve, there's a preservation order on it,' Portia had reasoned as she paced up and down the estate office for about the thousandth time. 'It may be crumbling around our ears but it is part of the county's heritage, there have been Davenports here for over two hundred years. Doesn't that count for something? Isn't there some Government department we could appeal to for help?'

He looked up at her from behind the desk he was sitting at and, just for a moment, their eyes locked. Without needing to say anything, they both knew that, in the history of useless, rubbish plans, that particular one took the biscuit. Any hope the Davenports would have had of gaining Government assistance had gone out of the window years ago, the day Blackjack wheedled a sizeable grant from the Heritage Department on the assumption that it would go towards the restoration of at least part of the Hall. A few months later, when an inspector from the department called to see what use the cheque had been put to, they discovered that Blackjack had used it to buy a racehorse, thoughtfully naming it 'Government Grant'.

Portia shrugged her shoulders and smiled wryly across the desk at him. 'Worth a try,' she said.

The new owners of Davenport Hall had graciously condescended to allow filming to continue at the Hall until they took up residence.

'Look here, Bridie,' Shamie had pleaded with her, flushed with the success of his trip to Las Vegas, 'how in the name of God would it look if I was to turf out that crew before they even finished the bloody film? Could ya imagine if that got into the papers? Jaysus, I can see the headlines now: "TD NOLAN IS A FAT PHILISTINE", and then none of them leftie actor types would ever vote for me! And I'd never get an Arts and Heritage portfolio then, not a snowball's chance in hell. No, let them finish whatever aul' shite it is they're filming and then the whole lot of them can go.'

Jimmy D. had breathed a colossal sigh of relief and treated himself to one of his biggest Havana cigars to celebrate this stay of execution. Had Shamie Nolan called a halt to filming, the logistics of the crew having to relocate would have been nightmarish. They had completed the exterior shooting, but now had to move inside to film the interiors, which included a ballroom scene with enough extras in it to make Cecil B. De Mille run screaming in terror. It was scheduled to be shot at the end of the week, which gave Johnny and the rest of the crew some much needed time to light the gloomy interior of the Hall and generally set up. It also gave the already overworked design department a breathing space to transform the crumbling, decaying Ballroom into something that would look semi-decent on screen, as opposed to a reception room with bin liners on the ceiling, which you would swear had just been bombed.

But as Jimmy D. puffed away, reclining on his favourite armchair in the Library, he felt more contented than he had done in weeks. Ella Hepburn was working out terrifically, better than anyone could have imagined. Christ, he thought, it was so good finally to work with a professional after weeks of acting as a referee during Montana and Guy's squabbling. She was a class act, gave no trouble, turned up on time, knew her lines and just got on with the job in hand. Not for nothing had she been at the top of her profession for over fifty years, he reflected. And she certainly had Guy in the palm of her hand, that was for sure. He'd been as meek as a little lamb since she'd arrived. Of course the rumour mill on the set had gone into overdrive with talk of the passionate affair they'd embarked on, but it sure as hell didn't bother Jimmy D. Film sets were always notorious hotbeds of sex and intrigue, and once all of his actors turned up for work at five a.m. each morning, what did he care if Ella Hepburn was sleeping with a boy young enough to be her grandson? The press permanently camped out at the front gate were running wild with the story and, as every producer and director in Hollywood knew, all publicity was good publicity.

Pity about Daisy Davenport though, he thought. She was such a pretty thing and Guy had behaved like a shit towards her, dumping her the minute Ella came along. If he thought this was some kind of career move on his part, he was sadly mistaken. Ella Hepburn had a reputation as a man-eater for whom the phrase 'doesn't count on location, darling' might have been invented. Married, single, gay or straight, she'd shag anything with a pulse and move on as soon as the film was in the can. And now, on top of being dumped so publicly, poor

Daisy, together with her older sister (who'd been nothing but lovely, kind and welcoming to the crew since day one) and their insane mother all had to move out of the home that had been in their family for centuries. He sighed and took another great puff of his cigar, surveying the room around him as though he owned the place.

What was happening to those women was such God-awful luck, they didn't deserve it. Surely there was something he could do to help?

Daisy had never been particularly attentive or academic during her miserable schooldays, but one phrase which her English teacher had drummed into her time and again now kept coming back to haunt her: 'When sorrows come, they come not single spies, But in battalions.'

It just seemed so apt now, with her world coming to an end, she thought, as she wrapped a towel around her naked body and limped on her swollen, bruised ankle from the bathroom back to her bedroom.

She'd cried so much in the last few days she could barely see straight and her head was thumping so badly she almost thought she was going to pass out. And as if things weren't bad enough, the bloody film crew had relocated inside the Hall and were crawling all over the house so the only place she could get any kind of privacy was in her bedroom. At least there's no chance of running into Guy and his old lady girl-friend here, she thought as she opened the door and slipped inside.

And nearly fell over with shock. The curtains had been pulled and just about every spare surface had been completely covered with candles, making the whole room twinkle like the fairy lights on a Christmas tree. And lying on the bed wearing nothing but a pair of Arsenal boxer shorts was Paddy, surrounded by dozens of chrysanthemums artlessly tossed all over the counterpane. He was smoking a cigarette and nearly jumped out of his skin when she walked in.

'Ah Jaysus, ya gave me an awful fright,' he said, stubbing out the fag into one of the burning candles.

'I gave you a fright?' she replied incredulously. 'Paddy, what are you doing?'

'I heard about your aul' fella selling the house and all, and I thought you'd like a bit of a pick-me-up,' he said, grinning at her and suggestively patting the bed beside him. Daisy looked at his long, skinny, spotty white body with his farmer's red-neck tan, thought for a moment, and then allowed her towel to slip to the floor as she snuggled in beside him. What the hell, she thought, any port in a storm.

'Just hold me, Paddy,' she whispered, with fresh tears start-ing to flow. 'Hold me tight.'

'Come here to me, luv,' he replied, locking his thin arms around her. 'It's not your fault yer aul' man's a wanker. And ya can come and live with me in my flat in Drimnagh anytime. Course, me ma would be there as well, but you'd get on great with her.'

Daisy gulped back more tears, thinking about how much she'd been coping with; how funny that in the midst of all her troubles, it was someone's kindness that made her want to cry even more.

'Now don't mash them chrysanthemums into the sheets whatever you do,' Paddy said, starting to sneeze. 'I had to go to three different garages to get them and now I think I'm allergic.'

Unlike her younger daughter, Lucasta wasn't going down without a fight. 'If my fucking bastard of an ex-husband thinks I'm going to take this lying down, he's got another think coming,' she ranted at Mrs Flanagan as they both sat at the kitchen table smoking cigarette after cigarette. Beside them lay countless empty wine bottles all soaking in basins of water to remove the labels before they could be miraculously transformed into Eau de Davenport. 'I came here as a child bride in the nineteen sixties, you know, surely I must have earned squatters' rights or something by now?'

'Yeah,' replied Mrs Flanagan, only half listening. 'I suppose ya could tell the press lads outside ya were going on a hunger strike or something by way of protest. Wouldn't do ya any harm to lose a few pounds either.'

Lucasta turned to her as though she'd just had a revelation. 'Mrs Flanagan!' she said in astonishment. 'You're an absolute genius and God knows that's something I don't get to say very often.'

'Don't fecking tell me, yer're going to go global with yer Eau de Davenport.'

'The press camped at the front gates! That's the answer! I'll march straight out there and appeal to them directly. I'll be like Joan of Arc crusading before the troops!'

'Joan Rivers more like. Before the plastic surgery.'

'Oh, piss off. I come from a long line of rebels, you know. My grandmother was a suffragette and her sister fought for Irish freedom in the GPO in nineteen sixteen.'

'With Pádraic Pearse and the lads? And was she shot along with the rest of them?'

'Emm, no. She only went in to buy a stamp and didn't realize there was a Rising going on. So she only really got caught in the crossfire by accident. I often wonder if anyone in history ever sacrificed their life as she did, just for the sake of renewing a wireless licence and buying a twopenny stamp. Anyway, the point is, the TV cameras and newspapermen at our front gates are like a PR goldmine, just crying out to be exploited.'

★

For six full days now, Portia hadn't heard a single word from Andrew. Not a whisper. From someone who'd barely left her side in the time they'd known each other. She'd had so much else to worry about that she'd done her best to push him to the back of her mind but, try as she might, he was rarely out of her thoughts for very long. After yet another mind-numbing day sweating blood with Steve in the estate office, scraping the barrel trying to find some way around the inevitable, she could take no more.

'Look at you,' Steve had said to her as they walked towards his Jeep in the forecourt together, 'you're making yourself physically sick from worry and exhaustion. You need to get out of here for a bit, clear your head.' He looked at her ghostly pale face with concern. She smiled wanly at him as she stood on tiptoe to peck him on the cheek before he drove off.

He's dead right, she thought, nothing like a good, brisk walk to take my mind off things. But just as she was about to set off down the driveway, she remembered: the bloody press were camped at the front gates and they still had her cast in the role of humble scullery maid lusting after the Earl of Ireland. They were snapping anything that moved on the estate these days and Portia wasn't in the mood to be used as tabloid fodder. Who needs that, she thought, jumping into the Mini Metro instead, and putting on a pair of sunglasses that she found in the glove compartment. I'll just drive into Ballyroan instead, she decided, making a quick mental list of various bits and pieces she could buy in Spar while she was at it.

She made it through the front gates in one piece. An electrical storm of flashes did go off into her face, but the sunglasses disguised her and she heard one wag remark, 'Doubt very much if Ella Hepburn's going to be driving around in a heap of crap like that.'

As she pulled out of the gates and headed for the town, her mind was racing. Maybe she'd done something to annoy Andrew without even realizing it. Whatever it was though, he'd have to spell it out to her; she was at a loss even to guess what was going on. It just seemed so weird that one minute they were practically joined at the hip and then he was gone, when he didn't come across as a messer or a guy who would behave like that. But then, she reasoned, I'm not exactly Madonna; it's not as though I have a vast back catalogue of relationships to compare this with. For all I know this could be perfectly normal, acceptable behaviour. It didn't feel normal, though.

A slow, sickening feeling began to creep over her. A nagging doubt which she'd been suppressing at the back of her mind for the past few days now came centre stage. When it boiled down to it, she actually knew so little about Andrew. She knew he was a man-about-town, that he thrived on the high-octane life he'd had for years in New York. Maybe this is what he does, she thought. He'd moved from Manhattan to Ballyroan in the blink of an eye and was temporarily stuck in this backwater until his super-cool, metrosexual stag pad was ready. He could have just been feeling restless and bored and then . . . enter the girl next door. Portia's heart was beginning to thump as a cold reality hit her. She was just a diversion to him. Someone to pass the time with, nothing more. Daisy often used to say that most men would basically have sex with a tree if they could, only women clouded the issue with emotions. And that was exactly what Portia had done. The time they'd spent together, which had meant so much to her, was obviously nothing more than a wham-bam-thank-you-ma'am job to him. And yet Andrew didn't seem to be a shag-and-run merchant . . .

I can handle it, she thought, feeling suddenly strong. If he's buggered off, I'll deal with it and, similarly, if he hasn't, if this is all just a big misunderstanding, I'll handle that too. The not knowing was the thing that was driving her insane. With a jolt, she remembered the magnificent bouquet of flowers he'd sent her the day after that horrific party in his mother's house, which seemed like it was last year, so much had happened since then. He'd written her a card and left his mobile phone number on it. She found herself fervently hoping to God that the card hadn't been thrown out in all the chaos that was going on at the Hall. Well, that's the answer then, she thought, I'll just call him when I get home, simple as that. At the very least he'd want to know that the Hall had been sold from beneath them. Her gut instinct was telling her something completely different though.

If he had any interest at all, wouldn't he just have called to see her, as he'd done every day since they'd met?

'We're all very sorry to hear about the Hall being sold,' Lottie O'Loughlin had sympathized with Portia as she packed her groceries into a plastic bag for her. 'But at least it's going to local people, not some rock stars from Dublin. Sure Shamie and Bridie Nolan will take great care of the place, won't they? And I'm sure they'll put a few bob into it as well. Let's face it, it's not exactly Buckingham Palace at the moment, is it?'

Portia couldn't bring herself to answer, she just nodded and got the hell out of there.

No sooner had she sat back in the car and turned on the ignition than her heart sank. There it was, that all-too-familiar chug, chug, chug sound the car made whenever it refused to start. She sighed tiredly and stepped out on to the pavement to retrieve the water bottle from the boot of the car and put some into the radiator; that usually did the trick. Just then, a black BMW coupé pulled up alongside her and an electronic window buzzed down.

'Car trouble?' asked Susan de Courcey from behind the wheel. 'May I be of any assistance?'

'No, thank you very much,' replied Portia, shocked, but trying to keep her voice calm. 'This happens all the time, the car just needs a little water.'

A silence followed as both women eyeballed each other. Portia was torn between asking her about Andrew: was he still staying with her, had she seen him, what was happening, anything, any information at all would have been welcome. But the dignified, proud side of her kept silent, thinking: Why should I bloody gratify you by even mentioning his name?

'I hope you enjoyed the Midsummer party,' was her best shot.

'What, do you mean apart from ending up in hospital with severe blood poisoning? Not a night that I'll remember with great fondness, no,' Mrs de Courcey replied, tapping her elegantly manicured nails on the steering wheel and glaring rudely at Portia, almost daring her to ask more.

'I'm very sorry to hear that,' Portia replied. 'I hope you're feeling better.'

'Much better,' she said, allowing herself a slight smile now that the conversation was going her way. 'Actually, Michael and I have had some wonderful news which has cheered me up and helped my recovery no end.'

Portia started to feel sick.

'Yes, we're both over the moon. Andrew and Edwina are back together again and their wedding is going ahead, as planned.'

Chapter Twenty

Portia couldn't quite remember getting home or how she got up the stairs and into the privacy of her bedroom, but somehow she did. She was sitting at her dressing table shaking like a leaf and barely heard soft knocking on the door, but the next thing she was aware of was Daisy barging in, wearing a flowery nightie and plonking straight down on her bed.

'Thought I heard you coming in, Sis. I have to talk to you, I've done something really daft and now I'm so upset—' Daisy began, then broke off as she clocked the look on her sister's face. 'Jesus, what happened to you?'

Portia couldn't hold it in any longer. Since the news about the Hall being sold had broken, she'd been nothing but a tower of strength, supporting her mother and sister and never for one moment letting her own guard down, but now she'd reached breaking point. The past few days of fretting and stressing over their homelessness and bankruptcy she could deal with, Daisy's devastation over Guy she could deal with, her mother's inability to do anything except make matters worse she could deal with, but not this. She let herself sink into Daisy's arms and sobbed out the whole story. Daisy held on to her tight and rocked her gently from side to side, totally unused to being the stronger one of the pair.

After a few minutes, Lucasta appeared at the door wearing her wax jacket over a filthy grey nightie.

'I thought I heard whingeing, girls, what on earth's going on?' she asked, taking in the unusual sight of Portia being emotional and Daisy being the one in control.

'Shhh, Mummy,' Daisy replied, gesturing for her to sit on the bed as Portia continued to sob. 'She met that old battleaxe Susan de Courcey in town and she told her that Andrew's back with his ex and their wedding's going ahead. He's a bastard, a bloody user bastard. Same as the rest of them.'

'You're fucking joking,' replied Lucasta, pulling a box of fags from her pocket and lighting up.

'I'm afraid it's true,' Portia replied, sniffling. 'Explains a lot, doesn't it?'

'But he'd practically moved in here, you and he were inseparable. I simply can't believe that he'd just up and away with someone else.'

'It's not just someone else, it's the woman he was supposed to be marrying this summer, they were together for years.'

'Well, I can't accept that,' said Lucasta firmly. 'He was knickers about you, Portia, absolutely knickers about you. And not forgetting the fact that he promised me he'd invest in my Eau de Davenport. I simply can't understand it; what is the matter with men these days?'

'If you saw his ex-girlfriend, you'd understand,' Portia replied, a little calmer now. 'She's so beautiful, I can't imagine that he wouldn't be happy with her. The whole thing makes perfect sense to me.'

'You're beautiful too, darling. You could do with breast implants, but apart from that, you're lovely.'

Tears started to fill Portia's eyes again; she was so unused to any degree of kindness or sensitivity from, of all people, her mother.

'What is it about us Davenport girls that not one of us can hold on to a man?' Lucasta went on, stubbing her cigarette out on the bare wooden floor. 'There's only one logical explanation and that's that there's a curse of some sort on us. Right, well, there's nothing else for it. I'll just have to cast a spell.'

'Oh Mummy, not base metal into gold again, I've still got that nasty green ring around my neck from the last time,' said Daisy.

'Oh no, darling. This time I'm calling out the cavalry.'

She was as good as her word. The next morning at sunrise, Mrs Flanagan was dispatched down to the entrance gates at the bottom of the driveway where the press were gathered, to issue an invitation.

'Good morning, lads,' was her opener. 'Now don't be bothered taking any photos of me, I've no make-up on for starters, but if youse would all like to follow me inside the Hall, Lady Davenport has the scoop of the century for youse.'

Much puzzlement ensued as the assembled press corps tried to figure out what the hell was going on, but Tony Pitt and the more hard-nosed hacks needed little encouragement. They were actually being invited into the Hall! Who knew what candid shots of Ella Hepburn and Guy van der Post they might be lucky enough to get?

All in all, about a dozen reporters and TV cameramen trooped indoors and were ushered by Mrs Flanagan into the Library. There, lying prostrate on a chaise longue was Lucasta, looking so frail and fragile that she could have given Elizabeth Barrett Browning a run for her money.

'I have something to say to you all, and I need you to pay very careful attention,' she began, checking first to make sure that the TV cameras were rolling. Then, casting her eyes downwards and looking as doe-eyed as possible, she began. 'I am speaking to you now not as the proprietor of Eau de Davenport but as the former owner of Davenport Hall. In the past few days a catastrophe of epic proportions has befallen us.' She sounded like a TV appeal to help starving babies in Somalia. 'This heritage house, this jewel in the architectural crown of County Kildare has been cruelly snatched from the loving arms of the family who for nine generations has lived here and worked the land. The Davenports were never absentee landlords, they never buggered off during Ireland's struggle for independence, oh no. They stood shoulder to shoulder with the people of Kildare through thick and thin. And now our illustrious story is at an end. The Hall has been sold out from under us and I, along with my two daughters, am about to be made homeless. As I speak, bulldozers are gathering like storm clouds outside, waiting to destroy the land our ancestors sweated blood and tears over – and for what? So that a vulgar housing estate can be built? So that a motorway can defile this beauteous countryside?' She was reaching a pitch now – starting to sound a bit like Winston Churchill rallying the troops. 'I urge you to help us! Hear my plea and let us snatch victory from the jaws of defeat! Please send what you can to Davenport Hall and help us to fight the barbarians who are seeking to usurp our home!' Then, with a tearful sigh, she sank back into the chaise longue, as though completely overcome by her passionate plea.

A polite ripple of applause broke out among the assembled hacks, which Lucasta graciously acknowledged with a wave of her hand.

'Now, before youse all leave, there's a complimentary bottle of Eau de Davenport for each of you,' said Mrs Flanagan, handing out bottles from a crate inside the door.

'Was that all right?' Lucasta hissed at her under her breath.

'You were like Princess Diana when she went on *Panorama*,' she replied. 'There wasn't a dry eye in the house.'

'Whoever would have thought that Mummy was such a good actress?' Daisy asked as she and Portia sat in the kitchen watching Lucasta's performance as it was broadcast on TV4's lunchtime news bulletin. 'Nice to see that all those years of watching the Queen's Christmas Day speech weren't wasted on her.'

'Right. Come on then, back to work,' Portia said, picking up a stack of old newspapers and continuing carefully to wrap up the china tea service.

'Oh, must we?' moaned Daisy. 'I don't see why we have to pack in the first place. If Mummy's appeal works, we'll only have to unpack all over again.'

Portia silently raised her eyes to heaven and continued to pack.

Steve had miraculously hammered out an eleventh-hour mercy deal with the Nolans whereby the Davenports could remain in the Hall until the film had wrapped (only a matter of two months anyway), and then could stay in the gate lodge until they found somewhere permanent to live. Which was yet another nightmare Portia had to face up to; where would they eventually go and how in God's name would they support themselves? She had carefully salted away most of the money Romance Pictures had paid them for using the Hall, but they couldn't live off that for ever. And apart from a few dozen bottles of Eau de Davenport which Lucasta had bullied people into buying, the family had no other source of income now that the Hall no longer rightfully belonged to them.

And look at me, Portia thought bitterly, who in their right mind would ever give me a job? There's absolutely nothing I'm qualified to do except mismanage country estates and I doubt if there's much demand for that.

'Hey, maybe we could get jobs as housemaids here when the Nolans move in,' Daisy said, as though reading Portia's thoughts. 'Or, better still, we could become style gurus to Bridie Nolan, she could certainly do with it. You know, a bit like Carole Caplin and Cherie Blair. Did you see the outfit she was wearing to the Midsummer party? Paddy said he thought she was a strippergram.'

'Paddy?' Portia stopped her wrapping for a moment. 'Paddy the sound man?'

Daisy grimaced and suddenly threw herself into the wrapping with a vengeance.

'Excuse me, missy, will you please tell me what is going on?'

'Well' – Daisy wondered how on earth she could explain – 'you know what men are like, I mean look at Guy! He took one look at Ella fucking Hepburn and that was the end of me. So, I've sort of been having mercy sex . . . it's just interim shagging really, to keep the juices flowing, you know . . .' she trailed off weakly but was saved by the bell as Mrs Flanagan waddled in, panting.

'Jaysus, I think I'm the only one that won't be a bit sorry to leave this kip, I'm worn out looking all over the place for ya,' she said to Portia.

'Is something the matter, Mrs Flanagan?' she replied.

'Phone call for you in the Library. It's Andrew and he says it's urgent.'

'Oh shit,' said Daisy, banging her hand off her forehead in exasperation, 'I knew there was something I forgot to tell you. He rang the other day too.'

Portia thought for a moment, feeling the full force of both of them staring at her expectantly.

'Thanks, Mrs Flanagan. Will you tell him I'm not in?'

Chapter Twenty-One

Lucasta's heartfelt TV appeal had a most unexpected consequence. Apart from a few minor contributions that were sent to the Hall ('Barely enough for us all to go on a week's holiday to Torremolinos,' Mrs Flanagan had moaned) it transpired that someone else had been watching her performance on TV with great interest. About a week afterwards, Steve was rushing into his office already late for a meeting when his secretary handed him a message.

'Chief Justice Michael de Courcey was looking for you, he says it's critical that he speaks to you today.'

Steve took the phone number, thanked her and kicked the inner door of his office closed before calling him back, totally at a loss as to what could be so urgent.

'Michael? Steve Sullivan here. I believe you were looking for me?'

'Yes, yes indeed,' came the reply in that booming voice which could be heard in Cavan. 'I'm in chambers all day but I wondered if we could meet for a chat tonight, if you're free?'

'Unfortunately, I have plans for this evening, but how about tomorrow? I could call at your house in the evening if you're in court during the day.'

'I'm afraid not. Loose lips cost ships, you know. I'm awfully sorry to inconvenience you, but we'll have to meet in Dublin and it'll have to be tonight. This won't wait.'

Steve did indeed have plans for that night, which he was very reluctant to cancel. It was the annual Hunt Ball to be held in the Four Seasons Hotel in Dublin and every year he escorted the Davenport ladies. In spite of the upheaval the family had been through in recent weeks, this year was to be no different; they were still going, as usual. Daisy had bewailed the fact that it was the most boring night of the year and that she was sick of all those hunting-shooting-fishing types looking down their noses on the unfortunate Davenports. But, as Portia gently but firmly pointed out, they had to arrange for the horses on the estate to be stabled elsewhere when they moved out, and where better for them to organize this than at the Hunt Ball?

So when Steve called Portia later that day to cancel, she didn't really mind, although her curiosity was piqued.

'Promise you'll tell me what old foghorn voice wants, won't you?' she'd pleaded.

Steve just smiled and said nothing, knowing there was something going on but not fully understanding the state of play between Andrew and Portia.

Lucasta also pulled out at the last minute, but for a very different reason. Along with half the country, Jimmy D. had seen her masterful performance on the TV news and had offered her a part in the film. He had long wanted to do something to help out his hosts and felt that casting one of them in the film was the ideal way to throw a little cash in their direction. A 'special extra' role, he had called it, which was a polite way of saying that she'd only have one line to say, but as far as Lucasta was concerned, she'd been discovered.

'Now I know just how Lana Turner felt!' she said, over the moon with excitement. 'Do you know she was discovered working in an ice-cream parlour somewhere in America? I really think this is the start of a whole new career for me! I could be another Greta Garbo!'

'And think of all the acting experience you already have, with all the times ya made up sob stories to tell the debt collectors,' Mrs Flanagan replied, not a little pissed off that she hadn't been asked. Especially as the part was that of a housekeeper.

'Oh fuck off, you're just jealous they asked me instead of you. Can I help it if I have these wonderful cheekbones that are just crying out to be filmed?'

To add insult to injury, Lucasta decided to spend the day trailing around after Mrs Flanagan to observe a housekeeper at work, so she could fully immerse herself in her role, but gave this up as a bad job after ten minutes.

'You're of absolutely no use to me whatsoever. For Christ's sake, all you're doing is sitting on your arse watching telly.'

'Get the fuck out of my kitchen and don't come back till after *Oprah*!' Mrs Flanagan had screamed back at her, unable to take any more.

Then disaster had struck just as Portia and Daisy were setting off later that evening. They had arranged to drive into Dublin with Steve in the comfort of his big Jeep, but now that he'd cancelled, they were left with no choice but to take the Mini Metro. No sooner had Portia turned the key in the ignition than, there it was, the all-too-familiar chug, chug, chug sound.

'Shit! Now what?' Daisy groaned.

'Are youse having trouble with that aul' rust bucket?' It was Paddy, carting a pile of cables into the Hall.

'Oh fuck it,' Daisy whispered. 'Did he see me?'

'Youse are both looking very well tonight,' he said, leaning on the window, unable to take his eyes off Daisy, who did indeed look stunning in a strapless blue crushed velvet gown. Portia had just pulled on the only decent thing she had, which was the same white dress she'd worn to the Midsummer party. She'd scraped her hair back into a ponytail and hadn't even bothered with make-up. What's the point? she'd thought.

'Givvus a look,' Paddy said, letting Portia out of the driver's seat and getting in himself. He turned the engine over a few times and then stuck his head out of the window. 'Yeah, I think I can tell yis what the problem is all right,' he said, like a doctor giving a diagnosis. 'It's fucked. Come on, I'll drive yis.'

'Paddy, you can't!' said Daisy, panicking. 'What about the scene they're filming tonight, won't they miss you?'

'Ah, sure, they can manage without me,' he replied, gazing at her like a teenager in the throes of puppy love. If she'd asked him for a packet of fruit pastilles, he'd probably have flown through the poisoned gases of Mars to get it for her. Before either of them had a chance to protest, they were sitting side by side in the front seat of his white Hiace van, which was adorned with just about every mascot Arsenal ever produced, zooming down the motorway to Dublin.

When they arrived at the Four Seasons (in record time), neither sister could fail to notice that theirs was the only van pulling up amongst all the assembled Mercs and BMWs in the hotel car-park. The Davenports arriving in style, as usual, Portia thought.

'Paddy, you must come in with us for a drink,' she said, clambering out of the passenger side, ignoring the filthy look Daisy was flashing at her.

'Ah Jaysus, yeah, cool. I'm dying for a pint of Bulmers,'

Paddy answered, delighted with the way his evening was turning out.

'What did you have to go and do that for?' Daisy growled at her in the Ladies a few minutes later. 'Now we'll be stuck with him all night!'

'Darling, he drove us all the way here, it would have been the rudest thing imaginable for us to use him as though he were a taxi,' Portia answered.

'But he's not even wearing a dress suit! We'll stick out like sore thumbs!'

There was certainly no argument there. As they walked into the bar together, they saw Paddy chatting away to a woman dripping with diamonds and a man in black tie. Paddy did stand out a bit, dressed in his Arsenal T-shirt, jeans and trainers with fluorescent lights shining at the back of them. As Portia and Daisy approached, they were just in time to hear the tail end of a conversation he'd been having.

'So do you ride?' asked the diamond-clad woman.

'Ah, here, luv, that's a bit bleeding personal!' Paddy laughed.

'Where do you keep your horses stabled then?' asked her husband.

'Eh, where I come from, we don't really have, like, stables as such, you know? There's plenty of horses knockin' around all right, but they mostly just wander around the green in the middle of our estate.'

'Right, well, thanks again for the lift, Paddy, but we'd better go into dinner, so I suppose we'll see you back at the Hall later then?' snapped Daisy, anxious to be rid of him.

'No way am I letting my girlfriend hitch all the way back to the back arse of Kildare, especially not dressed like that. Other blokes might try it on with ya. No, youse go into the dinner and I'll just wait here for youse. I'm starving and all but I'm sure they sell peanuts or something in a posh place like this, and I'll just get a kebab on the way home,' he replied, laying it on with a trowel.

Daisy stared furiously into space but emotional blackmail always worked like a charm on Portia.

'Paddy, of course we wouldn't dream of leaving you here on your own, starving. Steve was to be with us tonight but had to cancel so there's an empty seat at our table. Won't you join us?'

'Ah Jaysus, that's very good of ya,' he said, delighted. 'Now don't be worrying, I won't make a show of yis or anything – ya just keep yer hands to yerself during the dinner, Daisy, ha, ha, ha!'

As they made their way into the packed dining room, Paddy went over to a noticeboard where the seating plan had been posted up, leaving the sisters on their own for a moment. 'You are so fucking dead when we get home, Portia. How could you have invited him? He even thinks we're an item – didn't you hear him use the GF word?' snarled Daisy.

'GF?'

'Girlfriend, idiot.'

'I never would have had you down as being such a snob, darling. He may not be dressed appropriately but it was sweet of him to drive us here and besides, you told me you'd slept with him,' replied Portia, unfazed by Daisy's rudeness.

'You're such a bloody nun, you have so much to learn about comfort sex. I was devastated over Guy; I'd have shagged anything.'

'We're at table sixty-nine, but don't let that give ya any ideas, baby,' Paddy said, suggestively patting Daisy on the bum. She darted yet another filthy glare at Portia, who calmly ignored it as they made their way to their table. These functions were always excruciatingly dull and the best you could hope for was to have friendly faces sitting at your table. They were in luck there; Portia heaved a huge sigh of relief to see Agnes and Lucy Kennedy sitting beside them, two elderly spinster sisters from Newbridge in Kildare, whom Portia knew well from her hunting days.

'My dear, how wonderful to see you,' said Agnes, rising to kiss her warmly on the cheek.

'And how well you're looking!' said Lucy. 'And sweet little Daisy, you just get prettier and prettier! And who might this be?'

'I'm Daisy's fella, howayis all?' Paddy said, introducing himself.

'Oh, we're so pleased!' they chanted in unison. 'Because, you know, we've been following everything in the newspapers, all about the film they're making at Davenport Hall and we were horrified to hear about that Guy . . . whatever his name is . . .' said Lucy.

'Van der Post,' Daisy finished the sentence for her.

'Yes, that's it! Well, we couldn't believe it when the papers all said that he'd broken up with our darling little Daisy and gone off with Ella Hepburn, who's old enough to be his grandmother!'

'Do you know, I remember during the Emergency going to see her in *Rover, Come Home* at the old Ambassador picture house in Bray, do you remember, Aggie dear? Daddy took us in the Daimler and we both cried buckets at the end . . .'

'Oh yes, Lucy, and I remember, because of the wartime rationing, we couldn't buy sweets or chocolate or any treats so Daddy gave us lumps of brown bread instead . . .'

'Gonna be a long night then,' Paddy whispered to Daisy, lighting up a cigarette. 'And them two aul' ones are sisters, are they?' Daisy nodded. 'Just think then, luv, yourself and Portia coulda ended up like them in about another two hundred years, if I hadn't come along.'

'And that's why we're so pleased you've met another lovely

gentleman, Daisy dear,' said Lucy, beaming across the table, oblivious to the fact that Daisy looked like she was going to bolt for the hills.

'Yeah, I'm delighted and all,' Paddy answered. 'I call her my Lady Chatterley. Do yis get it?'

'And what about our lovely Portia?' asked Agnes, fondly patting her hand. 'Any sign of a ring on that finger yet?'

'Oh, but don't you remember, dear?' Lucy interrupted. 'Portia's stepping out with that wonderful-looking young man whom the papers kept calling the Earl of Ireland. We did laugh at that.'

'Oh yes, dear, and there were such a lot of photographs of you both and you did make such a handsome couple, you with your beautiful slender figure and he was awfully good-looking, rather like Edward the Eighth when he was Prince of Wales; of course you're all far too young to remember, but he was the George Clooney of his day, you know, and do you remember, Aggie dear . . .? Oh, look, there he is!'

'George Clooney?' said Portia, who hadn't quite been able to keep up with the meanderings of Agnes's train of thought.

'No, dear, your gentleman friend, the "Earl of Ireland". Over there, by the door, look!'

She was right. Portia glanced over and there was Andrew. He was with a group of men, none of whom she knew, but they all seemed to be really good friends and were falling about laughing at some joke one of them had just told.

Stay cool, stay calm, her inner voice kept telling her. He hasn't seen you and even if he has, it's all going to be fine. She even surprised herself by silently thanking Susan de Courcey for so deliberately letting it slip about him and Edwina being reunited. Could you imagine if I didn't know, she thought, and if I had to hear it from him, now, first hand? It was too awful to contemplate. At least this way she was forewarned and forearmed.

Daisy had clocked him too and leant forward to whisper, 'I don't fucking believe this! What's Andrew doing here?'

Portia just looked at her, imploring her to be quiet, and calmly resumed the chat with Agnes and Lucy as though nothing had happened. Both the starter and main course had been served and he still hadn't seen her. Or, if he had, Portia said to herself, he's avoiding me as well. She was doubly glad to be sitting beside the Kennedys whose stream-of-consciousness one-way dialogue didn't allow for any interruptions, which meant that she could get away with just smiling and nodding in response.

Pretty soon, the meal was over and the dancing was under way. Agnes and Lucy had kindly agreed to stable Daisy's horses for her, so their mission was accomplished and they could now get the hell out of there. But just as they stood to say their goodbyes, Paddy grabbed a passing waiter.

'That dinner was nicer than my ma's Christmas dinner any day, but I can't finish it. Can you get me a doggy bag?'

The waiter looked at him for a moment, wondering if he was serious. (Never in the history of the Four Seasons Hotel had anyone asked for a doggy bag, ever.) But his silver service training soon came to the fore and he politely asked Paddy to wait; that he'd see what he could do.

Next the band started to play a medley of Elvis songs and Paddy nearly jumped out of his skin. 'The King! Come on, luv, what are ya waiting for?' Then, without giving her time to breathe, he whisked Daisy off on to the floor and launched into a series of mad gyrations while she screamed at him in vain that her ankle was still dodgy.

Shit, thought Portia, who had wanted to slip quietly away as soon as possible.

'And how is your dear mother?' Agnes was asking. 'Still as eccentric as ever? I remember going up to Davenport Hall once and I interrupted a naked seance she was giving. She never forgave me . . .'

Portia was about to answer, when, without her knowing quite how it happened, Andrew was beside her.

'Oh look, there he is now, the Earl of Ireland himself. How do you do?' laughed Lucy.

Portia could feel her knees begin to buckle but she willed herself to stand up straight and meet his gaze. 'We're local celebrities, it seems,' she said, blushing.

He didn't reply, but ran his fingers nervously through his hair and shuffled around a bit. After what seemed like ages, he met her gaze. 'Just out of curiosity, do you ever return phone calls?'

'Andrew, there was no need for us to talk. We've nothing to talk about. I just want you to know that I'm really happy for you.' She was pleased she'd got that in first and only hoped her voice wasn't wobbling too much.

'Wish I had your generosity of spirit. I'll give you this though, you certainly don't let the grass grow under your feet, do you?'

There was no mistaking it, his tone was harsh and bitter. For the life of her, Portia couldn't understand him. You'd think I was the one happily reunited with an ex from the way he's speaking, she thought, instead of it being the other way around. She was just about to ask what he meant by that remark when he spoke again – gently and more like himself, this time.

'Portia, I really have to speak to you, can I call you tomorrow? Maybe we could meet up if you're free? It's just that—'

'Andrew darling, there you are.' Portia turned to see

Edwina, who'd glided up beside him looking as immaculate as ever. 'And you're Portia, aren't you?' she purred, stretching out an impeccably manicured hand. 'We've met before.'

'Yes, hello,' was the best Portia could come up with, silently cursing herself for coming out without make-up and thinking that she must look like a big unscrubbed potato beside Edwina, who looked effortlessly like a goddess. A silence followed whilst she desperately racked her brains for something to say that would make her sound casual and relaxed but she couldn't think of a single thing. Her eyes darted around the room frantically looking for either Paddy or Daisy to come and bail her out, but they were still dancing, or, in Paddy's case, mosh pitting.

'You know your picture was all over the tabloids,' said Edwina, breaking the silence with her tinkling, cocktail-party voice. 'We did laugh about it, didn't we, Andrew? They said you were a scullery maid in some creepy haunted house somewhere. And then there was a picture of you wrapped around some guy . . .'

Although not fully understanding her, Portia knew that she could take no more. Ten generations of breeding rose to the fore as she stood up tall and drew on all her reserves of dignity. 'You really mustn't believe everything you read in the papers,' she said and, turning on her heel, she was gone.

She made it as far as the sumptuous Ladies powder room, thinking that she'd lie low for a few minutes until Paddy had finished hurling himself about the dance floor and they could retreat to the safety of his van. Her heart was pounding and a weak, whooshing rush was beginning to come over her. The room was full, but at least there was no one there she knew, which spared her from the torture of having to make small talk. She was mistaken, though, if she thought that the agonies of the evening were over. Just as she was running soothing, icy water over her wrists and splashing it liberally all over her temples, the door burst open and in swanned Edwina, purring into her mobile phone for all to hear.

'Kate, darling, you must understand, I know it's one a.m. in the morning but you're my wedding planner and I'm paying you to be on twenty-four-hour call. I'm stuck at a ghastly do in the Four Seasons and we have an emergency! They have *exactly the same* cream linen napkins here which I picked out for my reception with *exactly the same* burgundy bows tied around them. Now, I'm trying my very best to stay calm here but you're going to have to get on to Brown Thomas first thing tomorrow . . .' The Ladies was so packed that Portia was able to slip outside without the other woman even noticing she was there. Well, at least that's one bit of luck, she thought on her way to the car-park to wait for the others, delighted at least to be out of there in one piece. Never once did it cross her mind that Edwina's performance had been a one-woman-show staged solely for her benefit.

If the evening had been disastrous, the long, bumpy drive home in Paddy's van did nothing to help matters. Daisy had bagged the window seat, as physically far removed from Paddy as she could get, and promptly fell fast asleep. All Portia wanted was a little peace and quiet to marshal her thoughts, but no such luck. She was completely squished up against Paddy, so that his swinging Arsenal mascots kept hitting her forehead. He was delighted, though, clearly seeing this as a golden opportunity to inveigle himself with his girlfriend's one and only normal relation. They'd driven as far as Newlands Cross, almost halfway home, before he even paused for breath.

'So, I'd have to say, definitely like, that nineteen ninety-eight was the happiest year of me life. Now, that wasn't the first time that Arsenal won the double, though; they won it in nineteen seventy-one as well, but I wasn't even born, so that's fuck all use to me. So, tell us, Daisy, how do you feel about Arsène Wenger's managerial record?'

'She's asleep,' said Portia.

'During me Arsenal story? Are ya sure?' he asked, not taking his eyes off the motorway.

'Mmm, out for the count,' she answered, envying Daisy all the more for her ability to conk out anywhere.

'Gift. It's just I've been meaning to say to ya for ages now, thanks for being such a good aul' skin.'

'Sorry?' Portia was genuinely at a loss.

'The night of the Midsummer party . . . do ya not remember? I was pissed out of me gimp, off me bleedin' bickies, I was so twisted, locked; totally out of me game I was . . .'

'Bit squiffy then, do you mean?'

'You said it, luv. Anyway, I just wanted to say to ya, yer're a grand looking aul' bird and all that. Jaysus, yer're a bit of a ride really, considering ya must be coming up to forty.'

Portia let this pass.

'Sure, I've a sister yer age and she's a granny now . . . not a word of a lie!' Paddy laughed. 'Anyway, it's not that I don't think yer're lovely looking, for an aul' one, but I just want to say sorry for crashing out on yer bed that night. And I swear I kept me hands to meself.'

With a jolt, Portia remembered. That was the night Steve had told her about the rezoning of the Hall; she'd been desperately upset and he'd given her a sleeping pill to help her rest. She had a vague memory of someone being in bed beside her, and had mistakenly thought it was Andrew.

'I just got a bit lost on me way to Daisy's room, ya know?' Paddy was saying. 'That house is like a bleedin' maze. But as soon as I woke up and saw that I was in bed with the wrong sister, I got the fuck out of there like ya wouldn't believe. So nothing happened, luv, I swear on Sven Goran Erikson's baldy head. But ya won't mention it to Daisy, sure ya won't?'

'Of course not.'

'Ah, yer're an aul' sport. I knew you'd be cool about it. But, Jaysus, suppose something had happened? Two sisters on the one night? I'd feel like I was in an episode of *EastEnders*. Could ya imagine if anyone had seen us?'

Chapter Twenty-Two

Bridie Nolan's day had not got off to a good start, she having spent a wholly unproductive morning in her brother-in-law's architect's office bashing out plans for the future of Davenport Hall.

'How many times do I have to tell ya, Bridie?' said Mickey as he mopped up some coffee which her five-year-old son Hughie had sloshed all over his blueprints. (His final design for the Mausoleum at Davenport Hall, as it happened, which was to be completely gutted and turned into a bowling alley.) 'Do yerself a favour and put a bloody match to the Hall and then we can start clean again from scratch. Here I am slaving away on plans for the fast-track housing on the Davenport land and you want to ruin it by keeping that ugly aul' shithole right in the middle of the estate.'

'Ah, Shamie has to be very careful in his position. He gave me a big fecking lecture last night about how Caesar's wife should be above suspicion or some shite like that. I think he's seen that film *Gladiator* once too often. Anyway, he's in enough trouble with the lads from the Inland Revenue without having an arson charge hanging over him as well. No, I've a miles better idea than that.'

'What's that, Bridie?'

'The Davenport Hall restoration project. I'm going to get a documentary crew to follow me around the kip and film me and Shamie and the kids lovingly putting our stamp on the place. Shamie has a pal, a producer in RTE, who'll direct it for us – mind you, Shamie says he can barely direct piss into a toilet bowl, but sure he'll have to do. Then I'll give guided tours of the place when it's all finished, to show the "before" and "after", you know. Jackie Kennedy did it in the White House and it did her no fecking harm. And it'll be a great vote-catcher altogether. Jeremy Irons with his pink castle in Cork can feck off.'

Then, as she and Hughie were leaving the office, she bumped into Lottie O'Loughlin on Ballyroan Main Street.

'Well, hello, cover girl!' said Lottie delightedly. 'I'm surprised you haven't been in to me to buy ten copies for yourself to keep!'

'What are ya on about?' replied Bridie, at a loss.

'Go into the shop and see!' said Lottie, crossing the street as though she couldn't get away fast enough. 'I'm on my lunch break, so just leave me the money on the counter.'

A less thick-skinned person would almost have got the impression that Lottie was avoiding them, but over-sensitivity had never been a failing of Bridie's. She dragged Hughie inside Spar, bribing him with the promise of an ice-cream if he behaved for two minutes. She quickly cast her eagle eye over all the titles on the magazine stand, but saw nothing untoward. Then, looking over at the stack of newspapers in the corner, she nearly passed out. There it was, in glorious Technicolor, the photo the press had taken of her when she was changing her laddered tights in the car on the night of the Davenports' Midsummer party. All you could see was the astonished look on her face as the camera flash went off, with her gusset huge in the foreground and her wobbly, thundering thighs straddling the dashboard of the car.

MEET THE NEW LADY OF THE MANOR! screamed the banner headline.

BRIDIE NOLAN CLIMBS THE 'LADDER' OF SUCCESS.

TODAY'S POLL: IS THIS BUM BIGGER THAN THE GRAND CANYON? IS THIS BUM LUMPIER THAN COTTAGE CHEESE? TO VOTE YES, PHONE 1850 123123, TO VOTE NO, PHONE 1850 223344.

Without even pausing for thought, Bridie whipped out her mobile phone and pressed the speed-dial button.

'Hello, Shamie Joe Nolan Junior speaking.'

'Shamie! It's a fecking *catastrophe*! Drop whatever it is you're doing and get on to your solicitor immediately! You'll be able to paper the fecking walls with the number of legal writs and libel actions we're going to take!'

'I don't think so, luv,' he replied nervously. 'I've a bit of news for you too.'

Meanwhile, Lucasta's big moment had arrived. She'd spent a wonderful morning being preened and pampered by the unfortunate Serge who was dumped with the task of transforming her into a nineteenth-century housekeeper.

'There's nothing like a challenge, as I tell all my paramours,' he'd cheerfully said to Jimmy D. earlier in the day, 'but I think I'll need a good two hours before she's camera ready. And, please don't think I'm teaching Grandma how to suck eggs here, but you might wanna think about using a lot of soft focus in this scene.'

Being the centre of attention was not exactly a hardship for Lucasta and, as Serge patiently washed and combed out her matted hair, she was in heaven.

'So, Lady Davenport, when is the last time you had your hair done?'

'Oh darling, do the words *Sergeant Pepper's Lonely Hearts Club Band* mean anything to you?' she laughed in response. Serge just smiled back, not having a clue what she was on about.

Exactly two hours later, Caroline knocked crisply on the door of the make-up bus, ready to escort her to the location, which happened to be the newly transformed Ballroom. 'Dear God, I hardly recognized you,' she said, on seeing Lucasta sitting in the make-up chair as Serge whipped off the plastic gown that was covering her shoulders to reveal the magic he'd woven.

I know!' squealed Serge, thrilled with the result. 'I'm so talented I need to have a lie down. David Blaine should really worry.'

The transformation was indeed miraculous. Lucasta was clad in a Victorian housekeeper's costume, which comprised a long black crinoline skirt and a tight black blouse worn high at the neck, with just a simple cameo brooch at her throat. Serge had painstakingly teased out her long hair and coiled it around her ears, with perfect attention to period detail. The corset she was wearing nipped in her expansive waist giving her an almost girlish, hourglass figure.

'Lady Davenport, you look wonderful!' said Caroline in a rare burst of enthusiasm.

'Thank you, darling, but I'm afraid I'm in character now, so if you could just address me as Miss Murphy from now on, that would be terrific,' she replied, doing her best to sound like Meryl Streep.

As they walked from the make-up bus inside the Hall and on into the Ballroom, Lucasta, never one to be at a loss for words, gasped. The design crew had indeed worked miracles and the result was astonishing. In just a few short days they had repainted the great domed ceiling, removed all the bin

259

liners that had been sellotaped to it and replastered every patch on the roof, which had gaping holes in it. Then they'd removed all the pots and pans strewn over the floor to catch the rain, and polished the wooden parquet till it shone for probably the first time in about a hundred years. In addition, they had draped lush velvet tapestries all over the walls, which covered the damp patches perfectly and also absorbed the awful echoing sound, which was the norm in that room. The final touch was the candlelight, which twinkled from the candelabra dotted tastefully around the room.

'Holy fuck, I didn't recognize the old kip!' gasped Lucasta. 'This is Davenport Hall, isn't it?'

Jimmy D. strolled through a group of extras who were practising waltz steps in the middle of the floor and warmly kissed Lucasta on each cheek.

'Well, don't you look fancy, Lady Davenport,' he said, simultaneously grinning at her and puffing on a cigar.

'I'm in character now, darling, so I'm only answering to Miss Murphy from now on, but what an amazing job you've done here! I feel like I'm stepping back in time, or having a past-life flashback, which happens to me quite often, you know. But you mustn't worry a bit, I want you to know that I'm very at home in Victorian times. And I've evoked all of our ancestral spirits to help me. Now, you're my director so go on then, direct me.'

'Piece of cake. In this scene, Brent and his mother Blanche are waltzing with the other couples while Magnolia looks moodily out the window. So when Johnny cues you, here's what's gonna happen. You're outside in the corridor and, on cue, you're gonna come rushing into the middle of the dance floor and call out for your mistress in terrible distress. Magnolia will go over to you, ask you what's the matter, you deliver your line and then we cut. Got it?'

'Oh yes, yes I think so,' replied Lucasta, not really following, 'I'm just a little nervous, that's all. You know, new career and all that.'

Jimmy D. then nodded at Johnny and sauntered over to his director's chair, where Ella and Guy were sitting side by side, deep in conversation and totally ignoring Montana who sat demurely behind them. Or rather, Guy was chatting away while Ella just smoked a Sobranie cigarette looking bored.

'Astounding how well this place can look with a little effort, isn't it, darling?' Guy was saying in his Southern accent. Ella gave the tiniest nod of assent, without even looking at him.

'You know, my love, if someone took this dump in hand and put a little money into it, it could be really something. A romantic Irish love nest about as far removed from LA as you can possibly get, huh?' he said, brushing a stray hair away from the voluminous folds of her crinoline ball gown. Now he had her attention. She looked at him with just a flicker of interest in her eyes.

'Ah, yer majesty, how's it going?' Paddy said cheerfully to Lucasta, delighted to see her.

'Not now, darling, I'm immersed in character,' she replied distractedly. 'I've got to dig deep into my emotional reservoir to prepare for this scene.'

'Oh right, yeah,' said Paddy, well used to actors behaving like self-absorbed loonies. 'So, like, what are ya thinking about then?'

'It's nineteen eighty-two. I've just given birth to Daisy,' Lucasta said with her eyes closed, as though she was in a trance. 'I'm lying in bed feeding the baby when my husband bursts in and takes her from me to use her as collateral in a poker game he was losing.'

'Jaysus, ya must have been in awful trouble with the social workers,' said Paddy sympathetically.

'OK, first positions, everyone, we need to go for this now!' cried Johnny at the top of his voice. There was a general commotion as the crew took up their battle stations and the extras moved into place, all of them looking resplendent in Victorian evening dress.

A silence descended on the set, broken only by the sound of a phone ringing some distance away.

'Disconnect that bloody phone while we're shooting!' Johnny bellowed.

'It's coming from the Library,' said Caroline, clipping out of the door. 'Don't worry, I'll get it!' Moments later she returned, nodding at Johnny to indicate that the problem had been dealt with.

'OK, people,' said Johnny, 'here we go, this is not a rehearsal! And roll sound!'

'Speed!' called Paddy, winking at Lucasta and giving her a thumbs-up sign.

'Roll camera!'

'Shot!'

'Mark it!'

'Scene seventy-nine, take one.'

'And . . . *action!*'

An invisible string quartet struck up a Strauss waltz and the extras launched into their dancing; gentlemen in white tie elegantly swirled their partners in huge crinoline hoop skirts around the makeshift dance floor. Lucasta went out into the corridor to await her cue, clutching a battered page of script which had her one solitary line written on it.

'Ya look like a right dog's dinner,' said Mrs Flanagan, who by a total coincidence had decided to scrub the skirting boards outside the Ballroom, the first time in about thirty years that they'd seen the wipe of a cloth.

Totally ignoring her, Lucasta paced up and down the corridor, whispering her line over and over like a mantra.

'Are ya going to say it like that?' said Mrs Flanagan, squeezing out a sponge into a bucket of water.

'Bugger off. Don't make me come out of character.'

'No, I'm just saying, I never heard anyone out of the serving classes talk in a posh accent like that. Ya sound like the bleedin' Queen Mother.'

Before Lucasta had a chance to respond, Johnny was frantically waving at her from the other side of the door.

'Cue!' he mouthed silently at her.

'Oh Jesus,' she said, momentarily startled, before making her grand entrance. Marching purposefully into the middle of the dance floor she almost bashed the poor waltzing extras out of her way before delivering her line.

'Miss Magnolia! The potato crop is after failing to be sure! It's famine, I tell you! And the dispossessed tenant farmers are baying for your blood at the back door, begorrah!' she delivered in a cut-glass accent which a 1930s debutante would be proud of.

'Cut!' called Jimmy D., getting out of his canvas chair. 'Take five, people! Lady Davenport, may I have a word?'

'Yes, of course, darling,' replied Lucasta as he took her aside.

'That was, em, an interesting interpretation of the role but I feel the character is a little more working class.'

'Do you think I'm too regal? Yes, I've been told that before,' she replied, nodding sagely.

'I told her that outside and she wouldn't listen,' said Mrs Flanagan, who was now miraculously scrubbing the floor right under their feet. 'And another thing. There's a historical inaccuracy in the script, let me tell you.'

'What's that?' said Jimmy D.

She picked up the tattered piece of paper which Lucasta had discarded outside in the corridor.

'Now I could have this arseways, but I don't think they had Hoovers in eighteen sixty-four, did they?'

'I'm sorry?' asked Jimmy D., taking the page of script from her.

'Look, right there! It says, "Magnolia Hoovers at the window." Now, they may have had brushes and sweeping pans then, but they definitely didn't have Hoovers.'

'Magnolia *hovers* in the background, you moron!' Lucasta hissed at her.

'And what about her accent? I see me fair share of films and I've yet to see a member of the working classes talk like that. She sounds posher than Queen Victoria.'

Lucasta was about to snap her nose off when Jimmy D. said, 'Mmm. Interesting. I'll tell you what. Lady Davenport, great work, we've got you in the can. Why don't you let Serge here take you back to make-up and get you back to normal? You must be exhausted after turning in such a professional performance.'

'Do you mean I'm finished?'

'That's a wrap for you, well done!' he replied, clicking his fingers at Serge, who jumped to attention and rushed to escort Lucasta back outside.

'Well, I must say, that was remarkably easy,' she could be heard saying to Serge as they left the Ballroom. 'Acting's a complete doddle really. So why do actors make such a great fuss over nothing?'

'Because they don't all have your talent,' replied Serge, his voice growing fainter.

As soon as they were out of sight, Jimmy D. bellowed at the top of his voice, 'Wardrobe! Get a costume on this woman immediately! Places, everyone, we're taking it from the top!' Then, beaming down at a shell-shocked Mrs Flanagan, he said, 'So. Like all good little understudies, are you ready to step into the spotlight?'

Chapter Twenty-Three

The last person in the world Portia ever thought she would have found herself arguing with was Steve, but, whether she liked it or not, that's exactly what happened. She had begged and cajoled him on the phone, but he just wouldn't take no for an answer. And so, completely against her better judgement, she found herself sitting in the passenger seat of his Jeep on their way to a meeting in, of all places, Chief Justice Michael de Courcey's house.

'I don't understand what your problem is,' Steve said as they sped down the driveway. 'You've no idea the favour he's doing us. He's only got about a half-hour to spare and it's incredibly decent of him to give us his time so freely.'

'But whatever it is, didn't you already discuss it with him at your meeting in Dublin? I just don't understand why I need to be here,' she said, pleadingly.

'Trust me. You do. Look, tell me where to go if you think I'm being intrusive, but is this something to do with Andrew de Courcey?'

For once, Portia was delighted to have the distraction of the hordes of press and TV cameras gathered at the front gates. As they sped through them, the crowd parted a bit and the customary round of flashes went off in their faces. Portia was well used to the photographers by now, was even on first-name terms with them, but Steve wasn't.

'One of these days those bastards will cause an accident,' he swore under his breath. 'Do you know what my secretary told me the other day? Apparently there was a photo of you and me in one of those bloody rags. She gave me a right slagging about it.'

'Oh, I shouldn't worry,' Portia replied. 'No one pays the slightest bit of attention to the tabloids. And besides, they've been big allies of Mummy's ever since the news broke about the Nolans buying us out, you know. "Save the Hall" and "The Fall of the Hall", all that sort of thing. Daisy and I think she creeps down here at dawn each morning feeding them stories. Nothing that woman does would ever surprise me.'

Steve smiled a bit, just at the mention of Daisy's name. 'And how is she doing after the whole Guy van der Post debacle?' he asked shyly.

Portia glanced sideways at him, unsure whether or not to tell him that Paddy was now leading the field in the race for Daisy's affections. She decided not to, on the grounds that discretion was always the better part of valour. Although she certainly would be letting Daisy know how Steve was practically busting a gut to help the family, probably with her foremost in his mind.

Well, that's the difference between him and Andrew, she thought. Steve clearly adores the ground Daisy walks on and is bending over backwards to help all of us for her sake. Whereas Andrew . . . needless to say, she hadn't heard a word from him since the Hunt Ball two days ago. For someone who'd always prided herself on being a good judge of character, Portia was now having to admit that she couldn't have been more wrong about him if she'd tried. Even thinking about all the promises he'd made her was enough to make her blood boil. She remembered the night they'd sat together in the Yellow Drawing Room till dawn, plotting about how they'd renovate the Hall and turn it into a super-posh country house hotel. He'd even offered to invest money in the scheme. Talk about lip service, she thought.

No. Whatever way she looked at it, there was only one conclusion that made any sense of his behaviour. He'd just been killing time with her, nothing else. He and Edwina were clearly very much a couple again, no doubt about it. There was nothing for it but to accept that she'd been simply a harmless diversion to while away the long summer nights for as long as he stayed at his parents, waiting on his penthouse apartment to be finished. And when Portia thought of his mother, it was hard not to blame Andrew for wanting to escape to Davenport Hall, if only to get away from that old cow.

Her eyes welled up a bit when she thought of how unlucky she'd been to fall for someone who was so clearly out of her league. It was just the callousness of it all that upset her. The way a guy could sweep her off her feet, make her believe that they really had something together and then . . . *hasta la fucking vista*, all over in a heartbeat. Like it or not, it was time she faced the hard, cold reality. He was just out of an eight-year relationship and was only interested in having a final fling before he inevitably went back to the perfect Edwina.

She glanced sideways at Steve, who was concentrating on the road. 'Why is it that I do this drive at least four times a week and still manage to hit the same potholes?' he was saying, intruding on her thoughts. For a moment, she was tempted to ask him if this was the way all guys behaved or had she just had rotten luck with Andrew. She decided against it, remembering that it had been a very long time indeed since he'd produced a girlfriend. So long, in fact, that Lucasta, with her customary lack of tact, used regularly to tease him about being gay. ('I think you and Serge would be sooo sweet together!' was her latest.)

And to think I was worried about barging into Andrew's parents' house for this bloody meeting, she thought. She was fairly certain that the chances of bumping into him were slim (his apartment in Dublin must be finished by now, she reasoned, so what would he be doing in Ballyroan?) but, after that awful episode in the Four Seasons, you never could be really sure.

Well, if he was at home, this time he could be the one to be embarrassed.

Portia was in luck. No sign of his Mercedes parked in the immaculate front garden. She heaved a sigh of relief as she and Steve crunched up the pink gravel to the front door, remembering the last time she'd been there and how Andrew had gallantly escorted her to the car and even helped pile Lucasta and Daisy in. And then sent flowers the next day . . . Automatically, she forced herself to brush the thought aside. That was then, and this was now.

Steve rang the doorbell and Portia wearily braced herself for another encounter with Mrs de Courcey but the Chief Justice himself answered.

'Come in, come in,' he said, struggling to insert a pair of gold cufflinks into a silk dress shirt he was wearing. 'Will you follow me into my study?'

Portia and Steve did as they were told, and he led them into a beautiful oak-panelled room just to the left of the hall door. Once again, Portia was struck by the huge contrast between Davenport Hall and the sheer, unadulterated luxury of this ultra-modern palace. She was almost walking on tiptoe across the deep white carpet, she was so afraid of leaving a mark; she could see Steve doing the same. As far as the de Courceys are concerned, I must live in a mud hut compared with this, she thought.

'Sit down, please,' said the Chief Justice, for once toning his booming voice down a little. Then, turning to Portia, he smiled kindly. 'My dear young lady, I must apologize for all the secrecy attached to this meeting, but as I said to Steve the other night, things are at a critical stage so we can't be too careful. That's why I insisted on our meeting here, where we can talk freely.'

Portia looked blankly at him, utterly at sea.

'You and your family have been through a dreadful time recently, I hear,' he said, sitting deep into his leather swivel armchair.

'Well, yes,' she replied, wondering what in hell he had up his sleeve. Surely it couldn't possibly be anything to do with Andrew? No, she thought, because then why would Steve be here?

'I don't wish to alarm you, my dear, but the fact is, I have some news which may be of great interest to both you and your family.'

Daisy often used to say that if the presenters of the reality TV show *How Clean is your House?* ever visited Davenport Hall, they'd have to be treated for shock. Her own bedroom was a case in point; every time she opened the door, she wondered if she'd been burgled, such was its customary disarray. But this time, she really did get the shock of her life.

Egged on by Portia, she'd tried to spend some time packing her things – or more correctly throwing all of her clothes on to the bed before eventually stuffing them into bin liners. But, never a great one for applying herself, she gave this up as a boring job after five minutes and went out to exercise Kat

Slater. When she came back a few hours later, she couldn't believe her eyes.

Every stitch of clothing belonging to her had been tidily put away, the bed had been made and for the first time she could ever remember, the windows had actually been cleaned. For a split second, she wondered if Mrs Flanagan had completely lost it and now decided to clean up the Hall, just as they were moving out. But then she noticed a CD player on her dressing table, with a stack of Metallica CDs beside it. And above the bed was a life-size poster of Elvis Presley. And hanging from the bedpost was a pair of Arsenal boxer shorts . . .

'Where is he?' she screeched, not caring who overheard. 'I will fucking *kill* him!'

'So what do you make of it all?' Steve said to Portia in a low voice as the Chief Justice briefly excused himself to answer the door.

Portia rubbed her temples and tried to catch her breath. 'If this was happening in a film, I wouldn't believe it,' was all she could say in reply.

'There's an awful lot of ground work to be done, but if we pull together, we'll nail him.'

'So what happens now?'

'As Michael just explained, a lot depends on this contact he has in the planning office and exactly how much he's willing to put on the record. But even if we can't get him to co-operate, we certainly should have enough to open a full judicial inquiry—'

'To hell with that!' interrupted the Chief Justice, who'd just re-entered the study and was pulling on a dinner jacket. 'We'll get a nice, juicy Tribunal out of this at the very least. "The de Courcey Tribunal" – doesn't that have a good ring to it? I could retire a wealthy, happy man after a few years in Dublin

271

Castle knowing that I was instrumental in putting Shamie Joe Nolan where he belongs. Behind bars.'

Portia smiled.

'What?' asked Steve.

'Oh, nothing, I just had a mental picture of Bridie Nolan visiting him in Mountjoy prison, wearing one of her outfits.'

Steve laughed. 'Yeah, the other prisoners will think he's married to a Russian mail-order bride.'

'It'll happen, believe you me,' replied the Chief Justice. 'None of his cronies or his golfing buddies in Government Buildings can get him out of this one. The facts are there, plain and simple. A senior Member of Parliament bought the Davenport land cheaply in the full knowledge that a motion to rezone it was in the bag, thereby trebling its value. It's cases like this that make me regret that we ever scrapped capital punishment.'

Portia turned to him, with her eyes beginning to fill. 'You've been so kind. I really don't know how to thank you.'

'I hate to see injustice, my dear, I'm just doing my job really. Although, if you ever saw your way to introducing me to the lovely Ella Hepburn, I'd be eternally grateful. Huge fan, you know. Ever since she appeared in that superb Hitchcock thriller *Mental.*'

She smiled up at him, and for the first time noticed that he and Andrew had exactly the same ice-blue eyes. 'It's the least I can do.'

'That really would make my day,' he replied and, for a split second, Portia reddened, remembering how she'd taken a dislike to him when they'd first met and wondering how on earth she could have misjudged him so badly. 'And now I'm afraid I'm going to have to be very rude and excuse myself,' he went on. 'That was my driver at the door so I really must dash, I'm already late as it is.'

'Going anywhere nice?' Steve asked politely as he showed them out.

'The Unicorn restaurant in Dublin,' he replied. 'For a wedding rehearsal dinner. And the wedding's not for another week, you know. Dreadful waste of time, if you ask me. In my day, you had one wedding day and that was it, but now all these Americanisms are creeping in – bachelor parties and rehearsal dinners and baby showers. But the bride wants it to be a three-day extravaganza. She's quite a famous model, actually; perhaps you know her? Edwina Moynihan?'

Chapter Twenty-Four

'YOU HAVE PULLED DOWN YOUR KNICKERS AND SHAT ALL OVER MY CAREER, YOU STUPID FUCK-ING BITCH!' Lucasta's screaming could be heard as far away as Ballyroan.

'That's showbiz, dear heart,' Mrs Flanagan replied coolly, standing at the door of the trailer she'd been given to rest in between takes. 'Get fecking used to it.' Then, calling out at the top of her voice to no one in particular, 'Security? Could this person be removed please? I've more shots to do this afternoon and yer one here is messing up me process!'

'Is everything OK, ladies?' Johnny asked innocently on his way to grab some lunch in the catering truck.

'No! Everything is not all right,' Lucasta snarled. 'I now know exactly how Bette Davis felt in *All About Eve* when her career was cruelly snatched from her by a conniving bloody bitch!'

'Excuse me, I've a few things I need in me caravan, Johnny,' said Mrs Flanagan, totally ignoring her. 'Can ya bring me a gluten-free meal and a bowl of M and Ms with all the brown ones taken out, and, emm . . .' She paused, trying to think of all the other ludicrous demands rock stars insisted on before live gigs, which she'd read about in gossip magazines. 'And twenty, no, forty John Player Blue and a twelve-inch portable telly. Oh yeah, and no snow, no show, whatever that means, so you better get me a bowl of snow, in fact maybe I should just get me own personal chef.'

Johnny rolled his eyes to heaven. 'You create a star, you create a monster, I've seen it ten thousand times before,' he whispered to Lucasta. 'Ehh, yeah, sure, I'll get someone on to that for you right away!' he called up to Mrs Flanagan, who was still standing at the door of her trailer, humming the theme tune from *A Star is Born*, just in case she hadn't pissed Lucasta off enough.

'With the Ascendant Masters as my witnesses,' Lucasta growled threateningly at her, 'I tell you this. By the laws of the universe, there is a boulder of bad karma on its way to you.'

'Oh, and another thing,' Mrs Flanagan called after Johnny as he disappeared from view, 'get me some carbonated water, with the fizz taken out of it. And none of that Eau de Davenport shite. I wouldn't flush me toilet with it.'

'Can I just ask what the fuck you thought you were doing?'

'Love, you're standing in me sun, can ya just move out of the way a bit?'

Daisy stomped furiously to one side and glared down at Paddy who was sunbathing at her feet. He'd stripped to the waist and his scrawny, spotty body was getting redder by the minute.

'Did you honestly think that you could just move in with me without telling me first?' she yelled, oblivious to the stares she was attracting from the rest of the crew who'd come outside to enjoy the sun on their lunch break.

'Don't be getting narky, baby, yer're wrecking me buzz,' he said, hauling himself up on to one elbow so he could light a fag. 'This is just a natural progression in our relationship. There's feck all point in me shelling out cash in that useless b. & b. in the town when we're sleeping together anyway. By the way, I hope me Elvis poster isn't a problem for ya, I broke up with me last girlfriend because she criticized his performance in *Jailhouse Rock*.'

'I don't give a tuppenny fuck about your last girlfriend! Are you listening to me? I want you and Elvis Presley out of my room *now*!'

Paddy lay back down on the grass again, cool as a breeze. 'All right, so, luv, yer're an old-fashioned chick, ya don't wanna live with me, I can respect that.'

'If your stuff isn't gone in the next five minutes, Paddy, I'm warning you, it all goes out the window!' she shouted over her shoulder at him, stomping towards the Hall.

Paddy nonchalantly took another pull from his cigarette. 'Nothing else for it then. Plan B it is.'

The combined furies of hell had no wrath to match Lucasta's as she stormed her way to the drinks cabinet in the Library. She was ranting something under her breath about wreaking vengeance when the phone rang beside her.

'Whoever the fuck this is, you've got a really shitty sense of timing,' she barked into the mouthpiece.

'Lucasta? This is Andrew de Courcey. I just wondered if I could have a word with Portia? It's really important.'

'You've some fucking cheek ringing this house. Now piss off and leave us alone before I set my cats on you, arsehole.' Banging the phone down, she poured herself a treble gin and tonic, lit a cigarette with a trembling hand and left the room.

Seconds later the phone rang again, but this time there was no one around to hear.

★

'If you think I'm just going to take the children and hide away in the Isle of Man like some feckin' fugitive, you've another think coming, Shamie Nolan.'

'Ah, it's not that straightforward, darling,' Shamie replied, shifting uncomfortably in his armchair. 'Ya wouldn't understand, it's complicated.'

Now he'd done it.

'Are ya saying that I'm some kind of thick? Is that it? Me, that hauled you up from fecking nowhere? I have not spent the last twenty fecking years of me life shaking hands and planting trees and freezing me arse off at the back of the halls while you made yer boring aul' speeches for this!'

'Now, darlin', it's not as bad as all that. Sure, the lads in the County Council are hardly going to do the dirty on an aul' pal like me, are they? There's not one of them would have their holiday villas in Marbella or their children in private schools if it wasn't for me and the odd brown envelope I'd throw their way. The Planning Office above in Dublin can try to clean up their act all they like but the fact is this is the only way anyone gets anything done in this country.'

'I hope to Jaysus you have a better defence than that worked out, ya thick gobshite,' replied his loving wife, 'or else we're all fucked.'

'Sure, darling, these aul' Tribunals go on for years and years and everyone knows nothing happens at the end of them. Maybe a couple of moany letters in the papers giving out about taxpayers' money being wasted, but that's about all. I'm just trying to get as much as I can out of the country while the going's good, just in case.'

'Just in case what?'

'Ah, don't be worrying, luv. It'll never come to that.'

★

Mrs Flanagan was a complete natural. After her first take, even Montana rushed over to congratulate her. 'You're sooo wonderful in this part!' she raved. 'It's, like, so rare when an actor blends seamlessly into the role, it's beautiful to see.'

'It certainly never happens to some people who call themselves actors,' said Guy, pointedly addressing Montana, 'unless they happen to be playing alcoholic porn stars.'

'You know, you were so realistic, when you said the potato famine had begun, I almost felt hungry,' laughed Montana, gamely choosing to ignore his jibes.

'Ooh, she's hungry, better lock up all your lettuce leaves,' he went on, 'not to mention your drinks cabinet.'

Montana blushed, but said nothing.

'I never realized he was such a wanker,' said Mrs Flanagan, shaking her head. Then, whispering conspiratorially to Montana, she said, 'Listen, if ya ever fancy a nice gin and tonic, luv, I'm yer girl, I'll sort ya out, no bother.'

Novice that she was to the pecking order on set, Mrs Flanagan then unwittingly broke the most important unwritten rule of all by sauntering up to Ella Hepburn and addressing her directly.

'Suppose ya didn't recognize me all done up like this, did ya?' she said.

Ella just looked straight ahead, totally ignoring her.

'By the way, you and me have more in common than you'd think,' Mrs Flanagan went on, under the mistaken impression that they were bonding. 'Do ya know, we were born in the same year?'

Ella, whose age was a closely guarded state secret, now turned to glare at her.

'Yeah, that's right! Now yer're looking a lot better than I am, what with all the work you've had done and all, but if ya don't mind me saying, yer hands are a bit of a giveaway, luv.'

I'm telling ya, when you die, the only way they'll be able to tell yer real age is by cutting ya in two and counting all the rings.'

Montana had to bite her lip to stop herself from guffawing.

'Come on, Mrs Flanagan, let's get out of everyone's way while they set up the reverse-angle shot,' she said, steering her well out of the line of fire.

'Reverse-angle what?'

'Oh. Basically, we do exactly the same thing all over again, except this time they set up the camera and sound from the opposite angle, so that Jimmy D. can intercut the scene later,' she explained patiently.

'Jaysus, I thought all that fella did was sit on his fat arse, smoking cigars and shouting "action" every so often. So tell me this then, luv, how do ya cope with the media intrusion into yer private life? I'm only asking so I can prepare meself for what's coming, ya know,' she said, as though a *Vanity Fair* magazine cover was only a phone call away. 'Oh yeah, and another thing, have ya any tips on coping with other people's jealousy about yer success? I've a feeling I might be needing them.'

She wasn't joking. About an hour later, when they were finally ready to shoot the scene from the reverse angle, disaster struck.

Sound and cameras were rolling away, and Mrs Flanagan was just about to launch into her soliloquy about the dis-possessed tenant farmers baying for blood at the back door, when the ground underneath them began to shudder. Not just shudder, but quake with a violence that should have been measured on the Richter scale. The windows began to rattle as though they might shatter at any second and the crystal chandeliers were swinging dangerously from side to side.

Mrs Flanagan went on with her speech, even though the walls were now reverberating and a loud, grating noise like twenty foghorns blaring in unison filled the air.

'Earthquake!' shouted Jimmy D. from his director's chair. 'Evacuate the building!'

'Earthquake? In the back arse of Ballyroan?' Johnny shouted back at him. 'Where do you think you are, San Francisco?'

'Everybody out!' ordered Jimmy D., ignoring him.

'No! Keep filming!' Mrs Flanagan screamed, seeing her stab at stardom evaporating. 'It's only the pipes, it'll stop in a few minutes! Keep rolling that fecking camera!'

'Remain calm and leave through the main door . . . actually no, just get the fuck out!' Jimmy D. was finding it hard to keep the panic out of his voice and, given that the Hall sounded like it was about to collapse, it was hard to blame him. There was almost a stampede as the extras and crew bolted for the door, leaving poor Mrs Flanagan all alone in the middle of the floor.

Twenty minutes later, she stormed into the kitchen where Lucasta sat calmly smoking a cigarette and soaking one of her cat's paws in a bowl of disinfectant.

'Finished already?' she asked innocently. 'So how did it go?'

'As if ya didn't know, ya devious aul' bitch!'

'What on earth are you talking about, you saggy old woman?'

'Somebody mysteriously turned on every tap and flushed every toilet in the bleedin' house *just as I was about to say me feckin' line!*'

'You know, I worry about you, Mrs Flanagan. There's no way you can have built up so much anger in just one lifetime, you're carrying over too much bitterness from a past life.'

'It's this present life ya should be worrying about.'

'Are you threatening me?' said Lucasta, covering the kitten's tiny ears as though he'd overhear the row and be sullied by bad vibes.

A devious look came into Mrs Flanagan's eyes. 'All I'm saying is, ya've probably got about two dozen cats by now. Must be very difficult, in fact it must be impossible for ya to watch all of them, all of the time.'

'This is the final boarding call for all remaining passengers on flight BA Three Six One Nine. Could the last remaining passengers please proceed immediately to gate B Twenty-seven.'

The British Airways ground hostess stood impatiently by the boarding gate as the last few stragglers filed past her, until there was only one youngish man left. Ordinarily she'd have given him a filthy look as he paced up and down the business-class departure lounge with his mobile phone clamped to his ear. But this guy was different. For starters, he was gorgeous-looking, tall and fair-haired with the most amazing blue eyes. Secondly, he seemed to be having a heated argument on the phone, to put it mildly. She didn't want to interrupt, but she knew he only had about two minutes before she'd have to close the flight.

'Operator, you've just got to try again, it's an emergency,' he was arguing loudly. 'I've spent the last few hours trying to get through to this number, it can't just be disconnected, there has to be something wrong. It's a Kildare number, 045 37210. Yes. Davenport Hall.'

'I'm awfully sorry, sir,' she said flirtatiously, 'but it really is the final call.'

'No problem,' he said, switching off his phone and tucking it into his coat pocket.

'May I see your passport and boarding pass please?' she

asked, clocking that he wasn't wearing a wedding ring as he handed them over. She was careful to check his name before giving them back.

'Thank you very much. Enjoy your flight, Mr de Courcey.'

Chapter Twenty-Five

Portia had wisely decided not to pass on Chief Justice de Courcey's news until all the family could be together, so it was well after ten that night when filming had wrapped before she could grab them in the kitchen. (This had the added advantage of Lucasta being well oiled by then; she was invariably easier to talk to after a few gins.)

Blissfully unaware of the ructions that had taken place during the day between her mother and Mrs Flanagan, Portia found herself innocently asking if there was any particular reason why they both adamantly refused to be in the same room as each other?

'I have spent the day trying to gather all my kitties together so that malevolent bitch couldn't inflict pain on them and I'm worn out,' wailed Lucasta. 'It's true you know, girls, what I've always suspected. Sagittarian women really are a shower of fucking bitches.'

'I'm sure she's insulting me,' shouted Mrs Flanagan from the kitchen garden, 'because her lips are moving.'

Portia sighed with the weariness of one who had quite enough on her plate without dealing with this.

'What's up, sis?' asked Daisy. 'But if it's bad news, I'm not sure that I want to know. I've sort of reached my quota for the day.'

'Well, it's news,' replied Portia. 'I'll leave it up to you to decide whether it's good or bad.'

A cackle of laughter could be heard through the open door, from where Mrs Flanagan sat smoking on a bench in the garden.

'Ignore,' Lucasta commanded. 'I mean it. Neither of you is to speak to that thundering trollop in the garden.'

'I feel like I'm watching an episode of *Poirot*,' she said, shouting to be heard. 'Jaysus, Portia, all yer're short of is a French accent and a moustache. Next thing ya'll be saying: "I suppose you're all wondering why I gathered you here." '

'Steve and I had a meeting with Michael de Courcy today,' Portia began.

'Andrew's dishy father?' said Lucasta, brightening. 'What the fuck did he want?'

'Mummy!' hissed Daisy. 'Let her get on with it, will you?'

'Actually, to talk about Shamie Nolan.'

'Oh, I'm just working on a spell to cast on that bastard,' said Lucasta, 'just to make sure he gets what's coming to him.'

'That could well be on the cards,' Portia replied. 'It seems that the Planning Office in Dublin are investigating some irregularities about land that he's bribed County Councillors to rezone. According to Michael, he's been getting away with this for years, and making a fortune out of it in the process.'

'But how does this affect Davenport Hall?' asked Daisy.

'According to Michael, Shamie Nolan had already secured rezoning for just about every acre of our land before he bought it from Daddy. Steve was at the meeting where Nolan managed to persuade the Kildare County Council to apply for permission to rezone and, well, you know Steve has been busting a gut for us ever since.'

'So, in other words, he bought it from Daddy knowing that

the land was going to be worth about ten times what he paid for it,' said Daisy, getting angry.

'Well, the slieveen little bastard,' Mrs Flanagan shouted from the back garden.

'In a nutshell,' said Portia, 'Michael told us that his contact in the Planning Office reckons our land was to be rezoned for high-density, fast-track housing.'

'What, do ya mean like poxy, scutty little holiday homes or something?' Mrs Flanagan shouted. 'Did Shamie Nolan seriously think he could turn the place into Albert Square?'

'That's exactly what he thought. There's such a huge demand for affordable housing in Dublin that he had planned to build about four hundred units here, two- and three-bedroom houses, duplexes and even an apartment complex. It would amount to an entire village, right here on Davenport land.'

'This beats fucking Christmas,' said Lucasta, stunned.

'And will they get the bastard for doing this to us?' asked Daisy with tears in her eyes.

Portia smiled at her. 'If only life was like that, darling. As Steve says, it's very unlikely he'll be hanging up his tartan cap and jacket on the back of a cell door in Mountjoy Jail. No, what's likely is that Michael de Courcey will set up a Tribunal to investigate all of his business dealings and all of the brown envelopes he's been bribing councillors with. All they have to do is follow the money trail.'

'So how exactly is he punished then?' asked Daisy. 'Or does he just get away with it?'

'If there is a big Tribunal, then his name will be plastered all over the papers, he'll be publicly humiliated and Steve says he'll be forced into resigning his seat in the Dáil. It'll certainly spell the end of any political ambitions he may have held.'

Daisy began to snigger.

'And imagine his awful wife turning up at the hearings in Dublin Castle in one of her rig-outs. They'll think he's married to a transvestite.'

'Yeah, but one thing,' said Mrs Flanagan, still shouting, 'Shamie Nolan may be the greatest tosser that ever walked this earth, but, now correct me if I'm wrong, he is still the legal owner of Davenport Hall, isn't he?'

Portia nodded.

'So, unless you got all six numbers in last night's Lotto and the Thunderball Plus and the bonus number, and we're rich now and you're going to buy the Hall back and we're all going to end happily . . . how exactly is this good news?'

Hours later, as Portia lay wide awake in bed staring at the ceiling, she reflected on what Mrs Flanagan had said. She was absolutely right, of course; the awful Nolans still owned the Hall lock, stock and barrel. No matter what public disgrace lay in store for Shamie, there was still no telling what fate held for the Hall. All the Davenports could be absolutely sure of was that Albert Square, as Mrs Flanagan put it, would not now be built on their land. But what was to stop the Nolans taking possession at the end of the month, as planned?

The grandfather clock in the entrance hall below her chimed four a.m. as she shifted restlessly from side to side. She'd bravely spent the day forcing herself to think about anything other than Andrew, but it was no use. Try as she might, she kept coming back to what Michael de Courcey had said. In a week's time, he would be married. She could remember so clearly the night of their first date, when they'd sat on Killiney Beach eating chips in the lashing rain and giggling like a pair of teenagers. She remembered what he'd said about Edwina and how unhappy he'd been with her in New York and all the reasons he'd had for calling off the wedding.

And in a week, they'd be married. And there was nothing she could do.

Paddy was leaving nothing, absolutely nothing to chance. Even if it meant having to have a conversation with the one person he loathed above all on the set.

'Come in!' said a disembodied voice from inside the make-up trailer.

'Ah thanks, emm, Mr van der Post, thanks very much,' Paddy replied, stepping in. 'I just wanted to radio mike ya for this scene, if that's all right.'

'Work away,' Guy replied as Serge painstakingly applied a prosthetic scar to the side of his ribcage.

'What's that?' Paddy asked, clipping the mike to the waistband of his cream linen suit.

'You like it?' Serge replied. 'Jimmy D. requested it specially. It's to make Brent look a little more butch, you know? More Alpha Male? Like he's been in a bar-room brawl or, emm, something . . .' He broke off, catching the insulted look on Guy's face in the mirror. 'Oh, not that your playing of the character isn't completely macho, it's just that . . .' he back-pedalled like a maniac.

'Get your fudge-packing hands off me, that's enough fucking make-up,' Guy snapped at him, rising out of the chair and walloping the trailer door shut behind him.

'Jaysus, I knew he was a wanker, but I'd no idea he was that bad,' said Paddy incredulously.

'Oh honey, I could write the book,' replied Serge, calmly taking a sip of Eau de Davenport. 'And you know, one day I will, and it'll be a bestseller and I'll call it *Film Sets Uncovered* and believe you me, I will kiss and tell. I've worked with some monsters in my time, but Guy van der Post is Godzilla compared with the rest of them.'

'Shite. I wanted to ask him something.'

'Well, maybe I can help?' Serge's curiosity was roused.

Paddy looked at him for a moment, unsure whether or not he could be trusted, and then decided, what the hell?

'It's about Daisy, actually.'

'Oh, you have come to the right person, sit down and tell me every sordid detail.'

'Don't overreact or anything, right? It's just that I tried to move in with her and she threw all me stuff out in bin liners. I think maybe she just wasn't ready for the kind of commitment I can offer her, ya know? Like, she's a bit raw after being with that fucking eejit Guy.'

Serge nodded, like a senior consultant listening to a patient's symptoms.

'So, I was thinking, OK, she's an old-fashioned girl, she doesn't want to live with me before marriage, so why don't I just . . .'

Serge clasped both of his hands to his open mouth. 'Oh my GOOWD! Don't tell me you're gonna propose!'

Paddy went red. 'Yeah. So I was just looking for a bit of advice on what I should do, ya know?'

'This is just so romantic,' gushed Serge, pacing up and down with excitement. 'It's gotta be a huge gesture, it's gotta be something that the lucky lady will remember for the rest of her life!'

'In my family, the bloke usually says, "You're what? Right. I suppose we have to get married now."'

'That won't do at all!' Serge was almost squealing by now. 'Know your prey, honey. Remember, Daisy is an aristocrat. Her family have probably been marrying their cousins for about three hundred years or something – you only have to look at the mother to see that. Boy, if ever there was a family crying out for fresh blood, it's the Davenports.'

'Gift,' said Paddy, delighted with his confidant, 'cos I was a bit worried about the class thing. I mean, I know I fit into her world really well, but the thing is, will she fit into mine?'

'She'll be with a man who truly loves her,' replied Serge, teary-eyed. 'What more could any girl want?'

'So, how do ya think I should ask her then?'

Serge breathed deeply. 'It should happen at the cast dinner tomorrow night, when everyone's together. I think you wait till dinner's over and then . . . oh! Oh! Inspiration striking! You have the mad housekeeper serve her a chocolate mousse for desert and you hide the engagement ring inside it!'

'That's brilliant!' said Paddy. 'Jaysus, I'm delighted I asked ya, yer're, like, really in touch with yer feminine side. And yer'll keep it a secret and all, won't ya? I really want it to be a surprise.'

'Honey, if there is a more discreet man in the northern hemisphere, then get me his number quick.'

Exactly ten minutes later, Serge barged into Daisy's bedroom without knocking and plonked down on her bed. She was midway through packing, or rather stuffing her jodhpurs into yet another bin liner, and looked at him in astonishment.

'You'll thank me for this later,' he said. 'Let me just say that I've been entrusted with a *huge* secret but my will to communicate is just too overwhelming.'

'Serge, if you're going to sit there talking shit then at least make yourself useful and help me pack.'

'Not in a million years will you ever prise it out of me, but I'll just give you this tiny little clue, you lucky bitch! The ring finger on your left hand isn't gonna be bare for very much longer!'

Chapter Twenty-Six

After yet another sleepless night, Portia wearily forced herself out of bed at six a.m., just as the film crew were starting to crank up for the day. Even if she had been able to sleep, it would have been impossible once they began setting up for the day, such was the noise level from the Ballroom below, where shooting continued. Needless to say, minus the tiny but pivotal character part of Miss Murphy the housekeeper, who had been unceremoniously axed from the scene.

'Your mother and Mrs Flanagan sure as hell are two mighty strong personalities,' Jimmy D. had explained to Portia the previous evening, 'and I really don't feel up to the challenge of refereeing between the two of them. I think even Kofi Annan would have difficulty doing that. So in the interests of non-violence, it's best that we just cut the part altogether.'

Portia could only feel that he was wise.

She pulled on the only clean pair of jeans she had, scraped her hair into a ponytail and threw on a warm, snuggly fleece jacket to keep out the cold. It was July, and the sun was actually shining for once, but the temperature at Davenport Hall remained resolutely freezing. Running lightly down the staircase, she made a mental note of everything she had to get through that day. Packing was such a massive job and she wasn't helped by the fact that every time Daisy or Lucasta tried to give her a hand, they invariably ended up in floods of tears. If she had to listen to either of them bewailing the unfairness of the situation they found themselves in once more, she thought she'd scream. Just get used to it, she'd patiently tried to explain to them, with Andrew not far from her thoughts. Where is it written that life is fair?

As she opened the kitchen door, an overpowering smell of bacon and cabbage hit her square in the face. Coughing, she reached for the kettle to make some tea as Mrs Flanagan came waddling out of the pantry clutching about five pounds of raw sausages in her bare hands.

'Ah howaya? Luv, there's fresh tea in the pot,' she said, seeing who it was. 'I'm just getting the ingredients ready for the cast dinner tonight.'

The cast dinner, Jimmy D. had explained, was the only night apart from the wrap party when cast and crew sat down for a meal together. A big affair, it was to be held in the Red Dining Room, which comfortably seated about sixty people. (The golden rule of cast dinners, according to Montana, was to arrive neither too early nor too late. Too early and you'd end up sitting beside the director, too late and you'd end up sitting beside the wardrobe department.)

'Smells really interesting,' Portia lied. 'What are you making?'

'A Dublin coddle. Boiled bacon and sausage swimming in milk. 'Bout time someone put a bit of weight on all these bleeding film stars; poor aul' Montana looks like she just got out of Dachau.'

'Tea?' asked Portia, reaching for two mugs from the dresser.

'No thanks, luv, but I must say, it makes a change to hear a polite word from a member of yer family. I wonder, if

I ever left, would yer mother even notice I was gone?'

Portia protested, knowing that all Mrs Flanagan wanted to hear were a few reassuring words to let her know that at least someone at the Hall valued her.

'Now, how can you even think that? You've been here since I was a baby, Mrs Flanagan, you've done so much to hold this family together and now we need you more than ever,' she said gently.

'I often wonder how ya turned out so normal, with mental cases for both yer parents,' sniffed Mrs Flanagan. 'I swear to God, if that woman has one more go at me, that's it. I'm gone. See how the stupid aul' cow likes having to pare her own corns without me.'

Portia wearily sat down at the kitchen table, well used to dealing with the love/hate relationship between the two women and its perpetual fallout. It'll blow over, she thought, it always does. Just then a copy of the *Kildare People* lying open beside her caught her eye. It wasn't the headline which grabbed her attention (ELLA HEPBURN DOES IT FIVE TIMES A NIGHT it screamed, with yet another picture of her and Guy. Where in God's name did they get their information from?). No, it was the fact that the jobs page had been torn out. And in her scrawly, spidery hand, Mrs Flanagan had circled several of them in bright red Biro.

'I've been in worse buckets of shite than this and still come up smelling of roses,' proclaimed Shamie Nolan as he and Bridie sat side by side in the Dáil bar. Government business had concluded for the day and the bar was packed with TDs availing themselves of the duty-free drink prices, in no rush whatsoever to get home. A television was blaring in the background, showing the commercial break, which went out just before the main evening news.

He loves me not . . . he loves me

'Will ya for Jaysus' sake listen to me, Shamie?' said his brother and campaign manager, Tommy, banging down his pint of stout. 'Can we just get the hell outta here before it comes on? I'm telling ya, I'm after being on me mobile phone to me pal whose cousin has a neighbour who has a pal that's the Controller General of RTE and there was feck all he could do to pull it.'

'Tommy Nolan, you just listen to me,' replied Bridie imperiously. 'Do you honestly think meself and Shamie are going to hide away like common criminals? Like we've done something we should be ashamed of? Over my fecking dead body. We're staying here for the news with our heads held high; let them report what they fecking well like.'

Tommy shifted in his seat, fervently wishing he was anywhere less public than the Dáil bar. All his brother's old friends and cronies were standing around, with one eye on Shamie and the other on the TV. Finally, the Angelus was over and the news theme blared out. The barman thoughtfully even reached for the remote control to raise the volume in case there was anyone from the planet Mars in the bar who wasn't aware of what was going on.

'Are you sweating yet, Nolan?' called one wag from the corner of the snug.

'Let's just hope you don't have to trade in your BMW coupé for a Lada yet, Bridie!' another invisible voice sneered.

'Don't think me offended by that remark or anything,' Bridie hissed to her husband, 'but when all this unpleasantness is over, you make sure that bollocks is fired.'

The lead story was about a car bomb explosion in Iraq, in which there were a dozen fatalities, and the report went on for a good four minutes of screen time. Next, there was an item about a missing schoolgirl from Liverpool who had just been safely reunited with her terrified parents. Shamie was just

293

beginning to breathe a bit easier when the newsreader announced with gravitas, 'And staying on home news, Shamie Joe Nolan, TD for Kildare South Central, is today at the centre of a number of allegations concerning planning irregularities. A report due to be published at the end of the week indicates that, on several occasions, Mr Nolan was involved at Government level in the illegal rezoning of private lands for commercial purposes. A report now from our political correspondent, Richard McHugh.'

The camera cut to a reporter standing outside the entrance gates to Davenport Hall (with graffiti on the wall which said 'Virgin Megastore' clearly visible in the background).

'It's hard to believe that Davenport Hall was once considered the jewel in Leinster's architectural crown, but there's no arguing that the land it sits in, over two thousand acres, is worth its weight in gold,' said the unfortunate reporter, looking like he'd rather be anywhere else. 'And it's this very land that's at the heart of the storm of controversy surrounding Kildare's beleaguered TD Shamie Nolan today. A report, which has been leaked from the Planning Office in Dublin, clearly implicates him in corrupt rezoning practices, which stretch to the highest levels of Government. It would appear that Mr Nolan knowingly purchased the Hall and its adjacent lands only after a motion to rezone the land for residential purposes had already been passed by Kildare County Council.'

The camera cut back to studio, where the anchorman said, 'So, Richard, what now for Shamie Nolan? Can we expect another planning Tribunal to spring from this?'

'It seems likely,' replied the reporter as the camera cut back to Davenport Hall. (This time Mrs Flanagan could be seen in the background driving the Mini Metro through the gates and waving like a lunatic at the camera.) 'Chief Justice Michael de Courcey has indicated that he has already been approached with a view to examining the minutiae of Mr Nolan's business transactions. In the meantime it seems the only honourable course of action for Shamie Nolan is to resign his Dáil seat immediately, and wait for the Tribunal to begin. Then, of course, this raises the question of his legal fees which are sure be substantial.'

The anchorman then continued, 'Thank you, Richard. Earlier, we caught up with Mr Nolan at Leinster House, and this is what he had to say.'

The camera swiftly cut to a close-up shot of Shamie, standing uncomfortably outside Government Buildings and sweating profusely.

'Well, sure, Jaysus now, listen to what I'm telling ya. If you were to examine the financial wheelings and dealings of every politician in here, sure we'd have enough Tribunals to waste the taxpayers' money till kingdom come. There's not a TD in the whole of Government Buildings that doesn't receive a calendar every January from one of their offshore bank accounts in the Cayman Islands.'

'And now, briefly in other news . . .'

The barman switched off the TV. In the awful silence that followed, it felt as though every eye in the place was fixed on Shamie.

Stammering, he said, 'They took that feckin' quote totally out of context, lads! The bastards cut out loads of what I said! Sure I'd never say anything derogatory about any of ye boys . . .'

A slow handclap started at the back of the bar, which gradually increased in volume until it became deafening. A couple of boos grew into a barrage of catcalls and cries of 'Resign! Resign!' could be heard loud and clear.

It seemed that the entire Dáil bar was jeering and stomping their feet in disgust; at least that's what Bridie thought as they sat there, heads held high.

Chapter Twenty-Seven

Steve was well used to the everyday drama and chaos at Davenport Hall, but nothing had prepared him for this. Along with the family, he had been invited to the cast dinner that night, but drove over a little earlier to brief them on the latest Shamie Nolan revelations. He was driving up the avenue approaching the Hall when the sight of a pair of bare legs topped by bright blue knickers and dangling from a first-floor window almost made him crash. As he drew closer he saw that it was Daisy, hanging precariously by her fingernails from an outside ledge, with her skirt practically around her neck. He pulled the car over and jumped out immediately.

'Need a hand?' he called up to her.

'Well what does it fucking look like?' she snapped back. 'Steve, I'm stuck!'

He couldn't help himself. 'So are you working as Montana's stunt double now? If you don't mind me saying, unless the film is X-rated, hadn't you better cover yourself up?'

'Steve!' she wailed, unamused. 'Just help me down!'

'OK, I'll come inside and haul you up; what room were you in?'

'You can't come in! Can't you help me down from where you are?'

'Not unless you jump for it.'

'I'm just recovering from a sprained ankle, I'll break my spinal cord this time!'

'No you won't, it's only ten feet at most. I'll catch you, trust me.'

'Oh God, why do these things only ever happen to me?'

'Look, Daisy, you can't cling on to that ledge for much longer. Now do you want the press boys at the front gates to take a picture of your delightful underwear or do you want to jump? I can just see the headlines now: BLUE MOON.'

Faced with choosing between the lesser of two evils, she jumped. Steve had been right, the drop was no more then ten feet and he easily caught her in his strong arms. They looked at each other for a split second, with Daisy panting to catch her breath back. He was certainly looking remarkably well and Daisy almost found herself doing a double-take. He'd clearly taken Mrs Flanagan's advice about smartening himself up a bit even further to heart and was now sporting a trendy navy linen suit, with a crisp white shirt, all crumpled-looking and sexy.

'Drive,' she said after a moment, wriggling out of his arms. 'Just let's get into your car and drive.'

'Where?'

'As far away from here as possible.'

Mrs Flanagan had really pulled out all the stops and was happily putting the finishing touches to the dining table for the big dinner that night. Linen napkins were unheard of at the Hall, but she'd gone into Ballyroan specially to buy paper serviettes, in marked contrast to the wads of kitchen roll they normally used. She'd even managed to root out candles to use as a centrepiece. (Unfortunately not in tasteful white, but in the green, white and orange of the Irish flag with 'World Cup Italia 1990' emblazoned in gold across them, which she'd been saving up for a really special occasion.)

She had just stepped back to admire her handiwork when a squealing noise from above caught her attention. She looked up to see one of Lucasta's favourite kittens, Uri Geller, who appeared to be caught in one of the crystal arms of the chandelier overhead. Ah, ya stupid gobshite of a cat, how did ya get up there? she said to herself. There was no budging him though; he looked helplessly down at her as the chandelier swung dangerously from side to side. There was nothing else for it but to grab a sweeping brush, which was conveniently at hand, and try to get him down. However, given that the ceiling was thirty feet high, this left her with no option but to haul herself up on to the dining table, broom handle in hand, and poke at him in the hope that he'd budge.

Just then, Lucasta came in, took in the scene and immediately jumped to the wrong conclusion, as was her wont.

'Leave that innocent little soul alone, you murderous woman!' she screeched.

'I'm trying to help him down, ya batty aul' bitch,' said Mrs Flanagan, continuing to prod at poor Uri Geller with her broom handle.

'Don't tell me you didn't have murderous thoughts in mind!'

'The cat is still alive, ya thick eejit; what do ya think I'm trying to do, sweep him to death?'

'Well, I wouldn't put it past you,' said Lucasta, gunning for a fight. 'And may I ask what the Italia ninety candles are doing out? Are you completely mad? They're collectors' items, you know, they're not to be used. Jack Charlton would spin in his grave, if he were dead.'

'Right, that's fecking it,' said Mrs Flanagan, throwing her sweeping brush to the ground and clambering down from the table. 'I'm here thirty-five years—'

'Oh really?' Lucasta interrupted. 'That must be why I'm so sick of the sight of you.'

'I've just about put up with enough from you,' snarled Mrs Flanagan. 'Ya treat me like shite, ya talk to me like dirt and ya pay me fuck all. Find yerself another bleeding white slave, I quit!'

Lucasta looked at her as though she'd been smacked across her face. 'Don't be so ridiculous . . .' she stuttered, shocked. 'You can't just quit!'

'Well excuse fucking me, that's exactly what I'm doing.'

'But . . . but . . . you live here! And you work here, and where in God's name do you think you'll go anyway?' Lucasta was starting to panic now that her bluff had been well and truly called.

Mrs Flanagan waddled over to face her square on. 'As a matter of fact, I went for a job interview today and I got it. I'm starting a whole new career.'

'As what? Don't tell me, you're the new face of L'Oréal.' Lucasta was red in the face by now.

'If ya must know, I'm after getting a job in the Crown and Glory in Ballyroan and they said I could start straight away. I wasn't going to take it, but I'm fucked if I'm putting up with any more of yer abuse!' she said, her eyes watering.

'The hair salon? And what in God's name do you know about hairdressing?' Lucasta was still shouting, but with a wobble in her voice.

Mrs Flanagan eyed her up and down, getting really upset. 'I know that the grunge look is out, so that's you fucked!'

'Well, look out, fashion world!' Lucasta shouted after Mrs Flanagan as she waddled past and went out of the door. 'It'll be the only hair salon in the country where you can catch nits from the stylist!'

'Well, you'll never know, because we don't serve Rastas!' she replied, banging the door behind her. Lucasta stood there alone for a moment in the silence.

In the space of a few short months, she'd dealt with her husband walking out on her, losing her beloved home and not having the remotest idea how she or her daughters would survive. But this was the first time that she cried.

'So do you want to tell me what's going on then?'

Daisy didn't answer, she just stared straight ahead.

'It's just that the last time I remember you climbing out a window to get out of the Hall, I think you were about fourteen and you wanted to go to some nightclub in Kildare.'

'And Daddy grounded me because he said nightclubs were only for tarts so I climbed out the Billiard-Room window,' she replied, smiling at the memory. 'There was a guy from my school taking me and I was so completely knickers about him, I think I'd have dug a tunnel to escape from the Hall. Then, of course, when I got to the club – the Galleria, or the Gonorrhoea as we used to call it – who was the first person I walked into but Daddy, with one of his girlfriends.'

Steve shot a sideways glance at her, just to check that she wasn't upset. On a bad day, the very mention of Blackjack's name was enough to have her in hysterics, but she seemed fine. A comfortable silence passed as they both sat side by side, savouring the view. She had bullied Steve into driving her all the way up to the Mausoleum and, gentleman that he was, he hadn't argued with her.

'This is my favourite spot on the whole estate,' she said. He nodded in agreement. The view was nothing short of spectacular, especially on a clear day like this.

'Did you know that the awful Nolans were going to demolish the Mausoleum and build a bowling alley here?' she asked. 'Mummy says, just for that alone, Shamie Nolan should be reincarnated as a toilet brush in his next life.'

He smiled, always tickled by Lucasta's eccentricities.

'Steve, can I ask you something?'

'Fire away.'

'Are all men either complete bastards or else insane stalkers? Is this it? Is this the spectrum I get to choose from?'

He was about to answer when she cut across him. 'I mean, first there's Guy, who I was mad about but who just wanted to shag me until something better came along. If you could call Ella bloody Hepburn something better,' she added bitterly. 'I may not be Hollywood royalty but I'm about sixty years younger than her, I'm not in danger of breaking a hip every time I stand up and at least I've got my own tits. And now there's Paddy, who's acting like he's totally obsessed with me. In warped Paddy land, he seems to think that we're boyfriend and girlfriend when nothing has ever happened to give him that idea.'

'Nothing?'

'Well, I slept with him, like, twice, but only out of lone-liness, you know the way it is,' she said, amazed at how frank she could be with him. 'And now he's turned into a stalker; he won't leave me alone for two seconds together. He's like a study in male psychology: the worse I treat him, the more he chases me. That's why I had to climb out the bathroom window. He won't even let me go to the loo in peace, he was standing right outside the door reading me one of his love poems.'

'Daisy, if you want my advice, the simplest thing to do is to be direct. Tell him you're flattered but just not interested.'

'But you don't understand!' she wailed. 'One of the crew let

301

it slip that he's going to propose to me. At this bloody dinner tonight! In front of everyone! What am I going to do?'

Although unused to being appealed to for advice when it came to matters of the heart, Steve thought for a moment, applying himself fully to the problem.

Daisy was kicking her heels off the moss-covered stone bench they were sitting on when suddenly inspiration struck. 'I've got it!' she said, beaming at him with her blue eyes sparkling.

He smiled back at her. 'What?'

'It's a piece of cake,' she replied. 'But, emm . . . Steve? Could you do me a favour?'

Mrs Flanagan was as good as her word. No less than an hour later, she had thrown her collection of housecoats into a tattered suitcase and flung it into the back of the Mini Metro. Portia stood beside her on the forecourt, hoarse from pleading with her to change her mind.

'If it was only yerself and Daisy, luv, I'd happily spend the rest of me days here. But . . . I know she's yer mother and all, but that fecking cow has me persecuted. I work so hard and I just feel so unappreciated . . .' She broke off, tears starting to flow down her lined, craggy face.

'Oh Mrs Flanagan, I know what she's like, but I'm begging you to reconsider. You're part of our family and losing you is unthinkable. I'm sure Mummy didn't mean the awful things she said, you know how hurtful she can be one minute and then it's all forgotten the next. She snaps my face off twenty times a day, and five minutes later, she's Mother Teresa.'

Mrs Flanagan dabbed her eyes. 'It's just after thirty-five years of slaving for her I can't take any more of her abuse. If she'd only apologize to me, that would be something, but she was vicious when I told her I had another job to go to, vicious.'

Portia hugged her tight, feeling close to tears herself. 'You know, I bet she's upstairs now, regretting every word and wishing you'd stay as much as I do.'

'Do ya think?' Mrs Flanagan was faltering a little.

'I'm certain,' Portia replied soothingly. 'She loves you so much deep down, she just has an odd way of expressing it sometimes.'

Mrs Flanagan looked at her with red watery eyes and seemed to be on the brink of changing her mind when a screech came from behind. They both looked up to see Lucasta's head stuck out of a third-floor window.

'May the curse of Apollo crash down upon you, faithless servant!' she was chanting. 'In fact, bugger that, may Apollo shit on you and your descendants from a height!'

Mrs Flanagan took one last look at Portia and said, 'Well, goodbye, luv. If ever ya need a wash and blow dry, ya know where to come. And thanks for the lend of the car.'

'MAY A PLAGUE OF LOCUSTS DESCEND ON YOUR POXY HAIRDRESSER'S AND MAY YOU DIE ROARING FOR A PRIEST!' Lucasta's screaming had swelled to a crescendo as the Mini Metro backfired its way down the driveway.

The last Portia saw of Mrs Flanagan was when she rolled down the car window, stuck her hand out and waved two fingers at the whole lot of them.

Chapter Twenty-Eight

Needless to say, the cast dinner was shaping up to be an unmitigated disaster. After Mrs Flanagan's departure, Portia had no choice but to enlist Daisy's help in the kitchen, to try and rustle up something to serve their guests. However, given that their cooking prowess would never cause Nigella Lawson to have sleepless nights worrying about her competition, this was easier said than done.

'But Mrs Flanagan must have left something for the dinner before she walked out?' Daisy moaned. 'Because if she didn't, then what's that rotten smell?'

'Dublin coddle,' replied Portia, throwing it into the bin.

'Why are you throwing it out? I know it smells like raw sewage, but won't it do?'

'Boiled sausage and bacon? For a table full of vegetarians?'

The sisters looked at each other. A moment of panic flittered between the two of them.

'We could order pizzas from Ballyroan?' said Daisy hopefully.

'And if all else fails, we will. But look, there must be the makings of something here, we just need to think laterally. You check the fridge and I'll check the freezer,' said Portia with authority. They both snapped into action.

Twenty minutes later and they had a solution – of sorts. Between them, they'd unearthed about two dozen eggs from the pantry and five family-sized bags of frozen chip wedges.

'How in God's name will we get away with this?' asked Portia.

'Simple,' said Daisy, tying an apron on backwards around her waist and looking like the world's most incompetent waitress. 'We just tell them that eggs are a traditional Davenport family staple, only eaten on very special occasions . . . because . . . emm . . .' she said, thinking on her feet. 'Oh, I know! Because during the famine the Davenports and all their tenant farmers survived by living off the hens on the home farm and so now we only ever eat eggs on St Patrick's Day and when VIPs come to stay.'

'And how do we explain the oven-ready wedges, Professor David Starkey? Do we say that although the potato crop had failed, the Davenports still had access to frozen chips?'

'Well, can you think of anything better?'

Dinner was at seven-thirty for eight so Portia almost fell over when the doorbell's foghorn blared out at six-thirty. The meal, if you could call it that, wasn't nearly ready and she and Daisy froze in panic wondering who this could be. Just then, Montana stuck her head around the door and cheerily said, 'Hi, ladies! I was just wondering if you could use some help in here?'

'That's so nice of you,' replied Daisy as she chopped up some onions finely. 'Do you think you could answer the door for us?' Montana was behaving angelically towards her ever since she'd been so publicly dumped by Guy. And at times like these, a little sympathy went a long way.

'Be right back,' said Montana, lightly tripping up the back stairs, which led to the main entrance hall. She stood on tip-toe to reach the huge latch which opened the heavy oak door and was surprised to see that it was Paddy, dressed in a 1980s *Miami Vice*-style suit and carrying a small bunch of garage carnations.

'Well, hey there, handsome, are they for me?' she asked teasingly.

'Piss off,' he replied, looking nervous and uncomfortable.

'OK, well, I think Lady Davenport is serving aperitifs in the Long Gallery so if you wanna go right on up . . .' she said, a little taken aback by a crew member speaking to her like that.

'Ehh, yeah, thanks very much,' he said, brushing past her and making a beeline for the gilt mirror above the mantelpiece to slick back his gelled hair and squeeze a zit that had really been annoying him. Pausing only to check that he was entirely satisfied with his appearance, he took a deep breath and bounced happily up the great staircase, humming a few bars of 'I'm Getting Married in the Morning' as he went.

'Who was that?' asked Portia as Montana rejoined them in the Korean sweatshop that the kitchen had become.

'Oh, that sound guy . . . what's his name?' she answered.

'Paddy. God, he's early, isn't he?' said Portia.

Daisy didn't reply, she just continued to whisk a big bowl of eggs and blushed a bit.

'And, you know, he's all dressed up like a dog's dinner.' Montana giggled as she picked up a tea towel and expertly tied it around her waist. 'In fact, he looked really cute. OK, so what needs doing?'

'Could you help me crush some garlic?' asked Portia.

'Of course, but, let me ask, are you trying to batter those eggs to death, Daisy?'

'I'm making an omelette,' she replied defensively.

'Oh honey, give it over. The idea is that you can eat the omelette, not plaster your walls with it. Here, let me show you how it's done.'

Both sisters stopped what they were doing to gawp at her in surprise.

'Well, don't look so shocked,' she laughed. 'I was an out-of-work actor in LA for years, which is code for saying I was a waitress. Do we have any chives?'

Less than thirty minutes later, Montana had everything under control. She'd even discovered asparagus in the kitchen garden and was scrubbing them at the sink to serve as a starter. 'It'll be fabulous with just a little lemon juice, trust me,' she'd said in between gossiping about Guy and Ella. It seemed the latest revelation (according to the good old reliable *National Intruder*) was that they'd swapped phials of blood and were now wearing them around their necks as love tokens.

'Ugh! That's vile!' said Portia, wincing.

'And you know, apparently the five times a night thing is true, according to Serge,' Montana went on. 'He swore he didn't have a glass pressed to the door of the trailer, but I wouldn't put it past him.'

'Well,' said Daisy, who'd now been made completely re-dundant in the kitchen because of Montana's efficiency, 'if the *National Intruder* ever want to pay me for my story, I'll sing like a bloody canary. Do you see this?' she asked, holding up a tiny frozen baby carrot. 'This is roughly the same size as Guy van der Post's willy. I'm serious. If they're looking for a headline, I'll give them one, no problem. I can see it now: WHEN I FIRST SAW GUY NAKED, I THOUGHT THE SURGEON WHO DID HIS PENIS EXTENSION OPERATION SHOULD HANG HIS HEAD IN SHAME.'

The three of them fell about laughing, especially Portia

who rarely indulged in girly sex talk and who hadn't had a good laugh in weeks.

'So how about you?' Montana asked her innocently. 'Whatever happened to that divine guy that the papers kept calling the Earl of Ireland? Weren't you kissing him at some stage?'

'Yes, I was, but not any more,' she replied simply.

'So what happened, honey? Do you wanna talk about it?' Montana was persistent, as though conducting a group-therapy session.

'Nothing to talk about I'm afraid, no headlines for the *National Intruder* here. He got back with his ex-fiancée and their wedding is going ahead. They were on a break when we met so I imagine I was just his rebound person.'

'Sweetheart, you mustn't be so hard on yourself. You're a beautiful, elegant woman and he must be some kind of fucked-up weirdo to leave a babe like you. That's the only explanation that makes any sense to me.'

Portia looked at her for a moment. 'You know, when women get dumped, they always say that the guy is either a messed-up commitment phobe or else a bastard from hell. The truth is, Andrew is neither. He's a wonderful man who just didn't want to be with me.'

Meanwhile, in the Long Gallery, most of the dinner guests had assembled and were knocking back extremely large home measures of gin and tonic supplied by Lucasta. 'The secret of serving shite food,' she always said, 'is to make sure your guests are far too sloshed to notice.' Which is why she never bothered with good wine, claiming that it had no effect on people whatsoever, whereas plonk got them completely twisted, and far quicker too.

Instead of bashing the living daylights out of a Broadway

show tune at the piano, as she normally would, this evening she had decided to play Lucasta the tragic, wronged employer, abandoned by her faithless family retainer. She'd spent the last hour smoking by the stained-glass windows and whining at poor Steve about the day's events.

'You know, darling,' she said, stubbing out a fag on the windowsill, 'at times like this, I really wish I had a dog.'

'But, Lucasta, you own about forty cats,' he replied patiently.

'I know, sweetie, but I really feel like kicking something up the arse.'

'Mrs Flanagan's only been gone for two hours, she's left you for longer periods when she's been shopping in Tesco's.'

By then, Portia had joined them, eschewing the gin and tonic Steve proffered and just in time to hear her mother moan, 'Oh, how sharper than a serpent's tooth it is to have nurtured such disloyalty! Nobody will ever know how utterly abandoned and alone I feel!'

'But, Mummy, you've still got us,' replied Portia.

'That's what I mean' Lucasta was well oiled by now and alcohol was loosening her tongue.

'So what would be so terrible about picking up the phone and apologizing to her? She's staying at Lottie O'Loughlin's until she finds somewhere else, you could call her right now if you're missing her that much,' Portia reasoned.

'Apologize? To that pig in knickers? I'd rather use Gnasher as an ashtray' Lucasta sniffed, managing to look wounded and betrayed at the same time.

At this point, Daisy walked in, no longer able to put off the inevitable. Paddy had been loitering by the door, almost giving himself whiplash each time it opened, in case it was her. When she finally breezed in, he was over to her like a bullet.

'Holy Christ' – taking in his suit – 'it's Don Johnson!'

'Do ya like it? I only wear it on really special occasions.'

'I'm guessing the first one was your confirmation,' she said, trying to sound as bitchy as possible.

'No, the last time Arsenal won the double. But, ya see, the thing is, Daisy, there's something I have to ask ya and it won't wait.'

Sensing what was coming, she launched her offensive.

'Stop! Stop right there, Paddy! Before you say anything, there's something you should know about me. We Davenports only ever marry our cousins, you know, we're totally inbred. I mean, why do you think aristocrats' eyes are so close together, for fuck's sake?'

'Ah, is that all that's worrying ya, luv? Cos I didn't exactly come from the deep end of the genetic pool meself, ya know?'

'And of all the useless institutions in the world, I think marriage is by far the worst,' she went on, her voice rising in panic. 'And . . . oh yes! I have no morals to speak of, you know. I worked in a massage parlour in Thailand for two years.'

'Wasn't Lucky Chang's by any chance, was it? I was there too! Years ago, when we were filming *Shanghai Noon.* Or, as we used to call it, *Shanghai Shite.*'

Daisy glared at him in utter exasperation. She was raising her voice by now and was aware that everyone in the room seemed to be staring at them.

'Paddy, you're not listening to me! I never ever want to get married, ever! For one thing . . .' She racked her brains for a good lie. '. . . I can never have children. I have no womb!'

'Luv, between all my sisters I've about thirty nieces and nephews; I couldn't give a shite if I never had to babysit again. Frankly, I'm relieved.'

'Right, that's it!' she said, falling back on to her final line of defence. 'You've forced the truth out of me. I never meant for you to hear it like this, but I don't have a choice. I'm in love with another man and I only want to be with him.'

'Who is the bastard? I'll sort him out for ya!'

Steve, who had been discreetly hovering on the sidelines, now sensed that this was his cue. Moving towards Daisy, he gingerly put his arm around her waist.

'There you are, darling,' she said, standing on tiptoe to kiss his cheek.

'Him?' said Paddy, aghast. 'I thought he was gay. I saw him wearing a pink stripy shirt once, for fuck's sake.'

'Darling, shall we go into dinner?' Daisy said, linking her arm with Steve's and steering him towards the Dining Room. 'I know that sounded dreadful, Steve,' she whispered to him as they left the Long Gallery, 'but sometimes you just have to be cruel to be kind.'

Paddy stayed rooted to the spot, staring down at the bunch of carnations he never even got to give her. Serge and Montana, who were standing by the mantelpiece, drifted over to him.

'You know what I always say, honey,' said Serge, chirpily. 'In with anger and out with love.'

'Sorry, lads, I'm just a bit . . . ya know . . . emotional . . .' he said. 'I think I need to go and express me feelings of rejection through song.'

'Or you could try to have a good night and come with us?' said Montana hopefully. 'You can even sit by me if you want.'

It was well after five a.m. before the party finally broke up. This was early by Davenport Hall's normal standards (where a good knees-up could last for anything up to three days, depending on both the amount of alcohol available and the mood of the hostess). However, Lucasta was in unusually

311

subdued form all evening and even refused to sing when asked, much to everyone's surprise. And relief in some cases. (Guy had threatened to smash the stained-glass windows piece by piece if she as much as opened her mouth.)

Daisy had dutifully sat by Steve all night playing the role of devoted girlfriend and surprised herself by having a lot more fun than she thought she would. He might not have Guy's looks or glamour but at least he was normal, not sad and obsessive like poor old Paddy. And after what she'd been through, there was a lot to be said for normality. He'd been sweet to her all night, lovely to talk to and just . . . easy. There was something so warm and comfortable and re-assuring about being in his company, he was almost like the human equivalent of hangover food.

She walked him across the gravelled forecourt to his Jeep just as first light was dawning and a gentle mist was lifting from the fields around the Hall. The moon was still high, and bathed the Hall in a silvery glow, making it loom out of the darkness like a magnificent stately ghost ship.

'Dear old Davenport,' he said, taking in the stark beauty of it all at that unearthly hour. 'I'm going to miss it every bit as much as you.'

'Don't talk about it, I'll start crying again. Do you know, it's only now that we're losing it that I've realized how much it means to me?' Daisy had started to shiver in the cold early-morning air and, without even thinking, he took off his jacket and gently covered her bare shoulders with it.

'Thanks for everything tonight, Steve.'

'Anytime.'

An awkward moment passed between them, a 'will we, won't we' moment, with both of them getting more and more embarrassed. Eventually, he broke away, muttering something about having an early start. She found herself following him to his car, surprised that he hadn't tried to kiss her. Surprised and a bit disappointed.

'Goodnight, Daisy Davenport,' he said, turning the key in the ignition and revving up the engine.

'I'll see you tomorrow, won't I?' she called after him as his Jeep sped off down the driveway.

But it was too late. He was gone.

Chapter Twenty-Nine

For the first time in ages, Shamie Nolan thought himself fortunate that there were film stars in residence at Davenport Hall, for the simple reason that press attention was deflected from him, if only temporarily. Mind you, it didn't stop his mobile phone from ringing every five minutes, with various reporters, radio stations and news programmes all asking the same question over and over again. 'Now that you've finally resigned your seat in the Dáil, Mr Nolan, have you any comment to make about the upcoming Tribunal of inquiry into your various business dealings? Chief Justice Michael de Courcey has indicated that no stone will be left unturned, that no paper trail will be ignored and that any hint of irregularities in planning practices will be dealt with by the full force of the law.'

Exhaustively coached by his legal team, Shamie gave the same standard reply to all comers. 'Ah now, lads, far from dreading the Tribunal, sure I'm actually looking forward to it. I welcome the chance to clear me good name, which has been so vilified by the media in recent weeks.' Then, checking to make sure his mobile phone was switched off, he rejoined the crisis meeting taking place around his kitchen table.

'Who was it this time?' asked his barrister, Harry Smith, as he produced yet another mountain of files from his briefcase.

'Ah, that fecking shower from Channel Six. I swear to Jaysus, when all of this shite is over, I'm going to sort out their Director General like ya wouldn't believe. By the time I'm finished with that leftie prick, he won't be able to get a job as the fecking social diarist on the *Tallaght Tribune*. And when I think of all the handouts I've thrown at his TV station over the years!'

'Mr Nolan, that's exactly the type of comment that will most emphatically not go down well at the Tribunal,' replied Harry coolly. 'Now, if we could just get back to what we were discussing about damage limitation?'

'Right, so,' said Shamie, sitting down, 'you think there's no other way around it?'

'I'm afraid not.'

'Bridie'll hit the ceiling when she hears this—' Shamie broke off, interrupted by the woman herself, who burst through the kitchen door laden down with armloads of shopping bags.

'Shamie Nolan, I'm after saving you a feckin' fortune!' she exclaimed, her standard greeting whenever her shopping sprees had run into four-figure sums, which they frequently did. 'Howaya, Harry? Did ya get a cup of tea?' she asked, bending down to rummage in the first of many bags.

'Yes, thanks,' he answered politely before she bulldozed over him.

'Take a look at this!' she squealed, producing what surely must have been one of the most garish outfits ever seen since Marc Bolan was top of the pops at the height of the glam rock era. Even a master of overstatement like Gianni Versace would have baulked at its fluorescent green hue and bat-wing sleeves with every square inch covered in giant diamanté insects. She

proudly held it up to her and pranced around the kitchen saying, 'Well, are yer eyes out on stilts or what, lads?'

'Very nice,' said Harry, an expert liar. 'Very, emm, Brazilian
rainforest.'

'I thought it would be fabulous to wear on the first day of
the Tribunal,' she went on. 'Do ya remember the way at Jeffrey
Archer's trial the judge took one look at his fragrant wife and
let him off? Well, wait till Michael de Courcey sees me in this!
And ya know, it'll do grand for all the entertaining we'll be
doing once we move into the Hall . . .'

'Yes, Davenport Hall,' replied Harry, relieved that she was
the one to have brought up the unpleasant subject. 'Your husband and I were just discussing that.'

In all fairness, Portia had to admit that even she never really
appreciated exactly how much work Mrs Flanagan did until
now, when it was too late. She and Daisy had spent the morning cleaning up after the previous night's revelries – not an
easy task.

'Can you believe the amount of wine we got through?' said
Daisy, yawning as she loaded up yet another trayload of
empties to cart down to the kitchen.

'I know, thank God Mummy has abandoned all her ideas to
go global with Eau de Davenport, or else she'd kill us for
throwing all those bottles out.' (Lucasta was a great one
for enthusiastically ramming her business scams down people's
throats ad nauseam, and then, just as suddenly, dropping them
the minute she got bored.)

'Where is she anyway?' asked Portia, emptying yet another
half-drunk gin and tonic into a slops bucket.

'Still in bed. She's lying in state today and refuses to
budge; she's communing with the other side to ask for a
solution to all our problems. She told me she's in touch with

a spirit guide who says he'll kick Shamie Nolan's arse for us.'

'Just out of curiosity, I'd love to know who the spirit guide is. Al Capone maybe?'

Daisy giggled.

'You're chirpy this morning, missy,' said Portia. 'Any reason why?'

'No reason,' she replied, tipping the contents of a stuffed ashtray into the bin.

'Right,' said Portia, taking charge, 'I need to go into Ballyroan to collect the car from Mrs Flanagan, do you fancy walking there with me?'

'You go, I'll stay here and keep on cleaning. And be sure to tell her how desperately we all miss her, won't you? And how much we need her back? Was I born so beautiful to spend my days emptying fag butts into bins?' she asked melodramatically.

Portia playfully threw a tea towel at her and ran upstairs to grab her tweed jacket from her room. As she walked down the upper corridor, she was just in time to hear chanting, or rather screeching coming from her mother's bedroom. The door was open and Lucasta, still in her long, grey nightie, was pacing up and down, as though in a trance-like state.

'I implore thee, I beseech thee, O benign one, in this our hour of direst need, to come to our aid and cleanse this house of the dark forces which are threatening us at this moment.'

'Need anything in town, Mummy?' Portia called, sticking her head around the door.

'Dark and evil spirits are clouding around me and only your intervention can save us now!' she went on, ignoring Portia. 'I call on you to take us from out of the darkness and into the light and GET TONIC WATER IN SPAR, WE'RE OUT OF MIXERS,' she screamed after Portia, not coming out of her trance for a second.

It was a cold, damp, miserable morning and Portia didn't

envy the film crew who were scheduled to film in the Yellow Drawing Room all day. Technically it was an indoor scene, but given the arctic cold in that room and the way temperatures would plummet whenever the north wind whistled through the gaping holes in the wall, they may as well have been shooting outside. Thank God it's not raining, she thought, banging the front door behind her, the ceiling in there leaks so badly, they'd have thought they were filming in Niagara Falls.

She was looking forward to a good, long, solitary walk (it was virtually impossible to get a moment's peace in the Hall these days) and was surprised to have only got as far as the stables when Daisy breathlessly caught up with her.

'I changed my mind, I'm coming with you,' she said, panting. 'I need to get out of there. Christ! When will this film ever be finished?'

'What's up now?' asked Portia.

'There I was, scrubbing for Ireland, when bloody Paddy creeps up behind me, like a fucking slithery bastard, nearly makes me leap six feet into the air and then shoves this at me,' she said, taking a handwritten poem from the pocket of her wax jacket.

Portia glanced down at it and saw that it was titled 'O Most Pernicious Woman'.

'Go on, you can read it,' said Daisy. 'If nothing else in your life makes you glad to be single, this will.'

Portia saw at a glance that it was every bit as long as *Paradise Lost* but maybe not quite as poetic. One verse, which caught her eye, went:

> You're nothing but a slag,
> You're nothing but a tart,
> You stupid bloody bitch,

You broke my fucking heart.
I thought you were my girlfriend,
I thought you were all right,
I thought you were a lady,
What a load of shite.

'Well, I don't think he'll ever be appointed Poet Laureate, but he certainly gets his point across, doesn't he?'

'I'm telling you, he's unhinged. He's a male bunny boiler. I'll go home and he'll have shredded all my underwear,' Daisy ranted, waving the wad of paper dramatically in front of her, looking like Neville Chamberlain in 1939. 'This, this, *this* is the kind of thing that . . . that . . .'

'That what?'

'That makes you appreciate the normal guys. Like, emm . . . Steve, for instance. Just, oh, you know, just off the top of my head . . .' she trailed off meekly.

Portia would have burst out laughing, given how dismissive bordering on cruel she'd been to him in the past, except that by now they'd arrived at the main entrance gates.

Ordinarily there'd be a handful of reporters standing around, moaning at each other and looking miserable. In the past few weeks, the Davenports had become almost friendly with the press, they were such an integral part of their daily lives by now. Inwardly, Portia would marvel at the information they managed to wheedle out about what was going on at the Hall. For instance, how did they know for certain that Ella Hepburn used Hellmann's mayonnaise on her hair as a conditioner, or that she had a chemical peel applied to her face and neck every other day? (THERE'S MORE OF ELLA'S SKIN IN THE BIN THAN ON HER FACE, the headline had run.) They even seemed to know the most intimate personal details of Montana's menstrual cycle (HORMONAL MONTANA'S AT THE

CHOCOLATE AGAIN, had been another one). Portia's own personal theory was that they were going through the bins. But how they were capable of gleaning so much from so little was beyond her. Their talents were totally wasted in the field of journalism, she used to think, they'd be put to far better use in the Secret Service, or as weapons inspectors in the Middle East.

But the media's favourite character by far in the ongoing soap opera they'd manufactured was Lucasta herself, whom they portrayed as a lovable cross between Barbara Cartland and Joyce Grenfell. Indeed, she was so regularly featured in the papers these days that she'd become a minor celebrity of sorts, with pictures of her bottle-feeding kittens making all the gossip pages. In recent days, the press had even turned the Nolans' purchase of the Hall into a cause célèbre, running photos of Lucasta and Bridie Nolan side by side beneath headlines like: WHOM DO YOU WANT DAVENPORT HALL TO BELONG TO? THE LADY OR THE TRAMP? Given that six months ago most people would have been hard pressed even to tell you where Davenport Hall was, all this media attention had really put it on the map. So much so that Portia often thought about how impossible it would be for Andrew not to know what was going on. Which could only lead back to the inevitable conclusion that he wasn't interested and didn't care.

The girls passed through the huge, rusting entrance gates and paused for a chat with the journalists.

'Simon, how's your cold?' asked Daisy, addressing one of them. 'Did the potion Mummy send down to you make a difference?'

'Much better, thanks,' he replied. 'Ladies, could we ask you one quick question please?'

Portia and Daisy exchanged puzzled glances. 'Of course,' said Portia, 'unless it's personal!'

All of a sudden, there seemed to be cameras pointing at them from every direction, microphones thrust in their faces and sound booms wobbling over their heads. Bright lights shone right at them, temporarily startling them both. 'So this is what it feels like to be one of the Beckhams,' joked Daisy, but no one laughed. Bloody hell, thought Portia, wondering what was up and inwardly bracing herself for a curt 'no comment'. Daisy didn't even have time to fix her hair before Simon posed the question.

'Would you care to comment on the impending sale of Davenport Hall?'

They visibly relaxed as Portia answered for both of them.

'Naturally, we're devastated to have to leave our family home, but, whether we like it or not, the Nolans take possession at the end of August, as soon as the film has wrapped.' Even though the cameras were making her a little nervous, it did flash through her mind that this was hardly hot news. After all, they'd bought the Hall weeks ago.

Simon paused to rephrase the question.

'Perhaps you haven't heard. An announcement has just been made by Shamie Nolan's solicitors. Given the contentious nature of his purchase of the Hall and mindful of the fact that his legal fees could run into seven-figure sums, he has announced, with regret, his decision to sell. Immediately. As of now, Davenport Hall is back on the market.'

Edwina's morning had started out badly and got progressively worse. 'Are you learning impaired?' she snarled at the unfortunate seamstress charged with the task of pinning her dress in at the waist. 'I lose a few pounds and you can't even take the dress in without losing the whole line of it? This isn't brain surgery, you know, I'm not asking you to build the Channel Tunnel here.'

Kate Egan, her wedding planner, discreetly stepped forward, knowing that nervous brides-to-be were usually snappy and irritable like this. Especially in the final run-up to the big day. Particularly for a huge wedding like this one. She instinctively knew that all that was required was for a few ruffled feathers to be smoothed down a bit. 'Oh Edwina,' she gushed professionally, 'you look divine! Yes, you have lost a little weight, but the tiniest tweak along this seam here will sort that out. He's a very lucky man, you know,' she added for good measure. Not for nothing did her services command six-figure fees each year.

Edwina stepped down from the dais she'd been standing on in the middle of the designer's studio, being ultra careful not to trip over her ten-foot train.

'I need a word with you,' she whispered threateningly to Kate. 'Now, I'm trying my best to remain calm, but do you see what I'm seeing?' She nodded over to the far end of the studio, where her two teenage nieces were being fitted for their bridesmaids' dresses.

'Aren't they adorable?' was the best comment Kate could muster.

'Kate, I need to be absolutely clear about one thing,' Edwina replied imperiously. 'When I chose them to be my bridesmaids, I did so in the full knowledge that neither of them was ever likely to win a beauty pageant. I was willing to overlook their imperfections, because I knew they could only make me look better. But, for Christ's sake, look at them!'

Kate dutifully shot a glance down to the opposite end of the studio. They did indeed look horrific. The coral colour of their Bo-Peep style dresses only brought out the pus on their acne-covered faces and the designer's carefully concealed foundation garments did absolutely nothing to secure their sagging breasts and prevent them from wobbling as they moved. Harland and Wolff would have been hard pressed to manufacture underwear that would hold them in place.

'It's the biggest day of my life,' sniffed Edwina, on the brink of tears, 'and I'll look like I have transsexuals for my bridesmaids. When I walk down the aisle, it's going to look like *The Rocky Horror Show*.'

'Leave it to me,' replied Kate calmly. 'Both bridesmaids' dresses will have to be completely remodelled, I'm afraid,' she said to the seamstress, 'even if it means working all night to get them ready in time. It's now four p.m. We have exactly twenty-four hours to show time.'

Chapter Thirty

The story travelled like wildfire. By the time Portia and Daisy had reached Ballyroan, the first person they bumped into was Steve, driving down Main Street on his way to Davenport Hall to discuss the news.

'So what on earth made Shamie Nolan decide to sell?' Portia was quizzing him.

'Money,' he replied. 'What else? I've just had a call from Michael de Courcey to tell me that he met with the Minister this morning. The Tribunal will start its hearings in the next few weeks and he thinks it could last for at least eighteen months, given the amount of evidence against Nolan there is to sift through. So his costs alone will be extortionate.'

'And how would it look in the papers if he and Bridie were spending millions renovating the Hall while all this was going on?' said Portia, thinking aloud. 'How much do you think it'll sell for on the open market?'

'Hard to say,' he replied, taking off a very cool-looking pair of designer sunglasses and slipping them into the 'V' of his shirt. 'Nolan got it for two million, but that was a bargain basement price. I imagine by the time you get home, he'll have an estate agent scouring the place to put the highest guide price on it that he possibly can.' He glanced over to Daisy, who instantly reddened. 'So, how do both of you feel about this?'

'Well, short of one of us winning the Lottery tonight, it's not really going to affect us, is it?' said Portia, ignoring the fact that Daisy was looking like a beetroot by now. 'We're no longer the legal owners anyway, we were just there on borrowed time. So unless you've got a few million stashed away you'd care to lend us . . .'

Steve smiled and turned away.

'No, I didn't think solicitors made that kind of money,' Portia teased. 'But at least one good thing has come out of all this. Whoever does buy it, they could never be as awful as the Nolans, not in a million years. Who knows, they may even take pity on us and give us jobs on the estate.'

Steve nodded sagely, then, suddenly changing the subject, he asked if he could offer them a lift home.

'No, thanks,' Portia replied, answering for them both, 'we've got to collect the car from Mrs Flanagan.'

'Actually, I'd love a lift home,' said Daisy without a second's thought. 'It's so wet and drizzly and I don't want my boots to get wrecked.'

Portia looked on in mild bemusement as Daisy clambered up into Steve's passenger seat.

She was wearing Wellingtons.

Mrs Flanagan too, had heard the story. The crackly portable radio in the hairdresser's had just broadcast the lunchtime news, so chances were the whole town knew by now. No sooner had Portia walked through the door of the Crown and Glory than she came waddling over to hug her. Portia hugged her back tightly, realizing all over again how much she really missed her.

'Well, I'm delighted that aul' bastard Shamie Nolan is finally getting his come-uppance,' Mrs Flanagan said. 'Sneaking off to Las bleedin' Vegas to con your halfwit of a father in the first place; he should have been jailed for that alone. And as for that aul' cow of a wife of his, do you know she comes in here all the time to get her roots done and never, ever tips?'

'Shhh,' Portia whispered, in case customers might overhear.

'Are ya afraid someone might be listening?' laughed Mrs Flanagan as she waddled back behind the empty receptionist's desk. 'Where in the name of Jaysus do ya think ya are? Vidal Sassoon?'

Portia glanced over her shoulder to see that the salon was completely empty.

'So, has she asked for me yet?' said Mrs Flanagan, lighting up a cigarette. 'Or has she even noticed that I'm gone?'

Portia paused for a moment before answering, knowing all of her inherent tact and diplomacy would be needed here. She had spent most of the previous day alternately coaxing and begging her mother to apologize to Mrs Flanagan, all for nothing. 'I'd rather cut off my left tit and eat it for dinner than apologize to that wagon,' had been her actual words. And once Lucasta dug her heels in, that was usually that.

'We all miss you dreadfully and we want you to come home so badly. I don't suppose there's the smallest chance that I could persuade you to—'

'Listen to me, luv. Hell will freeze over before I work for that mad bitch again. It said on the lunchtime news that Shamie Nolan is looking for five million for the Hall. Well, ya can tell yer mother from me, she'll be a long time turning tricks in the Kildare Arms before she'll buy it back at that price.'

The level of interest in Davenport Hall was phenomenal. Eamonn Cassidy, the estate agent who was handling the sale, had never seen anything like it. Almost as soon as it went on the market, his tiny office in Kildare town was flooded with phone calls, emails and faxes from as far away as Canada, all full of enquiries about the impending auction. Shamie Nolan's instructions on the subject had been clear and concise. 'Squeeze as much cash out of this as ya can and, for Jaysus' sake, try not to show too much of the kip when yer're having viewings. If a buyer was to see the real state of the place, sure they'd run a mile.'

And so Eamonn hit on the one ingenious excuse that was staring him in the face.

'Of course I'd be delighted to show you over Davenport Hall,' he would smarm down the phone to potential buyers, 'except that there's a film being made there at present, which makes certain parts of the property inaccessible to viewers.' He would then conduct clients over the land and when it came to viewing the inside of the Hall, he would try to steer them clear of the most decrepit parts of the house and concentrate instead on the Ballroom, the one room the film crew had jazzed up a bit for the interior scenes. Cleverly, he also arranged for private viewings only to be held at night, when it was less likely a buyer would notice the decaying ceilings and rotting floorboards, and he was also careful never to show it whilst it was raining for fear of bringing a whole new meaning to the phrase 'water feature'.

The level of media interest in Davenport Hall had certainly put it on the map, and Eamonn had his work cut out in distinguishing genuine potential buyers from tourists who only wanted access to the Hall in the hopes of catching a glimpse of a Hollywood star. (His rule of thumb was that if a client arrived at the Hall clutching a camera and an autograph book, chances were they didn't have a few million euros to throw away.)

However, there were a number of genuinely interested buyers, with a notable celebrity amongst them. Billy Toner, the lead singer with Ireland's most famous rock band, the Living Dead, had flown in by helicopter to inspect the Hall and seemed very taken with it. The fact that it was nighttime and that he didn't once remove his trademark wraparound sunglasses had helped to shield him from the worst horrors of the house. Billy Toner, it seemed, was the proud father of no less than nine children, all by different mothers, and felt that at least here they could each have their own bedroom.

'Yeah, man, sure it's a bit run down,' he said to Eamonn in his acquired mid-Atlantic accent, 'but I want my kids to grow up knowing what it's like to be underprivileged, a bit like I did, man. This house could be the nearest they'll ever come to living in a ghetto.'

Another serious contender was the leader of a religious cult called the New Age Loons. He arrived at the Hall with Eamonn late one night, clad entirely in white robes, and introduced himself to Lucasta by his spirit-guide name, Chasing Moonbeams. He then examined every square inch of the Hall, commenting on how poor the ley lines were. When he saw the Ballroom, he said that it would make a perfect temple to the Goddess of Isis, but that it would have to be feng-shuied from top to bottom first. Chasing Moonbeams was equally taken with the Yellow Drawing Room, saying that it would make a wonderful past life regression centre. Then, standing in the middle of the entrance hall, he claimed that he could sense a great number of lost spirits there who weren't fully at peace on the other side.

'Well, I hope to fuck he doesn't buy it,' said Lucasta, firmly banging the door behind them. 'I think he could be a bit mad.'

There was also interest in the Hall from a most unexpected quarter. Early one morning, as Guy and Ella lay in bed together, sharing a post-coital cigarette, inspiration struck.

'I win, darling,' said Guy, throwing his copy of the previous day's *National Intruder* on to the floor. 'My name is mentioned forty-one times and yours only thirty-six. Sorry, baby, I've counted. So, if I've tallied up right, that's a win for me two days running.'

Ella said nothing, just continued to blow smoke upwards towards the moth-eaten canopy of the four-poster bed.

'Now, according to the rules,' drawled Guy, 'if they'd printed a picture of you then that would give you ten extra points, but the only photo they got was one of me doing my yoga, so you forfeit the game, darling.'

Ella turned and fixed him with a smouldering stare.

'I know just what you're thinking, baby,' he laughed. 'Sure, they're going to take my picture if I practise yoga right in the middle of the driveway twenty feet away from the lenses, but, honey, that's what they're for. If they're going to make millions selling papers with me plastered all over 'em, then surely I deserve a little publicity in return? You know, that's probably the only good thing about this fucking hellhole, at least the press are willing to travel down here. Not like what happened to poor ol' Burt Reynolds when he bought his ranch in Nevada, remember, honey?'

Ella continued to stare at the ceiling.

'He thought the press boys would track him down' – Guy laughed, cracking up at his own gag – 'and that he'd be all, like, "Fuck off and give me some privacy!" But they all thought it was too far to travel, so they never bothered. Burt sold up within six months; he couldn't take his face being out of the papers for that length of time!' Guy was hysterical by now, thoroughly enjoying the media one-upmanship, and then the thought struck. Turning on to his side to face Ella he said, 'You know, baby, you and I could do a lot worse for ourselves than to buy this place.'

He must have been getting through to her, because her eyelids flickered for a millisecond.

'I'm serious, baby,' he went on, taking this as an encouraging sign. 'Sure, it's a shithole right now, but with the right architect and the right interior designer, it could really be something. And think of the parties, baby! The A list would fly in here by the planeload! If we built a golf course, we'd definitely get Catherine and Michael; of course we'd have to have a crèche for their kids, but that needn't be a problem. And if we had an Irish theme bar, then Leo and Brad and Tom would definitely come. Especially when I tell them that the press are camped right at the front door. A little holiday in the beautiful Irish countryside and a little press to tell the world all about it, what more could they want?'

Ella reached her arm across the bedside table and carelessly stubbed out her cigarette into a pot of Vaseline.

'I think it's a terrific idea, baby,' said Guy, lying back down again. 'I'm really glad we had this talk.'

It was the night before the auction and Portia had never known exhaustion like it. She'd spent the entire day single-handedly packing up the Library, putting one dusty tome after another into dozens of cardboard boxes and she still was nowhere near finished. Now I know why families stay in these great houses for generation after generation, she thought. It's just too bloody difficult to move out. Eventually, as the grandfather clock in the hall chimed midnight, she'd had enough. The best she could hope for was that whoever bought the Hall the following day would take pity on the Davenports and allow them a little breathing space so they could pack up two hundred years of their history into cardboard boxes and move out with what little dignity they had left.

Exhausted, she hauled herself downstairs to the kitchen to

make sòme tea. The Hall was deadly quiet, the film crew long since having wrapped up for the night. Lucasta had barely left her room, so intent was she on communing with the other side for help, and Daisy had disappeared all day. Rubbing the back of her aching neck with her hand, she switched on Mrs Flanagan's TV set. Anything to distract her from thoughts of what the next day would bring. It was Channel Seven, just coming to the end of the nightly news report.

'And finally on to showbiz news. In what must surely qualify as the wedding of the year, today in Dublin's Pro-Cathedral the Irish supermodel Edwina Moynihan walked down the aisle . . .' Portia stood rooted to the spot as the camera clearly showed a radiant Edwina gracefully stepping out of a vintage Rolls-Royce followed by the two most unfortunate-looking bridesmaids ever seen. The camera even caught one of them picking her nose. The bride smacked her across the wrist before waving to onlookers and lightly skipping up the cathedral steps.

Portia could take no more. She switched off the TV and slumped down into Mrs Flanagan's tatty old armchair.

Once the tears started flowing, she thought they'd never stop.

Chapter Thirty-One

The morning of the auction dawned bright and clear, much to Lucasta's disgust. She'd been up since six that morning chanting for rain in the vain hope that torrents of water gushing through the ceiling would put off prospective buyers. Over breakfast that morning, Portia reminded her for the thousandth time that the Hall would be sold whether they liked it or not, but, as usual, she was wasting her breath.

'No negativity around me today, sweetie,' Lucasta said, going upstairs to get dressed. 'You must trust me. I've been communing with the other side all week, you know, and they tell me everything's going to work out beautifully. And I've been chanting for a happy outcome too and we all know how powerful my chanting is.'

Daisy was agitated and nervous too, constantly looking at her watch and then asking Portia what time it was two seconds later. Between them, they had decided the auction would best be held in the Long Gallery. Eamonn Cassidy had told them to expect a large turnout and the Gallery was easily the biggest room in the Hall. The auction was to take place at midday and they both spent the morning arranging row after row of chairs to seat everyone, making the room look a bit like a parish hall on bingo night.

Jimmy D. had been most understanding and had kindly offered to suspend filming for the morning, until it was all over and he could have the run of the house again. Even Montana had sent a message of support from her room. *I can't watch,* her note had said, *but my thoughts are with you guys! I just wish this movie was paying me enough to buy the Hall and give it back to you as a gift.*

'She meant well,' Portia said on seeing Daisy's eyes well up with tears.

'I know, I know,' Daisy answered, glancing around the empty Long Gallery as though for the last time. 'It's just that, well, this is it, isn't it? This is really it.'

Lucasta's behaviour was nothing short of appalling. From as early as eleven a.m., buyers had started to throng the Hall, and the Long Gallery was soon bursting at the seams. She took it on herself to introduce herself to everyone and to inform them that the Hall was cursed.

'Let the buyer beware!' she said melodramatically, tossing her matted hair over her shoulders and clutching Gnasher, her favourite cat, tightly to her. 'He who usurps the family from their ancestral home will be cursed for generations to come. No good will ever come to the occupant of Davenport Hall, you only have to look at my daughters to see that, barren spinsters the pair of them.'

No sooner had Portia steered her away from one group of potential buyers than she was over to another. 'Well, I just hope you don't mind living with ectoplasmic manifestations from the other side because that's what you're in for. Your children might very well become possessed. Have none of you people seen *The Exorcist*?'

Then poor Billy Toner arrived, looking as conspicuous as ever in his trademark sunglasses, and she landed on him like a ton of bricks.

'How can you even consider turning us out of our ancestral home? We are the last of the noble line of Davenports. Apart from the one in jail.' She wasn't kidding. Their cousin Mad Jasper Davenport was currently doing a twenty-year stretch in Portlaoise maximum security prison for staging an animal rights protest. (Unfortunately, his protest was to shoot dead two farmers for speaking rudely to battery hens, as he subsequently testified in court.) He did say, however, that being in jail was like staying in a five-star hotel compared with Davenport Hall.

'You know, man, I felt really vibed out about that, so you can all crash in the gate lodge for as long as you want, man,' replied Billy, 'providing I get the Hall.'

Eventually, Eamonn Cassidy took his place at the end of the Gallery and tried to call everyone to order. Portia was at the back of the room glancing around to see if there was anywhere for her to sit when she saw Daisy waving to her like a lunatic from the front row. 'We're up here!' she called out and Portia gratefully made her way to the far end of the Gallery. There must be five hundred people here, she thought, never having seen the room so packed. Billy Toner sat down in the second row, clutching a rolled-up copy of the auctioneer's brochure. Chasing Moonbeams sat across from him, clad in white robes and surrounded by three women, all very young and very beautiful, and all smelling strongly of incense. There were also two very tall, handsome men, dressed in snappy black suits, standing right beside Eamonn. Portia correctly guessed that they were from the Criminal Assets Bureau, given Shamie Nolan's involvement in the sale. However, this didn't prevent a rumour from sweeping through the room that they were members of the Al Maktoum family who wanted to buy the Hall and turn it into a stud farm. ('Well, at least they might cut the grass,' she overheard one wag commenting.)

She slipped into the empty seat beside Daisy and Lucasta and was surprised to see Serge sitting with them, unscrewing a bottle of rescue remedy and passing it along. 'Take one big gulp each, girls,' he said, 'and I promise you won't feel a thing.'

'What are you doing here?' asked Portia. 'I thought Jimmy D. gave you all the morning off.'

'Oh yeah, he did, honey, I'm just so drawn to real-life drama, I can't help myself.'

As though on cue, the grandfather clock in the hall boomed out midday and, gradually, the room quietened down.

'Oh, this is just like *High Noon!*' said Serge. 'My piles are clenching with the tension!' An onlooker could easily have been forgiven for thinking that he was the rightful owner.

'I'm on tenterhooks,' said Daisy.

'And I'm on Zanax,' he replied.

'Ladies and gentlemen, you're all very welcome here today for the auction of Davenport Hall,' began Eamonn Cassidy, shouting to make himself heard. 'As you will see from the brochure in front of you, this important property was built by James Gandon in the mid-eighteenth century and is showing the effects of some minor wear and tear.'

'Minor?' whispered Serge, amazed at the brazenness of estate-agent speak.

'The Hall itself contains eight reception rooms, including a Ballroom, which many of you will have already seen, a Library, a Billiard Room and the Long Gallery you're seated in now. In addition there are sixteen bedrooms all of which are . . . emm . . . in need of refurbishment. The property also encompasses over two thousand acres of land, including woodlands, fishing rights along the River Kilcullen and Loch Moluag bordering the edge of the estate. So without further ado, may I have an opening bid? Do I hear one million euros?'

Portia didn't hear anyone reply, but someone must have because seconds later the bidding had leapt up to one point five and in lightning time it had reached two million. Eamonn then proudly declared Davenport Hall to be 'on the market'. From the word go, the bidding was fast and furious and in no time had climbed up to three million.

'Turns my stomach to think that Shamie bloody Nolan will make a profit on this,' Daisy whispered to Portia.

Very soon, it boiled down to a three-horse race between Billy Toner, who was sitting right behind them, Chasing Moonbeams and a third bidder at the back of the Gallery whom none of them could see. They were at the three point five million mark now and Lucasta was on the edge of her seat, as though she were watching a horse race.

'Come on, Billy Toner!' she screeched. 'You can do it!'

Eamonn Cassidy had to bring proceedings momentarily to a halt in order to ask for quiet before moving on. For once, Portia found herself in agreement with her mother. At least Billy Toner had a big family and there was something lovely about the idea that Davenport Hall would be full of children again.

'And he's all into cancelling Third World debt,' Daisy whispered, 'so maybe he'll cancel our debts too. Or at least give us jobs here.'

Poor Eamonn was about to continue when there was a further, most unexpected development. A side door which led into the Gallery suddenly opened and in strolled Guy and Ella, hand in hand and looking like they already owned the place.

'Now, don't tell me you all started without us,' Guy

announced to the room as autograph-hunters began to cluster around Ella. 'Why, I didn't think anything began on time in Ireland.'

'There are two seats here on this side, if you'd care to bid,' said Eamonn, almost falling over himself at the sight of Ella Hepburn. She did indeed look spectacular, in pale blue palazzo pants with a matching headscarf tied around her head, clutching her tiny Pekinese dog. There was a ripple of applause as she and Guy took their seats, which she acknowledged with the tiniest nod of her head.

'I'll set fire to Davenport Hall before I see them living here,' said Daisy, flushed with anger and not caring who overheard.

'Well, hand me a box of matches while you're at it and I'll set fire to her fucking dog,' replied Lucasta, glaring over at her. 'That fart of a thing is upsetting Gnasher.'

'I don't believe it!' wailed Serge, getting hopelessly swept up in the moment. 'They can't buy it, they'll turn it into a theme park for ageing movie actors.'

But it seemed that they had every intention of buying it, with Guy immediately jumping in and bringing up the bidding to three point eight million.

'Come on, go higher!' Daisy hissed at Billy Toner in the row behind her. 'Forget the Third World, you need to buy Davenport Hall!'

'Exactly!' said Lucasta, agreeing. 'Never mind all those African loser countries, you should spend your money here.'

Portia had clenched her knuckles so tightly as the bidding edged towards four million euros that she thought she'd cut off the circulation to her hands. By now, Chasing Moonbeams had thrown in the towel, shaking his head at Eamonn to indicate that he was out of the running.

'Thank Christ for that,' whispered Lucasta. 'Who wants bloody weirdos living here anyway?'

Eamonn ploughed on, with Guy pushing the price higher and higher until at four point five million euros, Billy Toner backed down.

'Bloody coward!' said Daisy, on the verge of tears. By now, the field had narrowed down to a two-horse race between Guy and the person at the back of the Gallery who was matching him relentlessly, bid for bid.

'And we are now at five million euros,' declared Eamonn. 'Do I hear five million?'

Guy and Ella conferred with each other. Then there was an embarrassed pause during which Guy was heard whispering, 'I know it's your money, but I thought we were agreed!'

'Sir?' Eamonn asked him, anxious to move on. Guy folded his arms and shook his head, throwing a filthy look at Ella.

'Do I hear five million euros? Yes? The gentleman at the back of the room, thank you.' Portia and Daisy were craning their necks to see who it was, but the room was way too crowded to make him out.

'Five million euros it is,' declared Eamonn. 'Going once, going twice, sold to the gentleman at the back for five million euros.'

There was a round of applause before Eamonn could bring the proceedings to order again.

'What name, sir?' he asked. But the reply was completely drowned out by the cacophony of voices in the room.

'Sir?' Eamonn was shouting by now. 'May I have your name, please?'

'Oh, didn't you hear me?' came a voice from the back of the room, which immediately sent a shiver down Portia's spine.

'I'm afraid not, sir,' said Eamonn. 'Could I have your full name, please?'

'It's Davenport. Jack Davenport.'

★

Portia felt her knees buckle from under her as she gripped on to Daisy's arm for support. Lucasta had passed out and Serge was pouring neat Rescue Remedy straight down her throat. There was no mistake. Through the crowds at the back of the room who'd milled around to congratulate him, she could just about make out the back of her father's head. He was shaking people's hands, smiling and laughing, like a king returning from exile. Steve was behind him, looking every bit as shell-shocked as they were by the outcome. She could see Blackjack clearly now, his usual dapper, flamboyant self in an immaculately cut suit, with his jet-black hair slicked back and his black eyes glowing. For a moment, she caught his eye and he waved regally at her and Daisy, indicating that he'd be with them in a moment. But it wasn't that which made Portia's nerves jangle and her breath catch in the back of her throat.

Standing right beside him, looking as tall and tanned and gorgeous as ever, was Andrew.

Chapter Thirty-Two

'Daddy!' squealed Daisy, jumping into his arms like a ten-year-old. 'I knew you'd come back to us!'

'My darling girl, did you honestly think that I'd allow Davenport Hall to be sold to strangers? This home that we all love so much?' Somehow, Blackjack always managed to sound about as sincere as a daytime chat-show host. His voice was oily and deep, and his eyes were dancing at the sight of his favourite child.

'Well, yes actually, that's exactly what we thought,' said Portia, unwilling to play along with the charade of a happy family reunion. She could feel Andrew's eyes on her and was determined not to look at him first, although in a million years she couldn't guess what he was doing there. Bugger it, she thought, I'll have my say if it kills me. 'You'll forgive me for not joining in the hero's welcome,' she said in a wobbly voice, 'but can I remind you that you sold us out? You gambled our home without even bothering to tell us.'

'Portia my dear,' he replied, 'a straight flush to the ace is not a gamble. You look so serious, darling, so grave and pale. Can't you at least be happy that you've got your home back?'

Portia looked at him disgustedly. As far back as she could

remember, this was what her father always did, smooth talk his way out of everything. The man was possessed of Olympic-sized quantities of charm, which he knew only too well how to use to maximum effect. As Mrs Flanagan used to say, 'That fella would charm his way out of a bucket of shite.' And here he was, at it again. Same old pattern repeating itself.

'Yes, I took Shamie Nolan's money,' he went on in his deep cigars-and-cognac voice, 'but I only ever looked on it as a short-term loan. I knew I'd win it all back and more when the stakes were right, and I did. Eight million dollars to be exact. Trust in Providence, what have I always said?'

'Daddy!' shrieked Daisy almost knocking him over. 'The first time in your life that you've actually won!'

'And how about your girlfriend?' Portia was really going for broke now. 'Is she with you? Because I'm sure Mummy would love a word.'

'You have every reason to be angry with me,' he replied calmly. 'But please understand that I really have tried to make amends. I don't expect you to forgive me, Portia, but you might at least thank this young man.' He indicated Andrew, who was standing a few feet behind him.

For the first time, Portia met Andrew's gaze. A moment passed where each of them wondered who'd speak first. After what felt like an age, eventually Portia cracked. 'I didn't expect to see you here,' she said feebly.

'Well, I'm glad you spoke first,' he said dryly, 'because for a second there, I thought this was going to be awkward.'

'Must have been the shortest honeymoon in history,' she said.

'I wouldn't know, I'm not married.'

Suddenly, she felt flushed and weak at the same time.

'Could you use some air?' said Andrew.

All she could do was nod in reply as he gently guided her through the crowd and out of the door.

341

Meanwhile, ably nursed by Serge, Lucasta had come round.

'Mummy, isn't it wonderful?' gushed Daisy with tears of joy running down her cheeks. 'He's come back!'

'Oh bollocks,' groaned his lady wife, 'I thought I was dreaming. You know that spell I did to make myself irresistible to men? *Big* fucking mistake.'

It was a magnificent day and almost as soon as she stepped outside into the fresh, gentle breeze, Portia felt her wits coming back to her. Andrew walked beside her, steering them away from the crowds dispersing in the forecourt and down the wooded dirt track behind the Hall, which led to Loch Moluag.

'Feeling better?' he asked, darting a sideways glance at her.

'Mmm,' she answered, still a bit unsteady and shaking like a leaf.

'Here, sit down,' he said, indicating a wooden bench which faced out on to the lake, 'you're still as white as a ghost.' She obediently did what she was told, trying her best to breathe deeply and calm down.

The view helped. When the sun was shining, Loch Moluag really was a sight to behold. The way the light dappled on the water was something no artist could capture and as they sat side by side under the shade of a cool willow tree, Portia gradually began to feel her composure flooding back.

Andrew took a box of cigarettes from his pocket and lit one up. He seemed a bit nervous too, jumpy and stressed-looking.

'The wedding was on TV, you know,' she began, deliberately not looking at him but focusing on the view ahead. 'I saw a tiny clip of it on the late news last night.'

'Well,' he answered, taking a deep pull of the cigarette, 'I wish Edwina every happiness, she certainly got her man.'

Portia looked at him, completely at a loss.

'I have the most wonderful alibi to prove that I was

nowhere near a church getting married yesterday, you know. I was flying home from Las Vegas with your father.'

'What did you say?'

'Portia, did you honestly think it was just a total co-incidence that he showed up today of all days like some deus ex machina? How do you think he knew about the auction? Who do you think talked him into buying the Hall back for his family? If all my years in corporate law have taught me anything, they've taught me how to be persuasive. As soon as my father filled me in on the Tribunal he's chairing, we both decided there was nothing else for it. Someone had to physically travel to the States to get Lord Davenport home, and I was the obvious person. If that gobshite Shamie Nolan could get to him then so could I. Blackjack is going to be one of my father's star witnesses, you know.'

'But what about Edwina? Your mother told me you were back together with her.'

'Well, that's certainly news to me.'

Portia looked at him in utter astonishment.

'You know, in spite of everything, I do think that you are a good person,' he said, pulling on a cigarette and staring out over the lake. 'You're straightforward and totally lacking in guile, I'll give you that much. I think it would be near im-possible for you even to comprehend the deviousness of some women, with my mother leading the field. That woman's talents are utterly wasted baking scones and doing meals on wheels for the Irish Countrywomen's Association, she should be writing soap operas for a living. She has by far the most devious, manipulative, twisted, inventive imagination I've ever come across – and I'm a lawyer.'

'Do you mean she was lying?' Portia's head was starting to swim. 'But why would anyone do that? Why would she go to such lengths?'

'At the risk of sounding conceited, she wanted Edwina and me back together and this was one sure-fire way of marking your card. No doubt the pictures and stories about you and me in the *National Intruder* spurred her resolve a bit.'

'So who did Edwina marry?'

'You know, I forget about the isolated existence you lead here, my lady,' he said teasingly. 'Hasn't today's carrier pigeon arrived yet with the news? It's been splashed all over the papers.'

She grinned back at him, surprised that they'd slipped back so easily into their old banter. 'Andrew, in case you hadn't noticed, I was sort of otherwise occupied all morning.'

'Well then, have I got news for you. Do you remember the first night I took you out and we bumped into her in that awful pretentious restaurant?'

Portia second-guessed him. 'No! Don't tell me she married Trevor Morrissey? But he must be at least forty years older than her! And he's got skin the colour of a Jaffa Cake. And his last album was brutal, even Mummy's a better singer than him.'

'He's also a multi-millionaire, which would help a lot, in her eyes.'

Portia sat back for a moment, scarcely able to believe it.

'So why didn't you tell me? About going to the States and Blackjack and everything, I mean. You never even called. I was going off my head and you never even called.'

Andrew bent down to stub out his cigarette. 'Oh, I called all right. It's like trying to get through to Stalinist Russia, ringing this house. I left messages with your mother and Mrs Flanagan, both of whom told me you weren't in. I think Mrs Flanagan's exact words were: "She says to tell you she's not in, luv." Then Daisy practically banged the phone down on me; it seemed you were too busy with Steve even to take my call. Message received, loud and clear. I kept trying right up until I boarded the flight for the States, but your phone seemed to be disconnected. When I met you that night in the Four Seasons in Dublin, I knew you'd instantly jumped to the wrong conclusion when you saw me with Edwina, even though I only went with her because we'd arranged it months before. And you wouldn't even give me a chance to explain.'

Portia didn't answer. He had her there, she had point blank refused to take his call.

'I've played fair with you, Portia. I was furious with you for what you'd done and furious with myself for having mis-judged you so badly, but I did at least try to explain where I was coming from.'

An alarm bell was beginning to ring at the back of her head. *For what you'd done?* Her mind raced as he kept talking, well on to his third cigarette by now.

'I don't think I'll ever forget that awful Midsummer party as long as I live. There I was racing back to the Hall like a complete idiot, straight from a meeting with Paul O'Driscoll—'

'Who?' she interrupted.

'A senior Kildare County Councillor whom I'd just persuaded to go on the record about the rezoning of the Davenport land. I'd spent the entire night talking him round, busting a gut for you, working my ass off on your behalf, and when I came here, dying to tell you about it, Mrs Flanagan casually tells me you've gone to bed with someone else.'

'*What!*' Portia couldn't believe her ears.

'My reaction exactly. So I hoofed it up to your room and saw for myself. I don't think I ever would have thought it of you, only I saw with my own two eyes. And seeing is believing. Then I see pictures of you with him in the papers

345

and I thought: Well done, de Courcey, you sure know how to pick them.'

Portia's mind was reeling. 'Oh Jesus,' she stammered, the penny dropping. 'Yes, Steve did mention that there was some awful photo of him and me taken that night that appeared in some rag, but, oh God, I think you're talking about Paddy. Bloody Paddy. I'd choke him if he was here now.'

'Yet another boyfriend you conveniently forgot to tell me about? Who the hell is Paddy?'

'Andrew, listen to me.' Portia tried to take a deep breath, thinking: Please, dear God, just let me get this out right. 'Paddy is the sound man on the film and he's totally fixated on Daisy. He was a bit the worse for wear and got lost on his way to her room and ended up crashing out in mine. I didn't even know he was there because Steve had given me a pill that knocked me for six.' I'm starting to sound like a witness panicking under cross-examination now, she thought. She shot a side- ways glance at him, but he was staring out over the lake.

'So now we're back to Steve.' Andrew's tone was harsh, cutting. 'Portia, I've sat through French farces that are less complicated than this.'

'Is it possible, just possible that you think I'm seeing Steve? You're mad! You're completely bloody insane. He's a family friend, he's like a brother to me, how could you even think that there was anything going on?'

'I apologize for not being able to read your mind. What was I supposed to think?'

'You could have trusted me!'

'And you could have trusted me.'

An angry silence fell during which Portia made a mental note never to get into an argument with a lawyer again. There was just no point, Andrew was running rings around her. Bugger it, she thought, nothing to be lost now.

'I thought I was just some rebound fling for you,' she said, calmer now.

He turned to look at her. 'It seems we've been at cross purposes with each other. OK, I'll put my cards on the table. I tried telling you this the day of the Ball but you wouldn't listen. So maybe you'll hear me out now. What happened between us had never happened to me before and I doubt very much that it ever will again. I'd fallen for you, Portia, really fallen for you. From the very first time I met you in my parents' garden and you doused yourself in a glass of champagne.'

There it was. 'Fallen.' The past tense. Portia was scarcely able to breathe.

'But then I figured things were moving too fast for you,' he went on, 'and Edwina in the background wouldn't have helped. And my mother didn't exactly make you feel welcome.'

She couldn't listen to any more. There was a time for silence and resignation and a time to bloody well speak up.

'Andrew,' she said, turning to face him. 'Things weren't moving too fast at all. In fact, things couldn't have moved fast enough for me. I'm stone mad about you. I mean I think I'm in love with you . . . I mean . . . Oh God, I'm making such a pig's ear of this!'

'Go on,' he said, still looking at her intently.

'It's just that I never felt I was good enough for you. I mean, look at you! You could have any woman you wanted and I could never understand why you'd want to be with me in the first place. And on the day of the Midsummer party I knew you were annoyed with me and I wanted to sort it out with you, but you disappeared, you just disappeared. I was gutted. I kept thinking you'd turn up at the Hall one day, but nothing.' She was beginning to get teary, now that she was finally

347

putting all her pent-up feelings into words for the first time. 'And then your mother told me you and Edwina were back together and then Steve and I had a meeting with your father in your house one day—'

'You were in the house?'

'Yes, it was the first I knew about the Tribunal. Your dad was lovely, so understanding, but he said he was off to a rehearsal dinner for Edwina's wedding . . .'

'Never go into law, Portia, your attention to detail is nothing short of pitiful. He said he was going to a rehearsal dinner for Edwina's wedding, not mine. Her father passed on years ago and she'd asked him to give her away. Dad was just too much of a softie to refuse.'

'But what was I to think, Andrew? I had no choice. I just had to accept that you were as good as married and try my best to get over you.'

Very tenderly, he lifted his hand to her cheek and brushed away a stray hair. 'Well, after all the trouble I've been to, I sincerely hope that you're not.'

She caught his hand and smiled up at him, her eyes filling up all over again. 'No,' she said, 'very definitely under you.'

'Well, thank God for something,' he said, putting his arms around her and running his fingers through her hair. She held on to him so tightly she thought she'd never let go. He ran his finger gently across her cheek before bending down to kiss her. She kissed him back greedily, waves of relief and happiness sweeping over her.

'So, my lady,' he whispered into her ear as he was kissing her neck, 'do you really think you could be with a commoner like me?'

'Yes please,' she murmured back, 'yes, yes please.'

Hours later, as they strolled arm in arm back towards the Hall, Andrew turned to her and said, 'You know, honey, you're looking pale and tired. You're exhausted. What do you say we get away for a few weeks together? Just you and me?'

'Oh Andrew, I'd love nothing more,' she said, stopping to put her arms around his neck and hug him tightly again. 'I don't care where we go as long as I'm with you.'

'Somewhere sunny and exotic maybe?' he said, kissing her forehead. 'We could always call it a honeymoon.'

Unbeknownst to Andrew and Portia, someone was watching them. As they passionately kissed each other like a pair of teenage sweethearts in the field behind the Hall, Lucasta just happened to be passing by an upstairs window and caught a glimpse of them.

Pausing for a brief moment to pick up Gnasher, she pointed the cat's tiny head towards the window. 'There you are, Gnasher, you see? My spells and chanting never fail, you know. Didn't I tell you everything would work out beautifully?'

Chapter Thirty-Three

The atmosphere at Davenport Hall that evening couldn't have been more different from the previous night. As everyone assembled in the Long Gallery for a celebratory drink, Portia was fit to burst with sheer happiness.

'Honey, you're positively glowing!' Serge had said to her when she told him her news. 'You know, I once read some-where that all a woman needs to be truly beautiful is to wear black and be on the arm of the man she loves, and, baby, you're living proof. So this hunk of sex must be the famous Andrew?' he whispered, so he wouldn't be overheard. Portia nodded and smiled. 'Why oh why are all the good-looking ones straight?' he said, shaking his green hair theatrically. 'Well, far be it from me to upstage the happy couple but do you wanna hear some hot, hot, *hot* gossip from the set today?'

'Yes, please, I love gossip,' said Daisy, who'd joined them, slipping her arms around Portia's waist. 'Isn't it the most amazing news, Serge?' she added, beaming at Portia. 'My big sister's getting married!'

'Gossip first, gushing later,' he interrupted, delighted to have an audience. 'Now, this is highly confidential, so only tell one person at a time, but I heard from Caroline who heard from

350

Johnny Maguire who heard from Jimmy D. that Montana and Paddy ended up together last night! So are you stunned?'

'I know, I know!' cried Daisy excitedly. 'Because when I was upstairs earlier, I saw him tiptoeing out of her room. He almost fainted when he saw me and made the funniest excuse. He said he was fitting her out with a radio mike on a very sensitive part of her body for some love scene they're filming tomorrow. I laughed so much I almost weed.'

'Shhhhh, speak of the devil!' said Serge, as the man himself walked into the Long Gallery. Paddy immediately spotted them and strode over, throwing his arms around Portia and congratulating her in his own inimitable way.

'Ya finally got a fella, I'm delighted for ya!' he said. Then, turning to Daisy, he whispered, 'Listen, luv, I hope ya didn't get the wrong idea or anything earlier. I was only having sex with Montana, ya know? I wasn't making love or anything, the way I was with you.'

'Emm, oh really?' stammered Daisy as Serge and Portia peeled off in fits of giggles.

'Are ya still seeing him then?' asked Paddy with a nod towards Steve, who was over by the stained-glass window, deep in conversation with Andrew and Blackjack.

'Yes, actually,' Daisy lied, 'but I want you to know, I think Montana's a very lucky girl.'

Paddy grinned back at her, delighted. 'Yeah, she's not a bad aul' bird, is she? And I don't care what anyone says about her, her lips are all her own.'

'So do you still need me to be on boyfriend duty?' Steve said, coming up to her as soon as Paddy went off to get a drink.

'Not a bad idea,' she replied, slipping her hand into his and making him blush bright red.

He held her hand tightly, in no hurry to let go. Daisy didn't know why, but for some reason, it just felt lovely to be standing in the middle of the room holding hands with him. Comfortable, somehow.

'What on earth happened since I was away?' Blackjack said to Andrew in his deep, gravelly voice, observing what was going on around him. 'I left a pair of Virgin Marys behind me and I come back to . . . well, you're far too young to remember the Profumo scandal but there was a saucy pair of minxes involved called Christine Keeler and Mandy Rice-Davis. Fabulous legs, you know. The girls, I mean, not Profumo.'

Egged on by Andrew, Portia did her level best to be civil to her father that evening. 'I know he hasn't exactly behaved well,' Andrew explained, 'but he really has tried to make amends, you know. I've spent so much time in his company in the past few days that I've grown quite fond of him. Just give him a chance, darling, he's actually a very nice man.'

But there was one person who was less than overjoyed to have Lord Davenport back in residence again. For the first time in as long as anyone could remember, Lucasta didn't waft into the Long Gallery for her customary stiff gin and tonic before dinner. After a while, Daisy began to get a bit worried and whispered to Steve that she was just going to discreetly check up on her. She found her in the kitchen, drip-feeding tiny droplets of milk to one of Gnasher's kittens by the Aga.

'Are you all right, Mummy?' asked Daisy, genuinely concerned. 'It's almost nine o'clock and you're sober.'

'Oh yes, sweetie,' Lucasta said, not looking up. 'Do you know, I don't think I'll bother with dinner tonight. I'm still having visitations from the other side, so I'd best not.'

'Mummy,' said Daisy sternly, 'you can't avoid him for ever. You'll have to face him sometime.'

Lucasta sighed and pulled out a pack of cigarettes from the pocket of her wax jacket. 'I know, darling. It's just . . . well, when he first buggered off of course I was upset, but then the film crew arrived and everything and, well, the last few months without him have just been . . . well, they've just been such fun! I've had a ball, darling. And now I've bloody well got to go back to being Lady boring Davenport again and, let's face it, that's fuck all crack. Why can't he leave us alone and we'll just contact him whenever we need his signature on anything?'

'But he's not staying, Mummy, that's the thing. He told me that he's only staying on for Portia's wedding and then he's going straight back to the States. I promise you, he's not here for good.'

'Are you sure, sweetie?' asked Lucasta, brightening. 'Are you sure he wasn't just saying that? I mean, you know what Blackjack is like. I swear that bollocks would say Mass. Not that he's a bad man or anything,' she corrected herself, seeing the hurt look on Daisy's face. 'A tosser, yes, but not a bad man. Do you honestly think he'll go back to America?'

'I'm certain. I think he's anxious to get back to . . .' Here Daisy faltered a bit, unsure how her mother would take it if she knew her husband still had a girlfriend. 'Well, he just loves it over there . . .' she trailed off.

'Best news I've heard all day,' said Lucasta, delighted. 'And, you know, it's much the best thing for him. I've always felt that Las Vegas was your father's spiritual home.'

Portia had never known happiness like it. With Andrew beside her discreetly feeling her leg under the table and only having eyes for her all night, she thought she'd died and gone to heaven.

'You should get married in Ballyroan Church,' Blackjack was pontificating from the head of the table, swirling brandy around in a crystal glass. He'd spent the entire meal scanning the table for a female over eighteen and under forty to flirt with but, apart from Montana, who was engrossed in conversation with Paddy, he was having no luck. 'And as soon as possible too,' he went on, sounding bored now. 'Nothing worse than a long engagement, no point in it.'

'Sir, I will marry your daughter tomorrow morning if she'll have me,' Andrew replied laughing.

'If I'll have you?' said Portia, leaning in to kiss him again, and not caring who saw.

Daisy and Steve were also sitting side by side further down the table, engrossed in conversation.

'You're doing a very passable imitation of a boyfriend so far,' she said teasingly, 'but I think you should snog me for good measure.'

'Now?' he replied, reddening.

'Now,' she answered firmly, taking the fork out of his hand and lifting her face towards his. Shyly, he pecked her cheek and pulled away, but Daisy was having none of it. 'Steve, when is the last time you kissed someone?'

'Let me see,' he said, sounding very lawyer-like, 'this is Friday, so that would have been . . . emm, nineteen ninety-five.'

'Well, things have changed a bit since then, so let me show you how it's done,' she answered, pulling him down towards her and bringing her mouth to his. She kissed him slowly and softly and then, just as he was getting warmed up, she pulled back. 'Mmm, not bad,' she murmured, 'but we need a lot more practice.'

Montana and Paddy sat opposite them, enjoying the sideshow. 'Do ya see what I'm trying to tell ya, luv?' Paddy was saying to her. 'The upper classes in this country are all slappers.'

Montana winked over at Daisy and smiled, probably a bit more clued into what was going on than Paddy.

Lucasta sat at the bottom of the table, as geographically far removed from her husband as possible. 'All these happy couples,' she chirped to Jimmy D. who was sitting on her left, 'have me to thank, you know. I was chanting for a result like this all bloody night and has one of those ungrateful bastards even poured me a gin?'

A fairytale wedding wasn't exactly something Portia had dreamt of since girlhood, and probably just as well. Neither she nor Andrew would look back on the day with any great nostalgia but, as he remarked to her in the taxi as they drove to the airport, the worse the wedding, the better the marriage. 'So you see, my darling, when we're celebrating our golden wedding anniversary, we'll look back and laugh.'

The day had begun well, with Serge putting the finishing touches to her hair and make-up while Daisy and Lucasta were downstairs bickering about who got to wear a tatty pearl necklace (the only piece of jewellery in the house). Serge was just stepping back to admire his handiwork when there was a knock at the door and in walked Blackjack. He was in morning dress, looking as immaculate as ever – as though he dressed like that every day of the week.

'I do hope it's not unlucky for me to see the bride before we go to church?' he asked.

'Oh no, your lordship, come right on in,' said Serge, gushing. 'Isn't she beautiful?'

'My dear, you're stunning,' he said, and for once he wasn't lying. Her dress was cream silk, long, plain and simple, and showed off her slender figure to perfection. Serge had knotted her hair up, so the line of the dress could be seen from the nape of her neck and, with just the lightest make-up and a hint of lipstick, she looked a million dollars.

'I hope I'm not interrupting,' he said. 'It's just that with you and Andrew going away after the reception tonight, I thought now would be an appropriate time for me to give you my wedding present.' Then, delving into his breast pocket, he produced a thick white envelope and handed it over to her.

Portia opened it, not knowing what to think, and almost fell over when she took out an ancient parchment, almost two inches thick, yellowing with age and covered in Latin copper-plate handwriting. She looked at her father, bewildered.

'Look closely,' he said. 'Those are the title deeds of Davenport Hall. I know how much you love the old place, Portia, and I want you and Andrew to have it. It's the least I can do. If I hang on to them, there's a good chance they'll end up on some nag in the three-thirty at Aintree.'

'Daddy,' she said, overwhelmed, 'I don't know what to say.'

'Well, I do,' Serge chipped in. 'Go hug him!'

'I just like the idea that perhaps one day I'll have grand-children, and perhaps one day I'll be welcome to come and visit them here,' he went on.

'Anytime,' Portia said, hugging him, 'you know you're welcome anytime.'

'And roll credits!' said Serge, beside himself. 'Oh God, I love a good reconciliation.'

Then there was Susan de Courcey. She initially refused her invitation and spoke so venomously to Andrew about his future bride and the family he was marrying into that there was nothing left to say. Thankfully, his father took a different stance and bravely turned up alone at Ballyroan Church knowing that the Third World War would await him as soon as he returned home. However, the minute Susan found out that Montana Jones and Ella Hepburn were going to be there with their press entourage, she instantly changed her mind. Shoehorning herself into a strapless designer gown she barged into the church just as the couple were taking their vows.

'Fucking latecomers!' Lucasta had bellowed just as Portia was about to say 'I do'.

The reception afterwards wasn't exactly the stuff of a *Hello!* magazine centre-page spread either. For a start, it was lashing rain so when the small number of guests assembled in the Long Gallery, the roof started to leak badly, drenching people to the bone and all but destroying the buffet spread out on a side table. Then Uri Geller, easily Lucasta's most territorial cat, got into a vicious fight with Ella Hepburn's Pekinese dog and they had to have buckets of water thrown on them to keep them apart. In the absence of anyone else for him to flirt with, Blackjack even tried it on with Susan and was rewarded with a clatter across his face and a cackle of laughter from Lucasta. Portia had done her utmost to be friendly towards her new mother-in-law, but met with such a brick wall of rudeness that she gave it up as a bad job. Michael, however, was perfectly charming.

'Never mind the old girl,' he'd said once Susan was well out of earshot, 'she'll come round. Just wait till the Tribunal gets going and she's plastered all over the papers going in and out of Dublin Castle in a different outfit each day: she'll be a pussycat.'

In fact, as the taxi arrived to take the bride and groom to the airport it would have been hard to say which of them was the most relieved to be getting away. 'And that was a mild display by the Davenport family standards,' Portia said, snuggling into his arms in the back of the car. 'I hope you realize what you've just married into.'

Andrew laughed and held her close. 'I told you, the worse the wedding, the better the marriage. And by the way, darling, the first thing we're doing when we come back is getting the roof repaired. Your mother and Daisy I can live with, the two dozen cats I can live with, but the indoor waterfall has to go.'

★

For the first time in as long as she could remember, Lucasta sat in the kitchen, completely and utterly alone. It was a few weeks after Portia and Andrew's wedding and they were still on their extended honeymoon. Daisy had gone out for the night with Steve; the pair of them were virtually inseparable these days. The film had officially wrapped and the crew had departed almost as suddenly as they'd arrived. It was like the circus leaving town, she thought dismally, the way all their trucks and vans just rolled down the driveway and were gone. The crew had been perfectly polite to her, of course, thanking her for her hospitality and kindness towards them. Ella Hepburn had graciously invited her over to the film's premiere in LA and Montana had generously offered to pay for her flight. Jimmy D. had even given her a parting gift of an engraved solid silver flea collar for Gnasher and had promised to come back and visit as soon as he'd finished editing the film. But after all the buzz and excitement of the past few months, the sense of anticlimax was awful.

'Well, Gnasher, they've all buggered off,' she said dismally. 'It's just you and me now, darling.' She switched on the tiny, flickering TV and was just in time to catch the tail end of a nightly entertainment show. They were covering a glamorous film premiere in Hollywood and there, swanning down the red carpet, was Montana Jones. She was wearing Versace and looked stunning, but that wasn't what made Lucasta squint at the TV in disbelief. Standing beside her, wearing a dress suit and looking like he did this every night of the week, was Paddy. The press had gone into overdrive, shouting, 'Over here, Montana!' and, 'Is it true your latest boyfriend is Irish? And that you met while filming over there?' A battery of flashes went off as Montana and Paddy approached them, with Montana gamely twirling around to show off the dress.

'Eh, lads? Excuse me, lads?' Paddy could clearly be heard saying in the background. 'I don't suppose any of youse got the score of the match, did yis? It's just that Arsenal were playing Sunderland last night and I just thought—'

Suddenly and without warning, the front doorbell blared out, echoing all the way down to the kitchen, making Gnasher jump out of Lucasta's lap in fright.

'Who the fuck could that be?' she said, stubbing out her cigarette and going upstairs. It was late, well after eleven at night, and the Hall was in pitch darkness.

'Who is it?' she called out nervously. 'I'm armed, you know,' she added, pulling an umbrella from the bottom of the coat stand by the door. 'And I have a guard cat!'

'Ah, would ya ever open the door, I'm freezing,' came an all-too-familiar voice from outside. Eventually, after struggling with all the locks and bolts, Lucasta finally got the door opened.

'So,' she said, seeing who it was, 'you've come back to me then.'

'Thought ya could use a bit of company.'

Tears began to well up in Lucasta's eyes. 'Are you back to stay?'

'Depends. Would ya have me back?'

'Oh Mrs Flanagan, of course I would,' said Lucasta, throwing her arms around her. 'I've missed you so much, although you're still a saggy old cow.'

'I missed you too,' replied Mrs Flanagan, hugging her back, 'although yer're still a mad aul' bitch.'

Lucasta picked up her suitcase and linked her arm, steering her inside the Hall and back downstairs to the kitchen.

'Do you know, Mrs Flanagan,' she said theatrically, milking the moment for all it was worth, 'I think this could be the beginning of a beautiful friendship.'

Mrs Flanagan smiled at her, shaking loose from her grip. 'Ah, would ya ever feck off and pour us a gin.'